How To Meet Your Match on the Moors

ALSO BY ELIZABETH COLE

Honor & Roses

Choose the Sky

Raven's Rise

Peregrine's Call

A Heartless Design

A Reckless Soul

A Shameless Angel

The Lady Dauntless

Beneath Sleepless Stars

A Mad and Mindless Night

A Most Relentless Gentleman

Breathless in the Dark

ELIZABETH COLE

How To Meet Your Match on the Moors

SKYSPARK BOOKS

MILWAUKEE, WISCONSIN

SkySpark Books
Milwaukee, Wisconsin
skysparkbooks.com
inquiry@skysparkbooks.com

Publisher's Note: This is a work of fiction. Names, characters, places, and incidents are a product of the author's imagination. Locales and public names are sometimes used for atmospheric purposes. Any resemblance to actual people, living or dead, or to businesses, companies, events, institutions, or locales is completely coincidental. This book was written by a human with no generative AI assistance.

Ordering Information:
Quantity sales. Special discounts are available on quantity purchases by corporations, associations, and others. For details, contact the "Special Sales Department" at the address above.

HOW TO MEET YOUR MATCH ON THE MOORS / Cole, Elizabeth. – 1st ed.
ISBN-13: 978-1-942316-65-7

Chapter 1

Spring 1816

NIGHT SATURATED THE CITY OF Edinburgh. Though it was late spring, the air was chilled by a grasping winter unwilling to retreat. Few people were out now—only the desperate and the dangerous.

One such figure strode over the mist-slicked stones on his way to somewhere only he knew. Once or twice, a shadow slipped out from a doorway or a close between buildings and began to follow him. But the huge man simply paused, his footsteps stilling, his right shoulder rolling like a prizefighter's. He didn't even look behind him. Each time, the pursuer slinked back and away. The shadows working the night were predators. But this man was not prey.

The man continued on his path until he came to a particularly narrow close. Turning down it, he stepped carefully, his broad shoulders grazing the walls on either side even though he moved almost sideways. The squeak of rats echoed off the building walls, irked that anything entered their domain, yet wise enough to disappear before the thundering gait of this larger creature.

The man reached a door and knocked. It cracked open. The clink of a few coins soon opened it wider. The visitor passed into the building, pulling the door shut behind him.

This was one of the city's many gambling hells.

"Where's James McGregor?" the stranger asked.

* * * *

A few floors above, the sought-after McGregor took a swig of his drink and glanced at his cards, willing them to be different than what he'd been dealt. Anyone looking at him would see the faint sheen of sweat across his brow, and the raised color in his face. He had the hunted look of the gambler who knows he has overstretched, and yet hopes against hope that he has one last, lucky turn to change his fate and restore his fortunes.

The cards had not changed, nor had his luck.

"Fold," he announced in disgust. He stood up, swaying a bit. "Excuse me, gentlemen, I must attend to a necessity."

Deep in the game, the others scarcely responded.

McGregor stumbled into the hallway, where he straightened up immediately, casting off his seeming drunkenness. He was so engrossed in planning his return to the card game that he didn't notice the gigantic shadow until the stranger stepped into his path.

"McGregor. You've not responded to my queries."

Identified and caught all at once, McGregor stared at the figure in shock, then dismay. The dingy hall was lit only by a candle guttering behind the foxed glass panel of a lamp. It showed little more than a coppery murk upon the other man. Perhaps he preferred it that way, if only to hide his ravaged face.

Some terrible accident could have caused the disfigurement, the scarring and the puckered skin that pulled his right eye into a permanent glare. The same wound also tugged the right side of his mouth into a scowl.

But it was no mere accident that had altered his appearance. It was a war. The man had served in the British Army during the war against Napoleon, as had so many other Scotsmen. He had returned alive, but not whole—at least, according to rumor. Yes, he had all his limbs, which was something, considering how many soldiers couldn't say the same. But, as the stories went, he'd gotten too close to an exploding shell, and survived only through pure chance.

"Oh, Christ. It's *you*." It wasn't surprising that McGregor was nervous, for he now spoke to the man who held the largest and oldest of his debts. Struan MacInnes.

His luck was getting worse and worse. If only the damned soldier had died, like so many others, this uncomfortable debt might have been lost or in some way discreetly wiped from the ledger...whether literally or figuratively. It was really most inconvenient that the scarred man continued to breathe, especially when no one would miss him much. For he was unmarried, from the Highlands, and of no significance in terms of family name, whereas James McGregor— a husband and a father—was well respected in the city. He rarely walked down the street without greeting somebody he knew!

And yet. Here he was, in thrall to a man who was just this side of dead. And there was also the incontrovertible fact that McGregor still did not have the money to pay him back.

"I expected your response some time ago," the tall man said, his voice gravelly as a stream bed.

"Ah, I've been...busy," McGregor said, in a way that was meant to convey a carelessness, but he couldn't hide a degree of servile fawning. Such was often the case when a man owed a great deal to the one he was speaking to. "I heard you were in Edinburgh. I didn't wish to bother you while you were getting your bearings, after...well, you know."

"I'm touched by your deep consideration for my comfort," the scarred man replied. His warped expression meant that nearly anything he said had a tendency to seem sarcastic. But this time there was no mistaking his sentiment. He went on. "I trust that you used the lengthy delay in my return to gather *all* the money required to repay the principal and interest from the loan I extended you before I left."

McGregor glanced down the hall, as if help would appear. It did not. "Well, sir, as to that… I had every expectation of giving you the full payment at the earliest opportunity. But I am, er, at present in a rather awkward place, and I cannot readily lay my hands on the funds required."

The scarred man glanced down at an open notebook in his hand. He tapped one line in particular and looked up at McGregor. He said nothing, allowing the uncomfortable silence to stretch on.

At last McGregor could no longer stand it. He said, "I beg you for some indulgence, just a little more time! Or if you prefer, I can pay a smaller amount shortly, and then gather the rest as soon as I may."

"Six and half years." The scarred man tapped a column of the ledger, which held a listing of dates. "I made this loan to you six and half *years* ago, and you have the audacity to avoid me and tell me you have nothing? By the quality of your clothing and your boots, to say nothing of the jewels you're wearing, I find it difficult to believe you're destitute."

"I never claimed such," McGregor protested. "You understand how important it is to appear respectable. I would not defame my wife or daughters by looking like a pauper! And of course I must pay to maintain their needs as well, you know. My daughter is expecting to make a great match soon, and the expenses related to that endeavor are considerable. A man would do anything for his family, anything at all."

"Anything. At. All," the scarred man repeated with an ominous inflection. "So this loan that I made you…you are telling me that you are spending it on your family rather than yourself. Excepting, of course, the fine clothes I see you in. And, of course, other incidentals from a friendly game of cards, am I correct?"

"Er, yes indeed, sir!" the man said, grasping the rope that he had been thrown—perhaps with too much eagerness, considering he did not know where the other end of the rope was leading. "I have every hope that my daughter will make a splendid marriage, and that of course will elevate my own situation."

"But you said *daughters*. Won't you spend just as much on the necessities for the next girl's season? And the one after that? When is it all to end?"

"Well, who can say with certainty? You know how the marriage mart is."

"I do not."

McGregor was not an empathetic man, but he did have a certain elemental awareness of others' moods, particularly when it came to matters of money. Now he sensed the tiniest chink in the armor of the man in front of him.

This wounded soldier had been away for years and returned in a state not at all conducive to entering the marriage mart. With that glimmering of insight, McGregor said, "I didn't mean to imply you would be caught up in that petty world. Not all men wish to marry. Some men have no interest in the life of a husband or father. Some men are meant to be bachelors."

"Some men are made so."

The words could be taken for an agreement, but McGregor sensed something else. The scarred man was acknowledging that his choice had been made for him by a shell on some battlefield. If things had been different, he would have waded into the waters of polite society in search of a wife.

Then McGregor's desperately spinning brain made a

connection, two gears clicking together at just the right moment, offering him an option so wild and unexpected that it made him suck in a startled breath.

If he could sell this notion, if he could persuade the scarred man to consider an alternative form of payment… well, that would be an extremely generous payout on an extremely daring wager.

The gambler in him seized the reins. "I did not say so yet, sir, but I wish to convey my sincere appreciation for your service abroad. Not all men are cut out for the risk, not to mention those like me who are too old. But your service and sacrifice is a mark of bravery. I can't say how much of a blessing for our nation it is that you've come back alive and well!"

The scarred man gave him a strange look. "I don't see what my wartime service has to do with the payment of your debt."

"Well, sir, I wouldn't venture to even suggest this idea if I didn't respect your character and strength of will. You have a fine reputation, and come from a most excellent family. Don't forget that I knew your father, and counted him a friend!"

This statement caused a new and uncertain stillness in the scarred man. "Go on."

"I perceive that your recent misfortune with regard to your appearance may—most unfairly!—prevent you from pursuing what you would otherwise already be seeking out."

"What am I seeking out?"

"Why, a wife!"

The scarred man pulled back a fraction, obviously not expecting that.

McGregor went on, more eagerly. "As a father concerned for his daughter's happiness, I can't imagine a more suitable match than to you, sir."

"I thought your eldest daughter was already expecting to make a brilliant match." The sarcasm was back again.

"Oh, no, sir. Not *my* eldest, who is a complete disappointment to me. And the youngest of the house is in truth a stepdaughter, and it is for her we have the great hope which I have mentioned. But her mother, my wife, would surely have something to say about any match made without her knowledge and approval! I had, in fact, pictured my *second* daughter for you. Her name is Elspeth, and everyone agrees that she is as pretty as a picture."

"They always are," the scarred man noted. "Though I am in no position to render judgment on one's appearance. So, your second daughter. What's wrong with her?"

"Wrong with her? Nothing! She's twenty years old, accomplished in matters of feminine and domestic pursuits, and has a most agreeable nature."

"Then why are you so eager to be rid of her?"

"Well, of course I wouldn't be, except that this opportunity arose."

"You speak as if I initiated the proposal. And yet I have never met, seen, or indeed known about your fair daughter's existence until this moment."

"What other prospects have you got?" McGregor said with a certain cruel edge. "Are you already married? Engaged? Courting?"

The scarred man's expression grew cold. "None of those things."

"Well then, what would your objection be? I assure you there is nothing to complain about when it comes to Elspeth's appearance or manner. I think that it would be an even exchange."

"You would pay your debt with your daughter?"

"Well, I would not put it in so direct a way," McGregor demurred. "Rather, I would hope that the joy to be found in your union would result in the debt being considered totally dissolved. We need not be mercenary about this."

"Oh, no. We wouldn't wish to be *mercenary*," the scarred man said. His eyes glittered in the candlelight.

McGregor smiled. "All I ask, sir, is that you consider the possibility. If you like, I could arrange a meeting between you and—"

"No. There will be no meeting."

While the words sounded like a rejection, there was a shred of something in the scarred man's voice. *Hope.*

McGregor knew that his fish was hooked. He could now play his catch with skillful tugs at the line. "Ah? Too direct. Too quick? If not a meeting, then I could make it so that you could see her at some public function, or along a street one day. You would not have to be introduced or even be noticed. But surely a man wishes to know what he is buying."

"I am not in the habit of buying people."

"Of course not, sir," he said soothingly. "A figure of speech! But once you see Elspeth—my sweet, dear, darling Elspeth—you'll understand that I'm offering a most fair bargain. Think about it, sir. Come by the house and see if you like her. In any case, contact me when you have made a decision."

And with those words, McGregor turned and walked away, back to the brightness and the relative safety of the card room. There was restored confidence in his step. Fate had once again intervened to save him from ruin. The cards would fall kindly now!

Yes, let his debt-holder take his daughter off his hands. It was the perfect solution for him. Whether it would be an acceptable solution to either the husband or the wife involved, he did not care in the least.

Chapter 2

STRUAN DIDN'T MEAN TO DO it. The whole proposal was daft. Struan had meant to tell McGregor to go to hell, and then press for the payment. Not because he needed the money, but because he didn't like the idea of McGregor wiggling out of an agreement. It had been foolish of him to offer the loan in the first place, but Struan had been young and too trusting of McGregor's acquaintance with his own father.

Since then, he'd learned the risk of trusting.

And yet, early in the morning after he met with McGregor, he found himself walking toward the street where the man lived, in one of the newer neighborhoods of Edinburgh, and then watching the door of the house that belonged to his quarry.

Come by the house and see if you like her. McGregor obviously meant that Struan should make a social call in the guise of being friends with McGregor himself, and then meet the daughter being offered up as a sacrificial lamb.

But Struan MacInnes was a soldier. He knew the hallmarks of an ambush, and he refused to follow the breadcrumbs McGregor was laying down.

He'd do his own damn reconnaissance. On his own terms.

So this initial foray was intended only to scout out the

house and grounds, perhaps to overhear servants talking in the back where chores were done in the yard, or in the working rooms with doors and windows left open.

He never expected to see the daughter in the flesh. But that's what happened.

He'd drifted down the back alley of the row of houses, barely fast enough to call it a walk. Just when he reached the backyard in question, where a group of servants were doing the wash, a maid with a voice a field marshal would envy bawled out, "Miss Elspeth, we need more soap!"

"Look in the cupboard below the stairs, Bri," a much more cultured voice responded. "I moved everything for washing day there last autumn."

"Aye, Miss Elspeth. Forgive me, I forgot!"

Struan was confused. *This* was Miss Elspeth McGregor?

A daughter of the family, doing the washing. Directing the washing. Like a housekeeper.

The young woman who'd answered to *Miss Elspeth* wore a dress in a hideous shade of purple, as well as battered boots that looked as if they'd once belonged to an old man. Her apron was shabby as well, but hid much of the purple dress, which was an advantage. It was tied around her waist in such a way as to highlight her figure, which he also found to be an advantage.

Her blonde hair was bound into a plait, presumably to keep it from dipping into the vat of dirty water. Even so, it was obvious that the hair would be long and light and wavy and weightless if allowed to fall freely.

The woman in purple laughed, sounding absolutely delighted to be there, in front of a giant tub of filthy laundry. The other women and the one older man seemed buoyed by her mood, and laughed and smiled as they continued the chore—a chore which Struan knew to be a grueling one. In the army, all the soldiers but the highest ranking officers had to do their own washing, and do it well, or live with lice and fleas.

What was going on? A daughter of the home's owner, this Elspeth McGregor, was inexplicably helping the servants on washing day. Was this why her father was so desperate to be rid of her? He couldn't afford to pay more servants to care for the house, and had to press a daughter into the duty?

No. That made no sense. Struan could count. He'd seen who passed in and out of the house—plenty of workers were employed. And the lady seemed perfectly content, even pleased to be participating in the ordeal.

Something was off in that house. Struan should leave it all well alone. Make McGregor pay his debt in coin, just like any other man. Or else face debtors' prison, just like any other man.

Struan should go home to the Highlands as he planned, and avoid whatever trap McGregor had set for him.

But. He stayed and watched, drawn to the easy, efficient movements of the young woman. And more than that, he listened. He could hear only some of the talk, but he heard laughter and joking and good humor, even if he didn't know precisely what was said.

And so often, *her* laughter above it all. Warm, sweet, unrestrained.

He wanted that laughter. What a stupid, intangible thing to want. But he wanted it. That joy.

And if she were married to him, he'd get to hear it.

Why would she laugh around you? a part of him countered, a part that had become far more talkative since his injury. *Are you the sort of man who makes a woman smile?*

No. He was not. But he still wanted that laughter.

After he tore himself away from the house, he walked the city until the clock spun to a more civilized hour. In the afternoon he found his comrade Calan Shaw at his favorite club, one that was popular with gentlemen of military background (indeed, membership required the good references of no fewer than six current members, so the pattern of veterans sponsoring other veterans was well established).

Struan was uncomfortable at the club lately. But at least Calan was here, instead of at one of the establishments that offered drinks but also provided feminine companionship for a price. Struan never liked such places, even before. Now, it made his skin crawl. The skin he had left to him anyway.

"Shaw," Struan said in greeting. "I'm glad I found you."

"I'm glad to be found." Calan was sipping a whisky that clearly pleased him, because he insisted Struan have some from the same bottle. A skinny lad appeared out of nowhere to offer a new glass.

Struan took it, thinking that he'd need a drink in him if he ever hoped to get the words out.

The two of them sipped in silence for a little while.

"It's good," Calan said, in the tone of one seeking confirmation, after Struan finished the dregs. The same lad reappeared to fill both glasses again.

Struan nodded. "You picked well."

Calan grinned. "Yes, I do that. But it's always gratifying to hear other people tell me so."

Struan shook his head but said nothing, not wanting to add fuel to the raging fire that was Calan Shaw's ego.

After another few moments, Calan gave him a different look. "What brought you out? Not that I'm not pleased for the company, but you've been damnably difficult to drag from your townhome ever since we got back to Edinburgh. Are you finally sick of brooding alone, and you'd prefer to brood among friends?"

Struan took a breath, then said, "I might be about to do something stupid." Yes, the whisky had helped loosen his tongue.

Calan raised an eyebrow. "Go on."

"I can't tell you what it is. I just need to be talked out of it."

"How can I talk you out of it if I don't know what it is?"

"You could say, Struan, don't do something stupid."

"I could, but honestly, I've never had to say that in my life. You don't make stupid decisions. You're always thinking ahead and considering the options." Calan paused. "You're not about to kill yourself, are you? Because that would be stupid."

Struan shook his head. "No. If I were going to do that, I'd have done it before now." Even in the worst time after his injury, when all he thought about was how much pain his body could hold, he never considered ending his life for more than a few seconds, which he figured was a natural reaction to such overwhelming agony.

But they could all name more than one soldier who chose to end it all, so Calan's question was fair. To reassure him, Struan added, "I promise that however stupid my current decision is, I'll be alive to regret it afterward."

"Excellent. I was worried for a moment." Calan took a long drink. "Give me a hint, at least. Is it about money? A woman? Something else?"

Definitely a woman.

"Let's say it's about money," Struan said, because it was also about money. At least partly.

"Are you considering some extravagant purchase?"

"That's one way to put it," Struan said. "Though not so extravagant that it would damage my finances. But it could be considered…unwise." And unethical, which was the larger problem. He clarified, "It's not legal. Or maybe it is legal, but it would be frowned upon. I think."

"I've never heard you so uncertain about anything." Calan was now fully alert, sitting up and facing Struan, his eyes intent. Calan could go from idle to intense within seconds, but Struan was rarely the focus of the other man's attention. It was disconcerting to say the least. "What the hell are you really contemplating?"

"If I told you, you'd not approve."

Calan let out a surprised laugh. "Well, if *I* wouldn't approve, maybe that's the signal that you shouldn't bloody do it."

Struan nodded, then looked down. It was hard to look Calan in the eyes when he was being serious. It was like talking to a wolf.

Calan let the silence stretch, then finally broke it with, "But you want it anyway. Whatever it is."

"I do. Or I want…the idea of it."

"You're talking in riddles."

Struan sighed, dragged a hand over his temples. "I know. Believe me, I'm not enjoying it."

"Yes, that's obvious. Struan, I'm your friend. If you tell me what's actually going on, I can help you. But if you don't, and then make a stupid decision without telling me, then what's the point of this…half confession you're offering?"

"I shouldn't have come to you," Struan muttered.

"Why not?"

"Because you would never have this problem."

"*What* problem, for Christ's sweet sake?"

"Never mind. I should go." Struan put his hands on the leather arms of the chair, preparing to get up.

"No, wait." Calan leaned forward. "Tell me, I'm begging you. And then we can figure it out. With the other men, or not! Though you know they'll be insulted if they can't help too."

Struan grimaced. He pictured his closest friends. They'd be not just insulted, but hurt that he didn't trust them.

"Yes, I know," Calan said. "It's such a bother, having friends who care about you."

"How do you know what I'm thinking?"

"I know what everyone's thinking," Calan said. His smile evaporated and his eyes suddenly went dark. "I can't help reading people. A lot of times I wish I could." Then he blinked, and said, "But I don't mind when my skill can help a friend. So tell me."

So, after one more slug of excellent whisky, Struan told him.

And Calan, after an achingly long period of silence, told him what would happen next.

Chapter 3

ELSPETH MCGREGOR REGARDED HER FATHER in disbelief. "You've *what*?"

It was Sunday. Morning sunlight filtered into the breakfast room of the spacious townhouse owned by the McGregor family. Her father liked nothing but the best. Elspeth loved Sundays for their quiet and peace. Most days, she awoke almost at the same time as the chambermaids, and directed the majority of the tasks as well as pursuing her own projects around the house. For instance, on Saturday, she'd worked on the kitchen garden to expand the plot for onions and garlic. The day before had been washing day, so the whole backyard had been occupied by the tubs of water and the lines of drying linens.

Sundays were meant to be a respite.

She normally enjoyed her morning coffee on her own, being the earliest riser in the family. However, today her father had appeared almost immediately. There was an edge of excitement in his face that she associated with long nights spent at card tables, so she attributed his glee to a particularly lucrative hand.

But then he told her the news.

"I said, I've promised you in marriage. You should feel honored," he said, patting her hand. The gesture was unlike him. He'd always been a distant man, his concerns never overlapping with her own. By her own choice, she confined herself to home and hearth, always striving to keep her household as comfortable and as efficient as possible. Her father, by contrast, was always about town, or at his club, or handling matters of business. He was an important man in the city of Edinburgh, at least according to him. So the fact that he had come *to* her felt like an event in itself.

She looked down at her hand, the light skin against deep-dyed fabric. Elspeth wore a plain day dress in a rather unflattering purple color, with an apron tied around her waist because she intended to prepare the morning meal for the rest of the household. If she had known what momentous news awaited her, Elspeth would have removed the apron.

"You are to be wife to a wealthy and important man. He has chosen you especially, so you should respect that decision."

"I do, of course. But I don't recall ever having met the gentleman," Elspeth said. Her voice was low and soft, as always. She had been instructed how to make the best possible impression on the people around her, which usually entailed keeping herself quiet and out of the way, so that she wouldn't bother anyone. Elspeth viewed a peaceful and harmonious home as the pinnacle of achievement. She'd worked hard to make that happen for her own family and she was alarmed by the revelation that she would shortly be doing it in another location entirely.

"It will be a good match," he said.

"I do wish to make a good match, Father. And I'm grateful that you have handled the matter so smoothly." By which she meant, *quietly*, or *quickly*, or even *stealthily*, though she would never say those words to the man in charge of her home. "But I thought that you wished both Mairi and Averill to be married before me."

"Well, that had been the intention, though Mairi..." He gave up the rest of the sentence with an aggrieved sigh. "But who am I to stand in the way of fate? This offer of marriage is a blessing."

Elspeth nodded automatically, having been trained to believe that blessings were good. "When is the formal announcement to take place?" she asked. Elspeth had always dreamed of a summer wedding, and it was possible that she would be able to be married by the end of summer if everything were to go as expected. She would have to prepare her trousseau, and pack what she owned, and make arrangements for the wedding, as well as what she would need to do in order to step into the role of wife to a gentleman. Yes, it was likely that she would not be married until autumn...

"The announcement will go out in the morning edition of the newspapers," her father declared. "You will marry on Friday morning, after which you both will travel to his home in the Highlands."

It took her far too long to process that.

"*This* Friday?" Elspeth asked at last.

Now her father showed a trace of irritation. "Of course this Friday. If it were to be a different Friday, I would have said. Thank God we're not in England with their banns and rules."

"That's less than a week! I can't prepare what I need by then."

"What's to prepare? Your new husband will provide for you," her father said. He smiled, showing gleaming yellow teeth. "Pack your personal belongings, and the rest will be handled once you arrive."

"But I don't understand. Are you and my stepmother... doing anything?" she asked. Elspeth never called the second Mrs McGregor *mother.* For similar reasons, she did not like to refer to Averill as her sister, though that was how her father introduced them on the rare occasions that the whole family attended an event requiring introductions.

"We'll attend the wedding ceremony, of course, but probably not the breakfast. If he has one—I am not sure what his plans are. But I believe he intends to waste no time in returning to his home, which I understand is far from here." Her father patted her hand once more, then released it. "Now why don't you get to packing? As you said, there isn't much time."

By his manner, the discussion was over. Elspeth rose, too flustered to ask out loud the thousand questions in her mind. One thing she knew above all. When her father made a decision, it was made forever. Elspeth *was* going to be married. But she didn't know who she was marrying.

At the top of the stairs, she rushed into her sister's room. Mairi groaned when Elspeth pulled aside the curtains. "It's far too early, Pest! Why are you tormenting me?"

"Mairi, wake up. Something has happened."

"Did someone die?" Mairi sat up as she asked it, looking bleary-eyed.

"I'm to be married!" Elspeth announced, hoping to jolt her sister into alertness.

"Better you than me." Mairi groaned, then asked, "Hold a moment. Were you being courted by anyone? Who's the gentleman?"

"That's why I'm here, Mairi. I don't know who he is! Father said he made the offer last evening, and he's admired me from afar."

"Very afar, if you don't even know him. He must have a name."

"Mr Struan MacInnes. He's got land up near Wick. Or Thurso? I'm not sure. And he was in the army, but he's not anymore."

Mairi sighed. "I expect many soldiers are searching for

wives now that the war is over. After the bleeding, the breeding."

Elspeth frowned at her sister's matter-of-fact tone. "Mairi, that's harsh of you!"

"It's true. Men are all the same." Mairi was a firm proponent of the rights of women, to the point of joining a local society for the cause: the League for the Advancement of Scottish Women. She read literally every book, pamphlet, tract, and newspaper article published about the issue. While Elspeth admired her sister's singular focus, she thought Mairi had acquired a few more radical notions than were strictly helpful to a young lady in 1816.

Elspeth herself joined no societies, and her singular focus was nothing more radical than the running of the house…a task at which she excelled. Elspeth felt close to her late mother when she worked at that. She had no memories of her mother doing such things—after all, Elspeth's birth had caused her mother's death. But her father sometimes remarked to visitors that there had been no finer lady than the first Mrs McGregor when it came to matters of homekeeping. The second Mrs McGregor, whose given name was Susan, showed no offense at this, her focus being much more directed toward her own daughter. So Elspeth strove to do the same work as her birth mother, though she had not yet earned the same level of praise.

But other matters were paramount this morning.

"You have to help me find out more about him!" Elspeth said to Mairi. "Where can we do that?"

"As unmarried young ladies with no connections to him? Nowhere," Mairi said. "Let me think. You could write to Uncle Nicholas. He might know something. Father really didn't say anything else?"

"Just what I told you."

"That's odd. One would think Father would vet the man,

if only to ensure he doesn't accidentally lower our family's social standing."

Elspeth nodded at that, for their father was intensely concerned with such things. A scandal or shame on one branch of a family tree could blight all other branches. She said, "Well, then it's certain that Mr MacInnes is respectable. That's reassuring."

"Is it? Many men are considered respectable without doing anything worth respect. All it means is that they haven't done anything bad enough to be ostracized."

"You are oil upon troubled waters," Elspeth joked with an exasperated yet affectionate smile.

"Your waters are never troubled, Pest," Mairi retorted. "I could lead a charge of elephants at you and you'd merely offer them tea and…whatever elephants eat."

"Straw or corn, I think," Elspeth said. "But Mairi, please pay attention! What can I do?"

"Run away, if you don't want to be married."

"Don't be absurd. Of course I wish to be married. But I don't wish to be surprised. If I can learn about my husband, I'll know what he likes."

"Sounds as if he likes you," Mairi said with a shrug. "Well, I'm awake now. We'll write to Uncle and see if there's any information to be had about your mysterious suitor."

Chapter 4

BY AFTERNOON OF THE NEXT day, the packing was largely done. In contrast to some of the other members of the household (that is her father, her stepmother, and her stepsister, Averill), Elspeth did not own much. She had a small wardrobe in her room, consisting of some sturdy dresses all in the same purple color, a pelisse, the usual accessories required of any respectable woman living in the year of our Lord 1816, as well as a few personal mementos acquired over the years. This last category was wrapped with extreme care and placed into one of the two traveling trunks that had been allotted for her use. The first trunk was Elspeth's own, and had resided in her bedroom since she was a child. The second trunk had been donated by her stepsister, who declared she didn't need it anymore. It might have been more accurate to say she did not want it anymore, for the trunk was old, battered, and smelled like codfish, no matter how many times Elspeth rinsed the surfaces with vinegar.

Even with only two trunks, Elspeth had a little room left over, which she filled with some fabric and accoutrements that she had been intending for her trousseau. However, now she would have to complete the sewing and stitching after her wedding occurred. She closed the trunks, locked them, and then sat on her childhood trunk (the one that did not smell like cod) to consider her strange situation.

Together, she and Mairi had written or sought out and inquired of everyone they knew about Mr Struan MacInnes. Her extended family, friends, and neighbors collectively had provided the following facts:

From Uncle Nicholas: He had been a soldier in the British Army, fighting in France until fairly recently.

From Aunt Rosalind: He was known to be well off.

From the scullion Jock, who had it from the holster at the Bell Tavern, who had it from the local constable who patrolled the night shift: He had been involved in some mysterious event recently—not scandalous, but worthy of gossip in that it had involved a small group of men, a rather eccentric woman of the city, and a house on fire.

This last bit was the most interesting, for it happened in connection to another member of the ladies' rights group to which Mairi belonged. When Mairi heard the news, she said, "Oh, yes! The fire at the Ross house! I met Catriona Ross on several occasions at League meetings. There was something strange afoot this spring, but our chairwoman, Mrs Roberts, would not countenance any discussion. She feared it would generate bad press about our group."

"Because a house caught on fire? Surely no one blames the ladies' rights movement for that."

Mairi said, "You'd be amazed at what blame can be placed at a woman's feet when it's convenient to do so. Do you not remember the matter of the apple in Eden?"

In any case, the connection to the League allowed the two sisters to lean upon the members for additional facts. From what they were able to glean, the group of men including Struan MacInnes had saved Miss Ross from the fire, and therefore were lauded as heroes by most of the neighbors. But evidently the local constables and magistrate had *also* been present at some point, and there was at least one dead body, giving the whole affair a slightly ominous cast.

"Perhaps Miss Ross will come to tea," Mairi wondered aloud. "She surely wants to get out and enjoy a home that isn't on fire."

"I can make my lavender shortbread," Elspeth offered.

"Pest, you're marrying a stranger in a few days," her sister said. "Leave aside the menu planning for a moment, would you?"

Aside from that, Elspeth had learned that the gentleman who'd offered for her owned a great house in the north of the country, possibly within view of the ocean. Or on the moors. Or in the mountains. Or in a deep forest. Actually, no one in Edinburgh seemed to have a clear idea of where the man lived, other than that it was to the north. *This is not helpful information*, Elspeth thought. Most of Scotland was to the north. The fact that he was wealthy came up over and over in her various conversations, and everyone seemed to present this as the singular fact anyone needed to know.

Elspeth would've been glad to learn *any*thing else, such as his appearance, or habits, or whether he objected to the smell of codfish (to choose a random example). But such information was not forthcoming. And in the end, it didn't matter. Her father expressed such extreme delight about the marriage that Elspeth considered it an immutable fact about the universe, like the sun rising in the east, or crocuses blooming in spring. Her stepsister, Averill, had seemed jealous initially, but was soon converted to the idea of Elspeth marrying first.

Later that day, Averill knocked on her door. "Elspeth, are you in there?"

"Yes, come in." It was rare that Averill came up, or indeed showed interest in speaking with her at all. Probably this was due to the fact that Elspeth's room was on the top floor, on the same floor that housed the servants, though their accommodations were down the hall and past a green baize door to mark the boundary between family and hired help.

Elspeth's room looked over the front of the house and the street beyond, and Elspeth enjoyed standing by one of the two dormer windows, looking down at the life bustling on the streets and the sidewalks below. But other than Mairi, no one came to visit her there. It wasn't a shabby room, for Elspeth did not believe in shabby. Everything was immaculately clean, and all the linens laundered regularly.

All the furniture in the room was there because her father deemed the pieces too old-fashioned to be tolerated by fashionable people. There was an old oak bedstead, an ornate chair, and a chest, all from different eras. Her small desk was at least three generations in the family. The intensely fanciful carving of the desk legs and the drawer fronts made it clear that this was an item once fashionable in her great-grandmother's day. There was even a little gilt paint applied strategically to the drawer fronts, making the desk gleam in the candlelight. Elspeth loved the desk, and wished she could bring it with her to her new home, but no provision had been made for furniture. And technically, she did not own the desk —it was the property of her father. Everything in the house was the property of her father, excepting only a few personal items of each lady. In fact, one might say that Elspeth herself was the property of her father, at least until her marriage, although this was a fact that Elspeth did not think much about.

In any case, she would miss the desk.

Now Averill walked into the room, her nose wrinkling a bit in either surprise, or distaste, or both. She had her hands behind her back, but at that moment swept them in front of her to reveal a package tied with ribbon. "I got you a gift."

"For me?"

"Naturally, you silly goose. You're the one who is to be married! You need a gift like this. I'm sure you have none to match it in your trunks." She shook the package a little bit, almost as if she intended to toss it into Elspeth's lap.

Elspeth took it in her own hands before that could happen. "May I open it now?"

"Oh, yes, I want you to. I bought it especially with the occasion of your wedding night in mind." At these words, her stepsister's expression grew sly. "You do know what happens on the wedding night, don't you?"

"Your mother sat me down earlier today and informed me." Elspeth hadn't enjoyed the conversation. Her stepmother hadn't either, to judge by her expression and the strain in her voice. And Elspeth couldn't say that the conversation had even been particularly enlightening. The gist of it was that Elspeth was meant to lie down in her bed and allow her husband to do…whatever it was he wanted to do, and she was to obey without complaint. Elspeth never liked complaining anyway, and didn't expect that she would like to complain to her new husband on the first night that they were joined as a couple. So she assured her stepmother that she would do as instructed. That seemed to be sufficient.

Averill was shaking her head. "Oh, Mama would've told you what you *ought* to do, if you're boring. But she didn't tell you what you need to know."

"And what is that?"

"Open your present."

Elspeth undid the ribbon and carefully removed the paper wrapping. It revealed a garment, folded up. It was made of some kind of silk, Elspeth guessed. "My goodness, this must have been expensive." Elspeth didn't own anything made of silk. Silk seemed an incredible extravagance, and it had no place in her daily life.

"Oh, it was worth it." Her stepsister covered a giggle with

one hand. "Shake it out and hold it up."

Elspeth did so. The tiny square of folded fabric unfurled like a ship's flag. The garment turned out to be some sort of night rail, though it was so ethereal as to be almost a figment of the imagination rather than an actual piece of clothing one could wear. Around the edges and the hemline of the garment, a slightly more substantial line of lace marked the outline of the gown, like an artist's sketch that detailed what would eventually be painted in later. Elspeth had the impression that if she were to put the gown on, it would conceal absolutely nothing, leaving her body completely visible, outlined by the lace.

"You must wear this on your wedding night," her stepsister said. "It will drive your husband absolutely mad."

"I don't think that that's a desirable outcome?" Elspeth said doubtfully.

"I mean mad with lust," Averill went on, her eyes gleaming. Averill was seventeen and must have read too many books not normally allowed to women. "Mama spoke to you about duty. But men aren't interested in duty. They're interested in pleasure. And if you don't please your husband, he'll look elsewhere, and it will be all your fault."

Elspeth certainly didn't want to displease her husband. (She didn't want to displease anyone.) "I don't know that I—"

"When he sees you wearing this, he'll be so randy at the sight that he'll take you then and there. Men always think with their cocks, and if you're going to be stuck on some endless moor for the rest of your life, you'll at least want him to pay attention to you now and then."

These were words Elspeth never ever thought of, put together in a sequence she'd never ever imagined.

"Averill! I...I don't know what to say."

"Say thank you. I know a lot more about men than you

do, and trust me, this is the best thing you could do to ensure a successful marriage. Though your father—" (Averill never called him *our father* or *my father*) "—says he's rich, and that will help." She sounded jealous as she spoke, and Elspeth wondered what her father might've told her stepmother and stepsister that he hadn't seen fit to share with Elspeth herself.

"Thank you for the gift," Elspeth said, recovering her manners. "Luckily I won't have any trouble adding it to the trunk."

"He'll have to get you some proper gowns once you're married. Those purple things you insist on wearing are truly hideous."

Elspeth did not mention that it was Averill who'd purchased the vast quantity of the purple fabric a few years ago, only to decide that she didn't like it after all when she saw it the next day. Loath to waste the purchase, Elspeth made several items of clothing out of the fabric, despite also not liking the color at all.

Meanwhile, Averill was still talking. "Though, of course you'll be up in the Highlands, so I don't imagine anyone up there knows how to make a fashionable gown. And of course, nothing compares to *London.*" Her stepsister thought constantly about clothing and had an incredible collection of fashionable gowns. She'd gone on and on about the modistes she'd seen on her recent long visit to London.

"I can sew my own," Elspeth said.

"I wish I could see his face when he sees you wearing that," her stepsister said with what Elspeth considered a shocking degree of curiosity. "I wonder if he's a big man."

"I don't know how tall he is," Elspeth said.

"I'm not talking about his height. I wonder how *big* he is."

Elspeth realized that this related to the discussion regarding the wedding night, and the intricacies of the act she was supposed to engage in. Evidently, she lacked important details about the specifics. "I just hope that I can be a good wife to him."

Averill sighed, disappointed in Elspeth's response. Then she gave a little trilling laugh. "Well, I hope your wedding night is one to remember. And if it isn't, it isn't for any lack of effort on *my* part. You leave Friday, don't you?"

Elspeth nodded. "Yes, that's right. After the wedding."

"The first of us to be married," Averill said. "But not the last! I will have a fabulous debut, and I will make such an impression on the gentlemen of the city that I will surely have heaps of proposals."

"I'm sure you will," Elspeth said, aware that already her stepsister's attention was returning to her own future, which was the only one she cared about.

Chapter 5

IT HAD BEEN A STRANGE week. Requiring a dose of normalcy after finding James McGregor once more and agreeing to the most daft proposal he'd ever heard, Struan had invited his friends to the townhome on Thursday evening before the wedding. (It would be impolite to say that he begged, but that was close to the truth.)

The home was originally purchased by his father. He'd loved the city, and instilled the same affection for it in his son. Struan remembered coming here as a young boy along with his parents, which happened several times a year, and always heralded excitement. His childhood bedroom was on the top floor. It was more like a nook than a room, but he loved it. He remembered being taken to see the castle, and all the various sights of the city, and often walking along the banks of the Lieth with his mother before she passed away, and later enjoying the city with his father until he passed too.

Struan always thought of the city as a second home, but after returning from France, it hadn't felt the same. His injuries from the war were too significant. While he appreciated the fact that the doctors in Edinburgh were incredibly skilled, and that thanks to his family's wealth he could actually afford the care, no amount of doctoring erased the outward damage.

As he moved through the streets, he could feel the eyes of

everyone else. A chance encounter with an old acquaintance became an exercise in awkwardness. They would either pretend not to notice what had happened to him, or worse, paper it over with platitudes. He used to love walking through the city, but now he mostly used a closed carriage, unwilling to let himself be seen by either friends or strangers.

The only exceptions to this rule were the men now in this room. His close comrades from the war: Calan, of course. And Thane MacPhearson, Duncan MacKenzie, Kai Buchanan. These men had been with him through the worst, and they were the only ones who could look him in the eye with complete honesty. They never pretended that he hadn't gone through hell, and they never made light of the fact. With them he could be himself, which felt like an increasingly rare opportunity. So many other people he encountered expected him to either be a hero of the war, or to dismiss it completely and behave exactly as if he'd never enlisted. He couldn't play along with either of those wishes. And he didn't want to. Not for the first time or the last, he was grateful for the few friends he had.

"I thought you were leaving the city last week," said Thane, as he took a sip of Struan's finest scotch. "You seemed eager to retreat to Linneliath." He smelled faintly of smoke, since he spent a large part of each day helping to restore Catriona Ross's house, because he was totally besotted with her.

"Yes, I assumed the same," added Duncan, who sat near the fire. "Though of course I'm glad you've extended your stay. I have a feeling that the times that we'll all be in the same place are limited." He looked a little haunted by his own prediction. He was a burly redheaded man who tended toward bad jokes. He was an incredibly steady presence, so a haunted look seemed especially alarming on him.

"I had planned to already be on my way, but a few small

matters need to be resolved first." Struan took a seat across from Duncan and gestured for the other men to sit as well.

Calan poured a second drink, and then sank down onto a leather-covered chair, looking as comfortable as if he were in his own home. Then again, Calan knew what Struan was about to announce.

"A few small matters?" Thane grunted. "I seem to remember you using that same phrase right before a battle. Please tell me that you don't intend for us to storm the enemy's lines after we finish our drinks. I think the citizens of our fair city would misunderstand."

"But what *is* keeping you here?" Kai asked as he sat down. "Not that I don't appreciate the opportunity to have a quiet evening in. I had no idea how many events occurred in the city, and how many of them require formal wear and polite conversation."

Calan looked at their younger friend with a smirk. "It's not as if you find either of those difficult."

"It's not that," said Kai. "It's just that the invitations don't ever seem to *stop*."

Struan cleared his throat. "Well, I'm afraid that I'll be responsible for each of you receiving one more invitation."

Thane asked, "Are you going to host some gathering larger than this one? Novel." His response was completely understandable. Struan hadn't been the most gregarious of men before the war and, of course, since returning he hadn't felt the slightest urge to entertain.

Struan said, "It won't be large by society's standards, but what matters is that it's happening at all. I'm inviting you to my wedding."

Silence fell over the room. Struan was conscious of all four men watching him. After a long moment in which Struan strongly considered getting up and leaving the room so that he could find a hiding place, Kai said, "Well. This is a surprise."

Duncan nodded. "You've been keeping secrets from us. I thought that your previous engagement had been ended."

"It was." That came from Calan, who nearly spat out the words. He said, in a fierce tone, "As if any of us could forget the words of that...*woman*."

The woman Calan declined to give a name was Struan's former fiancée: Isla Abercrombie. They had gotten engaged before he left to join the army, and he had assumed that after the war, their marriage would be one of his first steps toward the rest of his life. Instead, she had abruptly renounced the engagement upon seeing him. Struan had no illusions. She was repulsed by his appearance, though in the letter formally releasing him from the engagement, she did offer the dubious justification of having succumbed to the affections of another gentleman.

Struan explained, "That relationship is over. However, I have been..." He paused. He'd been about to say *I have been fortunate*, but the fact was, he didn't know if it was fortunate or not. He tried again, saying, "I'll be marrying a different young lady. I don't believe any of you know her." Of course, Struan didn't know her either, a fact he kept to himself.

"Who is she?" asked Thane.

"Elspeth McGregor. She lives here in Edinburgh, though after the wedding, we'll be moving to my home." He meant Linneliath, his home in the Highlands, which all of the other men implicitly understood.

"Well, that's wonderful news," said Duncan. "I'm relieved that the treatment you received at the hands of your former fiancée didn't cause you to shy away from marriage altogether. We all know how much family means to you."

It was true. Struan had made no secret of his desire to start a family as soon as possible after completing his service. He had always looked forward to having children, and watching them grow day by day. Part of that was surely the warm and loving home his parents had given him, and how horrible it had felt to lose them both too soon. But it was also true that he simply loved children. He found them to be fun and raucous and ever surprising. Children lived life at a different pace than adults. They saw the world in a different way. He'd always loved talking to children, being delighted by their insights and the way they could cut through the nonsense of the adult world with all its rules and strictures and simply tell you what *was*.

He dreamed of being a father, of raising his own children, teaching them everything, passing on the lessons his own father and mother gave to him. He had been unusually close to both his father and mother, who disdained the trends of ignoring one's own children and leaving them in the care of a nurse or governess. The dream of a son or a daughter had sustained him in the darkest moments of the war.

Then the war nearly destroyed him. And all but destroyed that dream. Even now he had his doubts that a family was in his future.

"So, when is the happy day?" Duncan asked.

"Um. Tomorrow morning. At ten."

"Tomorrow…as in the day after today," Thane said in a remarkably even tone. "Roughly fifteen hours."

"Er, yes. I hope you all can attend." He wasn't sure he could endure the process without his friends present. The idea of marrying a complete stranger, with only strangers looking on, was overwhelming. "I know it's short notice."

"Nothing like taking care of the matter quickly," said Thane.

"Wouldn't miss it," Calan said. "I'm curious to actually meet the young lady."

Struan knew that Calan had *seen* her, since he took it upon himself to scout out the family over the past few days to ensure there was nothing obviously wrong with them. He returned the news that the McGregors were not a family that he had any interest in getting to know better, but by all accounts (meaning the accounts of servants and neighbors that Calan had been able to subtly interrogate without their realizing it *was* an interrogation), Elspeth was the best of the lot.

"You're not allowed to steal her, Calan," Thane joked. Calan was a notorious flirt. Thane continued, "Of course we'll all be there. I assume the lady's family is hosting the wedding breakfast?"

"There won't be one," Struan admitted. "It's all being arranged a little hastily because I don't wish to stay in the city longer than I must."

"The lady must be eager as well," Duncan said with an unexpectedly sly smile. "And really, there's no sense in wasting time. I expect we'll all get invitations to a christening soon enough."

Struan merely grunted in reply. However, his reaction was taken as an unwillingness to engage in earthy jokes regarding a soon-to-be wife.

A knock at the door interrupted them. "Excuse me, sir," one of Struan's servants said. "A package arrived for you, and the delivery boy insists you inspect it first. I tried to explain that you're busy—"

"I'm sure I can take five minutes away from my demanding social…demands," Struan said, standing up. "I'll be back shortly."

The others laughed as Struan followed his servant out the door.

* * * *

After Struan left the room, Calan moved to the door, listened for a moment, then shut it softly. He turned to the other men. "I assume you have questions."

"Yes," said Duncan. "First, do we believe this story about a courtship with a woman he's never mentioned, conducted over weeks and months without us hearing about it, only to have a wedding announced the day before it's to happen?"

"We do not," Calan replied flatly.

"Why would he lie?" Kai asked, puzzled.

Thane frowned. "That's the question. Calan, you obviously know more than we do."

"I usually know more than everyone else does," Calan admitted. "But all the same, I'm not going to share what I know."

"Why not?" Kai objected.

"Because Struan's a grown man. He can choose whatever bride he wants. No one has the authority to stop him."

"It's not about authority." Duncan's voice was little more than a rumble. "It's about friendship. Struan's been through a unique hell, and he might not have his head on straight after it. This woman could be after his money, or have troubles of her own that a hasty marriage could solve. So we're looking out for him. Because that's what friends do."

"What do you think I've been doing?" Calan said, looking offended. "Struan did come to me for advice. And thank God, because I was able to verify that the lady isn't a fortune-hunter, at least."

"How long have *you* known?" asked Thane.

"Not long at all. Less than a week."

Kai gave a little shake of his head. "Which is your way of saying that even though you didn't discover any information that would put Struan off, you don't trust the whole situation. All right, what needs to be done?"

"Good man," Calan said. "Pour yourselves another whisky and we'll discuss it until Struan gets back. And not a word to him about anything. He thinks he's got to do everything on his own, and we'll let him continue to think that if it helps."

"But what if there's actually a problem with this woman?" Duncan asked. "Or her family?"

Calan shrugged. "Then we'll make them regret it."

Chapter 6

THE DAY OF RECKONING HAD come. Struan entered the church, flanked by his friends. Kai had managed to find an outfit that was both Struan's size and in fashion. Such miracles were typical of Kai, who possessed an uncanny ability to get his hands on virtually any item, which had led to his being appointed quartermaster at a shockingly young age.

The other men were also dressed in their best civilian clothes, Struan having rejected the offer of them wearing regimental colors. "I prefer to think of you as my friends, not my fellow survivors," he told them.

Struan was all too aware that he had completely failed to meet his bride before the fateful day, and now he was profoundly regretting that lapse. Calan had taken the initiative to send her flowers for the past four days, and told Struan he'd done so only this morning. "I knew you were distracted," he'd said kindly.

A few more people filtered in, most coming to greet Struan and his friends, even though they were strangers. One man introduced himself as Nicholas Alpin, Elspeth's uncle and McGregor's brother-in-law. He was joined by his wife, Rosalind, who was as unlike McGregor as it was possible for two siblings to be. She was an apple crumble personified: humble, sweet, welcomed by nearly everyone. She even had round, apple-like cheeks.

"So you've swept our little Elspeth off her feet, have you? About time! I thought the poor lass would never esc… that is, leave her childhood home," she said.

"Luckily we got Elspeth's letter this week, reminding us of the wedding. Can't think how the original invitation never reached us," Nicholas added. While his wife seemed completely sincere, there was a questioning note in the man's eyes. Not hostility, just an awareness that something was strange about this situation.

"It was good of you to come," Calan answered for Struan. "Don't mind telling you that I was surprised when I heard too. But glad. MacInnes makes a miserable bachelor."

Calan's natural charm worked as it always did, and the uncomfortable issue of the wedding's timing was passed by.

Then there was another flutter of activity at the church door. The McGregors had arrived. The father, of course, was dressed as nattily as he had been when he met Struan in the gaming hell. The wife was no less impressive, in a green ensemble that put Struan in mind of a fashionable dragon. Two younger women wore light-colored gowns that would not have been out of place at a London wedding (he knew that the dark-haired one was Elspeth's blood sister, Mairi, and the blonde one was her stepsister, Averill). The dark-haired one spotted Struan and his friends immediately, and glared at all of them.

"Should we check that one for weapons?" Calan murmured.

"Why bother?" Duncan rumbled back. "Safe to say she's armed to the teeth. Someone definitely doesn't approve of this marriage."

Struan ignored them, because he'd seen the third sister— his bride. He got only the slightest glimpse of her before the other women whisked her through to the parish house. But that was enough.

She looked completely different than she had when he'd spied on her doing the laundry with the servants. Now Elspeth McGregor wore a pale yellow dress. Like the gowns of the other women, it was high-waisted and loose below the waist. But he was uncomfortably aware of the young lady's figure, especially the upper part, which was so carefully framed by the low neckline of the gown. The color was not unlike watery sunshine coming through after a multiday rainstorm. But the woman's smile was anything but pale. She practically beamed, a joyous expression that frankly unnerved Struan.

He was sure she hadn't seen him.

Struan departed the semicircle of his friends, saying he wanted to speak alone to Elspeth's father, which was true. But it was more that he didn't want them to overhear.

McGregor looked smug when he saw Struan approaching. "Ah, the bridegroom in all his splendor!" he declared with obvious mockery. "I'm sure the bride will be speechless."

Struan pulled her father aside. He hissed, "She doesn't know the details of the arrangement, does she?"

"No. You were clear about that condition, and I happen to be in full agreement. Women are unreliable, and it's foolish to tell them more than necessary. I explained that you admired her from afar and preferred to do things your way. You will forgive the slight exaggeration about admiring her."

Actually Struan didn't think it was an exaggeration, though he recognized the man's meaning.

He said, "You don't think she has any inkling at all?"

"Elspeth is an exceedingly simple soul," her father said. "She believes what she's told."

"And you will never tell her the origins of this marriage arrangement. Even afterward." Struan scowled at him. It was easy, because the more he spoke to McGregor, the more he despised the man.

"I will abide by your wishes," her father assured him. "It's not as if it matters anyway. Soon she'll be at your home in the Highlands, and who will know the truth there, except yourself? I've not told anyone, and I'm here in Edinburgh. So the secret is as safe as it possibly can be."

The argument was sound, so why did Struan have a sick feeling in his gut?

* * * *

They had dressed Elspeth in one of Averill's older gowns for the wedding, after both Averill and her mother agreed that it would reflect poorly upon the family if Elspeth wore one of her own gowns, which could charitably be described as utilitarian. Averill condescended to offer Elspeth the use of a dress that would be appropriate for something as important as a wedding ceremony. It was wool, an acknowledgment of Scotland's often chilly weather, even in months that were nominally warm. But it was a finely woven fabric that took its daffodil-yellow dye well. Further, it was delicately enhanced with white lace edging that highlighted the lines of the dress.

"It's a little sweet for my taste now," Averill said as she presented the dress to Elspeth a few days prior. "I don't think I've worn it since before my trip to London, and I almost forgot I owned it!"

Thus Elspeth was outfitted extravagantly in her consideration, and the family proceeded to the church with plenty of time before the ceremony was to begin. Elspeth wondered if her father was expecting something to go wrong. Though what could go wrong with a plan when so little had been planned in the first place?

When they arrived at the church, her stepmother whisked Elspeth off to a side room in the parish house, and then kept her there so that she could make a suitably grand entrance at the right moment. Elspeth thought she was ready to get married when she left the house, but there were several more steps. She was fussed over to a degree never before experienced.

Mairi assured Elspeth that guests were arriving and taking their seats in the pews, and that the bridegroom's guests were there as well. Though small in number, they were evidently impressive in appearance. Averill kept peeking out from the end of the hallway, where she could occasionally catch a glimpse of one of them walking by every few moments or so.

"They are all remarkably good-looking," Averill reported without offering any useful details whatsoever.

"Well then," Mairi said, rolling her eyes. "Why not walk out and welcome them? Perhaps that's all it will take for one of them to start courting you. You're not much use flitting around here like a drunk butterfly."

"Oh, goodness, that would never do. I have a list of potential suitors and I doubt any of them are on it. I expect they're all fresh from the war. *I'm* not going to marry a sometime soldier."

Elspeth's stepmother, who had been adjusting the bow around the waist of the gown, now gave Averill a stern look. "Hush. In fact, come with me for a moment. I have something to say to you." Susan McGregor's ire toward her daughter was unusual, and it added to Elspeth's disquiet.

Then it was just her and Mairi.

In a low voice, Elspeth said, "I'm sorry I'm abandoning you to deal with Averill alone."

"I will endure," Mairi replied. "Or I'll kill her. One or the other."

"Let's hope it doesn't come to that. Maybe she'll go back to visit her relatives in England, like she did last year."

"Ach, that was a beautiful time, wasn't it?" Mairi said. "The house so was calm and quiet, and we didn't have to listen to Her Spoilt Majesty. Granted, after she came back, she would not shut up about the glories of London, which was almost as bad."

"Thanks to her reports, I think I could find every city landmark without a map," Elspeth agreed.

"The splendor of the Serpentine! The exquisite shops of Bond Street! The evenings at Covent Garden, when the glow from the lanterns among the trees is nothing less than other-worldly. Ugh!"

Elspeth laughed, for she could hear Averill saying exactly that phrase in her dreamiest tone (and a disdainful expression for certain young ladies who didn't ever visit London).

"I'm glad they left," said Mairi. "This is a good moment."

Her sister pulled out a small velvet pouch from somewhere beneath her gown. Mairi believed that reticules were ridiculous and all ladies' wear should have pockets. She'd slashed all her dresses and sewn in a pocket, regardless of how the resulting weight "ruined" the drape of the fabric (according to Averill).

"You'd never get away with such a look in London," Averill had declared when she'd first noticed.

"Do I look as if I care what the fashions are in London?" Mairi had snapped back.

This exchange had been repeated several times in subsequent months, with no change in either party's view, as is often the case.

Now, Mairi opened the little pouch and pulled out a strand of perfectly matched, creamy-colored pearls.

"Where did those come from?" Elspeth asked, astonished. "I've never seen them before."

"You wouldn't have, dear heart. They belonged to Mama and they've been lost for a long time."

"Lost?"

"I took them from her jewelry box after she died because she loved them so much and I needed something of hers to hold. I slept with them beneath my pillow for months. Along about when Papa began to court again, he asked me if I'd seen them. I guessed he meant to give them as a gift to the next Mrs McGregor. So of course I lied and said I had no idea where they were. I kept them hidden all these years." Mairi squeezed Elspeth's shoulders. "Until today. Because Mama would have wanted you to have them."

Elspeth was practically in tears at the story. "But Mairi, you love them."

"Bah. I was their caretaker, and now I give them to you, so one day you can give them to your daughter. It's not as if the family line will continue through me."

Mairi fastened the pearls on, tying them with the silk ribbon at the ends. It was a short strand that nestled about Elspeth's neck. She reached up to touch one of the silky smooth globes.

"They're so beautiful," Elspeth said softly.

"Father won't like it, but he won't see till you're in public, so he won't say anything," Mairi muttered.

Averill and her mother returned then. Averill's expression was sullen, so whatever had been discussed wasn't about how pretty she looked today.

Finally, some secret signal was passed, and it was time for Elspeth to walk down the aisle and become a bride. Averill and Mairi hurried out to take their seats, with Mairi giving her a hug and kiss before she went. "Best wishes, Pest. And if he makes you miserable, say the word and I'll curse him as strongly as any weird sister did upon a blasted heath."

"Oh, I do love you, Mairi," Elspeth whispered back.

Her stepmother remained a few moments to adjust Elspeth's gown and tuck her hair into its proper place.

"These pearls are lovely—did you just put them on?" she asked curiously.

"It was a surprise from Mairi," Elspeth said.

"Hmm. She is full of surprises, isn't she." Susan McGregor was unfailingly proper, but also cold, and Elspeth had never felt that her stepmother liked her much. But now she said, "You have always done what has been asked of you, Elspeth." The words had the feeling of praise, which was uncommon enough that Elspeth picked up her ears.

"I intend to keep doing so," she said.

"You deserve a good husband and a good life. I will pray that you shall have both, since your own mother is not here to do so." Her stepmother gave her an awkward kiss on her cheek and hurried away, leaving Elspeth in a rather confused state.

But she knew exactly what she had to do next, which was to put one foot in front of the other, and proceeded down the narrow passageway and into the nave of the church where her future lay.

She did so, hearing the familiar wedding hymn sung by a dutiful but indifferent choir. She walked down the center aisle in a perfectly straight line. She saw her father and smiled at him, only to see that his face had gone white and his lips were pinched. His gaze was locked on her neck, and she realized that Mairi was entirely correct about his reaction to the pearls.

After that, she kept her eyes on the floor about five feet in front of her so that she wouldn't suddenly trip or embarrass herself in front of her groom. But when she came to the end of the aisle and saw the dais in front of her, she looked up.

Aside from the minister, there was only one man standing

in front of her. Part of Elspeth wondered if she would recognize him in the moment. Had she seen him at some event or on the street? Maybe, even if he'd been to reticent to court her face-to-face.

But she would have remembered if she'd seen this man before, because he was unforgettable. Her first impression was that he was massive. He was well over six feet tall; Elspeth was five and half. His size was not just height, but also breadth, particularly his shoulders and chest, which made him dominate the room. His legs were also big, though only in the sense that they fit the rest of him. He wasn't portly at all, and if anything, he actually looked somewhat lean, if such a thing were possible for a man so large. It was a wonder, Elspeth thought suddenly, that he'd managed to live through a war, considering what a big target he made. But then she realized that he'd been close to a different fate.

He had turned toward her fully by that point.

She beheld a face that had been through some ordeal that she couldn't even imagine. The scarring was most prominent on the right side of his face, and the skin had been affected in such a way that his right eyelid was permanently pulled down a bit, as if he was constantly about to squint. The same scar that pulled at the eyelid also crossed his cheekbone and continued down toward his jaw. The right side of his mouth was also pulled out of alignment.

The result was that while he seemed to be able to laugh or smile or scowl or do anything the face would normally do on his left side, the right side did not follow to the same degree.

He was entirely clean shaven, perhaps because the scarring meant that it would be impossible to grow facial hair with any sort of even result. As Elspeth always liked the look of clean-shaven men, this was no disappointment at all. She looked directly into his russet brown eyes then, and saw a familiar expression. It was an awareness that almost bordered on panic, and she recognized it because it was the expression she saw in the mirror every time she looked at it this morning. He was just as nervous as she was, and that knowledge warmed her heart considerably.

She had worried that he would be cold and not really want Elspeth, but rather had selected her for some quality that was merely convenient. That was a logical concern, considering his courtship by proxy.

But, she reasoned, if he was nervous, that meant he cared. And if he cared about the situation, that meant he wanted it to be a success, just as she did. And now that she saw that he had suffered in a way that left him visibly damaged, she could understand why he had elected to seek Elspeth's hand through such unorthodox means.

He'd been concerned that she would be turned away by a poor first impression, and that would make all of the courtship more difficult and painful for him. But Elspeth was determined that she wouldn't disappoint him at this stage, for it was one of her most dearly held principles that she should never disappoint anyone if it was in her power to please them.

Glad that she now had the answer to her groom's reticence, Elspeth smiled at him and stepped up onto the dais, even as she stretched out one hand so he could take it.

She said softly, "Hello, I'm Elspeth. It's such a lovely day, and now that we have finally met, I believe it is time for us to marry."

Chapter 7

THE WEDDING WAS PERFORMED WITH remarkable efficiency by the minister, who kept looking at her as if he expected her to run away. Elspeth wanted to tweak the clergyman's nose. Why was everyone acting like she was a lamb to the slaughter? Elspeth was getting married to a gentleman. This was exactly what she was supposed to do.

"...man and wife," the minister concluded. "You may kiss the bride," he advised Struan quietly.

Struan hesitated, then took her hand and briefly lifted it to his lips. Elspeth tried to smile at him, but the moment she felt his breath across the backs of her fingers, she somehow grew hot, and gasped.

He stopped and dropped her hand abruptly, stepping back a pace.

At the gentle urging of the minister, who assured them that the ceremony was complete and irrevocable now, Struan escorted Elspeth back down the central aisle, where she accepted the congratulations of the small but intensely interested crowd.

Elspeth's few school friends and neighbors who'd come gave her best wishes and some conflicting advice about married life, most of which Elspeth didn't really hear.

The men who'd come to the church with Struan seemed

keen to talk with her. And she was happy to learn more about them, especially if they could tell her anything about Struan. However, she wasn't able to get much out of them, since the discussion was largely focused on her and how she felt about her new marital status. She had to keep reassuring everyone that she was delighted.

While they talked, Elspeth looked over at the man who was now her husband. Her father's words echoed in her brain: *He has chosen you.*

But *how* exactly did he do that? That was still a mystery. Elspeth didn't have a great many friends in the city, and she went to only a few entertainments—and most of those were largely intended for women only. Mairi sometimes hauled her along to the meetings of the League for the Advancement of Scottish Women, but men were rare at those! And she'd have remembered seeing Struan MacInnes, if for no other reason than his sheer size.

Then she realized how good Struan was at standing back, remaining still and unnoticed. He'd obviously made an effort to keep himself away from the center of attention, knowing that everyone made a fuss over brides at a wedding. Or maybe he felt uncomfortable about the scars he wore.

The gentleman's appearance was impressive, not frightening. And as for the scars around his neck and the rather long one on his face…well, her first impulse was sympathy. She hoped the scars were just scars at this point, and he no longer suffered pain.

"We ought to go home," Mairi said at last, nudging her. "We've got to get you in proper traveling attire and all that."

"Yes, don't dawdle," their father told them as he passed by. "Mairi said you wanted to walk back together, though you better get your husband's permission first. Not my concern now!" He grinned as if he'd told a marvelous joke.

Mairi remained by her side as her family departed the

church. Then she said, "I had hoped for better from Father and our stepmother, but to be honest, this is exactly what I expected. He ought to be ashamed of himself. Not even giving a wedding breakfast."

"He's only concerned about the future, I think," said Elspeth. "And after all, now I am in the care of my husband, who will surely feed me breakfast if I ask."

"Yes, but will you?" her sister wondered aloud. "You're not good at asking for what you want, and you can't survive on air."

"I suppose you think that I've failed womankind by marrying."

"You were always meant to marry," her sister responded, now with a softer tone. "It's in your nature. I shall never choose to do the same, but that is my choice. That's all a woman really wants—the choice. Whether it is what gown to wear, or whether to stay home or go to a party, or if she wants a husband or not. It ought to be her decision, instead of society making the decision for her."

"When is the next meeting of your ladies' league?" Elspeth asked with a laugh.

"Wednesday," her sister replied promptly. "Too bad you'll be in the Highlands by then, or I'd drag you along."

"Should it not be my choice to go or not? To the meeting, I mean."

Her sister burst out laughing. "You *have* been listening! Oh, that's encouraging. Pest, I'm going to miss you so much!" She suddenly flung her arms around Elspeth, who returned the tight hug with tears pricking her eyes.

"I'll miss you as well. But you can come for a visit. Or we shall return to the city from time to time."

Mairi said, "You'd better! If he keeps you up there forever, he's a beast."

It was unfortunate that Struan reached them just at that

moment, hearing only the last few words.

Elspeth felt horrid, and hoped that he didn't think her sister was referring to his scars. "We were just talking about whether you would permit my sister to come visit," Elspeth told him.

"It's a long way," Struan said to her sister. It certainly sounded like a no. He was frowning. But maybe he always looked like he was frowning.

"Then when do you expect to come back to Edinburgh? For the Season, perhaps?" Her sister's question was perfectly polite, but she issued it like a challenge to joust.

"Perhaps."

He wasn't the most talkative of men. Elspeth took a breath. "We will discuss all those details later. You must forgive Mairi," she added. "I'm afraid that she's rather blunt. But she's my sister and I assure you she means the best."

"I have always wanted the best for Pest," Mairi said, so quickly that the pet name wasn't caught by anyone but her. "Oh, that reminds me." Mairi reached over to Elspeth's neck and untied the pearls. She put them back into the velvet pouch and then handed it to Struan. "Will you kindly keep these safe for your wife? They're a family heirloom and it would be a shame if they got…lost in the commotion."

Struan took the pouch, clearly confused. Elspeth was also confused, because she didn't lose things. Not even her sewing needles, and certainly not her mother's jewelry. Then she remembered her father's glare when he saw the pearls, and she decided that Mairi was worried he'd demand them back if they were still around her neck when Elspeth returned to the house.

Then Aunt Rosalind called to her near the church door, and Elspeth nodded to show that she'd join her. "Goodness, everyone wants to talk to me today."

"Well, it's your wedding day," Mairi commented tartly.

All Struan said was, "You must see what she has to say. And you then need to go back to your house to prepare for the journey north. I'll come for you at three, if that's acceptable."

"Yes, of course. I'll be there. I mean, obviously I'll be there. It's my house. Well, my family's house. It was my house up until a few minutes ago. Now my house is your house," she said in a rush. The very thought of sharing a home filled her with joy.

He blinked, then said, "So three is fine?"

"Wonderful. I can't wait. I mean, I *will* wait…of course." Elspeth took a breath. When she was nervous or excited, she tended to chatter. "But don't be late, please."

* * * *

Struan regarded the woman who was now his wife.

Elspeth was hurrying toward her aunt, who'd been not so patiently waiting to talk to her. Her whole family seemed to think that Elspeth ought to always be ready to respond to anything they said or did.

But at least she had a family.

Now he did too, or at least the beginning of one. He had a *wife*. Who seemed happy to be his wife.

Why? What woman would want the Struan who returned from the battlefields? The one who didn't just look damaged on the outside, but was twisted inside, until he hardly resembled the man he once was. What woman could ignore that reality, and blithely step into Struan's old fantasy of a simple, happy family life?

It was madness.

And yet, Elspeth hadn't hesitated.

He wasn't fooled. She'd been startled by his appearance when she finally saw him. She must have a strong sense of duty to carry out the promise her father made on her behalf. Struan respected her grit, concealed behind that cheerful façade.

He just didn't believe that he could give her the future she was no doubt hoping for.

"She's really like that, you know."

Mairi McGregor was still standing next to him. He'd been so consumed with his sudden shift in fortune that he'd forgotten she was there.

"Like what?" he asked.

"Warm. Kind. Sincere. Selfless. Trusting." Mairi shot off the list of virtues like a challenge. "People often think she's putting on a good face, but that's her true face. She's pure sunshine. I see it easily because I'm all thundercloud. But she's my sister, and if I hear a single hint that she's unhappy, I will know that it's serious because Elspeth is *never* unhappy."

"I'll do my best to avoid making her unhappy."

"Do better than that, sir. It's not enough to simply decline to cause pain. It is your responsibility to cause joy."

"I'm not terribly good at joy," he said.

Mairi raised one eyebrow. "Elspeth will balance that out…so long as you don't mangle your own role."

"Thank you for the advice," he said.

"I offer it freely, in the hopes that you will take it. Because if you don't, and you make my sister miserable, I'll find a way to make you miserable too."

Struan took a deep breath, unsure if he'd actually just been threatened by this fierce creature disguised as a young lady. "You'd have to work hard to surpass the misery I've already endured."

Mairi inclined her head in acknowledgment, but not apology. "Then I have my assignment, and you have yours. Congratulations on your marriage, sir," she said, suddenly smiling wide. Struan realized that Elspeth was returning. "And since we are now all family, I trust that we shall never be long out of touch."

Elspeth heard that and took it at its surface meaning. *Trusting*, Mairi had said. She reached out to take her sister's hand. "Oh, yes, Mairi. I shall write three times a week! And I hope you will manage it at least once."

"For you, I'll endure the hell of weekly letter writing," Mairi replied with a grimace. "And I will read every single word you send me. Now let's go back home to get you ready." As they headed toward the church door, Mairi sent a glance at Struan over Elspeth's shoulder.

Struan knew that look. He used to get it from old sergeants and captains, men who expected instant and complete obedience to their orders.

So what else was he to do?

He raised his hand to his forehead and gave Mairi a light-ning-quick, subtle salute.

But his mind was on Elspeth.

"She's friendly," Calan said to Struan in an undertone as he joined him.

"Elspeth is. Her older sister, not so much."

"Well, that makes sense. My older brother is a complete arsehole. But your new wife…she's cheerful."

Struan said, "I'm just glad to have it over. The courtship and wedding part, I mean. I don't think I could have endured another humiliation like the first."

"Forget Isla," Calan advised. "This Elspeth McGregor is a better match for you."

"How do you know?"

"I just do." Calan said, "The fact is, I didn't like Isla. She was pretty, and knew the right things to say, but I never warmed to her."

"I'm surprised there's a woman in Scotland you haven't

warmed to," Struan replied, not bothering to keep the tight tone out of his voice. "Why didn't you tell me this before?"

"If I had, what would you have done? It's not as if you could've broken off the engagement without causing some scandal. Even though her reasons were shallow, and frankly disgusting, I'm glad she jilted you. It saved you a world of misery."

"We'll see." Struan regarded the gleaming blonde woman who was speaking to guests by the church door—despite Mairi's obvious impatience to get Elspeth back home. They were both speaking to Thane and his companion, Catriona Ross. Evidently Miss Ross and Miss McGregor were in the same ladies' rights group, a fact that was causing much discussion among the three women.

Elspeth gestured as she made some point he couldn't overhear. She was just as beautiful every time he looked at her. It scared him. How could a person with such a lovely face look on his face without repugnance?

Just then, the lady glanced over toward him. She dropped her gaze a moment later, but the smile on her face remained, looking for all the world like a woman who was pleased with her life.

Struan couldn't believe it. Her father had been desperate to get rid of her. There had to be *something* wrong with Elspeth McGregor. However, no matter how long he looked at her or observed her behavior, he couldn't for the life of him tell what that flaw was.

Chapter 8

AT THE HOUSE, PRECISELY AT three, Elspeth bid farewell to her family. Her stepmother offered her a surprisingly vehement embrace and wished her all the best. Her father, looking calm as a cat, told her that she'd done well and had the marriage she deserved, which made Elspeth glow with happiness. Averill reminded Elspeth not to neglect her gift (saying so with a wicked smile).

But it was Mairi who undid her, giving her countless hugs. "Oh, you're going away, my little Pest!" Mairi said, as if just now realizing that fact.

"Married, not buried," Elspeth whispered. "We'll see each other again."

Then she was in Struan's carriage, heading toward the harbor. Struan informed her that they'd make the initial part of the journey by ship to hasten their arrival at his—no, their —home. They would sail as far as Wick. At the small port town, they'd have a carriage waiting to finish the last part of the trip overland.

The journey north was a revelation for Elspeth, who'd never been more than two days' ride from Edinburgh. She had never sailed before, and she discovered that she loved it. Everything about the ship was well-ordered, tidy, and logical, which appealed to Elspeth's sensibilities. Once she learned how the ship moved beneath her feet, she enjoyed strolling on the deck, shifting her body weight side to side, tipping forward or back on her feet to meet the pitch in the waves.

When Struan came on deck, she waved happily to him. He slowly made his way over to her. He didn't seem to mind the ship's motion, but he took his time to reach her.

"This is so much fun!" Elspeth said when he was close enough. "I love my cabin. Everything fits perfectly into place and it's all bolted down just so. It's like…well, I don't know what it's like! Do you sail often?"

"When necessary."

"Do you not enjoy it?"

He shrugged. "It doesn't bother me. The sea's mild today. You might feel differently about sailing if we get caught in a squall."

"Oh, I'm sure the crew knows exactly what to do if that happens. How long will we be on the ship?"

"We should be back on land the day after tomorrow. So two nights aboard. Why?"

"Just wondering. I've never slept on a ship. Well, I've never done anything on a ship. Which includes sleeping. You must have."

"Whenever I was deployed, yes."

"And where did you go?"

"The Peninsula for a few years. Then northern France, until last year. After I was injured, I came back. Eventually."

At the tension in his tone, she hesitated before saying, "May I ask a rather personal question?"

"You're my wife," he replied, which wasn't exactly an invitation, but she plunged forward anyway.

"I wanted to know if your wound still causes any pain. I noticed that you don't turn your head when you look at something, you turn your whole body. Is that due to the scarring on your neck?"

He said nothing, but his jaw tightened further.

"Excuse me, it was an impolite question," she said in a rush. "I've no right to ask, but it bothered me to think of you hurting after so long. A year, you said?"

"Fifteen months," he said in a low voice. "And yes, to answer your first, rather personal question, it still hurts."

"Oh, I'm so sorry. Can a doctor not give you something?"

"Doctors have given me plenty. Mostly some form of laudanum or opium, which I don't wish to take."

"Perhaps a poultice? To aid the skin's healing so you can move freely. It must be annoying to not be able to twist one's neck without—"

"The scarring extends beyond my neck," he said abruptly. "And any *poultice*—" (he spoke the word with utter disdain) "—would require half a day to apply, not to mention leaving me looking like a well-wrapped mummy."

Elspeth felt thoroughly reprimanded for her careless inquiry. Why should she speak of doctors and remedies as if she knew better than those who already treated him?

"Forgive me. I didn't mean to add to your distress."

"I'm not distressed," he countered, obviously lying. "But I will thank you to not bring it up again."

Elspeth bowed her head. She'd displeased him. So much for the wisdom of admiring from afar! If he'd tried to court her the usual way, he surely would have decided she didn't suit him. Now he was stuck with her.

Well, she'd simply have to work that much harder to show him that she could be a good wife. Luckily, Elspeth was skilled at running a household, thanks to her years of experience keeping her father's home. She'd do her best at Linneliath, so Struan wouldn't feel that he'd made a mistake in that regard.

"I do have one more question."

"What a surprise," he said dryly.

She blinked at the hint of humor in his voice. "Did you just mock me?" she asked, unexpectedly delighted.

He didn't seem to know how to react to that. "I might have," he said finally. "I didn't mean to."

"No, it was funny. Do you know any jokes?"

"Was that your one more question?"

"Oh, no! I had meant to ask…well, obviously when we're in public I'll address you properly as Mr MacInnes. But I wanted to know if you had a preference for what I should call you at home, when it's just us. That is, if you prefer to remain Mr MacInnes, I am happy to do so—"

He put a hand up, cutting her off. "You could call me Struan, when we're not in public. Which will be most of the time."

She said, "Struan isn't a name that lends itself to any variations, is it?"

"No," he agreed. "Unlike Elspeth, which has a dozen. What does your family call you?"

"Just Elspeth," she replied, somewhat puzzled by the question. It was true that *Elizabeth* contained multitudes: Lizzie, Liz, Beth, Bette, Liza. Elspeth was the Scottish version of the name and she imagined that some people shortened that too. But her own father never did, and his wife and Averill followed his lead. Only Mairi differed.

"Mairi calls me Pest," she shared.

"Excuse me?"

"When I was little, I couldn't say my own name well. It came out as Els-pest. Mairi thought it was hilarious. But she uses it in an affectionate way."

"I don't expect you'd like your husband to call you a pest. How about Ellie?"

"Oh! Yes, that's nice." She smiled happily.

"Your mother never came up with a pet name for you?" he asked, now watching her instead of the ocean.

"She died giving birth to me."

"I didn't know. I'm sorry to hear it." He looked genuinely troubled at the revelation. "Your father didn't mention the fact."

Had he mentioned *any* facts about Elspeth's life to Struan? Increasingly, it seemed not. "It was a long time ago," she said. She realized his hand had dropped to cover hers on the wide wooden gunwale. The skin was deeply tanned, sinewy, and peppered with tiny scars. It looked like a hand that had done a great many things. Her own hand felt small under his, fragile. Not the hand of someone who'd done much at all.

"Twenty years isn't that long. You speak as if you're an old crone."

"Not yet," she said. "I suppose I have a little while before I sit by the fire all day and complain about my bones creaking." The image pleased her. "Perhaps I'll keep a cauldron over the flames and tell all the children that it's a potion I'm tending."

"What sort of potion?"

"Oh, depends on the child. If they're loud, it will be a potion that takes their voice. If they're anxious, it will be a potion that sends them to sleep. And if they're sad, it will be a potion that grants happiness. Really, of course, it will be cider. I like cider, especially in winter."

"You seem to have everything planned out. Though I think you'd make a terrible witch. You're too cheerful."

"I'm afraid that's true. But I don't expect to be a witch for a long time yet." She took a deep breath. "I'm excited to see your home. Can you tell me about it?"

"Linneliath is…rather large. More than what I need, but it was built for a big family, so there are rooms that are empty now but that I remember others living in."

"Is it close to a town?"

"A small village," he said cautiously, "so don't expect

must diversion there. There are a few shops for necessities. Everything else must be ordered from a larger town or shipped from Edinburgh."

"How many families live there? Or near there?"

"I'm not sure. Several dozen? Probably more. I...I've been away."

"You must be eager to come home at last. Or will you still have commitments in regard to the army?"

"No, I'm of no more use to them," he said, and the bitterness was back. "Once a soldier is done, he's on his own again."

She turned her hand under his, their palms now touching. "But now you have me."

Struan looked down at their hands, and seemed surprised to find them clasped.

Chapter 9

TRAVELING WITH ELSPETH WAS A challenge.

Not for the usual reasons one often heard about bad traveling companions. She never complained, she wasn't fussy, and she never ever wandered off (granted, the last was difficult to do on a ship).

No, the challenge came from the fact that she was so damned delighted by everything. She loved the ship, she was entranced by the coastline, she even enjoyed the meals. *No one* enjoyed meals on a ship.

Except Elspeth.

They'd been on the ship for less than twenty-four hours, and she'd charmed them all. The captain found every reason to chat with her, and all the sailors called her ma'am and doffed hats when she passed by. And everyone had the same look in their eyes when Elspeth stood near Struan, or smiled at Struan, or chatted with Struan.

The look asked *Why?*

Why was a woman like her with a man like him?

He never wanted to answer that question.

Fortunately, Elspeth was easy to steer. If she started asking about topics he'd rather avoid (his scars, his military service, his utterly appalling secret deal with her father that resulted in her being handed off like a calf at market), he could redirect her attention to literally anything, such as a rocky coastline or a bird in flight, and she'd plunge (rhetorically speaking) directly after it.

Maintaining physical distance from her was also a challenge. Though in some ways it was easier than he expected, in other ways it was impossible.

He'd been careful of her the whole trip, often asking if she needed anything or if she felt well. And he'd gone out of his way to, well, go out of her way. He had informed her as soon as they boarded the ship and he showed her to her cabin that he would refrain from seeking her out until she had actually reached her new home and had time to adjust.

He had expected to see relief in her face when he told her the news, but he had not expected the genuinely warm smile she'd given him as she said, "You are so thoughtful! In truth, I am a little worried that I might have some seasickness, and I assume that would hamper my experience of...anything else." She hadn't looked him in the eye as she said those words. She couldn't know what to expect on a typical wedding night, and he felt a stab of remorse when he realized that this lovely young woman wouldn't ever get a typical wedding night. In the first place, what was to have been her wedding night was spent at sea. And in the second place, she was married to him. That was going to entail a lot of adjustment from ideals to the more sobering reality.

After disembarking from the ship at Wick, they stayed at an inn not far from the harbor. Struan told her that they'd leave early the next morning and should reach his home by the end of that day. "No point in traveling in the dark to save a few hours tomorrow."

So he was sleeping alone again tonight. Which was why he was wide awake, staring at the top canopy of his bed, listening to each creak of the building, the muffled sounds from the common room below, the breath of wind and distant lap of waves. True, he rarely slept well now, due to the lingering aches and pains throughout his body. But tonight was worse, because he was also thinking of the woman in the next room. Elspeth, the beaming, kind-hearted woman who never seemed to think ill of anyone or anything, and who was now shackled to him, a morose bastard who really should be shut away so no one else had to put up with his brooding.

This marriage was a mistake. A failure on every level.

Well, not every level, because he'd certainly acquired a beautiful wife. He remembered watching her leaning against the side of the ship, her purple dress lightly dampened by the spray from the endless waves. He could see more than he was meant to, and it all rushed back now to plague him, alone in his bed.

Her nipples had hardened in the cold ocean air, and they'd pressed against the fabric of her bodice in a way that he couldn't ignore. Her hair had come slightly loose in the wind, and he'd wanted to both tuck the strands back in, gently, but also to unleash it all and wind it around his hands as he kissed that perfect pink mouth.

It was confusing to simultaneously feel aroused, feel like a heel for being aroused, and *then* feel like feeling like heel was actually being ungrateful because the woman arousing him was in fact his wife, and shouldn't he be aroused by his wife?

Yes, except for the fact that she didn't know *why* she was his wife. And if she ever saw him without the shield of his clothing, she would not be aroused.

She'd be horrified.

He woke in the morning in a mood halfway between sour and not-sour. He attributed the sourness to not sleeping, and not-sourness to the fact that he'd get home by tonight.

The remainder of the trip was overland in a closed carriage. They departed after an early breakfast, and the road thinned out to an increasingly bumpy track, through a decreasingly populated countryside.

"I thought there'd be more farms?" Elspeth asked at one point.

"There used to be. I remember seeing barns and crops and livestock. But many landlords have begun clearing the land for other uses."

She frowned. "Is not the best use of the land to provide a home and living for the people on it?"

He agreed, though he didn't have the clear head to discuss the finer points of the emerging Scottish economy. She smelled good, and it was distracting.

At one point, she said, "Oh, I remember something I meant to say ever since the wedding. I never properly thanked you for the flowers you sent each day before we married. They were all beautiful. How did you know I adore lilies? And you even got yellow, which is my favorite!"

Struan had some idea how Calan (who had sent the flowers without Struan's aid—or indeed knowledge) got that information. But he wasn't about to tear down the illusion his friend had worked hard to put up. So he said, "If I told you how I knew, you'd be less impressed."

"I assure you I wouldn't, but I can't for the life of me think how you figured it out," Elspeth said.

Because you're too innocent to think of bribing the servants to share information about the family. Aloud, he said, "A good magician never reveals his secrets."

"Oh, I knew it! I bet you did use magic. Waking up to such astonishing blooms, seeing them and smelling them… when they'll not be blooming for months in the outside world. It really is as if you cast a spell."

"Only the spell of paying for a grower at a glasshouse to pick them," he said wryly (for that was how Calan performed his "magic"). "I'm afraid the only spell I have is money."

"Yes, we asked around about you, me and Mairi."

"And? What did you learn?" he asked, keeping his impulse to panic at bay. Was she about to drop the mask of innocence and lay into him for his despicable bargain?

"Only that you were from the north and you were an officer in the army, and that you were thought to be wealthy. All of which was no use to me! I wanted to know if you were kind and noble."

"I try to be kind," he said, hoping that was true. "I don't know what it means to be noble." As soon as he finished speaking, he worried that it might be the other way around.

"That doesn't matter now. I could tell in the church that you were everything I hoped for."

"You could?"

"Yes, of course. And I thought that you might have gone about courting me the usual way, but I understand why you didn't, and really, it's all right because your way was wildly romantic. Few ladies can say they were swept away by a mysterious gentleman, but I'll always have that story to tell, even when I'm terribly old, and it will still be romantic."

Talking to Elspeth would require him to practice paying attention. She moved so fast in conversation that it was difficult to keep up. He normally rode alone, in quiet. But Elspeth wasn't good at being quiet. And she had so many questions. Elspeth was interested in all of it—the sparsely treed land, the shifting shoreline, and the occasional hints of prior habitation, like standing stones and ruins.

She may have asked Struan *how much longer* a few too many times.

"You'll know when we arrive," he assured her finally, "because we'll stop moving."

"Oh, very well," she said, chastened. "But do tell me the moment the house and land comes into view, please? I don't want to miss it."

Eventually, the inevitable result of traveling in a carriage occurred, and Struan started to doze. Even Elspeth drifted off, curling up on the opposite bench, looking astonishingly comfortable wrapped in the plaid blanket that was always kept in the carriage—Scottish weather not being known for its stability.

They stopped for a midday meal and to change horses, and then, at last, the carriage started to roll past slopes and ridges that were painfully, heart-achingly familiar to Struan.

Home was so near.

He looked across the carriage to his wife, who'd fallen asleep again.

In sleep, her natural enthusiasm was banked, and he got a glimpse of her unfiltered by her intense personality. Her face smoothed and softened. Her lips were pink, the upper lip indented in the center to make a perfect bow of her mouth. Light brown lashes rested on her skin, and slightly darker eyebrows made a nearly straight line above her eyes—not much of a curve there at all. It was, all in all, a pretty face, though not exactly arresting in repose. Much of Elspeth's beauty came from her animation, her interest in the world around her. Asleep, she looked much more...well, *fragile* wasn't the right word.

Innocent.

The sort of innocence that came from too much faith in others.

The sort of innocence that got people hurt.

Struan vowed that moment that he'd do everything he could to give Elspeth the happiest life he could manage. Even if he'd acquired her in an underhanded way, that didn't mean he wasn't going to treat her like a princess. She deserved that.

He reached forward, touching her shoulder as lightly as

he could. "Elspeth?"

"Hmmm?"

There was something alluring in that one murmured sound, that sleepy, lazy hum.

She stretched, arching her back and causing the fabric of her bodice to tighten across her chest. Her eyelids opened with a flutter, blue eyes half-lidded. And that pose was ten times as alluring.

You're not getting near that body anytime soon, he reminded himself.

"You wanted to see the house when it came into view," Struan said, trying to repress the most basic male response to anything even vaguely sensual.

"Oh! Yes, I do!" Elspeth leaned to the window, which meant that he now had her practically in his lap, which was not a terrible thing in itself. Not at all. She had put something in her hair that made it shine, and she—amazingly, considering the journey—still smelled like flowers and afternoon sun.

"There is Linneliath." He pointed. He had always loved his home, which stood on a long ridgeline of the moor. It was a rather haphazard house, because it was like looking into the past. The oldest part of the house, clearly medieval, was originally a small fortress to protect the inhabitants from attacks. It had been added onto throughout the years, following the broad top of the ridgeline. Tudor, then more modern additions every few generations. As the sections of the house were built, one could see the progression of the architects' skill, and the effects of improvements in things like window glass. For instance, the old narrow windows of the medieval part sometimes had no glass at all, while the newer section boasted large windows containing panes of clear, unrippled glass.

"Oh, I love it! It's so interesting!" Elspeth said. "Where is your favorite part of the house? And we will sleep where? Is any of it haunted? I hope so. I've never met a ghost, but I should like to, if they're civilized," she added with a laugh.

"If it's haunted, I've never seen evidence of it," Struan said. "As for where you'll sleep and spend your time? That I will wait to show you until we arrive. It's easier to show than to tell."

He was flustered by her simple phrasing of where *we will sleep*, and it reminded him of the gravity of his decision to marry her. At some point, they would be sleeping together, if only for a short while, Struan not deluding himself into thinking that she'd want more than what was expected for her to offer. He had avoided the question on the journey up, which hadn't been too difficult thanks to the natural discomfort of travel.

Now, however, Elspeth looked just as excited as she had starting out the journey. She sat in her seat again, which was good, since having her backside more or less in his face was incredibly distracting.

She beamed at him. "I can't wait to walk into your home. *Our* home. It will be so different from the house I grew up in, and I can only imagine how grand and romantic it must be."

"You may be disappointed. It's not fashionable in the way that a lot of the townhomes in Edinburgh are fashionable. You'll probably find it out-of-date and gloomy."

"Out-of-date and gloomy are not insurmountable problems. I do hope your housekeeper stocks a large supply of vinegar."

"Housekeeper," he echoed. *Oh, no.*

There was a problem approaching that, while also not insurmountable, did give Struan pause. He had written a few weeks previously from Edinburgh to inform the household that he would be returning by the end of the month and planned to stay indefinitely. This missive would be taken in the spirit it was meant: he had no wish to surprise the household, but also expected that everything would be in place when he arrived. The household, from the butler on down to the youngest stable lad, would understand that there was no trick involved but that competence was assumed, and anything less would not be tolerated, especially given the timely alert.

However, when Struan had sent word, he had absolutely no notion that he would be bringing along anybody else, let alone a *wife*. The sudden arrival of a new and unknown mistress would send the household into a tumult. What would the housekeeper and the maids think? How would they handle the sudden appearance of the lady who would have power over their livelihoods and lives from this point on?

Struan was now going to present to the household a woman who not only they had never seen, but who they had never even dreamed of existing. It was unfair, perhaps not in a technical sense, for Struan was the absolute master of his house and could do as he liked. But it would be an unpleasant shock to announce one thing and carry out another. He hoped they wouldn't react too badly.

The carriage pulled up to the house just as the sun was setting. The servants were already standing assembled and waiting, because the carriage had been sighted at least five minutes previously. Therefore, Struan was able to catch the astonishment in many of the expressions when he helped Elspeth step out of the carriage. The butler's eyes had widened to almost comical proportions, but fortunately the housekeeper, Mrs Negus, was more than equal to the occasion. She stepped forward and gave a little curtsey to Struan.

"Welcome home, sir. We have done our best to make the house ready for your return and hope you will find it satisfactory." She looked sidelong at Elspeth, so Struan picked up his cue.

He said, "This is my wife, Elspeth McGregor. We married in Edinburgh, just before our journey. I realize this is a surprise, but there was no time to send word ahead."

Elspeth took a step forward. "I'm happy to see Linneliath at last, and I can already tell that the home and all the grounds are exceedingly well cared for. I look forward to exploring everything." Elspeth smiled after she said this, of course, because Elspeth smiled practically as often as she breathed. And her beaming countenance had the usual effect, at least as far as Struan could tell, because everyone straightened up a little, gave minuscule nods, or a discreet smile back—that being the limit of expression a well-trained servant would permit themself in such a moment.

But that was enough for Struan to realize that Elspeth would have all of these people eating out of her hand within days. Whatever concerns he had about the state of the house, at least he did not have any concerns about the household. Elspeth's natural charm of manner was almost magical in its ability to turn potential adversaries into allies.

Feeling both hopeful and slightly terrified of the changes ahead, Struan offered her his arm. "Welcome home, Ellie."

Elspeth curled her hand into the crook of his elbow, and her smile seemed like it would crack the cloudy sky wide open.

Chapter 10

THAT EVENING WAS THEIR FIRST night in their house, so Elspeth wanted to look her best at dinner, though her wardrobe was not inspiring. It was also not extensive. Everything she'd brought with her in the two trunks fit into the small room adjacent to her bedchamber. Elspeth liked the idea of a room just for clothing and sundries. The maid, Agnes, told her that the master bedchamber which adjoined hers had a similar room, plus a dedicated bathing and washroom beyond. This was the newest part of the house, and whoever designed it was obviously forward-thinking.

Elspeth chose the most formal-looking of her purple dresses, the one with the cap sleeves made of jet taffeta, and the trim in black lace. Agnes helped her put up her hair into a simple chignon, and Ellie wore a small silver cross on a silver chain around her neck. She'd put her mother's pearls carefully away in a small case, having received them back from Struan on the ship.

The cross had belonged to her grandmother, and her aunt Rosalind had offered it to Elspeth on her sixteenth birthday. It was the only present she received that year (barring a copy of *Maria: or, The Wrongs of Woman* by Mary Wollstonecraft. That was, obviously, from Mairi).

"But don't you want to save this for Genevieve?" Elspeth

had asked, thinking of her vivacious young cousin.

Her aunt had replied, "Your grandmother had several lovely pieces, so Genny will receive her legacy in time. But this one made me think of you, darling. And I want you to wear it and know that you always have family."

Elspeth had been touched by the gift, even if she'd not fully grasped the significance at the time.

Their late dinner was served in a long room that featured tall windows set between buttressed stone walls on one side. The other side featured portraits of much the same size as the windows, all of them depicting stern men and women, presumably distinguished ancestors of this branch of the MacInnes clan. In the daytime, perhaps the sunshine would brighten the countenance of the portrait subjects. At night, however, the meager light from the candles only made the painted eyes gleam balefully from the dark.

Elspeth regarded these new family members, and decided she'd have to learn how to clean oil paintings.

The meal was plain but hearty, and Elspeth ate more than usual, which made it difficult to talk. And since Struan was not exactly loquacious, the room was nearly silent except for the clink of silver on the dishes.

"I'm excited to see the house and the grounds in daylight," she said at last. "It's dark in here, isn't it? Should I call for more candles to be lit? Or have the fire put on?" She just realized that the fire that was laid in the fireplace had not been lit, which seemed like an oversight.

But Struan gave one firm shake of his head. "No. I would prefer to not have the fire at all. Until it's absolutely necessary."

"Do you dislike fire so much?"

"I don't dislike fire. I hate it," he growled.

* * * *

Struan watched Elspeth's eyes widen.

"You hate it? But fire is just the same as air or water or earth or stone. It can be good or bad and thus there's no reason to hate the thing itself. It's how it's used."

"Well, I remember how it was used to burn off my skin."

Elspeth winced, and he chastised himself for speaking so harshly, but then decided that she'd had asked, so she had better be prepared to hear the answer.

Apparently she was prepared, because she pushed aside her plate and leaned closer to him. "Can you tell me?"

Could he? She ought to know. She was his wife. She'd eventually have to see the body that the fire had destroyed. He took a breath. "It's not a nice story."

"I didn't expect it to be."

"All right. It happened while we were moving through a village in France. To this day, I don't know the name of the village, or even whether it deserved a name. It wasn't much more than half a dozen cottages along a slightly wider part of the road. We were on our way to rejoin the larger part of the battalion, when someone yelled out *ambush*. There was a hill, and the enemy had concealed artillery among the trees growing on it. They didn't attack us in the morning when we'd gone through on our reconnaissance mission; they waited the whole day until we came back and we were tired, and we believed the way was safe. It was afternoon, and the sun was already low in the sky, so we couldn't see them as more than silhouettes among the trees. We didn't have a chance."

Elspeth already looked stricken, but he'd barely begun the story.

"The whole company scattered, taking cover against the cottage walls to keep something between us and the shells that were starting to come down, but we didn't have enough warning. Plus there were soldiers concealed in the cottages, and they would shoot any man who took cover in a spot. I had been minding one of the pack horses that had gone lame, so I was further away from the rest of the men, and I saw it all start to happen. Time seemed to slow down. I called out a warning when I saw the first man fall from the snipers' bullets, and I tried to direct the others to a different place, where they might have a better chance to shield themselves."

"Did anyone hear you?"

"Yes. The men you met at the wedding heard me. Thane heard me and grabbed Kai and Calan and started to run across the road while Duncan shot toward the place the first sniper was using as a blind. I was so focused on them getting to safety that I didn't hear the shell descending. It was just on the other side of the horse, and then there was no more horse, and that may have been the thing that kept me alive, at least in that moment. But the shell exploded, and there were sparks and they flew into the back of the wagon the pack horse had been hauling. It had been packed with weapons—that was what we'd gone to fetch that morning. And those crates were packed with straw with more straw in between them, to keep them from sliding and rattling, and also to conceal what they were from a casual glance."

"It caught fire," Elspeth guessed, horror in her eyes.

"Instantly. The straw was all in flames, and then a breeze sprang up and the sparks were just in the air floating like fireflies, but it was too early for fireflies, and then they landed on me and my clothes caught fire, and then all I remember was heat and pain and not knowing where to turn next. I don't know how long it took for the other men to reach me. The sniper, you see, thought I was a grand distraction, because everyone kept yelling and trying to help me from a distance, not that they could do anything. But any time a man moved out of cover, the sniper would take another shot."

"What did you do?" Elspeth whispered.

"I dropped to the ground. I rolled, thinking that that would help put the fire out, but there was something in that shell—oil or some other substance—and the fire just kept relighting and spreading, and everything was hotter and hotter. And I just remember clawing into the dirt itself, like I was trying to break into my own grave. The earth wouldn't let me in, but I did lose consciousness."

Elspeth had wrapped her arms around herself. He had to take a few deep breaths before he could go on.

"A few days later I woke up in a tent somewhere in our camp. I was in pain from top to bottom, and I couldn't move at all. I had been wrapped in a shroud. It took two nurses and a doctor to explain to me that it wasn't really a shroud, but just gauze that they had wrapped around my whole body because I was one gigantic wound. The fire had split my skin, burned it halfway. My right side especially felt like meat instead of my own body. I kept asking them when I would die. The doctor wouldn't ever answer. One of the nurses finally told me that when I first was brought in, they took me for a corpse, and tried to send me out to be buried with the others. But Calan and Duncan wouldn't leave until I was given a bed, and my wounds were washed and wrapped."

"Good!"

"The doctors said there wasn't enough gauze. But Kai brought some within an hour. To this day I have no idea where he got it. I was in that tent for two weeks, barely able to move. Waiting to die. Calan came every day to talk to me, even when I wouldn't answer. Even when I couldn't answer. Kai brought wine and whisky. Whisky was worth more than gold to anyone in our regiment. He got it for me to help with the pain."

"Oh, Struan."

"Eventually, we—the other wounded men—were put on a

ship home, if by home one meant London. Plenty of doctors looked at me there, but damn few had anything to say, other than that it was a miracle I wasn't dead yet. So, Thane and Kai, having got back to England, managed to put me on another ship for Edinburgh. The doctors are better here in Scotland. They found one who was willing to look at me. He came to my house every day in town. And he actually tried every method he could think of to bring about any improvement in my muscles and my skin. He said more than once that he wished he'd been there in France, because there were things that the doctors could've done immediately which would have probably allowed my skin to grow back in a more normal way.

"I tell myself that maybe it wouldn't have mattered. I would've always ended up looking like this. But the doctor did his best, which is more than I can say for the rest of them. And my friends listened to every piece of advice he gave, and made sure that I followed all of his instructions. It's likely that without returning to Edinburgh, and having that doctor's care, I would've succumbed to my wounds or infection, or any of the plagues that a bedridden patient faces.

"I did recover, though it took months. And I started to pick up the pieces I'd left behind when I went overseas to serve. One of those things was trying to regain some semblance of an ordinary life. Meeting friends for a drink around the corner. Visiting my club. Going to dinner."

"Finding a wife," she suggested.

"I didn't even try." Struan almost, *almost* mentioned the other reason for his second thoughts about marriage, beyond his physical appearance. But he couldn't tell her. Not yet.

Ellie looked concerned, but then chirped, "Until me!"

That's right, she believed he'd selected her long before the proposal. He wished it were true. To say something that wasn't a lie, he told her, "Yes, until you. I half expected you to run out of the church."

"Everyone expected that," she informed him, looking annoyed. "As if you were some monster."

He was. Did Elspeth just have poor vision? No, on the voyage north, she'd seen (and had questions about) literally everything.

She went on, "I'm so glad you told me what happened to you. And I hope that you don't think I was uncaring because I didn't ask before. I was afraid to bring it up if you didn't wish to relive it."

"I should have told you immediately," he admitted. "I suppose I kept putting it off because I do hate thinking about it. Not that it stops me from thinking about it. I wake up half my nights because I've dreamed I was back there."

"Oh." She stretched across the table and reached for his hands. "I want to help."

"What could you do about it?"

"Well, you could talk to me about it. Whenever I had nightmares, I could talk to Mairi and the awfulness of the dream would fade and then I could go back to sleep."

"I'm not coming to your room and waking you in the middle of the night to talk about bad dreams."

"But you could." She offered him a hopeful smile. "You can tell me anything you like. And you can ask anything you like. That's what it means that we're married."

He knew that. Of course he knew that.

He also knew he was not coming to her room late at night.

He was not going to scoop her up in his arms and take her somewhere and expose himself, emotionally or physically.

Because even in his most fantastical imaginings about Elspeth—and considering how short a time he'd known her, he'd had more than his share—he'd never had the imagination to picture himself as something she'd actually want to look at, let alone touch.

It wasn't that he thought her shallow or cruel. She clearly was neither. But she was naive. And even if she truly believed that his appearance wouldn't be an impediment to intimacy, the moment she saw all of him, the truth would set in. To say nothing of the…other issue, the possibility that he never could have a family, that he was broken beyond repair.

And he couldn't stand to think about that. It was bad enough that he'd essentially purchased her. It would be far worse to finally prove how pointless the idea of marriage was for him.

Because seeing regret in her eyes would be the worst of all.

Chapter 11

ELSPETH RETIRED TO HER ROOM after the meal, as Struan suggested. But she hadn't gone to bed, because she'd thought that he'd…well, join her at some point. Agnes helped her loose and brush her hair, then dress in a modest nightrail, then left. Elspeth quickly removed it and then put on the flimsy silk gown Averill had given her. She was too mortified to ask the maid to dress her in it, because really no one but her husband should ever see her in it.

Once dressed, she waited.

And waited.

But Struan never appeared. Never knocked. Never even made a sound from the other side of the connecting door. She'd been pleased about the private door when she first saw it. It meant that certain…visits wouldn't be noted by anyone else in the household. While there was nothing wrong with a man visiting his wife's room, obviously, she was shy about the idea of people keeping count.

But the candle grew shorter and shorter, until the flame sputtered in a pool of wax in the holder. Elspeth fought off sleep as long as she could, and then dozed, though she woke frequently, sometimes due to a sound like a creak of the floor somewhere, or the snap of an ember in the fireplace. She'd misunderstood something, obviously. Which was not a surprise, since Elspeth didn't have any experience.

In the morning, she woke late, thanks to her restless

night. No one had come in, either because no one expected her to rise by now, or because the idea of disturbing the lady of the house was anathema. She saw a bell cord in one corner. But rather than rise and pull it immediately, Elspeth instead got out of bed and removed the gown she'd put on the night before.

After finding her original nightrail, she put it on and then rang the bell.

"Does my husband usually break his fast downstairs, or in his own chambers?" she asked after Agnes came in with a breakfast tray, and then set it down to help her dress for the day.

"I don't know, ma'am," the maid replied. "He's not been in residence since I got my position, and I've not heard of any prior habits."

"Oh, yes, of course that would be the case." Struan's habits may also have changed greatly since he left Linneliath to join the army.

"Early this morning he just stopped in the kitchen to take some food along with him," Agnes shared. "He wanted to ride out and see the property."

"That's understandable," Elspeth said. "It's been a long time since he's seen his home."

Part of her was a little sad that he hadn't asked her to join him. But then again, it was so late in the morning. Perhaps he had waited as long as he could. There was also the sad fact that Elspeth didn't ride at all, having grown up in the confines of a city where transportation was always available.

And while he was attending to his duties of seeing the property and reconnecting with the tenants and the locals, she also had a task before her: learning about the house itself.

"Once I'm done eating," she told Agnes, "I must speak with the housekeeper as soon as possible."

"Yes, ma'am."

"And I wish it to be known that I *never* sleep so late. All the travel has unmoored me from my routine."

"Yes, ma'am." This time the maid gave her a little smile, one that suggested she didn't think it was travel that caused Elspeth's fatigue. But Elspeth was not about to confide anything of her personal thoughts to a stranger, and she certainly wasn't going to discuss anything of what passed between her and Struan—or what *didn't* pass.

A short while later, Elspeth followed Agnes downstairs to the part of the house where the servants worked in the kitchen, the pantries, and whatnot. There, Mrs Negus gave her a deep curtsey, a move that looked unfamiliar on the older woman's sturdy frame.

"Good morning, mistress. It is my duty to hand over the keys, and to give you a full accounting of the household." She offered a large ring to Elspeth, who took it with a nod. There must've been at least two dozen keys on the large brass ring, from the heavy and ornate one that must lock the front doors to the house to several tiny ones in brass and silver, which would open certain drawers in a desk or a tea caddy or perhaps a jewelry box.

Elspeth would attach the keyring to a chain later, so that she might wear them as needed. "Thank you for this," she said. "I'm sure you carried out all of the household responsibilities to your utmost in the absence of a lady." It was only in that moment that a thought occurred to Elspeth, which should've occurred to her far earlier. "From whom did you take over the management of these keys? Had my husband been married previously?" But surely he would have mentioned if he had a wife before.

"Oh no, ma'am. He'd been engaged, but she—" And here Mrs Negus visibly checked her flow of words.

Engaged! Elspeth's smile faltered for a moment.

But then the housekeeper started again, "I've been in charge since the master's mother passed away, over fifteen years now."

"Ah. Then you must know everything there is to know, and I rely on your wisdom as I settle in. Do you have the household account book? I'd like to see what state everything is in and what the household budget is so we may ensure that there's no disruption. And perhaps you will apprise me of the master's preferences and expectations in matters of meals, entertaining, and houseguests." For Elspeth knew none of these things, thanks to the fact that she'd gone from spinster daughter to gentleman's wife in the space of a breath.

Over the course of a normal courtship, she would have learned about her husband-to-be, but there had simply been no time at all, and Struan was not a forthcoming man. She was lucky to have the housekeeper to speak with, and said so.

Mrs Negus gave a nod at the compliment, though there was still a trace of wariness in her eyes. Elspeth guessed the reason. Having been more or less in charge of the house for over a decade, to say nothing of the previous years in which she had doubtless also had great control, it would be an abrupt change. Many women would resent a new and inexperienced mistress stepping in, having all the authority of a wife.

She slipped the large brass ring over her arm, like a bracelet designed for giants. "Of course I will need you to show me what all of these keys unlock. We have a busy day ahead of us, so let's begin, shall we?"

The housekeeper bowed her head once, and Elspeth got the sense that this genuflection contained considerably more respect than the initial curtsey.

"Aye, ma'am. Please follow me."

Elspeth might not know anything about being a wife, but she knew plenty about running a household, and she already felt a bit more comfortable with the keys to this one. Doubtless, the rest would come.

* * * *

Several hours later, Elspeth stretched her neck from side to side. Account books were not for the faint of heart! But she was pleased with what she'd seen, even if she was sure she could improve the efficiency of some aspects of the house.

"Everything seems to be in order. I do intend to make some changes and improvements to the house and the gardens. But that is in no way a rebuke to the fine efforts of everyone here, and I hope that you'll pass on my compliments to the staff."

"Thank you, ma'am, I shall," Mrs Negus said. "They will be grateful… Begging your pardon, ma'am, but your arrival yesterday was a surprise."

"I'm sure!" Elspeth replied. "If you had told me last month that I would be a wife this month, I would sooner have believed that I could sail to the moon."

"So it was a whirlwind courtship, then?"

"It was a lightning strike courtship," Elspeth confessed. "Str—that is, Mr MacInnes chose me of all the young ladies in Edinburgh, and though I don't know why he did so, I know better than to question my good luck. I will be the best wife in all of Scotland." Elspeth smiled, then registered an odd look in the housekeeper's eyes. "Oh! I beg your pardon. Are you married? I didn't mean to imply that other women were not good wives."

The housekeeper chuckled now. "Be at ease, ma'am. I'm not married. But even if I were, I shouldn't take it amiss.

Newlyweds think the whole world is roses. I'm glad the young master found a good match. I've known him since the day he was born."

"And I not nearly so long," Elspeth said. "But that will change."

She hoped.

Leaving the realm of the kitchen, she returned to the main part of the house. She asked a passing footman for Struan's whereabouts. He informed her that the master had just gone into his study, and directed her there.

Struan was leaning over a desk strewn with open ledger books. He straightened up when he saw her, and asked if she was settling in.

"Yes, thank you. I spoke at length with Mrs Negus. We'll get along well."

"That's good to hear," Struan said.

She said, more tentatively, "There is a thing I wanted to discuss. I thought you would come to my room last night, it being the first night we were both here, where we shall live together."

He had the grace to look abashed. "I should have reminded you I wouldn't come to you. I thought you might be tired, and you would still want some time to adjust to your new surroundings."

"Oh, I see."

"In fact, I will wait a few days...nights...longer. You'll be busy, and your new life will entail a lot of attention, and I don't wish to, um..." He trailed off.

"I understand," she said, though she didn't exactly. "We can discuss it at a later time."

"Yes." He looked relieved.

"And today you reacquainted yourself with Linneliath?"

"Yes," he said, more warmly. "It was good to see it. The people and the land, and the moors. The sea. I know it's not a pretty landscape, but—"

"I think it's wonderful," Elspeth said. "I'm used to the city, so all the open sky is impressive. I hope that you'll show me around soon?"

"Tomorrow, if you like," Struan said. "I've got more tenants to visit, but they'd probably be more happy to see you."

"I'd love that." She beamed at him, so excited by the idea of being beside him as they traveled through their home ground for the first time. "That is, if you don't mind a carriage, because I'm not able to ride."

"At all?" he asked, surprised.

"I never learned."

"We'll have to remedy that soon. But for tomorrow, I'll tell the men to have the carriage out."

"When should I be ready in the morning?"

"Er…eight? If that's not too early."

"Not at all. I *never* sleep in. This morning was an anomaly. At home—I mean, at my father's house—I'd always wake as early as possible, because there was so much to do."

"Like laundry," he muttered.

Elspeth blinked in surprise. "Well, yes. Only on laundry day, obviously."

"You won't be doing that here."

"Oh? But I'm good at it, and extra hands—"

"You're the lady of the house," he said, firmly closing the door on her argument. "Direct the servants on particular tasks if you must, but I won't have it said my wife is doing the same chores as the scullions."

"Oh. Yes, of course. Well, there will be plenty to occupy me anyway. Linneliath is about ten times larger than Father's house, and I intend to make many improvements so the house is more comfortable…if that's acceptable?" she added, worried that she was asserting too much authority.

But he just said, "You're the lady of the house. Do what

you like."

Something niggled at her, and then she realized what it was. "How did you know I helped with the laundry?"

After a long pause, he said, "I saw you doing it once."

"You did? When? Why?"

"It was shortly before we met at the church. I…I wanted to see you."

Elspeth smiled, thinking how sweetly romantic that was —that he knew he would soon marry her, but he still couldn't resist an extra glance beforehand. "I wish that I'd been a little more presentable when you peeked."

"You were lovely," he told her. "You were laughing about something with your maids, and I could hear it from where I stood. Your laugh is…"

"What?" she asked.

"Enchanting. You sounded so damned happy." He looked away, cleared his throat. "I hope you'll be happy here some-day, Ellie."

"I'm happy here today," she told him, wondering why he seemed suddenly reticent. "I hope you're happy as well."

He nodded, and she wished she believed him.

Chapter 12

A WEEK LATER, STRUAN STILL had no idea what the hell he'd been thinking when he agreed to marrying anyone, let alone someone as...*sweet*...as Elspeth. It was like inheriting a spaniel. There was no one she wasn't happy to see, there was nothing she wasn't happy to do. Every day since the third day, she led a brigade of servants to room after room, directing footmen to move furniture about, maids to take down draperies, and all manner of other requests. (They were never phrased as orders, but rather something like "Douglas, would you be so good as to take down that oil painting on the east wall? Do have Neil carry the other side. I have no idea who that old lady is, but she is frowning already, and we don't want to give her more to worry about, do we?") And the servants did everything she asked, quickly and without complaint.

This wasn't confined to when they were in her presence either. Struan overheard two of the maids talking as they cleaned and dusted.

"She said, 'The brasses are well polished, Jeannie. Excellent work.' She knew my name, after only a few days!"

"Aye, and she knows what we all do," the other marveled. "The lady of the house knows it's Young Angus scrubs the pots!"

"Do you think she'll hold fine parties? I'd love to see a

Christmas ball." Jeannie sighed.

"Who'd come to a fine party here? She'll go back to Edinburgh and have the party at the master's home in the city. That's what ladies do."

"How d'you know what ladies do?"

"Read about it, don't I? In the newspaper whenever Madame Mouse writes her column. New Town Tattle! Oh, she always describes what the ladies are wearing, down to the pins and lace!"

"She doesn't have a very fine wardrobe," Jeannie noted sadly. "I'd hoped for satin and silk."

"Oh, she'll have more coming soon," the second maid replied. "Ladies *always* have trunks and trunks of clothing. They've got mountains of boxes just for their hats and shoes. You'll see."

Struan walked on, thinking of the maid's last comment. *Did* Ellie have more things coming? She hadn't said so. And she didn't seem to care much for fashion, to judge by her staunch partisanship for that odd purple hue. He'd have to ask her about it. Struan sure as hell wasn't going to let someone say his wife wasn't as well-draped as any woman in Edinburgh. She was stuck with him for life—she ought to at least enjoy what she wore.

His intention to inquire about Ellie's clothing was swept aside by a minor catastrophe at one of the farms, however, and Struan spent the next few days helping to repair some homes and almost a half mile of damaged fencing.

He told himself that he wasn't looking for reasons to avoid Ellie. It was just that whenever he saw her, he was first struck by how damned pretty she was, and then by how little he deserved to be near her, let alone touch her or do any of the things he increasingly wanted to do.

So several days later, he wasn't prepared when Ellie emerged from a side room in one of her endless purple gowns and asked if he'd allow her to show him something.

"You can show me anything," he said, hoping he didn't sound like a man desperate with lust.

Ellie beamed. She didn't look desperate or lustful in the slightest, more's the pity. Damn, he didn't used to have difficulties with women. He wasn't on Calan's level of attractiveness or charm, but when it came time to meet with a woman he'd had no troubles…until he was injured. As he was slipping into this pit of despair, Ellie had taken his hand and pulled him down the hall. She said, "Come with me into the parlor."

He walked into the room and blinked at the brightness. He recalled the room as dim and cold, but it was now… golden.

The walls had been hung with warm yellow silk. No more of that heavy puce brocade that suffered after a rainstorm. The curtains were also different. The heavy drapes that blocked the light were missing. In their place hung white linen that allowed the light through and let the trees outside lay green shadows over the fabric, like stained glass but impossibly delicate. Even the furniture was different, the wooden arms of light-colored wood and the fabric seats now covered in pillows in shades of gold.

Ellie was standing the middle, smiling hopefully at him. "What do you think?"

"What did you *do*?" he asked.

"I simply spruced it up a bit. The room gets wonderful morning light, and it seemed a shame to not take advantage of it."

"Spruced it up? You've changed everything."

"Well, the old wall hangings couldn't be salvaged," she said. "But that's all that's new. Other than the pillows, of course. We sewed them from an old bedspread upstairs. You'll find the seating far more comfortable now, as I've restuffed it."

"What do you mean, restuffed? This furniture is all different."

"Struan," she said with a merry laugh, the laugh that he'd dreamed of hearing within these very walls. "It's the same. It's just been *cleaned*."

"What?"

"There is little in this world that cannot be improved with hot water, vinegar, and some effort. Have a seat."

He sat. He remembered the couch as somehow both stiff and saggy—a combination that led him to avoid the parlor in past years. But now he sank back against the pillows and found it surprisingly… "Good," he grunted.

"It will be an excellent room for entertaining now."

"Enter-what?"

Her smile faltered. "We spoke of hosting a dinner…for the neighbors. Do you not recall?"

He did not. "When? I mean, when do you intend to have this dinner?"

"I'm not sure, honestly. I don't know who to invite either. A neighbor called on us few days ago while you were working with the tenants, and I returned the courtesy yesterday. She lives on the south road."

"Who? Old Mrs March?"

"She's not that old! She's very sweet. But I think most people don't know you've come back to live. So I'd like to host a dinner."

"That sounds excruciating," he replied, although the actual spoken words were, "Yes, that's fine." He looked at the room again. "Out of curiosity, how much did this cost?"

"Oh, nothing!" she said hurriedly.

"It must have cost something."

"I mean, it cost *you* nothing."

"How is that possible?"

"I used my pin money. I didn't think it fair to make you spend more than you have already."

"You used your pin money for the house? Never do that."

Her face fell. "Why not?"

"Because there's a budget for the house. The pin money is yours to use as you like."

"I like to make the rooms homier." She gave him that hopeful smile again, the one that was increasingly making him woozy.

"That's fine, but use the house money for the house. Your pin money ought to be for…you. Whatever you like for yourself."

She looked puzzled, as if the idea of spending money on herself had never occurred to her. "But I don't need anything. You provide all I'd ever need."

Like hell. He'd given her precisely nothing.

"You could buy a new dress. Or a hat. Or some…I don't know, what do women buy when they're out and about a high street?"

Her expression clouded. "There wasn't much time for that."

He didn't know what that meant, but before he could ask, Elspeth unleashed her relentless cheer again. She said, "I'll see to it that the money is taken from the proper accounts. Forgive me for not understanding your preferences."

"I never explained them," he admitted. Then he added, "You have nothing to worry about when it comes to my worth, and by extension your worth."

"But isn't it always good practice to be careful with one's resources?" Elspeth countered.

"Ellie, I'm not poor. My family's land produces both tin and lead. In addition to my cut, the mines provide an income for the men who live in the area and help to support their families at a time when it's sorely needed. There's not much else to provide a living in this part of the country. Those who live along the shore will fish. Those who live inland can farm in a modest way, so long as they don't hope to grow much more than oats and vegetables. There are sheep, of course, which provide a little bit of income from wool and weaving.

"But the mines are the one thing that has allowed the people living here some real security, including myself. I've benefited from the income and investments made by my predecessors. And believe me, I've got more than enough to maintain you, me, and this household in a fairly comfortable way for the rest of our lives."

"So," Elspeth said. "Am I to understand that you wish me to be more silly in my spending?"

"Somewhat silly," he corrected her, enjoying the fact that he had not only managed to have a mature conversation with his wife about a typical household matter, but also that she seemed to genuinely want to be in the same room with him. He stood up and moved to stand by her. "I don't believe that you could ever be persuaded to fully change your philosophy at this point, seeing as you're such an old and crotchety woman."

Elspeth laughed again, and yes, he was more woozy than before. He might need to lie down. Possibly near her.

She said, "Well, I promise that I won't use my pin money for items that I require for the house. But I'm not entirely sure how I would spend it, since there's not a lot of opportunity for shopping on a high street. Not that I would do that anyway, even in Edinburgh. I was never good at indulgence."

"Do you wish you were back in Edinburgh?" he asked.

"No. I'm happy here. Of course, someday I expect that we'll go back and spend some time there. When the occasion calls for it. But you've spent so much time away from your home that it would be painful for you to leave it again so soon."

He paused, regarding her. "You're always thinking about how other people feel, aren't you?"

"Isn't that what everybody does?"

"Assuredly not. If that were so, there would be fewer wars."

Elspeth suddenly sobered. "At least here at home, you never need to worry about war touching you again. This has to be the most peaceful place in the whole world."

"Do you think so?"

"Oh, yes. It's so different from the city. Here there's just so much space in the sky and when you walk outside, I feel like the whole landscape is just waiting to be discovered. I could walk for miles in any direction…well, except for the sea, obviously. I think I'll always find something interesting. But not the sort of interesting that requires action. I could just sit on a hillside and contemplate. I never used to be able to do that before."

Struan couldn't take his attention off her face as she spoke, and without meaning to, his gaze caught on her lips. Ellie noticed at last, and her happy chatter faltered. Her chest rose and fell a little faster. While she wasn't a flirtatious person, he could tell that she was curious.

So he leaned down toward her. He moved slowly, giving her plenty of room to step away or refuse him. But she tilted her head up, those big eyes open and inviting.

He kissed her.

She was silk and sugar. He ran his tongue along her lower lip, wetting the skin. The little intake of breath, and the way her mouth opened for him, was heaven. He slipped his tongue in deeper, reveling in her softness, imagining all the other soft places of her body where he'd use his tongue later. He'd never been a particularly patient lover, and now after such a long time without any physical exchange with a woman, he was already aching to turn this kiss into something much more intimate.

Ellie's response added fuel to the fire, because she'd raised her hands to his head and was running her slender fingers through his hair as she pulled him closer.

He loved the way she darted her tongue in and out between his lips, like she was testing the waters. Which he supposed she probably was. Had she kissed anyone before like this, with open mouth and shuddering breath? He hoped not. He wanted to be the first person she craved.

Ellie's hands had moved downward while he was consumed with her perfect lips, and with a jolt, he realized that she had one hand on his neck, where the scarring was thick.

She wouldn't crave that, once she saw his skin. Struan was only fooling himself to think she would. He growled in frustration.

Ellie heard it and pulled away, her eyes wide. "What's wrong? Should I not have done something?"

"No, it's not you," he said, but it was too late. She'd sensed his mood shift and misread it as a rebuke.

He tried to correct his mistake. He kissed her again, as gently as he could. But her mouth was pursed now, worried. "You're perfect, Ellie." Unlike him.

Ellie's answering kiss was so frozen that he gave up. "I scared you," he guessed. "I didn't mean to."

"Of course you didn't scare me," she replied. "I'll do whatever you ask me to do. I want to do it to make you happy."

To him, it sounded like she was trying to convince herself of the words, and that moment of happiness he'd just felt was already shattered. "I don't want to push you into anything."

"I'm your wife. This is what we're meant to do, isn't it?"

"Not if you're not ready."

"I am!"

That was the reflexive answer of a woman who was used to saying yes to everything because she never knew she could give another answer. He'd heard that tone before, when men responded to superiors instantly and unthinkingly, because that's what they were trained to do.

He straightened up and kept his expression as blank as possible. "I have some matters to attend to. I'll see you at dinner, Ellie."

She nodded, and he tried not to notice the hurt in her eyes. He felt like he just kicked a puppy. But he also knew that there was nothing normal about their marriage, and she was definitely not ready to sleep with him. Probably she never would be.

So all he had to worry about was spending a whole lifetime failing to make her happy.

Fantastic.

Chapter 13

LINNELIATH WAS A GRAND HOME, and despite her difficulty in understanding Struan's shifting moods, Elspeth felt that she was truly where she was meant to be. Now that she and Struan would be living here permanently, and hopefully adding to the size of their family soon, it was absolutely time to bring light and life and color back to the house.

Fortunately the housekeeper and the staff in general seemed to be in agreement. A few of the maids even offered suggestions for what sort of styles seemed to be popular at the moment. Elspeth listened to everyone, and noted when someone pointed out a particular issue with the house, or had an intriguing thought about fixing it. But first and foremost, she trusted her own impulse, honed by a life dedicated to maintaining and improving the household.

Elspeth also ordered the gardens and the grounds to be given a more thorough attention than had been offered over the past decade or so. Unfortunately, it wasn't an easy matter to bring in new plants or trees on short notice, but Elspeth could dream. No one would mistake this place in the wilds of northern Scotland for any tidy and trimmed property further south. The sky still stretched above the house, wild and untouchable, and the moors still rolled away into the distance, making the house feel like a little toy boat upon stormy seas. But it was trim and clean and had great potential, and Elspeth felt a sense of accomplishment.

While the cleaning helped, there were still real improvements to be made to the house if she ever hoped to make it feel welcoming for family and friends—and she hoped for large numbers to eventually visit and stay. She spent several days overseeing the movements of various pieces of furniture in all of the bedrooms so that by the end half a dozen rooms were bright and clean and contained everything a guest might want.

She thought about wall hangings and draperies and sconces and chairs and cushions, and also dreamed about a nursery filled with new toys and games and dolls for the children who were destined to run through these rooms, filling the home with their laughter.

But those children wouldn't arrive if she couldn't make inroads with her own husband, who remained polite and often kind, but still reserved and reclusive, and certainly not eager to come to her bedroom at night. Yes, he'd kissed her, and the kiss had left her trembling, ready to either faint or possibly throw herself at him to chase more of that wildly exciting feeling. But as quickly as he'd begun to kiss her, he'd stopped.

And of course he told her that it wasn't her fault, but whose fault could it be? Of the two of them, one knew how to kiss (Struan) and one did not (Elspeth). He was a man with experience, as nebulously mentioned by her stepmother in that stilted and unhelpful talk back in Edinburgh. Clearly, she had done something she should not have and disappointed him. Though honestly, how anyone expected a lady to have experience without *experiencing* anything previously... Elspeth gave a little annoyed huff. Why could things not be simple?

Mairi would have something to say on the subject on the

inequality of expectations, something forceful and witty. Elspeth, however, was not a naturally forceful person, so she wasn't sure how to proceed, and it was perhaps not a surprise that her method of avoiding the issue meant that she spent even more time working on improving the house.

Elspeth already loved Linneliath, but after over a fortnight of living there, she had a short list of items she hoped to purchase in the village. Struan's tour the second day had ended early because rainclouds had been threatening from the west by the time they'd got through most of the property, and then events had conspired to make it impossible for him to take her on another, lengthier excursion. So while she'd met several tenants, she'd yet to see much of the land beyond what Struan personally owned.

She didn't want to wait for the next delivery from the village, so she decided to take a journey there herself. She didn't like to think that her curiosity about her new home would result in any of the servants being forced to linger for an excessive amount of time, while Elspeth stuck her nose in all the shops and interesting places the village would have.

She dressed in her sturdy, but admittedly drab purple day gown and put on her wool cloak to ward against the stiff north breeze that had been blowing steadily all night into the morning. She set off down the track leading from the great house to the main road. In this part of Scotland, it seemed uncommon to make much of a point of specific property lines, which meant that there was no fence around Linneliath, and little to demarcate it from the world beyond. Elspeth turned onto the road, which was two worn parallel tracks exactly the space of wagon wheels apart. It being spring, there were plenty of places where the track had turned to mud or puddles had formed. When she encountered those, Elspeth stepped to the side, and proceeded along the way until she passed each obstacle.

Occasionally, this meant going into a farmer's field, but in reality, most of the land around here was given over to pasture, and Elspeth saw the fluffy shapes of Highland sheep, or goats, or the occasional cow as she went.

At the sound of wagon wheels churning up mud, Elspeth turned to see a farmer approaching. She gave a friendly wave, and the driver stopped to offer her a cautious greeting, obviously wondering who this stranger was.

"Good morning!" Elspeth said. "Are you going into the village? I live at Linneliath, and I'm walking that way myself. But I may have underestimated the distance."

"Live up at the big house now, do you?" the farmer said with interest. "What's your name, lass?"

"Elspeth McGregor I was born," she told him with a smile. "And you, sir?"

"No sir for me," he replied with a chuckle that sounded like two rocks grinding against each other. "You've met David Dunbar, my lass. Hop in the back, there's plenty of room for a passenger."

Elspeth wasted no time in clambering aboard, and she soon found herself sharing her seat with bales of raw wool. She squished the contents experimentally, thinking that the farmer must be intending to go beyond the village with this product, for surely it would be sold to markets well beyond this corner of the world.

She asked him exactly this, and received a thorough education regarding the economy of the wool trade, from raising the sheep to the eventual purchase of bolts of woolen cloth. The man was clearly an expert, despite his humble appearance and his disdain for being called *sir*.

They passed a low building that looked like an old farmstead with children running around outside. Elspeth asked, "Is that the village school?"

"No, my lass. The village school is just by the old kirk on

the high street. This school is for teaching and boarding the young ones who haven't homes."

"An orphanage?" she guessed.

"Not in name. It can't be an orphanage because some of the children there aren't officially orphans. Ye ken?"

"So they are *un*official?"

"They're children whose parents or guardians are gone for long stretches of time, and have no one to watch over them till their fathers or mothers return. Some sail on whaleships, some are soldiers serving overseas. Others traveled to Canada or elsewhere to work and make their fortune."

He went on to explain that these children lived at "the far school" for months or years at a time, alongside a few children who *were* official orphans, and would stay until they came of age, when they'd have to make their way into the world as best they could. And yes, sometimes the children in the first category moved into the second category—the world was a dangerous place, and not all letters home contained good news.

When they reached the village, a newly enlightened Elspeth jumped out of the wagon when he pulled up to the building that seemed to serve as the tavern and the central gathering spot. She offered a cheerful farewell, wishing Mr Dunbar good luck in selling his wool, and a hope that she would see him again.

She made her way down the main street, looking this way and that with intense curiosity. Struan hadn't spoken much of the place, and had intimated that she would find it small and dull after experiencing Edinburgh. But it seemed to be busy enough, to judge by the number of people she saw walking down the street, or in the several buildings to either side.

She didn't enter the tavern, but did stop in a shop with a sign advertising dry goods and sundries. A woman with red hair braided so that the plait fell over her shoulder greeted

Elspeth. Elspeth inquired if the woman sold any buttons. The woman pulled out a wooden box and sorted through it, holding up several options, until Elspeth pointed to one and told her she would take half a dozen. The woman seemed flummoxed when Elspeth informed her that she was living at the so-called "big house" now.

"I'd heard that the young Mr MacInnes was back, but I didn't know he was bringing anyone along with him. So you must have lived in Edinburgh, correct? For I can tell you're not English or French. You would not have met him overseas."

Elspeth laughed, and admitted it was so. "Yes, we sailed part of the way from Edinburgh, and then took the rest of the journey by carriage. It's far north indeed. I'd not appreciated the distance from one end of Scotland to the other until now."

The woman smiled a little wistfully, and said that perhaps sometime Elspeth could tell her more of Edinburgh, for the woman had never been there herself. But it was also clear that the time was not now, for several people had come in, and she didn't want the merchant to lose a sale on account of chattering with her.

She paid for her buttons and gave a polite nod to the red-haired woman, as well as the others in the small shop, all of whom were eyeing her without appearing to do so. Elspeth continued strolling down the street, taking in each building, whether it be some sort of business enterprise, or somebody's home—though most of the buildings appeared to be a combination. When she came to the small stone church in the middle of its green and somewhat wild-grown graveyard, Elspeth turned and walked down the white gravel path, curious to see the inside of what appeared to be an ancient building. However, before she could reach it, she was distracted by the inscriptions on the moss-covered stones. Or rather the inscriptions she could actually read, for several of the stones were so weatherbeaten that only a few letters could be distinguished. She saw a date from the early 1600s and she suspected that most of the graves were older than that. She recognized Struan's family name, though she wasn't sure if it was actually the same family, considering that so many surnames in Scotland were shared.

She was contemplating a small headstone with an indistinguishable name underneath a carving of a much faded cherub when she heard a man's voice behind her. "A kirkyard is no place for a fresh-faced thing like you. Only the dead here."

Elspeth turned and saw a young man standing on the gravel path, regarding her with eyes of bright blue. The curiosity in his face was plain.

"You're new," he went on, stepping closer. "Why don't you let a local show you the sights?"

"I think I have seen the sights," Elspeth replied. She smiled back, but there was something about him that made her slightly uncomfortable. While his demeanor and words were perfectly friendly, something in her warned her not to come too close to him. She said, "I must start back home now."

"I'll walk you there," he said easily.

With no reason to deny the offer, she turned to leave the small graveyard and retrace her steps down the main street. The man, keeping up a patter of anecdotes about every building and person they passed, was amusing enough. But when he suggested a stop in the tavern for a drink with him, she started to lose her patience.

"I must get back."

"Ach, who will miss you?"

"Well, at some point my husband might. I *am* married."

"Huh, there's been no such ceremony in this church for

weeks. I'd know if there was."

"I was married in Edinburgh. I've only just arrived here to live at Linneliath."

"The big house, eh? What do you do there?"

"Why do you mean, what do I do?"

"Chambermaid? Seamstress? You ain't no lady's maid, for there's no lady there."

She stared at him, dumbfounded. "*I* am the lady."

He stared back, then burst out laughing. "Oh, you are good, aren't you? I didn't see that coming. Oh, you the lady! That's rich."

"It's not a joke."

He was still laughing. "Aye, it is. And a bold one. You the lady, looking as you are. Anyway, the young master isn't married."

"He is, because he just married me. In Edinburgh." She resumed walking, eyes to the front. The sooner she was away from this boorish man, the better.

But the man reached for her, catching her shoulder. "No need to pretend, lass. I'm no clergyman, for all that we met in a kirkyard. I don't care if you're his piece. If he's back and brought along a plaything from the city, that's all to the good. The girls around here are boring. But you're a puzzle. Pretty little puzzle too. Come, give me a taste of what you're giving him."

Elspeth twisted away. The street seemed suddenly deserted. And she knew no one in this tiny town. Mairi would certainly know what to do in this situation. But Mairi wasn't here. Elspeth was, and she was all alone.

Chapter 14

STRUAN HAD SPENT THE MORNING in a cold room hunched over books, along with Mr Kerr, his man of business. Kerr had *also* been his father's man of business and thus knew virtually everything about Linneliath, the village, the mines, and indeed the whole region.

Just when Struan was ready to call for a midday meal, Kerr pointed to a small book and said, "I almost forgot. There is the matter of this debt to you, which is labeled as *McGregor*. It's been over six years since the money was first loaned, but I don't see any record of repayment of interest, let alone principal. I must have missed some information. Who is this person? How do you wish to proceed with this matter?"

Oh, hell. Struan had forgotten that the record of the debt would be visible to Kerr. He prayed that the other would not connect the name to his wife's, though it was not an uncommon name. He cursed his own inattention, for not making some innocuous-looking notation to indicate how unimportant it was.

"I'm not concerned," he said, aiming for nonchalance (which was not a tone he did well, or at all). "You don't need to take any action."

"At all? A loan of that size cannot simply be ignored!"

"It's not as if I'm relying on the repayment of any single loan. You've just told me that the mines are doing unexpectedly well.”

“I did, but mines are by their nature chancy. The veins the men are working could run dry next week. You yourself have said you don’t wish to be dependent on any one source of income. It sets a man up for disappointment later on.”

“Well,” Struan said, seizing on Kerr’s words, “if the mines run dry next week, I’ll revisit the matter of this particular debt. But not now. I’ve a lot to think about.”

“Yes,” said Kerr. “Your new bride must be occupying nearly all of your attention. It’s too bad your parents couldn’t meet her. They would have liked her.”

Struan felt terrible when he saw genuine pleasure in the man’s face, because, yes, his parents would have liked her. But if they were present, he never would have been able to maintain the fiction of how he had come to be her husband in the first place. Neither his mother nor his father would have approved of the arrangement he’d made with McGregor. His mother had been a romantic soul, and she had often told Struan that true love was not merely available to every person on earth, but that patience, goodwill, and a little bit of luck would make it happen. His father was more prosaic, but he too would have been appalled by the idea of buying a bride. No matter how charming and lovely that bride ended up being.

Struan sighed as he turned to look out the window. “Is there anything else I need to know?”

“Everything is in hand, sir,” said Kerr. “The mines have been a boon when it comes to the bottom line. The increasing practice of clearing the land elsewhere in the Highlands has worried many of your tenants, who fear you’ll order clearances here. But farming is only part of our local economy, and we have fishing and the mines to reduce our reliance on it. With attentive stewardship and with proper investments in new equipment, your land will continue to thrive and the people will continue to make an adequate living."

"That's my aim," Struan said. "Now that the war against the emperor seems to finally have come to an end, maybe no more young men will feel the need to take the king's coin. Soldiering is always an option for the right type of man, but there are too many who have no business on a battlefield, or on the deck of a Royal Navy ship. I don't want any lad to feel it's his only option."

"Aye, sir." Kerr shut the books in front of him, tucked them under his arm, and gave a slight bow. "Inform me if I can be of any further service."

After Mr Kerr left, Struan considered the land outside the window and how calm it looked. Yet there were forces moving in the world that seemed hell-bent on shaking the landscape and the people as well. Strange forces, hovering just over the horizon, whether innovations born of enlightened but sometimes reckless thought, or the ever-shifting political tides of countries far away, or the changing attitudes of his own country's elite.

The practice of clearances had once seemed fantastical to him, but it was happening with more frequency all over the country, as already wealthy landowners learned that they could evict tenants who had farmed the lands for generations, and turn that same land over to the production of sheep. Struan had been disgusted when he first learned of the practice, but perhaps that was because he'd never truly felt the bite of poverty himself. His family had been fortunate, as well as blessed with several generations of careful managers. Yet all too many members of the upper class had land or title, or both, yet little income to support their lifestyle. He remembered Elspeth's reaction to the notion of clearances, and thought he'd go find her to ask her about some ideas he had to make them unnecessary at Linneliath.

But that task proved to be more difficult than he expected. He first looked in the library and then the eastern parlor. He asked the cook if Elspeth had requested lunch yet, only to be told that the mistress had not been seen since she finished her morning coffee. With a slight feeling of trepidation, Struan knocked on her bedchamber door, the one that opened onto the hallway rather than the one that joined his own room. Though Elspeth was his wife, he'd been raised to believe that any woman's chambers were sacrosanct, and no gentleman would ever intrude upon them without excellent reason and explicit permission. But when he knocked, it was one of the maids who opened the door, and Elspeth wasn't in the room at all.

"Where is my wife?" he asked.

The maid looked at her companion, who shrugged. "I am afraid we don't know, sir. She may have gone out to the gardens?" she offered.

"I'll ask downstairs again," he said, leaving. There was no reason why a housemaid should know the location of the mistress, and it was certainly a large house, so it was possible that no one knew where Elspeth was precisely at the moment, but Struan couldn't help but feel a twinge of annoyance, which he knew was his mind's deliberate attempt to hide a different feeling that surged underneath.

Fear.

Losing track of his companions on the battlefield could lead to injury or worse. Struan had learned to always be scanning just to make sure that he hadn't misplaced one of the other men. They did the same for him. If it hadn't been for his friends, he never would have survived the ordeal he went through in France.

True, Linneliath was not a battlefield, and true, Elspeth was not a soldier. He had no reason to think that something had gone wrong, and yet he worried. Overtrained. That's what it was. He wouldn't feel secure again until he saw her, and that meant he would simply have to find her.

He wasn't distressed by the first couple of interviews with another maid on the ground floor or the footman, neither of whom had seen her that day. But when he ran into Mrs Negus, who informed him that Elspeth inquired as to the direction into the village, Struan's concern spiked.

"Are you telling me that she rode into the village?" But wait. Ellie told him she had never learned to ride.

"I couldn't say, sir," the housekeeper replied, not showing the slightest worry. "Though if she had, surely the hostler spoke to her when he saddled up a horse, and she probably has one of the stable lads riding behind her as escort."

Struan didn't remember if he replied to that, but he did remember rushing out to the stables and he did remember when the hostler and the two stable boys assured him in no uncertain terms that the mistress had not requested either a horse or for the carriage to be prepared. "She must have taken a walk through the grounds," the hostler said.

Struan retraced his steps as far as the gravel path that wrapped around the house to the only place even faintly resembling a formal garden, this part of the country not being amenable to the endeavor. He barely got around the corner when he encountered the gardener wheeling a wooden cart rattling with tools. Struan asked if he'd seen Elspeth, and the gardener gave him a cheerful nod. "Aye, sir. Told me how well the hedges looked, and hoped the winter wasn't too harsh on the more tender plants."

He exhaled in relief. "So she's in the garden now?"

"Oh no, sir. She took a turn and then asked me how far it would be to walk to the village. And I asked how *far* or how *long*, for they are not the same. And then the lady said she wished to know both, for she expected to make the journey regularly and she enjoyed walking. So I told her that she could reach the village by foot in less than half an hour if she took the main track out the gate. She bid me good day and walked off. Must've been nearly an hour ago now."

The gardener took up his cart again and moved away, humming.

Struan stood still for a moment, debating the foolishness of the action he was about to take. It was stupid to chase after Elspeth. It was broad daylight, the weather was fine, and this was Linneliath. It was perfectly safe, and the village no less so. It was laughable to think that any harm could come to Elspeth on a mere stroll to the village.

And yet.

Struan did not like misplacing people.

He returned to the stable and ordered the man to saddle up his horse. It would be a short ride and he would discover that Elspeth was perfectly well, and indeed probably would have charmed the entire village by the time he found her again.

And yet.

In the village, he tethered his horse and strode into the largest shop, where anyone might be expected to stop in. He asked if his wife had done so, and received only blank stares. Yes, of course. Barely anyone here knew he was married yet. He described her: blonde, Edinburgh accent, purple dress.

"Oh! The lass in the purple gown, sir?" the redheaded proprietress said. "Why yes, she was in here not half an hour ago—well spoken, she was."

"Did she say where she was going?" Struan asked.

"No, but there aren't many places to go, are there? Walk down the street toward St Magnus and you'll surely see her or someone who's just seen her."

Struan proceeded down the main street. He noticed several figures strolling along both sides of the track, but the moment he spied a purple-clad woman further down on the opposite side of the street, he quickened his pace to meet her.

Ellie hadn't noticed him yet. She was over a dozen yards away, and she was walking oddly. Her arms were crossed over her chest and her hands gripped her upper arms, as if she were cold. Her head was tilted downward, so he couldn't see her face. Why the hell was she walking like that?

Then he realized that she wasn't alone. A man was striding alongside her, talking earnestly. She was not responding in kind, and in fact looked rather…

Hunted.

Then the man reached out and put his hand on Elspeth's shoulder.

She jerked away.

Struan's vision narrowed to a tunnel. He crossed the street in a blink, grabbed the man by the collar, and pushed him against the wooden wall of the nearest building.

"Get your hands off my wife."

"What? This lass?" The man struggled, but Struan was not merely big, he was furious.

People within sight were now turning to them, most of them coming closer.

"This lass is my *wife*. And you scared her."

"I was only chatting! No crime in talking to a lass. No harm done."

"There was no harm," Elspeth echoed faintly.

"He touched you."

"I must not have been clear enough that I was not interested in…chatting." Her cheeks went pink as she noticed the other people within earshot.

"I expect you were clear enough." Struan turned back to the man. He pitched his voice lower, so it couldn't be overheard by the growing audience.

"What's your name?"

"Robbie Davies," he declared, as if his local fame made introduction unnecessary. "Who're *you*?"

"I am Struan MacInnes." He waited a moment for that to sink in, then said slowly, deliberately, "If you ever speak to my wife again, I will kill you. If you speak *of* her, I will kill you. If you look at her, I'll kill you. Am I clear enough?"

All the belligerence had drained from the other man. "I didn't know she was your wife, sir! I thought she was joking. Look how she's dressed! She said she just moved into the big house. I thought she meant she was a new maid or undercook or something."

"Whether she looks like it or not, she is the lady. And even if she were an undercook, dressed in rags, that's no invitation to you."

Elspeth looked like she was about to be sick. "May we go now?" she asked in a low voice.

"Aye. We're going." Struan started walking and didn't look back. If he stopped or turned around, he was liable to go after that man again, and this time do permanent damage.

Elspeth hurried along next to him, her hand curling around his right arm, trying to slow his progress. "Struan," she whispered urgently. "Why did you do that? Everyone's going to be talking about it now."

"Good," he grunted out. "Then I won't have to do it again."

"We'll be lucky if anyone speaks to us now. Though if there are more in the village like him…"

He turned. "Are you all right?"

She nodded quickly. "He was just overly familiar. But it was only words, Struan."

"Words matter. He shouldn't have said that about you. He shouldn't have thought it. And he did touch you."

"My arm. I'm fine. And you're fine. And that man is still alive, which I imagine is a rather near thing. I've never seen you act like that before."

"You don't know me very well, do you?" he snapped.

"I suppose not."

Ellie's muted voice cut through his rage.

He stopped and faced her. "Ellie, I just don't want anything bad to happen to you. Ever."

They were standing next to a little side passage by the bakery, to judge by the smell.

Elspeth raised her hand to touch his face, just above the scar along his lower cheek. "Struan, I'm fine. Truly. Please don't be angry."

He was angry anyway. Not at her. But angry all the same. His wife. *His* wife. His *wife*.

He'd got possessive quickly, hadn't he?

They didn't linger in the village. While Struan had ridden in alone, he didn't think twice about lifting up Elspeth and riding back with her. Though now he did have to deal with the fact that she was all but curled up on his lap. Every minute along the track brought a bump or a shift that sent her body sliding into his, and sweet Christ, those curves pressing into him were a torment. To have Ellie's soft body nestled on him was distracting as hell, and he prayed she didn't realize just how aroused he was growing.

But this was also the closest they'd ever been, and he wasn't sure he wanted it to end.

Chapter 15

ONLY JUST THIS MORNING, ELSPETH had been pondering how she might become closer to her husband, but she didn't anticipate being in his arms while riding on a horse, and she certainly wasn't prepared for how *much* of him there was. His chest and shoulders were broad enough to blot out the village behind them. He must have shaved that morning—he was rigorous in his habits—and she could smell the lingering scent of the soap he used. Something in her made her want to curl her arms around him and simply cling to his massive frame. His thighs reminded her of tree branches…though definitely more comfortable to sit upon. Firm, but with a bit of give, and a warmth that quickly spread to her own body.

She squirmed, realizing just how close she was to certain parts of his anatomy.

He let go of the reins with his left hand and lowered it to her leg, holding her in place.

"Please don't do that."

"Oh, I'm sorry." She twisted a bit to face him. "Does it make it harder to ride?"

"Yes." He was resolutely not looking at her, and his jaw was clenched.

Was he angry at her? Of course he would be. Her heart began to thud

Then, just as she was about to beg his forgiveness, he said unexpectedly, "I apologize for how I behaved back there. I overreacted."

She exhaled. Maybe he wasn't angry at her. She said, "And I'm sorry that I didn't fully comprehend how much my absence would concern you."

"I don't like misplacing people," he muttered.

"I'm here," she assured him. "I won't leave Linneliath again without leaving word. I'm not used to anyone noticing where I've gone."

"How is that possible?"

She gave a little shrug. "Father was busy with his own pursuits. My stepmother spends most of her time attending to Averill. And Mairi doesn't have the patience for the sort of things I like to do…tasks around the house or going to the market or—"

"What does Mairi do?"

It would be impolite to say that Mairi was plotting to overturn the bedrock of Scotland's social structure…although it would be accurate. "She's active in a particular ladies' society in town. She attends meetings and reads a lot of books and meets her companions for tea and such."

"You mean the League for the Advancement of Scottish Women? I'm aware of it," he said dryly.

"Oh, yes. You were part of that mysterious event with Miss Ross this spring."

"A small part. You didn't wish to join the League with your sister?"

"If I did, who would mind the house?"

"A housekeeper, perhaps?"

"Well, that's not the same at all."

Just then, the far school came into view. Elspeth noticed Struan looking at it, and asked if he ever visited.

"It's not part of Linneliath," he said. "I've no authority

there. My father did donate some initial funds to build it," he added.

She guessed the donation covered more than "some" of the cost. She said, "I thought I might visit. The school is almost a sort of neighbor, if you think about it that way."

"You can if you like. I'm sure the children would be happy to see you."

"Would you join me?"

He looked away. "I don't think it would help."

"But you like children."

"Aye."

"And they're children."

"Aye, I'm aware of that."

"I suspect they're curious about you," she said.

"I doubt they know I exist."

Elspeth didn't bother to hide her skepticism. "You think that local children, who are naturally curious about everything, wouldn't be curious about the most important gentleman in the whole region, who happens to be a military hero and also happens to employ half the countryside, and who lives in a mansion that's far larger than anything else they've seen in their lives?"

Struan gave a faint smile. "Fine. They're probably curious."

"So come with me."

"You go first. I'll join you on a later visit."

It was not quite a promise, but Ellie liked that he was willing to talk about it. He seemed much calmer now.

A breeze ruffled her hair, and she inhaled deeply. "I can almost smell the sea."

"When the wind is from the east, you can catch the salt sometimes. From that rise," he said, pointing to his right, "you can get a glimpse of the water."

"Oh, really? I thought we were too far inland."

"The coastline is deceptive." He paused. "Do you want to ride over there to see?"

"Yes!"

So he rode off in the new direction and she clung to him. At the top of the hill, Elspeth stared at the world before them.

"Oh, it's gorgeous. So wild and open. Why was the house not built here?"

"Because it's bloody cold, that's why. This ridge protects all the others further inland. There used to be a lookout tower here. But it fell to ruins even before my grandfather's time."

"Oh, how wonderfully romantic. A ruined tower and the open sky. I hope someone wrote a poem about it."

"If they did, I've never read it. And I'm no poet." He was looking at her now, and there was something in his eyes that made her breathing quicken.

"Alas, I'm not either. I could clean the tower if it were still here, though."

"It would be the tidiest ruin in Scotland," he agreed, obviously thinking of something else. He put his fingers to her chin, stilling her movement. "Can I kiss you, Ellie?"

"Yes, please," she breathed. Suddenly, her heart was racing.

"You can say no."

"I'm saying yes."

Yet he hesitated, and so she stretched to kiss him. She wasn't skilled, but he seemed not to mind. He cupped her face in his hands and let the kiss spin on, and then gently sucked on her lower lip. She felt so good she let out a little delighted moan. She put her hands flat against his chest, aware that he wore only a few layers of clothing.

She wore only two, and even with the heat building in her body, her skin prickled from the cold breeze as much as the excitement. Even her breasts were pebbling in the chill, pressing into the bodice of her gown.

Still, she didn't want to stop. She took a breath and leaned into him. Only when the wind nearly took her cloak from her shoulders did she pull away.

"The wind *is* strong up here," she noted, not pleased about it. "When will it warm up to be summer?"

"Mmmm, possibly tomorrow. Or never. This part of the world is not known for its summers."

"I see."

"Do you wish to go back to Edinburgh?"

"Not at all. But I may wish for a thicker cloak."

"We'll inform the seamstress of your wish."

"Oh, I didn't mean to add to—"

"Ellie. Hush." He kissed her again, silencing her worry about overspending.

She liked it when he kissed her, and she also completely forgot about the wind, because his hands were threading through her hair, and his mouth was so warm. She inhaled at the slow slide of his lip along hers, hot and slick and nerve-tingling. There was something almost sinful in the way that he slid his tongue between her lips.

"Let me in," he breathed as she opened her mouth wider.

Why should those words hit so low in her belly? Why should she want to hear them again, and again?

Another gust of wind hit her side, and she shivered.

"Damn it," he growled, also feeling the cold. "This is not the ideal location, is it?"

"It's private," she offered. "And has a lovely view."

He laughed, surprising her. "Always looking for the best in things, aren't you, Ellie?"

"It's not difficult."

Struan shook his head. "Maybe not for you. We should go back to the house. I won't be responsible for you catching a chill."

"I'm hardy, I promise."

"I believe you." But he was already wheeling the horse around to return to the path. As soon as they descended below the hilltop, the wind lessened, and she sighed in relief.

Struan wrapped one arm around her shoulders and pulled her against his chest. "Better?"

"Much. I hope it's not a bother to carry me."

"Are you asking me or the horse?" It was often difficult to tell when Struan was joking, but she saw a little glint in his eye, and smiled.

"Either. Both."

"We don't mind. Anyway, it's not far. Just down the slope there. You can see the smoke from the chimneys."

Elspeth sighed. "That's good. I know it's only been a few hours, but I can't wait to be home again."

"You mean Linneliath."

"Yes. Home."

He didn't reply, but she felt his arm tighten around her shoulders, holding her closer.

Maybe that's what made her bold enough to say, "When we get back, later tonight, I mean, maybe we could…resume the kissing?"

He seemed to grow brittle, wary. "Maybe."

"I liked it. That's all I meant."

"Good. I want you to be…comfortable."

"I am. So we can…continue. If you like. Soon."

He nodded. "Soon."

* * * *

Once they were back at the house, Struan wasted no more time about Elspeth's wardrobe. He went to the maids who were in charge of his wife's room and all her things.

"Tell me something about my wife's wardrobe. Does she

own only purple?"

"There's a black dress in case of mourning, sir," Agnes said.

"So truly all the rest are that same shade? That's astonishing. She must love it."

"I don't think so, sir. She mentioned that she wished to be done with them, but that she never could stand to discard good fabric. She takes good care of all five."

"All five what?"

"All five purple dresses, sir. I gather she'd sewed them herself out of the same bolt of fabric that she'd been given."

"Wait. She owns five purple dresses, and one black one she never wears. I thought she owned twenty gowns and they all just look the same."

"No, sir. She only came with the two trunks, sir. Didn't take long to get her settled."

Struan felt like an idiot. He'd heard the maids talking before, and he knew how much luggage Ellie had on the ship. So why did he assume that she magically had some infinite wardrobe?

Of course she didn't.

But now that she was married to him, he could at least use the only magic he had access to—money—and get her one.

At dinner, he said, "We're going to get you a proper wardrobe."

"Oh, what I have is sufficient," she said quickly.

"It's not. That incident in the village occurred because you appeared to be a member of the servant class."

"It occurred because that oaf would not leave me alone even after I asked him to," she corrected him.

"A mistake I hope he's learned from," Struan muttered.

"You certainly imparted a lesson," she said. "Whether he was a good student is another matter."

"Nevertheless, I don't want anyone to be able to use such an excuse again. You're my wife, you're the lady of Linneliath, and you ought to look the part. Where's your yellow dress, the one your wore at the wedding?"

"That was Averill's."

"Well, you're going to need more gowns of your own."

"I'll write to Mairi and ask her to send a few of her dresses. She has several that she no longer wears. Averill won't give up anything. Really, it was rather astounding she offered the use of the yellow dress. I should have begged clothing from Mairi earlier, but I suppose I was distracted by the speed of the wedding."

Struan paused a moment, feeling that she was blaming him for the situation. Not that he could tell her that her father practically pushed her out the door.

Seeing his expression, she added, "I didn't mean—"

"Never mind what you meant. You will not have your sister send you her castoffs. You will acquire new items, made for you. Items of the proper quality. First, if you'll entertain here, you need actual evening wear, ideally clothing you actually like for every day."

"I like what I have."

"No you don't. I asked your maid."

"Oh." She fell silent.

"What's the matter?"

"Nothing. I knew my gowns weren't de rigeur, but I thought because you didn't seem to put much stock in…social gatherings, you might not care what I wore to dinner when it was just us."

"I want you to like what you wear, Ellie."

"My pin money will cover the cost of a few gowns," she said.

"You're not using your damned pin money for this. I'm making you get a wardrobe, so I'm paying for it."

"I don't want to be a burden. I hope to run the house well enough that I won't fall onto the side of your costs."

Christ, did she know that the marriage settled her father's debt? Was that why she was so obsessed with the household funds? Struan thought he'd made it clear to her father that the arrangement would never be discussed. And her father seemed eager to agree.

But Ellie was already discussing the sort of gowns she'd need, and he understood that she was still blissfully ignorant of the truth behind her so-called courtship. He breathed a sigh of relief.

Then he remembered something he'd retrieved from his room before dinner. He pulled a velvet pouch from his pocket and slid it across the table. "This is for you."

"What is it?" Ellie asked, not reaching for it.

"You don't believe I can provide for you."

"Oh, Struan, of course I do."

He waved off her protest. "I've decided to prove it in a more material way."

"How so?"

He opened the pouch and pulled out a necklace: a thin gold chain that seemed almost too delicate to support a single large amber cabochon.

"Oh," Ellie whispered.

"The amber piece was found by my great-grandfather on the shore near Linneliath. He had the necklace made for his wife, and it's been passed down since. If you ever doubt that you'll be taken care of, you need only touch this."

"It's magnificent. I think it's too extravagant to wear on ordinary days, though."

"Wear it, Ellie. It suits you. Your hair is gold. So is your smile." He hadn't expected to wax so poetic. But being around her tended to make him do a lot things he never thought himself capable of.

She fastened the chain around her neck. "How does it look?"

"Like it was meant to be yours. I want you to wear either that, or your pearls, or some jewelry every day. No more denying yourself."

"I'll try to take your advice. Perhaps you should also?"

"Also what?"

"Also stop denying yourself." She blushed as she said it, making it clear what she was referring to.

He didn't enjoy denying himself at all. But he couldn't exactly demand to come to her room immediately after gifting her the amber necklace. It felt too much like…buying her.

Which he had.

Once again cursing himself, Struan said, "Soon."

Ellie, to her credit, did not instantly reply with the natural question: *how* soon. She just nodded and said, "As you wish."

He wished a lot of things, but the main one—not looking like he'd been burned over half his body—wasn't going to come true.

Chapter 16

Since Linneliath was so isolated, it was decided that Ellie's best fitting gown (ironically, the black mourning gown) would be sent to a seamstress back in Edinburgh, along with her measurements, as taken by her lady's maid, and a detailed list of the items she'd need for a new wardrobe. Then the items could be delivered much more quickly than if she made the trip down herself. Ellie made out the list, which she felt was far too long, and handed it to Agnes to be sent in the post along with the gown. She was unaware until much later that both Agnes and then Struan made some changes to the list.

The next day, Ellie walked to the far school, intending to introduce herself and offer her aid if it might be helpful. When she got there, she asked to speak with the headmistress if it was convenient. Though Elspeth didn't realize it, news about MacInnes's reaction to Robbie's disregard for Elspeth had got around. No one intended to disregard MacInnes's wife after that. So despite having to flee a Latin lesson and quickly don the lace shawl that she wore only to church, the headmistress assured the new wife that certainly it was no inconvenience *at all*.

Ellie smiled at her and said, "I wished to see the school, and also to ask if there is anything the students need. Since

Linneliath is so close, I would be happy to bring food, or fuel…or help with the children?"

The headmistress, Mrs Hardie, insisted on giving her a tour, and then introducing her to the class, all of varying ages.

With wardrobes on her mind, Ellie noticed that many of the children were dressed in clothing at the absolute end of its useful life. A dress that began good enough for a lady to wear to church eventually became a workaday gown for a daughter or sister. Then the spans of fabric in the best condition would be shortened or refurbished to make a dress for a younger girl, who didn't need to be at the height of fashion, only decently turned out. And as she outgrew it, perhaps the skirts would become an apron.

Scottish practicality (not to say stinginess) meant that most women, no matter their class, would reuse, take in, take out, mend, patch, and repurpose virtually any item of clothing until the fabric would bear not a single more stitch or snip. Only then would clothes become rags, and even so they'd be pressed into service for cleaning, being stuffed into furniture or bedding…and perhaps at the ultimate end, to be shredded and pulped to be made into paper.

These children needed more than rags. It gave Ellie an idea. "You know, I shall soon have some gowns I'll no longer need. I shouldn't like the fabric to go to waste. How many children attend here? How many boys and how many girls?"

The woman told her the numbers, and Elspeth silently decided that in addition to clothing, she would also make sure the children had enough to eat. The village seemed to be doing fairly well overall, probably as a result of the income from those who worked in the mines. But that didn't guarantee good fortune trickled all way down to the lowest—namely, the children with no strong family connections to ease their way.

"I do hope everyone likes purple," Elspeth murmured as she headed home.

Back at Linneliath, the servants were surprisingly receptive to the idea of doing yet more work, since the efforts of several would be required to cut and sew the new outfits.

"Oh, we could dye the boys' clothes black," one maid offered. "Black is good because it doesn't show stains or wear as quickly, and a boy will rip or stain a shirt the moment he puts it on. It's fate."

Mrs Negus, who knew what mischief boys could get up to, nodded in agreement. "Black for the boys, then. The girls will wear the purple, though. As soon as the mistress's new gowns arrive, we'll get to work on the purple ones."

Later that day Ellie told Struan, "I intend to visit the school often. I don't have enough tasks to occupy me, what with having a score of servants who all know their jobs. The school doesn't have enough hands for the work."

"How often?"

"Three or four times a week, I think. Is that acceptable?"

"You do whatever you like, Ellie. As long as you're back in the evening. These moors aren't safe to travel after dark. There are too many places where a person or a horse or even a whole carriage could stumble and get into serious trouble."

She nodded, unconcerned. The approaching summer meant that the days were already getting long. Soon the twilight might linger till ten in the evening.

A few days after the first of her new gowns were delivered, Elspeth was delighted to carry the resewn children's clothing to the school, helped by two maids who'd done much of the sewing. They presented the items to Mrs Hardie, who accepted them with a trace of surprise.

"Did you not think we'd finish so quickly?" Elspeth asked.

"In truth, ma'am," the woman said, looking down, "I did not expect you to start. The few times a person of means has noticed the school, we've gotten promises of aid. But promises are cheap."

"Does Mr MacInnes support the school at all?"

"His father was most generous in his time. Mr MacInnes, the young man I mean, has been away."

"I see."

"We get an annual gift, dispensed by Mr MacInnes's man of business."

"And is that sufficient?"

The woman looked away again.

"I see," Elspeth repeated with a sigh. "Let me guess. The amount of the gift has not kept up with the rising costs of goods and food."

"That's exactly the case, ma'am."

"I will speak to my husband. And until then, at least the children have new things to wear."

"It is a most excellent solution, madam. With all our girls in the same color, now they'll be easy to find no matter where we all go."

"Well, that's something. No one likes to misplace people," Ellie said with a laugh. It was only on the way back that she remembered where she first heard the phrase: from Struan. *I don't like misplacing people.*

Elspeth was optimistic when she returned to the house. She had made great progress in bringing the house up to the standards of a modern woman such as herself. Elspeth didn't like how dark and gloomy many of the rooms were to begin with, especially because Scottish skies tended toward dark and gloomy on their own. So she ordered new fabrics for the window hangings and instructed the household on how to whitewash surfaces that could be treated.

She gathered all the lamps and candelabra she could find

from the forgotten corners of the house, moving them into the more regularly used rooms. Then, when it was cloudy or dark, the rooms could be lit in defiance of the weather. Her back ached from all the climbing stairs and going from room to room, but it would be worth it.

She hoped to surprise Struan with the newly brightened dining room this evening. The dining room chairs were just reupholstered, and the drapes had been replaced with a much brighter color than the drab olive shade some previous person had chosen years ago.

Ellie herself dressed with similar care, wearing one of her new gowns. This one was a pale pink wool that seemed eternally springlike. She wore her hair only half up, allowing the rest to fall freely down her back, since there was little need for full formality when it was just a couple dining alone. She wore the pearls around her neck.

She was waiting there when Struan entered, and he stopped short, looking at her with an inscrutable expression.

"I know you were out visiting the tenant farmers all day," Elspeth said, "so I asked Cook to prepare an especially hearty meal. If you wish…"

But Struan wasn't fully listening to her. He looked her up and down, and then said, "You have your hair down."

* * * *

Struan went still, struck by the vision in the doorway.

Elspeth was a beautiful woman no matter what she wore, proven when she wore the aggressively purple gowns that didn't do a thing to flatter her.

But to see her now, wearing clothing meant for her, in a style that matched her personality, and with all the accessories and jewelry expected of a lady…she was a vision.

Her hair was put up in a style that seemed almost haphazard but somehow accentuated her face perfectly, as a few blonde curls cascaded down to settle on her shoulders.

Now she touched her hair. "I didn't feel like putting it all up tonight. Do you wish me to fix it?"

"Fix it? No, I like it." He loved it.

"Thank you," Elspeth said. "And I'm wearing one of my new dresses."

"Yes, I can tell because it's not purple."

Elspeth beamed at him. "I picked the color out myself. What do you think?"

"It's pretty." Christ, *that's* all his brain and mouth managed to say? "I mean to say that *you* look very pretty," he corrected himself. "As you always do."

But then his gaze flicked around the room, becoming more troubled. "There are more candles than usual."

"I had more brought into the room. I thought it was too dark before. I could hardly see my meal most evenings."

"There are too many."

"Tell me which ones you would like me to extinguish, then," Elspeth said quickly.

They both moved toward the nearest sconce at the same time, and ended up blocking each other's way, and Elspeth naturally laughed because even being half-knocked over by a lumbering giant was somehow delightful to her. Struan instinctively put out his hands, intending to move her to the side, but she had lifted her arms up for some reason and he found himself holding her by the waist, looking into her eyes, the reflection of too many candles making them bright and dangerous.

Her laugh faded, but she held his gaze. And tilted her head up, her lips parted.

And then they were kissing. He didn't know if he decided it or she did, but it felt so damn perfect that he didn't care.

Elspeth's mouth was hot under his, her lips silky and

sweet and why not bite her lower lip just a little, and hear her gasp and push into him, kissing back with a sudden fierceness that sent heat plunging downward.

He lifted one hand to her throat, stroking the smooth flesh, feeling the patter of her heartbeat under his fingers.

Unsure if he'd alarmed her with the intensity of his kiss, he hesitated, almost stepped back.

"No, don't stop," she said quickly. "It feels so nice, like…brandy without the burn."

Brandy without the burn. Sweet. Warming. Intoxicating. Yes.

She was soft and inviting, her arms reaching up and her hands grazing his shoulders, then her fingers were curling around the edge of his jacket as if to keep him close.

He kissed her again, more slowly, trying to savor the taste of her. Not wolf her down the way he'd started.

It was difficult, because she was luscious and he was starving. But he forced himself to take a little time, notice all the details. The way she leaned into him, her curves pressing against his body like a different kind of kiss. He took a breath, and used the moment to lean back and look at her— now with a flushed face and open mouth, her eyes half-closed, the lashes fluttering. He laid his thumb on her lip and then tipped it into her mouth, letting her taste it.

Curious lips circled it and she flicked her tongue against the pad of his thumb, and she may as well have shot lightning into him. He bit back the moan that threatened to burst out, and withdrew his thumb before she accidentally finished him standing right in the middle of the dining room.

Except…they weren't in the middle of the room. They'd somehow moved to the wall, his body pinning hers. He could lift her up just a little and it would be the perfect angle to…

No. Not in the damn dining room.

Not for the first time anyway.

Even as he thought that, Ellie was kissing him again, open-mouthed and urgent, uninhibited, eager. Like she enjoyed it. Like she wanted more. From him.

Struan was so overwhelmed that it took him a moment to respond when her tongue slid against his. The raw sensuality of the move made his vision blacken at the edges.

He held her exactly where he needed her to be so he could lean in and...

"Um. The soup course is ready."

Struan glanced toward the interruption. The footman who announced that from the doorway was staring at the ceiling, face wooden. Good man.

Elspeth giggled, the sound mostly lost and only the vibrations of it going into his chest, where she'd pressed her face. "The soup course is ready," she told Struan.

"Yes, so I've heard."

"We should probably eat the dinner prepared for us."

"It had better be the best soup ever made," he muttered.

Ellie smoothed down the fabric of her gown and walked gracefully to the table, allowing the blank-faced footman to pull the chair out for her. Which was good, because Struan needed those precious few seconds to adjust himself so he could walk at all.

It was perfectly fine soup. But not at all worth interrupting the previous course.

From where she sat, Elspeth looked at him, smiling over her uplifted spoon. "I wonder what the dessert will be," she said, her eyes sparkling.

Chapter 17

ELLIE ENJOYED DINNER IMMENSELY, AND not just because of the appetizer. She was anticipating dessert, but after excusing herself after the meal to attend to her bladder, she saw red in the bottom of the chamber pot, and groaned.

"Oh…bloody hell," she whispered. She wasn't comfortable with vulgar language, but this felt appropriate for the situation. She wanted so badly to know all the aspects of marriage, especially after that kiss in the dining room that had her pulse pounding and her body smoldering. She'd sensed that the kiss—and how intense it had grown—represented some kind of breakthrough. But now she was unfit for any intimate relations for at least the next five days, if the past was any guide. While Elspeth's courses had never been particularly punctual (unlike Mairi, who could set a clock by her cycle), when they did arrive, it was never for fewer than five days and sometimes up to a week.

Well, that explained her backache.

She returned to the dining room in a considerably less happy mood.

"What's wrong?" Struan asked, noticing immediately.

"Nothing."

"It must be something. Perhaps we could discuss it upstairs." His tone was so hopeful that she felt like she was about to crush something precious.

"Um, I would like that, but I can't."

He frowned. "Do you have another appointment?"

"No. It's actually that for the next several days, I will be…" She trailed off, because discussing something as intimate as her monthly courses arriving was not something she'd prepared for. "Indisposed," she finished awkwardly. Ugh. Her cheeks might as well be on fire "I'm sorry. The timing is…not good."

"I assume you don't have control over the timing," he said.

She shook her head. "Life would be much simpler for women if they did. But all the same, I'm sorry. I'm your wife, and I know what that means, and I don't want you to be disappointed."

"Of course not." He didn't sound disappointed, though Struan was sometimes impossible to read.

"I will inform you when…I'm…not indisposed again. Just the usual disposed." She sighed. "And I should warn you that I can be a bit cranky at these times."

"That I don't believe," he said. "You don't know how to be cranky."

"Oh, I do, when circumstances warrant. Are you angry at me?"

"Why would I be angry?"

"Because you wanted…and I can't…"

"Stop it," he said, his tone clipped. "We won't talk about this anymore. It doesn't matter."

"But will you spend the evening with me? In the parlor? I thought we might…just spend time together. We could talk. Or not talk! We could read."

He reached out to take her hand. "Yes."

"Yes?"

"Yes. We'll go to the parlor now. I've got some books

I've been meaning to get to."

"Oh. Good." Ellie bit her lip, but she couldn't stop smiling. "That's what I want. Well, the second most."

Ellie was annoyed at her body for thwarting her plan to actually get to spend a night with her own husband, but at least she could spend the evening with him. The new parlor proved to be a comfortable place, especially in the evenings after dinner. They'd found that they both liked to read books on the long couch which sat in front of the low fire.

Elspeth commandeered several mirrors from unused rooms in the house, and had them hung in the parlor, then had tables placed in front of the mirrors and stood either a lamp or a candelabrum on each surface. When each was lit, the mirrored surface reflected the light back, and doubled or tripled the intensity.

"See?" she said proudly on the first evening she demonstrated the effect to Struan. "Now you can get more light from each flame—which reduces the chance that any one candle could start an accident, and it's also frugal, as it means fewer candles and less lamp oil to replace. Plus I think it's pretty the way the glass sends the light back into the room. Don't you think?"

"Very pretty," he agreed, his attention on her.

Now they settled into the newly stuffed couch. Struan read a book while Ellie opened a letter from Mairi, delivered that afternoon.

Dearest Pest,

I never imagined how painful the loss of your company would be when you first left for your new home. I was prepared to endure my own melancholy, because I could always reflect upon your happiness, which I'm pleased to hear about from your letters.

Since your departure, life has been much the same. Father and our stepmother continue to entertain and make calls upon their circles and attend nearly every event to which they have been invited, even those I know no one looks forward to. Father continues to spend prolifically on his wardrobe and accoutrements, so that he may dazzle every eye that passes over him, in the continuing hope that he will cut an impressive enough figure to gain the esteem of those worthies in town. Ha! Susan and Averill follow his lead. It is all so much that I worry they will run afoul of the sumptuary laws set in place by our ancestors.

Averill, of course, continues to be a trial. She has, finally, set her sights on one particular gentleman, God help him...

"Once Averill is properly engaged, they won't strut about so much," she murmured to herself.

Struan looked up. "What's that you're reading?"

"A letter from Mairi."

"Isn't that good? She hinted that correspondence wasn't her strong suit."

"I'm delighted to hear from her, of course. But she has shared news that...well, never mind."

"Too personal to share?"

"You're my husband. You should know everything that touches my life. Mairi seems worried. She doesn't include details, but life with my father has grown more difficult for her."

"To think that life with Mairi would ever be turbulent."

She laughed once. "You only met her for a moment, but you know, don't you?" Then she held up the letter. "I just wish I knew what was going on! I realize now that my presence in the house probably...smoothed things over among the others."

"I expect it did." He hesitated, then said, "You could return there. Go for a visit."

Part of her wanted to do that, but she'd practically just

arrived! To leave when she hoped that her relationship with Struan was progressing? She couldn't.

"I won't rush to Edinburgh over a few complaints," Ellie said, putting a smile on her face. "The next letter from Mairi will be all about her latest effort toward allowing women to serve in Parliament, or something like that."

"Good luck to her."

"You sound like you mean it."

"Why not?" He shrugged. "Men have been in charge for a long time, and it's hardly a utopia, is it?"

"You're telling me you'd be happy if women suddenly had control of the whole country? How would you like me acting as administrator to the people of Scotland?"

"You do well with the house. Why not the country?"

She laughed. "You're just saying that because there's no chance it will happen."

"I'm saying it because I believe it, Ellie." He took her hand in his. "Why don't you?"

Ellie had no response. No one had ever asked her that before. To hear the question from this man who she was now bound to, but also was still getting to know, seemed incredible.

Struan hadn't released her hand. He ran his thumb over the tops of her fingers, back and forth. Awareness crackled in her body, and when she noticed him looking directly at her, she couldn't meet his gaze.

He actually laughed a little, a low rumbling sound that she found wildly exciting. She liked to make him happy, even if she didn't understand how she did it.

"When you look at me like that…"

"Like how?" he asked.

"Like you're thinking of…I don't know…eating me up."

"Maybe I am." Another low rumble of laughter, his lip curling into a half smile.

He raised her hand to his lips, and kissed her fingers. Ellie suppressed a little gasp, and then wondered why she was suppressing it, and let it out. When he heard it, his grip tightened.

"Yes?" he asked, and she knew he was asking if she liked it.

"Yes," she breathed.

His lips grazed her skin again, and she let her eyes close, concentrating on the new feeling surging through her. How could such a limited touch—his lips on her fingers—spark little fires all over her body?

She held his hand, thinking that she'd like to get to know how he felt under her lips. All the lines and ridges and scars that made his hand his. "I could kiss you back."

But he winced slightly, and pulled his hand away. It was done gently, but it still felt like a rebuke.

"Another time," he said.

"Why not this time?"

"If we start something, I'd like to finish it. But you're indisposed, remember?"

How annoying that he was correct.

Dealing with cramps was bad enough, doing so without a book was far worse. So she grumpily stood up.

"I need a book," she announced.

"There are a few to choose from," he said, gesturing to the walls.

She looked at all the books, delighted by the sheer volume, even though she knew many of them were ledgers and account books or law books that were profoundly boring.

After surveying several shelves, she saw a guidebook for London, and pulled it out on a whim. The title was *Walton's New Traveller's Guide to London and Environs.*

She opened a page and began to read. *No visit to London is complete without an evening in Covent Garden. This re-*

markable space is truly magical at night, when the glow from the lanterns among the trees is nothing less than otherworldly.

She laughed. She'd heard Averill say exactly that when recounting her many visits to Covent Garden. Perhaps this author had been there the same night.

She flipped to another page. *The exquisite shops of Bond Street, lined up like so many cakes, contain delectable wares. These shops are of high quality, and ladies will find everything they could dream of and more behind the doors of these respectable and august establishments. Several have been known to provide goods to the royal household, and it is not uncommon to spy a foreign dignitary or European princess on a shopping excursion.*

Now Ellie frowned. Hadn't Averill also talked about that? She'd mentioned seeing some princess in a shop, that was certain.

"What have you found?" Struan asked.

"A guidebook to London. Walton's."

"Are you planning on visiting?"

"Based on this? Definitely not. It sounds like everyone has the same experience."

"Come back and sit by me, then," he invited.

Deciding that was an excellent idea, she did so.

Chapter 18

A FEW NIGHTS LATER, THEY were both seated on the couch again, facing toward the fire. Struan was reading something that looked rather heavy, while Elspeth had a novel that she had brought from Edinburgh but then immediately forgotten that she owned, since it had been put away in a drawer by accident.

Though fond of reading, that night she couldn't keep her eyes open. She sighed as one passage in particular eluded her.

She scooted over to him and pointed to the line on the page. "This here. There's a passage in French, and my French isn't good. What does this mean?"

He squinted at it, then said, "All hail our queen the marmalade cat."

"Struan!" She laughed even as she swatted his arm (an ineffectual move if ever there was one. Twelve Elspeths could not hurt someone of Struan's size). "Tell me what it really says."

"Oh, fine. It says guard well your…um, body. It is for me alone and I will…mmm how to say…slay both the beholder and the beheld." Struan paused, parsing it. "I guess he's vowing to kill her if another man looks at her."

"That's ridiculous! How can she control whether someone else *looks* at her? Does it really say that?"

"I'm sorry, but yes." He pointed. "That word there means *execute* or *murder*."

"What a stupid man."

"Is he the hero?"

"No, he's the villain who's kidnapped her and taken her to the castle on the cliffs."

"If he's the villain, he's supposed to be cruel."

"But he's not just cruel, he's irrational."

"Doubly villainous, then," Struan said. "I hope your heroine escapes."

"She may die tragically. I'll read on and see."

"Do report back," he said, giving her one of his sideways smiles, gone in an instant. But always enough to warm her heart and quicken her breath.

She stayed next to him as she resumed her book. Or tried to. "You speak French well," she noted.

"I learned enough to get by while I was on the Continent. My friend Brodie Ross spoke it much better. And Spanish. And German. He was gifted."

"Was?"

"He died in the war."

"Oh, I'm so sorry. Was it…was it at the same time you were injured?"

"No, it happened afterward. I wasn't actually there then. I was recuperating in London."

"So you're still mourning him."

"Yes," he said simply. "When I'm not mourning myself."

"But you're still alive."

He shrugged. "For a long time, I didn't believe that."

She thought about that. Maybe that was part of the reason he avoided intimacy with her—he was coming out of such a dark and death-filled place that the mere thought of living was too much.

She leaned closer to him. "You know you can talk to me."

"I'm aware of that, yes."

"I mean, I want you to know that I'll listen."

"Always a nice benefit."

"Struan. You know what I mean. I want to be someone you can talk to, should you ever need to talk."

He gave her a look that was half alarmed, half pleased, then said, "Read your book."

She tried. She really did. But reading when one was already sleepy was difficult, and especially so when one could think only of the man next to her on the couch. The novel dropped to her lap, unheeded.

"Ellie?" he said quietly. He nudged her. "Ellie? You're asleep."

"No," she protested…sleepily, it must be admitted.

"You ought to be in bed."

"I like this. Being with you. Don't send me away." She cuddled into him, hiding her face.

He moved his arm to better hold her, and she reveled in how warm he was, how solid and yet comfortable.

But after a few blissful minutes, he touched her cheek. "Ellie. Come, you can't stay here if you're falling asleep. Get up."

"Don't want to. Bring a blanket, I'll sleep here."

"You will not." He leaned over and slid his arms under her shoulders and knees.

A moment later, he was carrying her out of the parlor, not seeming in the slightest bit inconvenienced.

Upstairs, her bedroom was empty—Agnes would be downstairs, listening for the bell. But Struan didn't go for the bell. He yanked the top cover away and laid her on the bed.

Then he began to unbutton, unlace, and unwrap everything he needed to in order to slide her gown off, lifting her where her body pinned it down.

"Are you going to take everything off?" she wondered.

"No." The word was muttered quickly, and she hoped with regret.

And indeed, while he removed her stays, he didn't touch her chemise. He did move down to her feet, still clad in stockings…which went up to over her knees, held in place by ribbon through the top hem.

He slid his hands over her right calf. There was nothing precisely sexual in the move, but his touch lingered, testing the curve of her calf and stopping only when the fabric of her stocking did. He found the tied ribbon and worked it loose, his fingers grazing bare skin once or twice, creating a flash of heat that made her wish she was wearing more articles that could be untied.

He leaned over her. "Ellie? Are you comfortable?"

As she turned her head to answer, her lips met his. And that was all she needed to be comfortable. There was something so lovely and solid about Struan. She craved his closeness, like she could build a wall between her and the whole world. And his kisses were just intense enough to make her lose her breath, and then he pulled away.

"You're kissing me," she whispered when he paused.

"I'm sorry."

"I like it. You could do it more. I'm…almost disposed again."

"I can't anyway. The things I want to do can't be done to a sleeping woman."

"But I'm not asleep. I'm talking to you."

"You're also not awake," he told her.

She frowned. "Am I dreaming?"

"You can think that if you want to."

"I want you to kiss me."

He kissed her once more, a kiss that was meant to be soft and quick but somehow failed to end, both of them too entranced by the slide of slick lips and hot breath to break it off. Elspeth dreamily thought that sometimes having was far better than wanting.

Struan went still, and she realized she'd spoken out loud…or whispered anyway. She said, "Stay with me. For a little while, until I'm really asleep. The rules allow it."

"I know the rules," he muttered. But he shifted lightly, so his weight was on the bed next to her, and he laid a kiss on her forehead. "All right, I'll stay till you sleep."

"Mmmm, good." She smiled, thinking how nice it was to have his comfortable warmth next to her, and his mouth occasionally grazing her skin in a way that sent a glow throughout her veins. "I'm going to stay awake."

"You will not," he returned. "But I'll stay with you till you drift off."

"I love you," she murmured. "I'm so lucky you chose me."

He didn't respond, but she felt his hand close over hers.

* * * *

The idea of leaving Ellie, barely dressed and drowsily seductive, was an exercise in pain. The only reason he would do it was the knowledge that if he fell asleep there, it was likely he'd be there when daylight returned, and he couldn't stop Elspeth from seeing what he looked like in full light.

But those few minutes—all right, the better part of an hour—he absolutely feasted on how good it felt to be so close to her, to see the beauty of her figure, hidden only by a layer of thin cotton, but the curves temptingly prominent under the drape of the fabric. He couldn't stop himself from skimming one hand over her body, noting that her hip fit perfectly under his hand. He watched her breasts rise as she inhaled, wanting to feel that part of her under his palm too. But he resisted, because she wasn't able to tell him he could, and he didn't deserve to have something so beautiful in his hands anyway.

Yes, she'd asked him to stay, told him the rules allowed it, and they did. The rules allowed him almost anything he wanted from her. But he needed her to want it too.

And she was now fast asleep, her breathing even and slow, her lips just a little open, and her lashes occasionally twitching in the midst of some dream. He moved his hand to take hers, and died a little when even in sleep, she tightened her grip and gave a sigh.

Christ, he was in hell. A hell of his own making because not only had he lied to Elspeth, he lied over and over, letting her believe the story she'd half made up and he was so willing to push. He had to tell her the truth about how she'd been offered to him as a way to escape a debt, but every single day he didn't, it seemed like a more impossible task, with the stakes higher each time. Because if Elspeth learned the truth and then chose to hate him—an extremely rational choice on her part—he would not recover.

Everyone thought Struan was some unmovable rock, uncaring and unemotional. He'd thought that himself some of the time. It was how he got through his injuries and the general hell of the war. But Struan was a maelstrom of feelings; he just never let anyone see it.

And now the maelstrom was worse than ever, because Elspeth was fueling it with her onslaught of sincerity, which ripped him up inside because he wanted to return it. He really did. But he couldn't, because he was a lying bastard.

But he still wanted her. Painfully.

Not tonight.

He was so hard that he winced when he eased himself off the bed and walked to the connecting door to his own room, where it was, thankfully, completely dark (Struan having made his feelings about unattended flames known).

So he could wrestle his clothing off and then get his hand on his aching cock, working with an urgency that even his younger self would find embarrassing. Breathing hard, he cleaned up and staggered to his own bed, praying that he'd have no dreams. Not the usual nightmares of fire, but also not the tantalizing dreams of Elspeth that had recently invaded his brain. Both were torture, and he couldn't escape either.

* * * *

The next evening, they had dinner as usual, with Elspeth sitting at his right hand, temptingly close to him, wearing the amber necklace, her hair half-down again…and an absolute scandal of a gown. Struan had dismissed the servants the moment the soup course was served. Granted, he dismissed the servants promptly every evening, since Elspeth had instituted the practice of she and Struan serving themselves when not entertaining (so in reality, all the time). It was more intimate, certainly. The servants probably also appreciated that fewer of them had to be on call throughout the meal.

Tonight, however, he was just glad there was no one else to see Ellie.

"Do you like my outfit?" she asked, probably because he couldn't keep himself from looking at it.

"It's lovely." Which was true. What he couldn't say was that it made her look ravishing. Or ravishable. The way the gown's neckline dropped practically down to her chest, the laughably scanty sleeves that revealed her shoulders and her arms, the overall sheerness of the silk that clung to her figure…it all made him think of exactly one thing.

"The seamstress's note said that it was an evening gown designed to make an impression," Elspeth said.

"It does."

"What impression does it make on you?" she asked. There was a challenge in her tone, almost a demand.

He knew exactly what she was driving at, and he knew it was past time to get this…issue between them out in the open. So he said, without softening his reaction, "It makes me want to take it off."

"And will you?" Elspeth was clearly done being patient.

He wanted to. Christ, he wanted to. But there was the stubborn issue of him looking like walking death.

"I thought this whole marriage was about you getting an heir," Elspeth said more gently. "Don't you want that any-more?"

"Of course I do." He wanted children more than anything else in the world, other than perhaps wanting Elspeth.

She took a deep breath, steeling herself to say something. "Then why do you refuse to…to bed me? You've kissed me, and I think you enjoyed it."

"Yes." Hell, yes.

"But you won't do more than that. You're making it im-possible for me to do my duty as a wife, and when I can't fulfill my duty, I feel like a failure. Every night, like clock-work."

She might as well have punched him in the gut. Struan had thought a lot about bedding or not bedding Ellie, but he'd never even considered that aspect of the issue. "You could never ever be a failure. Christ, you've taken the thank-less role of my wife and turned it into a triumph. Look at this house! The grounds. You've done all of that."

She set her jaw. "And yet you continue to ignore me."

"I'm not ignoring you. I've *tried* to ignore you, and if you want to talk about a failure, that's one for the books. You've never needed a gown like that one to make an impression. No matter how much I've tried to avoid wanting you, it's all

I can think about."

"Truly?"

"God, yes."

"But must I beg you to do more than think about it?"

The image of her *begging* caused an instantaneous stiffening of his cock. But then he remembered his appearance. "I appreciate your…willingness, but you don't know what you're asking. I'm not…you would not like the sight of me."

"You'd prefer me not to look?" she asked, puzzled. "If that's all, then I can keep my eyes closed. Or you could blindfold me."

Oh, *Christ.* A blindfolded Elspeth, naked beneath him on the bed…. He silenced the groan of anticipation rising up within him.

Wait. Had she just offered him a solution? A simple, obvious solution that he'd been too stubborn and stupid to think of?

"Would you do that?" he asked her.

"Do what? Keep my eyes closed? Make the room dark? Wear a blindfold? I'll do all of those. Whatever it takes to please you."

If she kept talking, he was going to need a cold bath. Or to jump into the sea.

"Struan?"

He inhaled. He could do this. "May I come to your room tonight?" Formal language for this formal arrangement— finally making Elspeth the wife everyone assumed she already was.

Maybe she hadn't believed that he'd actually get on with it. But then she nodded, apparently resolved. "You may. I will be expecting you."

Chapter 19

ELSPETH PACED THE ROOM. DESPITE her best efforts, her nerves were wound so tight she thought she might fly straight out the window if she got startled now.

She'd brushed and arranged her hair loosely down her back, and she wore the same flimsy fantasy that she'd worn on her first night at Linneliath. Perhaps this time her husband would actually see it. As they came up from supper, Struan had said he'd give her a half an hour to prepare for bed, and then he'd knock on the connecting door.

But her preparations took far less time than that, which left Elspeth pacing and fretting. What if he changed his mind? What if he did come in and *then* changed his mind? What if he didn't change his mind, but she did? What if she was a horrible disappointment to him and he decided to never come to her again?

Ellie twisted her hands together, mostly to avoid fidgeting with the silk and wrinkling it beyond repair. She looked around the room. In deference to Struan's wishes, she had doused every single candle, and the fire grate held only the half-consumed remains of a single log, which occasionally spat forth a yellow flame for half a second before subsiding back into colorless, smoldering heat.

When would he knock?

She got up and walked to the connecting door, as if that

would speed his arrival. Then she wheeled around and paced to the far corner, afraid of seeming overeager, a shameless woman desperate for a carnal act that she'd never actually experienced.

Two short, soft raps against the oak door made her start.

"Come in," she gasped.

Struan opened the door but didn't step in. His own room was dark as well, so she couldn't see much of him, other than to notice that he wore a banyan-style robe, belted at the waist.

"Please come in," she said again, trying for a more welcoming—and less terrified—tone.

He closed the door softly behind him. "You made the room dark."

"I thought you would prefer that." She moved toward him, half afraid he'd turn and leave. When she put one hand on his arm, he went still. "Thank you for…listening to me."

He sighed. "It was a mistake for me to wait this long. I never meant to hurt you by staying away. It's just that we didn't know each other at first, and then I wasn't sure how to proceed."

Ellie smiled, though he couldn't see her expression. "What's done is done. Shall we just pretend that tonight is our wedding night?"

"Aye," he agreed, his voice warming. "And speaking of that, I've brought a gift."

"You have?"

He pulled something out of his pocket and handed it to her. Ellie touched a roll of buttery smooth satin, and soon unwound the coil to discover a long sash of black.

"I've never received a blindfold before," she joked, despite the shivers rolling up her body.

"I've never given one." Struan took it back and stepped around behind her. He tied it around her head. "I didn't catch any hair in the knot, did I?"

She shook her head, and suddenly found herself pulled against his chest as he put his arms around her, his own big limbs covering her shoulders and practically her whole upper torso.

He said, "Ellie, this is daft."

"Nonsense. I don't mind."

"You're far too trusting." His tone was filled with amazement more than warning.

She relaxed against him, realizing that all her nervousness had fled. "I think you trustworthy," she murmured. "Now, tell me what I should do."

"Nothing," he said as he shifted to scoop her up in his arms. "You've done enough."

He walked her to the bed and laid her down on it. Thanks to the blindfold, Ellie's other senses were heightened. She felt the softness of the linen sheets and smelled the smoke of the dying fire, then heard Struan's breath quickening.

"You're beautiful, Ellie," he said. "It's not right that you're so beautiful when I'm…"

"Stop that," she ordered, her lack of sight somehow giving her more latitude to speak her mind. It was easier when she couldn't see Struan's often forbidding expression. "I'm glad you think me pretty, because I want to please you. So you don't find this task difficult."

That earned her a low laugh, and heat spread though her belly at the sound. "Ellie, the only difficulty I'll have is delaying the inevitable. Just thinking about you makes me hard. Now, seeing you…"

There was shift in the mattress as he climbed onto the bed, kneeling next to her. The sensation of his bare leg sliding against hers sent shivers up her body. He'd disrobed while they'd been talking.

"I'm going to touch you now," he said. "If you don't like

anything I do, you have to say so. Yes?"

"Yes," she agreed instantly.

"I mean it, Ellie. I don't know you well enough to guess, and I don't want you to dislike any part of this. So you'll speak up?"

"Aye. Yes, Struan. Please go on." She hadn't fully accepted how much she'd been aching for this. She was wildly curious about this mysterious act that was so important and yet so secret.

His hands were gentle, moving over her so lightly, as if checking that she was all there, and not a mirage. His fingertips grazed her flushed skin, and she raised her own hands, only to have him capture her wrists and lift her arms up to the pillow.

"Don't touch me back," he cautioned, his tone low. "I can't let you do that. Not yet."

"When?" she asked, unconsciously straining against him. There was something surprisingly arousing about being held like this.

"When I tell you that you can. Can I trust you to obey me on that, Ellie?"

"Yes," she said, meaning it. She'd agree to nearly anything when he asked it in that voice.

He slowly released her wrists. "But keep your arms up like that," he said. "It's a pretty picture."

"Is it?"

"Aye. Bare arms against your hair. The blindfold against your face…and what you're wearing…Christ. What the hell is this?"

"Do you like it?" she asked nervously. "I wore it on our wedding night, but you never got the chance to see it."

"That was my mistake," he muttered. He skimmed his hands over her breasts at the same moment, and her nipples hardened instantly at the heat through the silk. She gasped, and he groaned.

Then she gasped again, because his mouth was where his right hand had been, sucking her breast through the silk. Ellie twisted beneath him, heat spreading through her.

"Struan!" she whispered.

"Do you not like it?" he asked, stopping immediately.

"No! I mean I did like it. Keep doing it?"

"I'm going to pleasure you, Ellie," he said. God, she loved his voice. "It took me far too long to be here, but now that I am, I intend to make it count."

He'd resumed his suckling and she lost the ability to explain her thoughts, or even have thoughts. Struan's lips roamed her breasts, creating havoc wherever he went. Ellie arched her back in an attempt to give him more of herself, to bring their bodies closer.

Only when she was whimpering with need and the silk negligee was soaked with moisture did he sit up.

"How does this damnable thing come off?" he asked gruffly.

"There are ties at the back."

"Turn over," he ordered.

She flipped onto her belly. He pulled up the fabric around her legs and hooked his thumbs into the ribbons at the shoulders, tugging until the fabric untied. He lifted her enough to slide the negligee over her head, but then kept her in that position, her back pressed to his chest.

"Get your knees under you," he urged. "Christ, I like you like this."

In this position, she couldn't see him even if she weren't blindfolded. He must feel better that way. She'd have to remember that.

"Keep me like this, then," she gasped out. "Please, Struan. If you like me like this, I do too."

"Oh, Ellie." He held her against him with a strong left

arm, while his right moved freely over her breasts, fondling and petting until she didn't know how to breathe. Then his hand moved down to her stomach, long smooth strokes that took pleasure in the softness of her bare skin. She inhaled, smelling salt and sweat and the smoky air, and whatever that smell was that was uniquely Struan. A male scent that she was fast learning to love.

His hand continued exploring, pausing at the curls between her legs.

"Spread your knees a little more," he told her, his voice low, commanding.

She did, and then his fingers were there, slipping into the folds of her sex, teasing her with light caresses. He paid special attention to the hardened nub at her center, drawing the moisture from her body to glide his fingertip over it with maddening slowness.

"Struan," she moaned.

"You like that?"

"Yes, and you must know it, beast, or why do you linger so?"

His chuckle reverberated in his chest and seeped into her own. "Would you have me finish you so soon?"

"Is it soon?" she gasped.

"Too soon, but I'll do it if you say so."

"What is…finishing?" she whispered, wishing she could see the man who was doing such wonderful things to her.

"Bringing you to your peak. Or have you never touched yourself like this?"

She shook her head. "Not like this."

He stilled for a moment. "You've not felt an orgasm before?"

"I don't think so?"

"Christ, what are they teaching women these days? Ellie, you'll have to trust me."

He renewed his attentions, slowly at first, and then speeding up to keep pace with her gasps. Ellie sensed that she was nearing some border, and that crossing it would bring her to a new place. Struan murmured encouragement, his mouth by her ear, his body searing hot against hers, his arousal hard and insistent, pressing into her bottom in a way that only heightened her desire.

She rocked her hips against his as she chased the finish he hinted at. Lord, his touch was magical, stirring up so much want in her that Ellie had no words for it.

She realized she was gasping out his name with every exhale, and that her voice was so urgent it sounded panicked. "Struan, Struan, please, oh, please, oh, please, oh—"

And then she broke off, sailing into new waters, where the panic passed into peace. Her body climaxed and then went limp as her muscles all decided to quit on her, pleasure melting her into some newer, softer form.

Struan held her against him, his hand stopping, though he kept it where it was, cupping her gently.

"Ellie?" he asked after a moment. "How do you feel?"

She smiled into the darkness. "Like you meant me to feel. Wonderful."

"Lie back," he said, turning her around so her back settled against the mattress. "Christ, you're the most beautiful thing I've ever seen."

She warmed at his words, at the raw honesty in them. "Do you like looking at me?"

In answer, he moved enough so she could feel his erection against her thigh. "What do you think?"

Then before she could ask what was next, he nudged her legs apart with his knee, and his right hand returned to her sex. But this time he slid a long finger all the way inside her, and she learned that she barely understood her own body. But he did.

Ellie cried out and arched her back as another intense wave of pleasure hit her. He laughed softly and proceeded to tease her until a second orgasm took her and her limbs had turned watery.

Unconsciously, she reached for him.

"No," he told her sharply.

"But I need to hold something after what you did to me. Twice."

"Hold the bedposts," he ordered. "And hold tight, because I aim to do it again."

"Do you?"

He moved to place himself above her, his erection pushing against the damp folds of her body, eager to enter her. "Ellie, it's time. If you'll let me."

There was a warning in his voice, but she just nodded. This was what she asked for. Begged for.

"I'm yours," she told him.

She waited for the intrusion, but instead she felt his lips on her own, a kiss that tangled need and gentleness until she was dizzy.

"Struan," she whispered when she took a ragged breath. "*Please* don't wait any longer."

"I don't think I could," he admitted wryly. Then he added, "It may hurt. That's not my intent."

"I know." Lord, how could he think that she was worried about that, after the way he'd pleasured her?

He once again settled between her legs, which she spread as far as she was able to accommodate his huge frame. He pushed into her, the slickness from her previous orgasms making his entry smooth.

She moaned at the sensation of being filled like this, of taking this man into her body, an intimacy that all her imaginings could not prepare her for. He was hot and hard and huge—was this the real reason he'd kept her sightless, to not scare her with his size?

Still he pushed, and pushed. She wriggled, tilting her hips, trying to hold him but also flying apart with every minute shift of him inside.

"Struan?" she asked, not even sure what she was asking.

"You're doing well, darling," he told her, his own voice tight with effort. "You feel so goddamned good...."

And then he stopped, his body joined to hers. She inhaled once, twice.

"That's it. Relax. Do you hurt?"

"I don't think so," she breathed out. "Is this it? Is this what you wanted?"

"Not remotely." She heard the smile in his tone—dear God, the joy of hearing him sound happy!—and then he began to move.

His thrusts were slow, an in-and-out that was a gentle rocking more than anything else. Pleasure exploded in her, as parts of her body never before touched in such a way were caressed, teased, explored. She wanted nothing more than to have this last forever, and she ached to grab him by the shoulders and hold him tight to her.

"Struan, I'm not touching you," she moaned, turning her head to the side in her distress. "But I want to. I want to hold you so close."

"You're a marvel," he told her, his breath hot and desperate. "I'll hold you, darling."

And his hands came to her hips, guiding her movements as he timed his thrusts to bring her to another peak. She cried out his name, and he went stiff.

She felt the moment he finished inside her, a pulse of heat and the sense that things would never be the same for her, and she gripped the bedpost so hard she could feel the wood grain marking her palms.

Struan withdrew, and fell onto his back beside her, his

breath still rapid. His hand covered her own, prying her from the post. Then they lay side by side, their hands clasped in the space between. Belatedly, she let her free hand settle on her belly.

Elspeth waited until her heartbeat slowed. Struan didn't seem to want to speak, so she'd have to. "I wouldn't mind doing this again."

Struan exhaled next to her. "I'm glad to hear it. A woman may not conceive after just once. Usually not."

"But I could be with child after tonight?"

"It's possible," he said.

"I hope so."

"I thought you were open to the idea of repeating the act?" Now he sounded a little disappointed.

She laughed. "It's not that. I meant that if I carry a child, then you'll be happy with me."

"Elspeth, I'm already happy with you. You're better than I deserve."

"I wish I could see you," she said.

"Christ. I forgot about that." He sat up, and pulled the sheet around them both. He leaned over and slipped the blindfold off, the silk moving over her soft curls with no resistance. The room was even darker than before, the fire having subsided to almost nothing.

Ellie looked him full in the face and smiled. "Perhaps one night I'll able to use my eyes...or my hands," she suggested.

"Perhaps," he said, not committing to anything. "But for now, you relax and then sleep."

* * * *

Ellie woke up with a sigh of happiness. She'd done it. She was properly a wife now, and it seemed that Struan's façade was beginning to crack. And really, it all had to be a façade. He treated her so tenderly last night, proving that his essential nature had to be much more gentle than what everyone assumed. Certainly than what she had assumed. He'd cleaned her body with a cloth and warm water. He'd tucked the blanket over her, he kissed her before telling her good night and leaving for his own room. She wanted him to stay longer, but she also realized that pushing for too much too fast might spook him.

To think that she missed out on weeks of that particular pleasure, simply because she hadn't been bold enough to ask and he'd been overly careful of her feelings to press the matter. But now…she bit her lip as she recalled the absolute bliss she'd experienced the night before. Struan's hands on her skin, his mouth on her body, and the unique joy of having him inside her… The only thing missing was a visual memory, denied by the blindfold.

Well, that wouldn't last forever. And then she'd not just feel and hear and smell her husband, she'd see him too.

Chapter 20

ELLIE DIDN'T KNOW WHAT SHE was doing wrong. It had been a week since that fateful evening. Yes, Struan now came to her room every night. And yes, he did things to her that she didn't even know could be done, and every time he asked if she liked it, she said yes, yes she did. He seemed to know exactly how to touch her.

But the room was always pitch black and she always had to cover her eyes with that satin strip, and she was never allowed to see him or touch him. There was nothing more frustrating than being so close to her husband and yet being prevented from truly knowing him.

And yet how could she complain of ill treatment? Especially when he treated her so very well, and incited reactions that left her damp with perspiration, limp, and practically breathless after experiencing the most exquisite pleasure at his hands and his mouth and his…

Elspeth assumed it was wrong for her to say cock, but after all, that's what he called it when he wanted to know if it was time. *Are you ready for my cock?* he'd ask—or demand—depending on how intense the lovemaking had gotten so far.

And she'd always respond, yes, yes, she was ready, don't make her wait any longer. But more than feeling him, she wanted to see him. She wanted to touch him back, and explore him and make him feel the way he made her feel.

But she had no idea how to do that.

Otherwise, life at Linneliath had begun to take on a familiar shape and pattern. Ellie spent her days either at the house, working on the older, more run-down spaces, or trying to improve the efficiency of the day-to-day tasks. But she also went to the far school multiple times each week, getting to know the teachers and the children, and thinking that someday it would be lovely to introduce some of these students to her own children…if she were so lucky.

And then in the evenings, she'd meet Struan for dinner, and they'd eat, and talk a bit about the land and the tenants and the mines. They'd sometimes read for a few hours. But most often, they seemed to find some reason to retire. Ellie craved their nights, even as the prohibition against touching him or even seeing him chafed at her soul. Psyche herself couldn't have been more frustrated at the rules, even though Ellie could sense how much Struan needed that prohibition. But she didn't know how to break past that barrier, and her natural desire for harmony made her keep quiet.

One afternoon, Ellie had an errand in the village; she rode in the carriage, accompanied by Agnes (she was getting lessons in riding, but she wasn't very confident yet). From the window, she saw another carriage waiting in front of the dry goods shop. It was well appointed and two matched horses stood at the ready, so Ellie deduced that someone of the local gentry had arrived. Delighted at the opportunity to meet a new person, she got out and proceeded directly to the shop.

Ellie slowed when she saw an elegant woman step out of the doorway. From the black boots to the heavy wool tartan skirts visible beneath a dark blue pelisse, everything about the lady suggested quality. She was taller than Ellie, with a narrow build and face, but a wealth of silver hair that gleamed under her flat straw topper, which sported a tartan ribbon that matched her skirts.

"Hello!" Ellie said before she lost her nerve. "I do wish we had someone to introduce us, but I couldn't bear to pass the moment by. I am—"

"You're MacInnes's wife!" The lady smiled at her. "I am Margaret Kerr. My husband serves as MacInnes's man of business. I'm so glad to meet you, and I hope that you'll accept an invitation to dine with us soon."

Ellie beamed at the kind words. "I...we...should be happy to. I have yet to host anything at Linneliath, but when I do, I will certainly ask you and Mr Kerr to join us."

"No hurry, dear," Mrs Kerr said with a gentle laugh. "Fixing up that old pile is the job of a lifetime."

"Oh, it's coming along. Everyone is pitching in."

"Including yourself, I hear."

"You do?" Ellie asked, surprised.

"Gossip is meat and bread around here. I've heard about your efforts to make Linneliath shine again. Though it hasn't been long that the big house has been without a family, we're all relieved that a MacInnes is back in residence. Houses like that should be full of life."

"Yes!" Ellie proclaimed. Here was someone who understood. "I hope that someday that will be true again."

Mrs Kerr gave her a knowing look. "Soon, I imagine. I've also heard your courtship was terribly romantic. Too often, women marry for the wrong reasons. It's always nice to know when a marriage is a love match."

Afterward, Ellie was driven back from the village in the carriage, of course, but she felt as if she floated home on a cloud. When she saw Struan back at the house, she excitedly shared her encounter with Mrs Kerr. "She said people are gossiping that we're a love match!" she concluded.

"Well, I'd prefer not to be mentioned in any gossip, but that sounds like the best outcome if people must talk," he said after a moment. "At least they're not saying you married me for my money."

"Oh, no! But what if some others do think that?"

He backtracked immediately. "Ellie, no. Forget I said that. Anyway, it doesn't matter what others think. I know you didn't."

"But the truth is important. I wish everyone could just know the truth about *every*thing."

Struan pulled away. "That's a dangerous wish. That's what Brodie used to say."

"Brodie Ross. The one who died."

"Yes. His death was…unexpected. Which is a stupid thing to say about a soldier dying during a war, but he shouldn't have died when he did. And we're all still angry about it."

"I can't imagine how it feels."

As Elspeth spoke, she reached out and slipped her arms around his shoulders, giving him a tentative hug.

He hunched over for a moment, then relaxed. She felt the rise and fall of his breath, slowing slightly as he accepted her embrace.

"I don't mean to depress you with war stories," he said finally, his voice gruff. "It seems they're all I have."

"If they're part of your life, I want to know everything. Everything you wish to tell me, that is. I am yours completely, and you must never feel that there's any part of yourself I don't wish to be part of."

Struan's hand tightened over hers. "You're too open-hearted, Elspeth."

"Only with you," she said, kissing his cheek on the scarred side.

He gripped her hand even tighter and seemed about to say

something. Then he let go. Aware that he was getting uncomfortable, she unclasped her arms and stood back. Struan was like a dog or horse sometimes—a moment of affection was welcome, but too long and he began to act confused as to what to do next.

Elspeth smiled. Day by day, he was thawing. She'd be patient. He'd been alone too long and suffered too greatly to simply behave as though nothing had happened to him. It was just a matter of gentle, persistent encouragement. Eventually, Struan would be able to say the words she hoped he already felt. Words like *I love you.*

It was just that he wasn't comfortable yet. And Elspeth didn't know the full facts about his life. Like the previous fiancée. Like the extent of his wounds. What other secrets might he be keeping from her out of some misguided belief that it was for her safety?

Her household tasks as the mistress of Linneliath occupied her hands, but not nearly enough of her mind. It was one thing to sew for an hour every day, or take an hour or two learn to ride a horse from the patient servants who worked in the stables. Those activities were too simple to occupy all of her brain. She couldn't stop thinking about how Struan was keeping her at arm's length…or at least keeping her from using her arms to touch him. It had gone beyond frustration directly to maddening.

One afternoon she was getting rather lost in the depths of contemplating the inequality of their nightly exchanges—it wasn't fair at all that he was doing more than she was—even though he assured her that she was perfect.

She decided it was high time to confront him about the matter, and not wait till nighttime, when she would be naked, sightless, and thoroughly distracted.

But finding Struan proved to be a less than simple task. She inquired with all the usual people, and while no one had seen him lately, everyone was certain he was still within the house.

At last she entered a room she had never been in before. She stopped short, seeing a massive bath in the center of the space.

The bath was not empty. It held Struan.

* * * *

Struan liked a hot bath. It was a little odd, considering that he hated fire. But the bath was water…obviously…and the heat and steam helped soothe his physical discomfort. So he made a practice of lying in a hot bath much more frequently than the average man. This bath was especially nice, since it was gigantic, and held much more water than the average tin bathtub. Struan remembered his parents explaining that one of his great-great—great?—grandparents had commissioned it to show off the production of the family's tin mines.

Thanks to its volume, the bath stayed warm for a long time. He liked to sink into the water and pretend that the rest of the world didn't exist for an hour, and all the things that happened to him during the war would magically wash off.

But today it was difficult to relax. His mind kept darting back to Elspeth. He lived for the nights when he could touch Ellie and explore her and act on the fantasies that had been eating him from the inside ever since he met her. He saw her face practically every time he closed his eyes. Which he tried to do again.

And then she burst through the door.

"What the *hell*?" he growled before he even registered who had entered his private sanctum.

"Oh! I didn't know you were—" Elspeth broke off. "Oh," she repeated more faintly, her eyes locked on his chest and torso, then to his right side where the scarring was thickest and had warped his shape most distinctly.

"Enjoying the view?" he asked, not bothering to hide the tension pulling his muscles taut. He knew the strain came out as anger, but he didn't make a move to hide himself. She'd sought him out; she couldn't leave well enough alone. Now she'd learn what she'd married.

"No. I mean…"

"You should leave."

"But I've spent the last hour looking for you." Then she started walking toward him.

He edged back against the wall of the tub. "Don't."

"Don't what?"

"Get close to me."

"Yes, that's been your plan since you chose me." When she reached the edge of the tub, Elspeth's gaze flicked up to his face, and now there was a challenge there. "Acquire a suitable wife to fulfill your own duty to get an heir. No thought beyond that, though, was there? God forbid I might actually get to know you."

Struan was not prepared for that line of attack. "I meant you should stop moving toward me. Physically."

"I know what you meant." Her voice sharpened. "I'm not an idiot."

"I never thought you were."

"You certainly hoped that I'd be malleable, though. A simple girl you could put on a shelf once I'd done my own duty and got you a son."

"What? Ellie, no." Though in fact that had been the original plan, the safe plan, the *before-Ellie-smiled-at-him* plan.

"Were you going to keep me here at Linneliath after you'd finished with me? Maybe in a nice suite of rooms in the east wing, so you can keep living your own life in the west wing? Would that be more convenient?"

"I wasn't thinking about convenience."

"Were you thinking about anything?" she asked, leaning over the tub edge, her hands braced on the rim.

Struan inhaled, wondering if he'd look like a coward if he jumped out of the tub and ran away.

Yes. That's the definition of coward.

She smelled good, like springtime. God, he was sitting here naked, all his scars and injuries on display, having a fight with his wife, and all he could think was that she smelled good? "Ellie, what do you want?"

"What do *you* want is the better question! Tell me plainly what you expect, and no more games. You buy me gowns that no one sees me wear. You nearly kill a man for flirting with me, but you don't touch me for weeks afterward. And then you finally consummate the marriage, but you don't—" She broke off, and he realized with a jolt that she was near tears. Oh, hell.

"Don't what?" he demanded.

"It doesn't matter." She looked down again. "You were right before. I've intruded and made you reveal what you never intended me to see."

Himself.

Ellie turned away, but before she could take a step, he leaned forward and seized her hand. "Stay," he said, not knowing that's what he'd say until it came out.

Over her shoulder, she cast him a glance filled with doubt.

"Stay," he said again.

Her body was almost as tense as his, he could tell.

"You can look," he said. After all, she already had. What was the point of hiding anymore?

She was already looking again, surveying him with an expression he couldn't read. He was looking for pity, but he couldn't find that. He found concern, yes, but nothing of the condescending *oh-how-tragic-for-you* that he remembered from the days and weeks following his injuries.

He searched for the slightest sign of disgust, but was surprised at just how calm she was. Well, why not? She was calm at the wedding, when any normal woman would have fled.

"You're taking your time," he said, mostly because Ellie's silence was becoming uncomfortable for him.

"If you'd let me look before, I wouldn't have to catch up now. And there's a lot of you to look at," she added with the tiniest smile.

Something in her voice hooked into him and tugged, and yes, he was getting hard. How? This should be humiliating. The opposite of erotic.

And yet. Her tongue darted out to moisten her lips, her gaze skimming up and down him, and he was stiff as a rod.

"I could join you," she offered, making it his choice.

But what other choice could he make? He said what he wanted to say. "Join me."

Elspeth stripped off her gown, letting it pool at her feet. She had a moment of difficulty with the stays, but then they too dropped to the floor, and she stood in just her chemise. She began to gather the fabric up, intending to remove it, but Struan said, "No, leave it on."

"Why?"

"Because I want to see what it looks like wet." And he wanted to take it off her with his own hands.

Elspeth stepped into the hot water. Cautious, careful. The chemise clung to her body as she moved over him, molding to hips and breast, highlighting her curves. She stood with one leg on each side of his hips, and he loved that view.

"This is an extravagant bath," she said, lowering herself so she sat across his lap.

"It's insane. Some ancestor's whim. The hot water helps

me relax." Not that he was relaxed now.

Ellie regarded him from this much closer angle, her eyes moving over the scarred and unbroken skin alike.

"I wanted to spare you the sight," he said.

"The sight doesn't trouble me. You look like you, and I want to know everything about you. So of course I must see your whole body. You've seen *my* whole body."

"But you're beautiful," he said. "Everything about you is beautiful. I can't believe I get to touch you."

"I love it when you touch me," she said, taking his hands and raising them to her breasts. He rubbed his thumbs across them, feeling the slip of wet fabric over her skin. She gave a little gasp, her mouth opening into an O that sparked dirty ideas in his mind. She said, "In bed you never let me touch you back. It's cruel of you."

"I didn't mean it to be."

"Can I touch you here? In the bath?"

"Yes," he breathed. "But you must stop if I tell you. That's a rule."

"I'm good at following rules," she said, which was a sentence he longed to test in all sorts of ways.

But then she was touching him, carefully and gently. "Would you tell me to stop because I might hurt you? I always worry that you're in pain," she said softly, splaying her hand over the largest area of scarring.

"I'm not in much pain, mostly. Unless you consider being aroused like this and not doing anything about it pain."

"Is it? Painful to…get stiff like you do?"

"Is it painful for you when you get warm and wet for me?"

"There's an ache," she told him. "And it aches until you make it end. And then it feels so good."

His breath caught as she leaned over him.

"I had wondered about this part of you," she confessed.

She slid one finger along his shaft, and just that touch made him want to grab her and spread those pretty legs and sink into her. He said, his voice taut, "What do you wonder?"

"Well, what it looks like, obviously." She was still running her finger up and down its length, until she traced the ridge along the underside and he groaned.

"Oh? You like that?" she asked, looking up at him with an expression that was part shy, part sly…a woman learning about a man after a lifetime of being forbidden from doing so.

"I'm very sensitive there."

"Hmmm." She wrapped her hand around him, and he closed his eyes as he felt her strokes, slow and maddening. He kept teasing her breasts, completely saturated from the fabric. He longed to peel off the sopping-wet chemise and lick off the water with his tongue.

When she reached his stones and started playing with them, he thought he might pass out from the sheer unexpected pleasure.

"We need to leave this tub," he got out between groans.

"Oh? Is the water getting cold?"

"No, but if we continue what we're doing, I'll never be able to take a simple bath again. I'll always be remembering the one time I took you in here."

She laughed a little, actually turning her head in a shy gesture. "Maybe someday. But for now, if you like, we can go to…your bed? It's closest."

It was about fifty feet closer than hers, but Struan didn't want to waste a moment, so he nodded.

Ellie released his cock, damn it, and put her hands on the rim of the tub to balance as she stood up and finally peeled off the soaking chemise.

"I wanted to do that for you," he said.

"Oh, sorry."

"I'll survive." Struan slid his hands along her legs until he reached the apex, and then slipped one thumb into the folds of her sex, just for a second. The sound she made would keep him up nights for a long time.

Somehow, they both got out of the bath.

There was only one towel, so he wrapped it around her, drying her off. Ellie responded by stepping next to him and running her hands over his still-damp flesh. He shivered, more from the sensation of her delicate touch than from cold. She took her time, keeping a leisurely pace as she inched downward, enjoying making him impatient. Then she stepped back to regard his cock again, arrowing out eagerly, tip already beading with moisture.

"Does it have a taste?" she asked. Before he could say anything, she knelt and licked the tip of his cock, her tongue curling to catch the bead of liquid.

He was going to die if she didn't do it again.

"Ellie." It was meant to be a warning, but it sounded like a plea.

"Salty," she said, looking delighted with herself for finding out. "A little salty."

"Bedroom," he ordered, his voice gone hoarse.

Ellie tossed him the towel and strolled away, casting a glance over her shoulder as she went. "Coming?" she asked.

Very soon.

Struan toweled himself off as he followed her, catching up just as she reached the bed, where she turned and put her hand on his chest, stopping him short.

She climbed onto the bed and then beckoned him to join her, which he'd do even if he were dead. But she held up a hand when he moved to lay her on her back.

"Can I lick you again?" she asked, hope in her eyes.

Yes.

"Lick, suck, kiss, bite. Whatever you want," he agreed. Then added, "But bite gently."

Ellie's laugh was soft and so erotic. "Very gently, I promise. Lay back."

He did, and then she put her mouth on him again, tasting and teasing at a languid pace. She really didn't know what to do, so she did a little of everything, and God he loved it so much. She kept asking if he liked this, or liked that, and laughed that maddening silken laugh when he admitted each time that *yes* he liked it.

"Are men just not particular?" she wondered at some point.

"Not very. Not always. I'm particularly obsessed with you, though, if it matters." It would be crude to tell her that seeing her gorgeously pink lips circling his cock would make him hard every time he remembered it, but it was the truth.

"I do like to make you feel good," she said softly. "Could I finish you with my mouth? Would you mind doing it that way? I'd like to try."

"Christ, you've got a way with words."

"Is that not a thing men want?"

"Oh, we want it." He hesitated. "It's usually something done by a woman who's being paid."

She looked even more intrigued. "Why is that?"

"Because ladies don't... Look, it's messy if you don't swallow, and expecting you to swallow is…"

"Treating me like a whore?" she asked with that bluntness that she sometimes displayed.

He winced. "Yes."

"Nonsense," she declared. "I want to please you. And if I can, why shouldn't I? It will save the cost of a whore anyway."

He nearly choked on a laugh. "Ellie!"

"What?" she asked. "I do pride myself on my frugality."

And then she proceeded to drive him to a point of desperate need, her tongue swirling over flesh so primed for her touch that he had to keep back a howl of pleasure.

He wanted to enjoy this feeling a little more, but within minutes, he was at the edge.

Struan gasped out her name, intending to warn her, but then he was over the edge, and his whole body convulsed as he came. Bliss followed, interrupted only by the aftershocks caused by his wife's wicked little tongue. Ellie continued to lick and suck, until he couldn't stand it anymore. "Enough," he moaned. "It's so good, but you're killing me."

She released him and moved upward so that she could lie beside him, putting her head on his chest. He reached his hand up to stroke her hair, loving the silkiness of the curls against his skin.

"Did I do it correctly?" she asked with a trace of nervousness.

"Perfectly. Beautifully."

"You'd let me do it again?"

"Any time, love." As if he'd ever say no to her.

"Good. I like it when you look like you're enjoying yourself."

That was one way to put it. "You know, I never dreamed *frugality* would be the last word I'd hear before coming," he said, laughter bubbling up in his chest. He couldn't remember the last time he felt so happy. And it wasn't what Ellie just did to him—well, that helped. It was what she was doing *now*, curling up against him in the light of the afternoon, her soft curves molding to his body without any restraint at all.

"Why not? We are Scottish after all." Ellie giggled into his chest. "Oh, I'm terrible, aren't I?"

"You're wonderful. I've been terrible," he said. "I don't know what I was thinking, staying hidden from you. I didn't want you to… I don't know. I didn't want to frighten you."

"You mean you didn't want to disgust me. You were the one who was afraid, Struan. Afraid that I'd not like what I saw. Which is silly. You're a fine man, every inch of you."

"Stop it. You don't have to be nice about it. I know what I look like."

"You know what you look like *to you*," she said with a heat that silenced him. "You can never know what you look like to another. Nor do I, though I consider myself adequate most mornings. I've seen beautiful girls stare at a mirror and cry because they believe they're hideous. Nose too big, they say. Hair too dull. But it's not true at all. I think sometimes it would be better if all mirrors got broken. People are poor judges of themselves."

"My little Ellie, dispenser of wisdom."

"No charge," she told him, and then dissolved into giggles again.

* * * *

Ellie never wanted to leave Struan's bed. It was so comfortable to lay with him, skin to skin, and *see* him at last.

He'd been angry when she first confronted him in the bath, and she almost fled. But her need to see him transcended her fear. And once she looked, she refused to stop looking.

She'd been appalled by the extent of the damage, because it drove home how close to death Struan had been. Half his torso was covered in strangely smooth, shiny, reddish skin, devoid of the hairs sprinkled over the other half of his chest and then narrowing down his stomach to his groin. The only disconcerting thing was the fact that one nipple on his chest, the right one, seemed to be gone. Only the new, smooth skin remained. And she could see how the scarring fit on his frame like too-tight clothing, sometimes making him hunch or bend oddly, perhaps because he moved in such a way to avoid pain remembered from recovery.

But even though the burn scars had left a bitter reminder of what he'd gone through, he wasn't any less a man because of it. Indeed, she thought wryly, no one seeing his naked body could doubt his manhood, especially when she saw his arousal.

Ellie had grown heated herself seeing that, knowing it was a reaction to her presence. It made her feel powerful, like she could work magic on him. And she wanted to learn what kind of magic worked best. Happily, he seemed to enjoy her explorations. She enjoyed them too, though she still felt that ache between her legs.

Stretching and tipping her head up to find his, she kissed him.

"You don't think it's wrong of me to want you, is it? I mean, you say you were afraid of scaring me, but you meant disgusting me. But what's the opposite of disgusted?"

"Gusted?" he offered, sounding more languid and open than she'd ever heard.

"Stop it!" She had to laugh before recalling herself to the topic at hand. "You thought I would be repelled by your appearance. I'm not. I'm drawn to you. I like touching you. Learning you." She felt shy about admitting this, and kept her eyes on his body as she ran her hands over his skin. Scars made little ridges and islands. Muscles rose into plateaus.

"I don't like touching me," he admitted. "For a long time I felt like I was just a broken-apart shell."

Ellie shook her head. "But you're healed now. Scars aside, you're whole."

"Maybe."

"What do you mean?" she asked.

Struan hesitated before he spoke again, and when he did,

his voice was low. "While the most obvious wounds were to my skin and muscles on the right side of my body, there's a chance that my injuries may have…other effects."

"Such as?"

"Such as not being able to…" He touched her belly.

It took her a moment to understand exactly what he meant, and just how upset he was about the possibility of not being able to father a child. He couldn't even *say* the words. She wanted more than anything to comfort him. But she was hardly an expert.

"Has a doctor told you so?" she asked, carefully stepping around her own ignorance.

He shook his head, his eyes still clouded. "No. In fact, the ones who treated me went out of their way to tell me that it's not a concern. But the army taught me that when anyone voluntarily tells you not to worry about something, you should definitely worry."

"They were army doctors?"

"The first one was. I've gone to other doctors in Edinburgh since then."

"Who have no reason to lie to you."

"They probably didn't want to be the bearer of bad news."

"Or there was no bad news to bear. So to speak," Elspeth added.

He let out a laugh, then looked surprised at his own reaction. "Ellie, this is serious."

"Unless it's not. I mean, we've not been…*together* for long, have we? But if we keep…um, being together, then I may be carrying a child in a few months. And you'll know that there's nothing to worry about. Truly. Because I'm not part of the army, and when I say not to worry, I *mean* not to worry. And for what it's worth, I've seen no evidence at all that you suffer from any…lack when it comes to the act of…

procreation."

Struan said, "My desire was pent up for a long while. I assure you, I'm not typically so randy."

"I'm not objecting in the least. It was nice to see your desire."

"I guess you've no more need for the blindfold."

"Well, don't lose it," she said. "I enjoyed that too."

He raised one eyebrow. "That's useful to know." He kissed her, hungrily, then said, "We don't have to wait till dark now."

"No," she agreed in a breathless voice. "No."

He pulled her atop him, and she rose on her knees to allow him access.

"Christ. Are you so wet for me already?" he asked, one knuckle dipping into her folds. "Should I play with you more this way, or do you want my cock?"

"Yes. Don't make me wait," she gasped.

"You're in charge, love."

She lowered her body onto his stand, moaning as he filled her.

He kept one hand on her hip, guiding her movements. The other hand reached up to tangle in her hair. "Ellie, you feel so good."

She ran her fingers over his face, lightly skimming his cheek and jaw. "There is something in particular I want."

"Name it."

"Make me a mother."

He groaned and held her tight to him as he began to thrust hard. She reveled in the sensation, and arched her back as the pleasure built. He seemed to feed on her desire, and within moments, they both were lost.

Chapter 21

THE NEXT DAY, ELLIE TOLD Struan, "I'm going to the far
school in a little while. Won't you come with me?"

"No one there wants to see me," he muttered.

"I thought we slayed that dragon," she said. "I talk about
you there, and everyone wants to see you. You're the most
important person around for miles and miles. Plus they respect you, and they're curious about you, and they need to
know you're part of this community. Your father and mother
were involved with local folk, yes?"

"Of course."

"Then follow their example."

He narrowed his eyes at her. "You know exactly what to
say to get me to do what you like."

"I'm learning." She smiled, then leaned forward to kiss
him. "Speaking of you doing what I like…"

As it turned out, they were a bit late in leaving the house,
but both were content when they did. They rode, Ellie having
learned the basics by now. The hostler had found an extremely staid black mare for her, who went by the unimagi-
native name of Midnight.

Being at the school wasn't horrible, not at first. He met
Mrs Hardie, and the other teachers at the school, and several
of the older students. They all greeted Ellie with smiles and

familiar, friendly words. Everyone had obviously been told to be on their best behavior for the master, but children are naturally curious, and soon he'd been invited to join some boys in a game while Ellie stayed and chatted with the headmistress.

Struan was actually having a good time, which of course meant that he had to be punished for daring to experience joy. The school was in a state of controlled chaos the whole afternoon, with girls and boys running about, charging through the doorway to go inside or out, according to some obscure pattern that only the children seemed to understand. The adults spoke as best they could amid the happy chatter and occasional excited shrieks of children.

Seeing them in there, the girls in identical new outfits made from Elspeth's purple fabric, made him laugh. The boys wore black, but if it was possible to have a purple-tinted black, that's what the shade was. The new outfits guaranteed that it was all but impossible to differentiate one child from another.

He turned around when he felt a child careen into the back of his legs, and said with mock seriousness, "Watch your step or you'll end up like me."

The young boy had fallen onto his seat and looked up at him with wide eyes. His mouth worked, but no sound came out.

"I was only joking," said Struan to the boy.

The boy took a deep breath, and then screamed.

As if suddenly inhabited by a whirlwind, the boy jumped up and spun around, rushing out of the building, screaming his head off the whole way.

Struan knew exactly why he did it. Though he made no outward sign, he felt his chest constricting and his whole body shutting up.

Elspeth noticed, of course. And she said something, of

course.

"Struan? Are you all right? That boy was very rude." Elspeth's eyes were wide, her posture stiff.

"Aye, he's more like a feral cat than a boy," Mrs Hardie added, her hands on her hips. "I'll fetch him in and make him apologize. I assure you, sir, we strive to teach manners to all our children. But I'll admit that some take to the lessons faster than others."

"That won't be necessary," said Struan. "I must go. Elspeth, you may stay if you wish."

He didn't wait for her reply before he strode out of the building, his eyes straight ahead as he made his way to his horse. The other children continued to play around him, seemingly undeterred by his presence. He mounted up as quickly as he could, and rode off toward home.

It had been a mistake to come. Elspeth was far too optimistic that he could resume anything resembling a normal life. He knew it wasn't her fault that the child had been scared of him, but he couldn't help thinking that his first mistake was listening to Elspeth, or rather, believing her words that the excursion would be good for everyone.

It clearly hadn't been good for the boy. As for the other children, well, they were simply a bit better at pretending. The headmistress had announced that she taught them how to behave. But he thought back to the carefully averted eyes and the shy voices and the way that very few of the children dared to come near him, and knew that his appearance was upsetting to them.

He would avoid the far school in the future. It was for the best. No one needed to see him, as long as the income from the mines and the fields kept coming in, and everyone was paid properly. It was foolish for him to think that he had a place among them anyway. He was to the manor born. They were common folk. At best, they viewed him as a tolerable landlord. He certainly wasn't a friend or part of the community. He wasn't one of them before, and he certainly wasn't now, not after what happened to him.

On the way, he hesitated, then rode onto the hill closest to the coast, the one he'd shown Ellie before. Today it was grey and sullen and cold, not at all suitable for lounging and looking over the water.

But it suited his mood. Dismounting, he sank down slowly onto the long grass and stared out over the distant water. The wind flattened the grass, pushing it down in a pattern that mimicked the waves of the ocean. It whipped his hair around his head, sending the ends into his eyes. He blinked away the irritation. Putting his hands down, he felt the grass, each stem rough under his fingers.

The popular conception of meadow grass as soft and green and lush was a product of other lands, those with more gentle climates. Here in the Highlands, the plants covering the moors were tough and unaccommodating. They had to be in order to survive the endless wind, the harsh winters, and the roving sheep and cattle that sought out anything tender enough to consume.

No wonder that the edge of each grass felt like a blade. The grass wasn't even green up here. It was a dull grey-brown, half bleached by the sun. It wasn't that Scotland didn't have rain. It had more than its share. But the rocky landscape and the steep slopes meant that the water all seemed to roll down into ravines, and then out again to the sea. It was as if some magical creature, capable of bestowing grace, briefly visited the land, and found it unworthy.

But this was Struan's land, so here he would stay. He didn't mind that the view was uninspiring, and he didn't mind that he was alone. If anyone else was here, they would insist on talking. Struan didn't want to talk. No amount of talking would change anything.

He didn't know how long he had been sitting there, other than that it was long enough for the wind and the damp to make him cold. But when his horse nickered, he realized that someone had ridden up. Looking back, he saw Ellie on Midnight, and he suppressed the urge to tell her to go away. He knew she meant well. Elspeth always meant well.

She dismounted awkwardly and strode toward him, stopping a few paces away. She looked down at him with an expression on her face that he couldn't interpret. After a moment of hideous silence, she turned and walked back toward her horse.

Struan exhaled. So he didn't have to speak after all. His own expression and his posture had sent the message. A part of him wished that Ellie didn't understand what he meant. But he couldn't blame her for leaving him. It wasn't as if he was someone people wanted to be around.

Elspeth had reached her horse, but instead of finding a way to remount and ride off, she unbuckled something behind the saddle, and walked back toward him, her arms now burdened with the bulky shape. She shook it out and he realized that she had brought a whole blanket along with her. She draped it around him, and the thick, heavy wool cut the wind to almost nothing. He was about to grunt a thank-you when she sank gracefully down beside him. She lifted one edge of the blanket and tucked herself under it, nestling against his side. Without thinking, he slid one arm around her waist to hold her close.

She didn't speak, she didn't even look at him. Instead, she gazed out at the sea, regarding the endless ocean and the relentless rhythm of the waves with calm eyes. He glanced at her profile, and found it soothing to see her refined features with the wild landscape in the background.

He knew he should say something, anything, but he didn't know how to begin. He wondered if Ellie was angry at him. But if Ellie was angry, she wouldn't have brought him a blanket. She wouldn't have sought him out at all. And yet here she was, sitting silently next to him, watching the grey sea.

The only thing different from before was that she was there. And then he realized that *was* the difference. He'd been alone, and now he wasn't. He didn't have to say anything. The fact that she was there was enough.

"You didn't have to come after me," he said.

"Yes I did. Would you like to have an argument about it?" she offered.

"No. I'm grateful you found me."

She smiled at him. "You found me first."

So he had. But she still didn't know how he found her. And he could never tell her the truth of it.

He tried to put the conundrum from his mind. After going back home, they dined as usual, then they retired to the parlor as usual. He still found the ritual of just sitting in a room with his wife to be as comforting as it was. They both read books or letters, enjoying the end-of-day calm. Ellie often asked him things about the house or the property or the land surrounding it, and he was surprised by how much he remembered from his younger days. Both his parents, and several friends and neighbors loved telling stories, and he must have soaked them up. Ellie usually had something to say no matter the topic, often some idea for how to improve something. She seemed to have a knack for solving problems.

Just then, Ellie yawned. She slid her thin leather shoes off and dropped them to the carpet, before curling up next to him.

"Rather messy, for you," he said.

"I'll put them on again before we go up," she promised.

He looked down at the shoes and noticed a folded letter on the floor. He bent to pick it up. "Look. This must have fallen off the table. It's a letter from Mairi, must have arrived today. Would you like to read it?"

"Yes! But you read it to me, please. I'm too tired to stare at handwriting now."

"You're sure? What if your sister has secrets she doesn't want me to know?"

"What secrets could Mairi know?" Ellie asked, giggling at the thought. "If she learns a thing, she tells the world that instant."

"Whether the world wants her to or not," Struan muttered. "The letter begins, 'Dear Pest.' Must she call you that?"

"It's said with love."

"I prefer Ellie. All right, *dear pest*." He began to narrate, "'The household is utterly consumed with preparations for Averill's Assault Upon Society. If I cared for society more, I'd feel badly for them all. But I have instead absented myself from the field, and taken refuge elsewhere.'" Struan snorted, and then added his own commentary, "Best thing she could do, actually. Retreat isn't cowardice when it's strategic."

"Go on," Ellie ordered.

He continued reading, "'You remember meeting Miss Catriona Ross at the wedding. We have spent some time together since, both at meetings of the League and beyond. Catriona spends much of her time restoring what she can of her damaged home. The fire was limited, but the smoke ruined most everything.'"

"Oh, I should write back with my method for getting the smell of smoke out of fabric. I'm sure much of the curtains and upholstery are salvageable!"

Struan laughed. "You don't need to clean everyone's house, you know."

"But I like to improve things. It gives me such a feeling

of accomplishment to see that my actions have transformed something from broken to mended."

He gave her a considering look. "Not just because you think someone else will approve of it, or to earn your keep?" She tried to be the perfect daughter and housekeeper for her father, and that had resulted only in him handing her off like a used cart.

"No, I'd do it even if I were all alone," she said. "I think that one of the things I love best is to leave the world more beautiful than I found it."

"Well, you do that just by existing."

She blushed. "Keep reading."

"'Catriona and I have decided to write a series of essays in the hopes that a newspaper will be brave enough to print them. If not, I may start my own newspaper. Catriona has been preparing speeches as well. Did you know she was once shot at during a speech? She says it wasn't actually related to the speech itself, but I think she should consider it a badge of honor. You must meet her aunt Tacita, who is not in our League, but is delightful. Time spent at Cat's smoky home is much nicer than time spent at our own. Only once was there an interruption. The men who were at the wedding—your husband's compatriots—called for a visit. Apparently Mr MacPhearson asked Cat to marry him, but she refused.'"

"That's true," Struan added, seeing her astonished expression. "Thane already proposed to her, and she told him no."

"But he asked again?"

"He told us that he'll ask until she either says yes or tells him to go to hell."

"Oh," Ellie said, eyes wide. "What else does Mairi report?"

He looked back at the letter."'...though it is apparent that she does *not* discourage his advances! I think she loves him. He is fairly handsome, I admit, and his handsomeness is better than Mr Shaw's, because that man knows how he looks, and it makes him insufferable. Mr MacKenzie and Mr Buchanan, however, are pleasant.'"

At this Struan had to stop reading to recover from laughing. "I wish I could read this to Calan."

"That's Mr Shaw?"

"Yes. She's exactly right. He's used to women falling all over him, so to be in a room where neither lady is besotted must have been confusing."

"Perhaps it will build character," Ellie said. "What else?"

He read silently for a moment, then said, "Mairi tried to smuggle a dog into the house, but your father heard it barking and had it removed. One of the footmen took it home."

"Mairi loves animals. She can't stand to see one suffer. I'd wager it was the brown dog in the mews with the bad back paw."

"Correct," he said, still reading. "You remember everything. Do you miss your old home?"

Ellie pondered a moment, then shook her head. "No. I thought I'd miss it more, but I don't. Isn't that funny?"

The way she smiled at him, with such open innocence, he didn't think it was funny at all.

Chapter 22

OVER THE NEXT FEW WEEKS, Elspeth continued to visit the far school regularly, happy to be of use and to be surrounded by all the children, vibrant and hopeful despite everything that had brought them here over the course of their short lives. She liked the other women who worked there as well, finding them solid and steady souls who quickly adapted to Elspeth's presence and soon spoke to her (and around her) in much the same way as they did to anyone else.

A letter arrived one day while Elspeth was there. The headmistress read it over, her stern demeanor softening into sorrow. Then she said, "Will someone bring Aileen to me, please?"

Elspeth replied, "I'll get her. Is it bad news? Shall I prepare her at all?"

"If you can, dear. Tell her only that she will hear something very sad, and she must be strong."

A few minutes later, Elspeth sat beside the slender child on a bench, facing the headmistress. The girl gripped Ellie's hand as if it were a lifeline.

"My dear, I am so sorry to tell you that your father passed a few weeks ago."

Aileen didn't wail or shriek, but she began to shake, and tears rolled silently down her cheeks.

"He never got better?" she asked, knowing the answer.

"No, my child." Mrs Hardie's tone was low and gentle. "You do remember that he wrote to you from London, saying he was ill. Now his friend has written to say it was consumption after all. He went quickly, it seems."

"Will he be buried with Mama?" Aileen asked.

Elspeth exchanged a glance with the headmistress. She understood Mrs Hardie's expression instantly. The man was a poor laborer, barely able to save money and send it home when he was healthy. He'd have been buried in a potter's field in London, at best. She spoke up quickly. "I'm afraid that's not possible, dear. But it is certainly proper to have a stone set next to your mother's grave, with his name and dates, even though he is buried elsewhere. It's common for sailors, you know. When men are lost at sea, their families erect a memorial so they are not forgotten."

"That's what I want for Papa, then," she said. "How much does it cost?"

Elspeth's heart broke for the girl, forced to reckon with cold, practical, grown-up tasks far too early. "We will inquire, but I would like to pay for it, as a favor, if you will let me."

"Why, ma'am?" she asked with wide, wet eyes.

"I lost a parent when I was young," Ellie said. "I know how it feels to miss someone. And what sort of friend would I be if I didn't try to ease your burden?"

"Oh, ma'am. *You* know." Aileen embraced Ellie tightly. That was when the sobbing truly started, and Ellie simply held her and let her cry. Mrs Hardie offered her a clean handkerchief from the drawer of the desk.

After a while, Aileen wiped her face and solemnly asked to be excused. "I wish to lie down on my bed for a while."

"Go rest, dear. I'll check on you in a half hour," the headmistress said.

After the girl gave Ellie a final hug, she left.

"The worst part of my duties here," Mrs Hardie confessed with a sigh. "Poor child, now alone in the world."

"She has the other students, and you and the teachers. And the village. And me. We must not fail her by letting her think she is alone."

"Well said," the woman agreed after a moment.

"And I will pay her school fees until she is of age," Ellie told Mrs Hardie in an undertone.

"Ma'am, you must not let yourself be taken advantage of. Aileen is a good child who would not presume to exploit the fact that she knows a lady like yourself. But not everyone is like that."

"A matter I will deal with if and when it happens."

* * * *

Most days, fortunately, were not as dramatic. Later that week, she was tidying some scrap paper and pencils that several boys had dumped out of the box in the middle of a game of hare and hounds (Mrs Hardie had been so annoyed she ordered them outside before remembering that they ought to clean up their own mess).

Elspeth found herself thinking that the boys in particular would fare better if they could see more adult men in their lives. If only the boy who'd upset Struan had been quicker to explain that his reaction had been because one of the other children had just related a scary story.

Not that the explanation would ease Struan's mind, or get him to return here. At least she'd managed to convince him to come every day to collect her and bring her back to Linneliath when she finished her tasks. She hoped that by slowly getting him more comfortable with the idea of other people, he'd come out of his shell.

She sighed. For every step forward she took with Struan, something seemed to pull him back to an unhappy place. She'd just have to be patient, and work diligently. After all, she knew that happiness was a matter of perspective.

A shriek came from behind her. "Molly, no!"

Elspeth whirled around at the sound of the young girl's cry of dismay. A lantern had been knocked over, the oil spreading in a pool on top of the scrap fabric that had been so carefully piled at the end of the table. The flame leapt from the wick to the fuel-soaked fabric and flared up immediately.

She grabbed the girls and pulled them away from the flame, calling out as she did so for everyone to get out of the building. Her words didn't seem to have the desired effect. Half a dozen girls stood stock-still, gazing at the burgeoning fire with horror in their eyes. In a panic, one of the teachers ran to fetch a pitcher of water, then rushed toward the fire and flung the water at it.

But she managed to hit about only half of the fire, and the other flames seemed to rise up in defiance. Elspeth steered the girls toward the exit, pushing them along until they reached the doorway. "Go on! Go outside and let the boys know so they can help bring water from the stream."

The girls nodded, frightened but now past their initial confusion. They dashed outside, presumably to spread word of the accident. Elspeth turned and stepped aside to help move more of the girls through, one by one so the doorway would not be blocked.

"Is everyone out?" Elspeth asked one of the teachers. They both looked back into the room, rapidly filling with dark smoke.

"I think so," the teacher replied, though with doubt and fear in her voice. "I didn't see Thora. Did you?"

Elspeth thought of the dark-haired girl, and shook her head. "She always sits by the stove, doesn't she? I'll go look."

"No! You won't be able to breathe. We must go."

"I'm not leaving anyone behind. Go out and start a bucket brigade." Without waiting for a response, Elspeth walked back into the room, lifting her arm to cover her mouth and nose. She crouched to avoid the cloud of smoke that hit the ceiling and was growing darker every moment, dropping down closer to the floor as it did so. She saw the outline of the stove, and also saw two skinny legs next to it. Thora was evidently too afraid to move.

"Thora! Come with me," Elspeth said, removing her arm from in front of her mouth for just a moment. Even those few words required her to suck in a breath that was too hot and too dry, and she began to cough. "Come! We haven't any time to lose."

"I can't, ma'am! I just can't," the girl cried out, panic in her voice.

Elspeth looked behind Thora to the window in the far corner of the room. She could smash the glass and push Thora through. The window was too high for Ellie to climb up after, but she could make a final dash through the room and out the door.

Taking Thora's arm, Ellie pushed her toward the window. She grabbed one of the wooden stools set by the wall and hurled it at the glass. The cloudy, pockmarked glass shattered, and two things happened at once. Thora screamed, and the fire inside the room suddenly exploded in size, fed by the influx of fresh air from the outside. Elspeth placed the stool below the window and set Thora onto it, her little feet teetering on the seat.

"Thora, put your hands on the windowsill and pull yourself up as hard as you can." Elspeth lifted her by the waist as

Thora reached for the windowsill, and together they managed to perch Thora on the sill, teetering half in and half out. There must have been a growing crowd outside, because a man shouted, and seconds later, Thora was being pulled through the window by unseen helpers.

She could hear Thora crying out, "She's still inside, she's still inside!"

"I'm going through the door now," Elspeth shouted at the window. Frantic voices gave conflicting orders from the other side, but Elspeth couldn't make sense of them, and in any case she saw only one option. She took one deep breath of the relatively smoke-free air by the window, lifted her sleeve once more, and turned.

That main door now seemed impossibly far away. Even within the last few minutes, the flames had spread over every surface, the wooden building and all of the items within being flammable. Smoke billowed black and thick, with only the bottom couple of feet above the floor being somewhat less dense.

Elspeth made her way forward in a zigzag fashion, avoiding the largest spouts of flame. Her skin seemed to crack in the oven-like heat, and she desperately wanted to take another breath, but she knew she couldn't. Her eyes watered, making the flames seem to sparkle and move about, so that she was no longer entirely sure if what she saw in front of her was really what was there. She dropped down to her knees, crawling toward the door.

She had only a few more seconds before her body would force her to breathe, and that would be her death. Her lungs burned with the desire for fresh air. Her linen gown began to scorch and blacken as the flames found it. A instinctive cry broke out of her throat when she saw the bottom of her skirts catch fire.

Even that was enough to send her to the floor, unable to

keep moving forward as her limbs weakened from the lack of air in her body. Just then a crashing sound reverberated through the room. A portion of the roof gave way, falling in front of her. It didn't entirely block the way out, but would force her to move further around to the side. Elspeth willed herself to get to her hands and knees, and she began to crawl around the mass of burning beams and thatch.

A shadow darkened the doorway, in the hazy silhouette of a man. He shouted her name.

Elspeth called back, her own voice thin and weak, with nothing in her lungs to support it. She crawled a few inches more, just enough to catch his attention.

He stormed toward her, a dark figure without definition. He bent down and gathered her in his arms. *Struan.*

Then he spun about and retraced his steps, avoiding the ever-growing flames.

He carried her through the doorway sideways, and managed a few yards more before sinking onto his knees, and placing her gently on the ground. She was coughing uncontrollably, and could hardly move her limbs.

Struan bent over her, asking in a hoarse whisper if she was all right. Hands touched her gently, but even so Elspeth cried out in pain. Had she been burned?

Struan howled at the crowd for water, and then one of the villagers was running toward them with a bucket that sloshed over, it was so full. Struan dipped his hand into the bucket and then made Elspeth drink out of his cupped palm. He lifted her up so that she wouldn't choke, but wouldn't let her move until she had drunk several times, since much of the cool water spilled out over her face and onto her chest.

"What the hell?" he demanded.

"Lantern. Knocked over." Elspeth was too overwhelmed to give a full explanation, and surely one of the girls or the teachers had already announced what had happened.

"I thought you would die." Struan's voice was harsh, but his eyes were haunted. He had been terrified for her.

All at once, Elspeth realized that he had run into the middle of a raging fire by choice, just to find her.

"You went into the flames," she whispered. "You *hate* fire."

He paused for a long moment, then said, "Aye, I do. But I would not let that fire have you."

* * * *

In the nearby field, Struan knelt next to an exhausted Ellie and watched the efforts to douse the fire, everyone bringing buckets and pitchers of water to fling at the building and then quickly switching to soaking the nearest neighboring buildings so the fire wouldn't spread, since the wind was brisk.

When the main danger was over, Struan arranged for Elspeth to be brought back to the house, bathed by her maid, and put into bed. Though the ordeal itself couldn't have lasted more than an hour in total, he felt like he'd lost years of his life.

The local doctor arrived at Linneliath not long after. He examined her under Struan's watchful eye. He announced she had no permanent damage or serious burns.

"Her skin is *red*," Struan spat.

"But not blistered much, nor bleeding. That's all to the good." The doctor pulled something out of his bag. "She must use this salve. It should be applied twice a day, and again after the skin is bathed."

"I'll do it," Struan replied. "I've plenty of experience with burns."

After the doctor left, Struan sat on the edge of the bed, as close as he dared to Ellie.

"You need to rest. I'm not in any danger," she said, watching him. "You got me out in time."

But Struan shook his head. "You breathed in smoke, and that takes time to recover from. Your skin was burned. And your hair was singed." He reached toward her hair, which had been gathered into a low ponytail after her bath. The hair was mostly dry now, and he saw just how much of the length of it had been lost to the fire, and then the scissors, as Agnes cut off the burned ends.

"It'll grow back," she said.

"God, Ellie," Struan said in a lower tone. "I thought I'd lost you."

"No," she told him, reaching for his hand. "I had to get Thora to safety. The fire spread much faster than I expected," she admitted.

"You must never put yourself in that kind of danger again." Struan lifted her hand to his lips and kissed her palm. The back of her hand was too red and raw to bear touching.

Ellie made a huffing sound, but submitted willingly when he lifted the bedsheet and surveyed her body. Her hands and forearms were the worst off, whatever had been uncovered by her garments in the school. Then her neck and face, to a lesser degree.

She was still red all over, though, a physical response to being exposed to too much heat, too quickly. Her body was attempting to expel the heat through her skin.

Struan uncapped the jar, and inhaled the familiar sharp, cool scent. Crushed, macerated mint was the main ingredient. He remembered it well from his own treatments. The mint would provide a cooling sensation, and the fat that made up the salve would protect and soothe the skin so it wouldn't crack and pull from being too dry.

He scooped some out and carefully smoothed it onto her skin, a layer thin enough to allow the skin to still breathe.

Ellie said, "It's so tingly."

"That's the mint. Does it feel cool?"

"Yes. You used this before?"

"By the gallon," he said simply.

"Who put it on *you*?"

"Jealous?"

"Maybe."

He grinned. "Whoever the hospital could spare. Not one of them was a pretty nurse who slid her soft, smooth hands all over me. Alas." In fact, most of the time, he'd done it himself, once he was strong enough. But he was enjoying Ellie's obvious concern that another woman had touched him so gently. If she was worried about that, she probably wasn't dying.

He got off the edge of the bed, standing and looking down at her. "Rest. I'll check in on you frequently."

By the doctor's orders and Struan's strong enforcement, Ellie was confined to her bed for days. She objected, but everyone ignored her, as he'd told them to.

Struan went back to the far school each day, working with the local men from the village (even Robbie Davies) and the servants from the house to see what could be salvaged. The answer, sadly, was not much. In their haste to get all the people safely out, they hadn't been able to fight the fire until it was raging. The stone husk of the building was black from smoke, and every scrap of wood from the beams to the furniture turned to ash.

"At least no one died," said one man, tossing aside a twisted mass that had once been a tin lantern. "But with no school now, where'll the children go? The school in the village is too small for more."

"Tavish," Struan called to one of the men who worked as a gardener at Linneliath. "That old barn by the mineshaft that closed down in '08. What condition is it in?"

"Roof's fallen in," Tavish said after a moment of thought. "But the walls are solid as ever. Clean out the inside and put up new thatch, it'd serve for a schoolroom. No room for beds, though," he warned.

"The students who lodged at the far school can lodge at Linneliath for now," Struan decided. "Elspeth, that is, Mrs MacInnes, pointed out that the house is underused. We'll set up some of the bedchambers in the Tudor wing for the boys and girls."

"You don't intend to rebuild the school?" Robbie asked. This was the first time he'd dared speak directly to Struan since he'd offered to kill him for flirting with Ellie in the village.

"It will be rebuilt," Struan announced. "It's necessary. But it'll be done right, and that takes time. Until then, we improvise."

No one said much, but Struan could tell that they all approved. A new school would mean more work for the locals, which was always needed, and Struan was suddenly excited by the idea of having more people, particularly young children, at the house. He realized that he'd been so consumed by the idea of making his own family that he'd forgotten that his home was already surrounded with people he knew from birth. And none of them cared that he now bore scars. All they wanted was someone who cared about the land and the people living on it. And he could be that person.

"Pick some men to start work on the barn," he told Tavish. "I'll speak to the headmistress about lodging the children, and then see about the rebuilding."

"Aye, sir." Tavish gave him a short nod, the Highland equivalent of thunderous applause.

* * * *

Each day, Struan came to sit with Ellie frequently, giving her reports on what was happening, and he religiously applied the salve the doctor had made.

On the fourth day, she said, "I'm bored. I really am able to get up."

"Absolutely not."

She groaned. "What am I to do? Lie here naked and alone forever?"

"It won't be forever. Soon you'll be healed and you definitely won't be alone at night." That last was delivered as a promise.

Now she closed her eyes. "Struan. Is being with someone…like we are…"

"You mean fucking?" He kissed her bare shoulder softly.

"I can't say that word."

"Why not? It's what we do, isn't it?"

"But doesn't that word…"

"Fucking."

"Yes. Doesn't that word…"

"Say it, Ellie."

She bit her lip. Inhaled. Then whispered, "Fucking."

"There you go. Now, what about fucking?"

"Well, just that…that's not what married couples do, is it? There must be another word for when…"

He was puzzled. "For when…what?"

"When it's not just two…bodies. It's not just about taking pleasure. What's the word for…fucking but when you're in love?"

Struan stared at her for a long moment. "Love?"

"Yes. I love you, so when we're together, it can't be something as base as…fucking. It has to have another word to describe what's happening, not just in my body, but in my heart. I mean, not the heart in my chest that beats. The heart in my…the heart that falls in love with you."

"In love?" he echoed. "With me?"

"Who else? Every time you touch me I want to stop time so I can hold all the feelings up and just look at them. I'm so happy I could cry, and I want you to be happy too. Happy that you chose me. That's what love is, yes?"

Stunned, he said, "Yes. Yes, you're right. I'm sorry, Ellie. I'm no good at words. I won't call it fucking again, if you don't like it."

"I just want to use the *correct* word. And *fucking* sounds too harsh."

"Does it? What if we just say it more gently?"

She laughed then. "How would that sound?"

He leaned close so he could murmur in her ear, "Fucking."

The little noise she made nearly killed him.

Then she turned her head to give him a quick kiss, and she said, "I love you. You can say whatever words you like, Struan. As long as you let me love you."

Blood surging though his veins, he stood up. "I'll…I'll check in again later. Sleep, Ellie."

She smiled even as her eyes slid closed.

He left the room, left the house. Struan couldn't sit still, he couldn't stay caged inside. He needed to be out in wind and rain, away from the home he'd been dying to return to for years. The home that Ellie had made bright and welcoming. Ellie so innocently saying she loved him cut like a blade in his flesh.

He reached the high place where he could see for miles, the whole wild moorland surrounding him with its desolate beauty.

It hurt more because he loved her too. He loved her when she'd pulled all the mirrors together to create more light out of fewer flames. He loved her when she curled up next to him and told him she would listen. He loved her so fiercely that it scared him. But saying the words out loud seemed like inviting disaster into his life. How could he dare to feel any happiness or hope at this point? If he told Elspeth how much he loved her, who knew what vengeful god or demon would overhear and decide to punish him for the audacity to be joyful? He didn't deserve to feel this good, this at peace. He had lied to Elspeth from the moment he met her, and let her believe a fairy tale because he was too weak to tell her the truth.

He wasn't sure how long he remained there, but the sky was going dark by the time he stood up to head back.

Struan took a deep breath, letting the cold air fill his lungs. He had to tell her. He knew that. He'd always known that. Calan had told him something when he confessed his dilemma to his friend. *The truth is like water. You can dam it up, divert it, try to contain it. But it will find the tiniest seam in the rock and emerge. Sometimes as a trickle. Sometimes a flood. But it will come out.*

So Struan would tell her. No matter how much it hurt him, it couldn't hurt more than it did to hide it. The lying and silence were clawing him hollow. He turned to face the direction of his home, where Ellie lay.

Ellie deserved to know. And she needed to know he loved her.

Chapter 23

ODD HOW A NEAR-TRAGEDY could wake one up. Despite the fire, and despite how close she'd been to danger, and how much even "minor" damage had hurt to recover from, Ellie found herself so happy with her life she could barely stand it. She'd been cheerful before, of course, because she believed in being cheerful as a way to make the world easier to bear. But the joy that came from being in love was so much more than mere happiness.

A few hours after Struan had left her following their discussion of, *ahem*, semantics, Ellie rose from bed and got dressed. She wanted to embrace the whole world. She beamed at every chambermaid (even the ones who told her she was supposed to stay in bed). She wanted to sing back to the birds in the sky. She greeted each person she saw in the house with an ebullient smile that was probably disconcerting to the average Highland denizen.

Yet how could she do otherwise? She had a lovely home, filled with more than she'd ever need to live and thrive, and she was matched to the most perfect man ever created.

Not literally perfect, of course—nothing short of the Divine was without flaw. But his flaws were really just how life had shaped him into what he was, which was caring and thoughtful and always attentive. He both sheltered her and shocked her, a combination she never knew she needed until she came to live here.

How absolutely wonderful the world was, bringing them together in this way. Of course it had to be that Struan couldn't court her in the usual way, because he wasn't the usual man. He'd been through too much and he had to keep himself distant even as he admired her from afar. But he'd then gone to her father and asked for her hand just like in fairy tales, and it was all terribly romantic and this was the result…her confessing her love to him, and knowing (almost certainly) that he would say he loved her too, if only he said that sort of thing.

Eventually, she went to the parlor room—now one of her favorites in the whole house —and took up a seat on the long couch in front of the fireplace, where a low fire burned, the smoke peaty and comforting in her nostrils.

She was just debating whether to call for some tea or wait for Struan when a maid entered.

"A letter for you just arrived, ma'am," the maid said, handing Elspeth a folded paper. Elspeth took it from her and saw with delight Mairi's handwriting. She flipped it over and worked her finger under the flap to break the seal. Mairi had folded in her usual pattern, and the act of folding back each corner of the paper was as familiar to Elspeth as the shape of her sister's script. She began to read, hoping for happy news from the city. However, that was not what she got.

Dearest Pest,

You must prepare yourself for my next words, and re-member that any pain I give you now is that of the surgeon whose scalpel cuts, but only in the cause to save a life.

Elspeth almost put down the letter. Was Mairi ill, hence the discussion of surgeons and scalpels? Was there some death in the family that came suddenly, not allowing for Elspeth to return to the city in time? Mairi always leaned toward understatement rather than histrionics. If Mairi said something would be painful, then it would be excruciating. Elspeth only hoped that she could provide some comfort to whomever Mairi was speaking of. She took a deep breath, and continued.

Through happenstance, I learned some most disturbing facts regarding our father's financial standing and his future expectations.

This wasn't the sort of news she had been expecting, and she was unsure how it could necessitate such a daunting preamble.

Not only has he been most imprudent in his spending habits, he has gone so far as to require multiple loans in order to maintain the appearance of solvency.

Now Elspeth guessed where this missive was going. She had sometimes suspected her father of living beyond his means, because he was always so concerned with others' regard of him. It was in his nature to equate a person's moral worth with their outward presentation. She hoped his behavior wasn't going to hurt Mairi's happiness. If he had spent her dowry, it would considerably limit her options…should Mairi ever want to marry after all.

I don't fear poverty, and I dare say that of our whole family, I am most likely to tolerate a greatly reduced income, should he not be able to repay what he has borrowed this time. However, I do fear losing what little freedom I possess, and I pray you will forgive me for the truth I am about to impart.

Elspeth considered finding Struan before she continued,

thinking that she might require some strength outside herself to bear the blow that was coming. But Struan was somewhere else, no doubt hard at work, and after all, she was a grown woman. She could hear bad news, no matter how upsetting it would be. Her hands shook slightly as she read the rest of Mairi's letter.

Our father has not only borrowed a staggering sum from money lenders, he has proved fiendishly inventive when reimbursing his creditors. Perhaps inventive is the wrong word, for what he has done is one of the oldest and most repugnant of trades. In short, he has sold a person in payment for his debt. And not just any person, but one who I hold most dear. It is you.

Elspeth couldn't make sense of those words. Did Mairi have brain fever? But if she did, how could she write and fold and seal her bizarre letter so perfectly?

He had borrowed from the man who is now your husband, and rather than coin, Father rendered payment in the form of your hand in marriage. It is my understanding that the bargain was settled upon by both parties with little discussion. And I am afraid that explains all too well why you had never laid eyes upon your husband before your wedding. Our father implied a tenderness that never existed, and the notion that MacInnes was too reticent to court you in the usual manner was a fiction. It rends my heart to know how happy you were, thinking that you had received a most loving partner, when in fact your name, your body, and your tender affections were nothing more than an item in a ledger.

Elspeth had to read the words several times before they truly penetrated. It couldn't be true. Struan wasn't some coldhearted figure in a counting house. He had shown every evidence of regard toward her. He would have told her if he had made such an arrangement with her father. Wouldn't he? Her mind aflame, she read on.

But Father has not learned any lessons or changed his ways since his unnatural bargain with your husband. When I discovered the foundation of your marriage, I also discovered that Father has borrowed yet again, from a different lender. This amount is even more extravagant, and at an interest rate which the law calls usury. He and Susan are spending like mad things in preparation for Averill's impending engagement (though Mr Farquhar, the most favored man, has not come up to scratch just yet). They are pinning all their hopes upon a match to this gentleman, whose income will justify the risk our father has placed upon all of us.

She was sweating. Her heart was racing. Elspeth could hardly hold the letter, her arms were shaking so badly. The physical effects of these revelations were as real as what the fire did. Mairi went on.

I fear that, having already performed the act once, our father will not hesitate to do it again. Am I to be shortly offered up upon the auction block? Am I also to be called wife to some man I have never met and will be forced to marry? Am I soon to be an indentured servant across the sea? There is worse that I could imagine, though I will not commit such nightmares to paper, for no woman should ever have to contemplate such a demeaning future.

Did Mairi mean to come north? Elspeth couldn't imagine it.

Alas, your home is no safe haven. I have never been as full of rage and disappointment as I am now. If only we were together. If only we had wings. Write to me as soon as you may. I will be in agony until then, not knowing your heart after learning this news. Please trust that I am always

Your sister and your friend,

Mairi

Elspeth attempted to read parts of the letter again. Her eyes must be wrong. She'd misread the words, it was a joke, it was a mistake, it was some ridiculous crossing of intentions.

But the words remained the same.

On the fourth attempt, the words blurred as tears welled up, turning her vision glittering and unreliable.

"It's not true," she whispered, but that did nothing to make the truth fade.

She could toss the letter into the fire right now, and make the words disappear.

But words once read cannot be unread, and she couldn't toss herself into the fire. Struan would be furious....

Elspeth took in a harsh breath, unfamiliar feelings billowing up inside her, dark and sooty. Emotions too big to stay inside, but too big to let out...for Elspeth anyway, who never succumbed to feelings that would disrupt the tranquility of others' lives.

What about my life? she thought with a savagery that was sharp as a new blade.

And then Struan walked into the parlor, looking a little disheveled after being outside in the constant wind. But moving easily and confidently, the lord of the manor. The man who'd chosen her to be the lady of the manor. Just not in the manner she'd thought.

"There you are, Ellie," he said with the smile he only gave to her. And it made her heart skip a beat, even as it raged in her rib cage.

But as he stepped toward her, she steeled herself, stood up, and asked, "It is true that I am payment for a debt?"

He went completely, utterly still.

"What?"

"You heard me. Is it true?"

"Who told you that?"

"Is it *true*?"

His posture and form changed from surprise to the forbidding attitude she'd seen early on. Then he said, his voice flat, "Yes. It's true."

She closed her eyes, the words like a physical blow.

He moved toward her. "Ellie, it's complicated. If you let me explain…"

She held her arm out, stiff, keeping him away. She swayed.

"Ellie. You're going to faint." He sounded concerned. Well, why not? He'd bought and paid for her. He wouldn't want her to break before he got his money's worth.

"Don't touch me," she snapped. "Don't come near me."

He stopped in his tracks. Other than the rise in his chest, he could have been made of stone.

"I intended to tell you," he said at last.

She glared at him. "*When?*"

"I suppose it doesn't matter when. Because someone told you first."

Elspeth held up the letter. "Mairi."

"Mairi?" His brow wrinkled. "How did *she*…never mind."

She gathered her nerve for the next question. "How much was I priced at? I'm curious, you understand. A lass does like to know what she might fetch on the open market."

He told her.

Ellie blinked, sure she'd misheard. "*What?*"

"Your father failed to pay back any interest over six years, which increased the total amount owed significantly. I was busy on the Continent for a while—the war, you understand"—the way he mimicked her phrasing cut her—"so I couldn't press for payment. And by the time I did get around to it, he was in no position to return even a portion of the loan."

"So you took me instead."

"He offered you," Struan growled. "He knew I wanted to marry."

"Father said you *chose* me."

Struan shrugged one shoulder. "That is a matter between you and your father. I told him I'd take you for a wife, and then his debt to me would be forgotten, if not forgiven. You came to the church. You went through the ceremony. You chose to accept."

"Under false pretenses! I thought you wanted me."

"I did." Now he looked at her for a fleeting moment. "I do."

"No, you wanted any woman who'd say yes. It didn't matter who it was. I'm just to be a vessel for your eventual heir. Oh, Lord, Mairi was right this whole time. Marriage is a lie. It's just a lie on top of a lie on top of another lie."

"It's not. I..." He seemed to be having difficulty speaking. "I care about you, Ellie."

How she wanted to hear that. How she craved it. But wasn't craving a dream what got her into this mess? "You say you care. But not enough to tell me the truth. You let me believe a fantasy. So you can't care all that much."

"I went through fire to get you," he said, and his voice crackled in her ears.

She shook her head, too overwhelmed to fully take in his words. She could only catch the sound and throw it back. "Then you can go through fire to leave me. I never want to see you again."

Chapter 24

ICE HAD DESCENDED ON LINNELIATH.

Not that anyone could see real ice—the weather was in a stretch of sunny, almost balmy days.

But inside the house, a frozen, deadly pall covered everything.

The servants knew that the master and mistress quarreled. A person would have to be dead to not be aware of that.

But it was generally assumed that it would pass after a day, or two, or three. Surely no more than that.

"Newlyweds always have a tiff or two," Mrs Negus said knowingly on the first day. "It's natural, and they'll get over it sooner or later."

It did not happen sooner. Or later.

For days, the mistress refused to leave her rooms, taking her meals alone, and scarcely changing from her bedclothes to half-dress in the daytime.

Meanwhile, the master left the house entirely, riding away on horseback at first light, and not returning till after darkness fell.

They did not cross paths, they did not speak.

"Should we do something?" one of the maids asked.

"Do what?" Agnes replied. "I don't know what they're quarreling about, and even if I did, I'm not such a fool to think that any of us could just walk into a room and say the right thing to make them all smiles again."

"If someone doesn't take steps, he'll never smile again.

And he might even leave the house altogether. Go back to soldiering. Can a man repurchase a commission? Anyway, this place could be shut up for years, and we're all without jobs."

"But the mistress…" Agnes began to say.

"Her family's in Edinburgh. Why would she stay here if he doesn't?"

Agnes pursed her lips, unhappy with the conversation. "You're making a mountain out of a molehill. Odds are that we'll all forget about this by Wednesday next."

"Odds are, eh? Care to wager?"

"I would not! One doesn't wager on whether folks are going to fight forever. Anyway, I haven't got any coin to spare. Sweep the corner again—you're not paying attention to your work."

"Oh, aye. Might as well work while we have work." With that portentous statement, the maid grabbed the broom.

They were not the only inhabitants of the great house considering the future. Up in her room, Elspeth thought about little else. She had made a bargain with the marriage ceremony, and even if Struan hadn't been sincere, she was. Perhaps she could shame him into feeling remorse for his actions.

And she was so sick of being alone in her room.

So, late in the evening a week after the fatal letter had arrived, she wrenched open the connecting door and strode into his chamber.

Struan looked up, alarmed, then angry. He was sitting in a chair by the fireplace, though there was no fire now. A single lantern burned on a table.

"What are you doing in here?" he growled, putting down his book.

"I'm reporting for duty," she replied. She opened the outer robe. Underneath, she wore only the flimsy silk lingerie that had been intended for her wedding night.

Struan's eyes locked on her, but he didn't move. Instead, he ordered, "Leave my room. Go to bed."

"I am going to bed," she told him, advancing toward his massive, heavily carved, four-poster bed. "Yours. Isn't that the reason you purchased me? To bed me and get an heir? Well, I am here to acquiesce, without complaint, of course."

"I said leave." He got up and strode toward the bed as well, arriving at the same time.

"And neglect the sole duty for which I exist? Don't be silly."

"If you stay, you'll regret it."

"I'm here. You wanted me here, and you have to deal with me now, *husband*."

With a snarl, he grabbed her and spun her around so that her back was to him.

"Oh, that's right," she said, ignoring the frisson running up her spine, now pressed tight to his chest. "I'm not supposed to look at you."

"No, you're not."

He pulled her robe off her shoulders and jerked the braided cord meant to be tied around her waist out of its loops, then lifted her so she lay with her belly on the bedspread. Keeping her pressed there so she couldn't wiggle free, he tied her ankles to the lower bedposts, ignoring her outraged protests. There was lead on each, but she couldn't pull her legs together.

"Are you scared now?" he asked. "Do you wish you left?"

She bit her lip. "I'm not scared, and I'm not leaving."

"No?" He snagged the thin straps of her flimsy gown and simply broke them. Bunching fistfuls of the silk in his hands, he yanked the whole thing away from her body, and she heard the seams rip as the gown fell into tatters onto the bed.

So much for mending that, she thought.

"Last chance, wife."

Oddly, she was so annoyed about the silk that she wasn't scared. "You can't frighten me."

"You have no idea what I can do to you." As he spoke, he pulled his own robe off, and she realized he pulled the belt out of it as well. He stretched over her to take her hands, and twined the woven belt around them several times.

"What are you *doing*?" she demanded.

"Evaluating my purchase." He ran his hands over her. He'd done that before, many times. But this felt different. Now he seemed to be measuring her, testing her.

She wished it didn't feel so arousing.

She wished he didn't know her body so well, because every touch was working to turn her into a mindless creature of need. His fingers, the palms of his hands, his *teeth*.

She was half kneeling, and she leaned back enough to brush her bottom against him as he stood at the edge of the bed. He hissed and pulled away, but not before she felt how hard he was. He absolutely wanted her...or he wanted release. She let out a keening sound, a desperate plea for him to proceed, to slide that hardness in her.

He didn't. All he did was scrape his nails across her bottom, making her go hot with longing. "You don't decide what I do," he told her, his voice tight. "Try to push me and I'll make you regret it."

"You'll hurt me?"

"Does this hurt?"

His fingers slid between her legs. Slowly, softly.

Ellie moaned, twisting in response. "Oh, Lord."

He kept circling that agonizingly sensitive bud, bringing her ever closer to the inevitable end. But he seemed in no hurry to get there. His fingers may even have slowed down. Yes, now he was stroking her folds as if he had all night.

Which he did. Ellie couldn't move until he let her go.

And she didn't want to move.

Instead, she endured this soft, sensual torture that made her writhe under his touch. She whimpered and begged him to finish her, or put his cock into her and finish himself. "You said you like making me wet, Struan. I've never been this wet before."

His breathing grew ragged behind her, but he didn't say anything. He just kept teasing her, playing with her, toying with her.

"Why won't you…why are you not…" *penetrating me*, she meant to say and couldn't. He was supposed to value her only for her ability to bear a child. And yet he was refusing to do the one act needed to create one.

"Why not?" Struan hissed next to her ear. "It's simple. Because you want me to."

"But you want it too. You're denying yourself pleasure just to spite me."

"Does that upset you?"

"Yes!" she burst out.

"Good."

"I'll scream."

"Go ahead. You think anyone in this house will charge into my chambers and intervene?"

She did not.

"You belong to me, Elspeth McGregor," he told her, his voice hot with hate. "I can do whatever I want to you."

"You can't."

"I can." He flicked his thumb over her flesh in a very deliberate move.

She came apart all at once. She'd been kept on the edge of it for so long that it was a surprise to fall over into the dark swirl of orgasm.

She felt dirty at how good it was. She moaned into the

softness of the bed. Now he would enter her, and complete the ritual. Wouldn't he? Limp, sweaty, spent, she looked over her shoulder for him. There was no one there.

He'd walked *away*.

Ellie was so shocked by the fact that he'd left her that she didn't move. Not that she could move much anyway.

A few moments later, he returned from the side room, but didn't come back to her. Instead, he casually put his robe back on, sans belt, and walked over to the window to gaze out at...nothing.

"It's dark out," she said, knowing she sounded petulant and needy. "What are you looking at?"

"Why are you still here?" Struan asked. "I thought I made it clear we were finished."

She bit her lip to stop herself from screaming in frustration. She said slowly, "You need to untie me, husband."

"Untie yourself, wife. You could have done so at any point." He spoke to the window, still not looking at her. There was no inflection in his voice, just...boredom? Fatigue?

Furious at his inattention, Elspeth worked her wrists out of the twined-around belt, then reached down to her right ankle, and discovered that the cord had been looped in such a way that by tugging the end, the whole knot simply disappeared.

So easily undone, she noted from a vantage point very far away. *Just like my marriage.*

With both hands available and her right leg now free, she had no trouble loosing the left one either.

The whole time he'd been tantalizing her, torturing her, she only thought she was restrained. Was there something insulting in the way that Struan had tied her so ineffectively? Or was there something humiliating in the way that she'd not even tried to free herself?

She hadn't wanted to escape him. Not when he was making her feel like that.

Elspeth stood uncertainly at the side of the bed. Part of her wanted to storm away from him, and part of her wanted to storm *at* him. Make him notice her, to acknowledge her. He said they were finished, but that couldn't mean…finished. She was still his wife. He was still her husband. They had to come to some understanding, didn't they?

"You haven't left," he said then. "I can't imagine why."

"You've ruined my clothing," she said, the first thing age came to mind, and not at all what she cared about. *You ruined our marriage. You ruined my happiness. You ruined my trust.*

"Anything that enters this room is liable to be ruined," he told her. "I did warn you to leave at the beginning."

"I suppose you'll not buy me a replacement. Averill hinted that it was expensive. "

"Then she overpaid. It's about two pence worth of fabric," he noted harshly. "You can use your pin money to get something new, should you wish to seduce some lover in the future."

"*Me* take a lover?" The suggestion alarmed her more than it should. "Why? Because you'll be busy with your own lovers?"

Struan turned to glare at her. "Oh, aye. I don't know how I'll choose from all the women beating a path to my door. Warped ex-soldiers in remote houses are so sought after."

"You could pay," she suggested, lacing her tone with sickly sweetness. "It's not as if you haven't before."

"You forget. I was the one *being paid*. In retrospect, I should have insisted on cash rather than chattel."

Elspeth inhaled. Struan had never once struck her, even when he was enraged. But those words felt like a slap to the face. As they were clearly meant to. *Chattel.*

She bunched the flimsy, tattered silk of the lingerie and the robe in her hands. "You're a beast. I'm leaving now."

"Thank God. Don't ever step into this room again," he warned her.

"So you shall come to my room in the future, until I'm pregnant and have fulfilled my duty? Seeing as you did nothing to further that goal tonight?"

"Your room is your own. And your imagined duty was already over when you invaded my room tonight. So however you feel about what I did, just remember that *you* came to *me*."

"Go to hell," she spat.

"I've already been there."

"Then go back. And when you get there, I hope it's hot."

In her own room, Elspeth crawled into the bed, pulled the curtains around her and hid under the blankets.

She wanted to be anywhere but here.

This place she'd tried so hard to make into a home, only to discover that she was just another possession of the man who owned the house, like the clock in the hall or the chairs in the dining room.

And what was worse than that was how much she'd wanted to be possessed.

It was bad enough that their final encounter was so…*violent* wasn't the right word. *Cruel* was closer. Or just *unloving*.

Yes, that was it. All the previous times they'd slept together, he'd always been so careful to ensure that she was prepared for whatever came next: he told her what he meant to do, and how it might feel, and asked if she was ready.

This time he hadn't done any of that. He tortured her without the slightest hint that he cared at all how she felt. That the torture was just as careful, and it came in the form of physical pleasure, was somehow the worst part of it. If he'd simply beat her, she could have called him a monster. But how could he be a monster when he made her feel the way she did? And he'd deliberately denied her the one thing they *both* wanted.

Which was upsetting.

But not as upsetting as the realization that she'd still wanted it.

Wanted him.

Struan withholding himself from her was a special kind of cruelty, because she knew that it meant she'd never achieve the dream *she* wanted. To be a mother.

As a child who never had a mother, Elspeth raised the idea of motherhood up to religious heights. She just hadn't fully realized it until Struan had shared how much he wanted children. And then Elspeth had been so excited because at last she could make someone happy just by being herself. By becoming what he needed her to be: the mother of his child.

How pathetic.

Elspeth didn't know what to do next, because she didn't know what *she* wanted, because she didn't know who *she* was.

Well, she knew that she was miserable.

She curled up on her wide, lonely bed, and sobbed.

* * * *

After a naked, furious Elspeth finally stormed out of his room, Struan didn't sleep. He couldn't even sit down.

Why the hell had he done all that? To punish her? He thought so at first, but now he couldn't remember what he thought he was punishing her for, or what he thought it would accomplish.

Other than making him painfully aware of how much he desired her. Even when he was angry. Though again, he couldn't remember why he was angry. She should be angry at him. She should hate him.

Well, she hated him now.

Maybe that was what he'd meant to do. Make her hate him so she'd never love him.

She wouldn't love him after that. He wanted to hurt her by showing her he didn't need her. That he could resist her. That she meant nothing to him.

It was the most painful torture he'd ever experienced, because he did need her and he couldn't resist her and she meant everything to him.

Struan had to flee to another room before he could humiliate himself, before he gave in to temptation and slid his cock into what he knew would be the sweetest, hottest part of her body, because he'd made her that way. Primed for him.

God, he was an idiot. He pretended he was torturing her. But he was torturing himself.

Hiding in the side room, he'd come so fast that he almost screamed. And even after that, he still wanted her. When he returned to the bedroom, his stupid cock was already threatening to stiffen again at the sight of her deliciously ripe figure tied to his bed.

So he'd refused to look and said hateful things until she finally ran from him.

Was that supposed to be a victory?

He moved to the connecting door to Elspeth's room. And heard the muffled sound of her crying.

Yes, he was definitely going to hell.

And he deserved to be there.

Would it be as hot as Elspeth wished it to be for him? Struan didn't have to close his eyes to summon the memory of the day he was burned—the memory was always there, just under his warped and scarred skin.

Chapter 25

A FEW DAYS LATER, ELSPETH received a letter written in Averill's handwriting, which surprised her so much she actually blinked, assuming she would see Mairi's familiar style when she opened her eyes.

No. It really was from Averill. The letter was short and mostly served to contain a formal invitation to a succession of events celebrating Averill's impending engagement. At least, that's what it sounded like. Elspeth wasn't sure, but there was a list of parties on one card, including a masquerade where the happy announcement would finally occur.

It sounded over-the-top, extravagant, and untraditional. In other words, very Averill.

She should go just to see the spectacle.

Mairi had also written, her letter a tiny folded square enclosed with the invitation. It said: *Please come home.*

Elspeth didn't need more encouragement. She would go.

If Struan didn't keep her here.

Keeping watch the rest of the afternoon, Elspeth cornered him as he walked back from the stable.

"There is a matter I must discuss with my husband," she said.

"That means you'll have to discuss it with me," he replied without changing his pace.

It was difficult to keep up, since Struan's legs were so much longer. "Will you not stop and talk?"

"I'm going to my study. You can talk at me there." His jaw was set, and he hadn't looked at her once.

In his study, Elspeth found him just as cold as he'd been outside. He pointed to the chair opposite his desk while he reached for a leather-bound ledger. "You have something to discuss. Discuss it."

She held up the letter she'd been clutching. "I must go home. Apparently Averill is finally engaged. Or is about to be—the invitation isn't terribly clear. I am invited to attend the festivities," Elspeth said, looking out the window at the endless grey moors.

"And you must go?"

"I wish to go."

"Do you?"

She glanced at him. His tone had been flat before, but now there was a faint note of…something. *Did* she wish to go? Elspeth wasn't entirely sure. But with everything so miserable here, and with her and Struan barely speaking to each other, going anywhere seemed preferable to remaining.

She said, "It's important to be there for one's family at a significant event like this. And I need to see Mairi." Surely, if they were together, then they could formulate some sort of plan to at least ensure Mairi's freedom. Elspeth tried not to remember that her own freedom was already gone, and in fact, had disappeared in the very moment she thought she was gaining it. She would not allow Mairi to suffer the same fate.

He frowned. Well, he had been frowning before, and now the frown deepened. "You know what your father was willing to do before. I've already sent—" Here he broke off abruptly. Then he asked, "Why would you think it's safe for you to entrust yourself to his care?"

"I'm not trusting myself to anyone's care. All I'm doing is traveling to the city, attending some events, and then it will be done. You own me now, and my father is a man who will respect another man's property." Elspeth never would have spoken so cruelly to anyone just a few days ago, but now she felt the words coming naturally to her. Perhaps she had always been a cruel person at heart, and it had been restrained only by her upbringing and the constant pressure to behave like a perfect daughter. She saw now where her obedience had got her.

"They didn't treat you well before."

"You're one to talk. And in any case I'm an invited guest. Surely you don't think that they're intending to mistreat all their guests?"

"I wouldn't put it past them. But you won't be staying in the same house, so they won't have as much of an opportunity to misbehave."

"What do you mean I won't be staying in the house? Why wouldn't I stay with my family?"

"Even if they begged you to stay in their finest bedroom, I wouldn't permit it. You will stay at my townhouse."

"I didn't know you had property in Edinburgh." But as soon as she said that, Elspeth realized the foolishness of her assumption. Of course Struan would own a home in town. He had told her before that he frequently had dealings in the city, and both his father and grandfather before him had enjoyed living in Edinburgh. She said, "Even if you do own a house, I'm sure that it would not be worth the cost to open it up and arrange for staff to manage the place for the short time we'll be there—"

"Your arrival will be accommodated with no question."

Elspeth tipped her head to the side, contemplating his phrasing. "You speak as if I'll be going alone."

"I'm being honest, as you so deeply desired me to be.

You don't want me near you, and I have no particular need to go to Edinburgh. It's as if your wish has been granted." He walked to a table, poured a little whisky from a decanter, then took a drink. He still didn't look at her.

And while she couldn't pretend to be surprised by his refusal to go to her family's parties with her, she still experienced a sting. How would it look for Elspeth to return to the city on her own? She had left as a newlywed wife, but would be coming back without any husband at her side. At a series of parties where courtship, engagement, and marriage would be the major topics of conversation.

Elspeth said, "I thought that you wouldn't permit me to leave."

"You're not a prisoner."

She didn't know what to say to that. No, she technically wasn't a prisoner. But she was a wife, subjugated to her husband and the expectation that she would spend most of her life in his presence. Although there were endless women who got married, and then found themselves living essentially alone in their houses, as their husbands continued the same social rounds that they had before, going to clubs and spending time with their own friends and mistresses, only returning to their homes to sleep, to change clothing, or to extract marital duties from their lonely wives.

Elspeth hadn't realized that would be her story as well, but it seemed her future was set.

She said, "If you give me permission, I will travel to the city and stay there until the end of my stepsister's festivities." She did not ask him to join her. It would feel too much like begging.

"I give you permission. Provided you avail yourself of my townhouse, rather than stay with your family."

"Is that an order?" she asked.

"I won't order you to do anything. I trust that you will

consider the wisdom of putting yourself too close to your father when you don't have to."

"Give me the street direction of the townhouse, so I may find it," said Elspeth. She carefully avoided promising she would actually stay there.

Fortunately, Struan seemed to think he'd convinced her. He took a fresh sheet of paper to write the information down.

"When do these events start?" he asked. "I will arrange transportation. You may have to wait a day or two at Wick to catch the next ship."

"Will that ship sail to Edinburgh? Or do you intend to send me off somewhere where I will be less of a bother?"

At last he looked at her, and she wished he hadn't. His eyes glittered like black ice. "That is beneath you, Elspeth."

"But perhaps not beneath you," she retorted. He made no reply to that, so she turned and left the room.

And that was it. No attempts to keep her here, and no expression of interest in joining her. Elspeth wanted to cry. After learning of his betrayal, she hadn't imagined that Struan could still mean so much to her. But he didn't care whether she stayed or went, and that was a blow to her dignity. She told herself that's all it was. It couldn't be a blow to her heart, because she didn't love him anymore.

Everything happened quickly after that. Later that day, she went up to her bedroom to find the maids in a tizzy, and footmen bringing in some empty trunks. Elspeth's original trunk, the one that smelled like codfish, was not among them.

"What's happening?" she asked Agnes.

"Ma'am, I'm to pack your things for your journey to Edinburgh tomorrow morning."

"Tomorrow! Even if I work all afternoon, I'll not have my things ready for a journey tomorrow. I'd hoped to go to visit some of the children from the far school before I left."

"Er, ma'am."

"Yes?"

"*I'm* to pack your things. Me and the other maids."

Oh. Elspeth kept forgetting that she wasn't supposed to do anything for herself. She was meant to act like a lady. She sighed. "I need all the ballgowns and what goes with them, I'm afraid. I'm attending a number of parties."

"Yes, ma'am."

"When I return from the school, I'll go over what's been packed."

"Yes, ma'am." It was clear that Agnes thought Elspeth was being ridiculous, and Elspeth was starting to feel ridiculous.

"I suppose I need a lady's maid to help me when I'm there. Do you…care to come to Edinburgh?"

"Oh, ma'am! Yes!"

"Then pack your things and make any arrangements you need to."

"Yes, indeed, ma'am." Agnes was glowing as she left the room.

When Elspeth was alone again, she walked to the connecting door, lifted her hand to the knob, and found it would not turn. Struan had probably also locked the door to the hallway, simply to keep her out.

Not that she wanted to go in anyway, she told herself. She'd just wanted to know that she could.

Now she knew she could not.

Chapter 26

ELSPETH COULDN'T COMPLAIN ABOUT HER journey back to Edinburgh, because Struan ensured that everything was managed so that she had the finest carriage, the best lodging, and the fastest ship passage home. Alas, unlike the earlier calm and sunny voyage, the high, rough seas this time made her horribly seasick, no matter how beautiful and swift the ship was. She was also perhaps a little feverish. When she got to Edinburgh, on the street of her family's house, for a moment she thought she saw two of the gentlemen who'd attended her wedding. But by the time she really looked, they were gone.

When she arrived at the door of her childhood home, she expected that her family would be surprised. However, she did not expect them to be annoyed.

"What are you doing here?" her father asked, looking at her as if she were a rat slinking in from the street.

"I'm here for Averill's engagement festivities," Elspeth said. "I received an invitation."

"Aye, it had to be sent. For appearances. No one thought you'd come."

"Well, I did."

"We don't have a guest room for you. They're all given to guests."

"What happened to *my* room?" She'd been gone only a few months!

Her father looked blank. Then he said, "Oh, right. Well, you can have that. We wouldn't put guests there." There were bags under his eyes, and while his outfit was made of the finest materials, and clearly well-tailored, the overall effect was that of a man stuffed into something that didn't suit him. His skin was greyish, and he gripped a glass of brandy like a lifeline.

Was he always like that? It had not been terribly long since Elspeth had left this house, so it was all the more surprising to register several differences in the place…or perhaps to recognize some things had always been different from how she'd perceived them.

Her stepmother was also different. Still effortlessly elegant, and still lovely of face and form, even two decades beyond what most people in society considered to be the bloom of a woman's life. But there was a dullness to her complexion that suggested some greater struggle, and downward lines at either side of her mouth that had not been there before—had they? Elspeth always pictured her stepmother as a woman of ultimate leisure and supreme serenity. How could such a woman show any signs of hardship?

"Elspeth, you're looking well," Susan said, getting over her surprise at last.

"Your clothes *are* infinitely better," Averill allowed with a sniff. "Who did you go to? Someone who made all the decisions, for you never showed the slightest genius for dress."

"I suppose not," Elspeth said softly, not answering the rest of the question. She recognized at long last that Averill didn't care about the answer, and the inquiry was made solely for the purpose of appending the insult.

"Your gown is finely made," her stepmother agreed. "But I was referring to your health. You've gained color, and you've filled out a bit. The Highland air must agree with you."

"It's a beautiful country," Elspeth said. "Though not to everyone's taste."

"The Highland food must be to your taste," Averill sneered. "You used to be so slender."

Because she'd worked all day long and scarcely remembered to eat, Elspeth thought, recalling the effort she expended to keep this house at its shining best. Even the maids used to tell her to rest. And when a *chambermaid* thought you worked too much, that was saying something. Struan's firm injunction against her doing most domestic labor had forced her to rest, to live the life other members of her family had been living for years.

"Where is Mairi?" she asked, striving for a new topic.

"At some dreary meeting with her coven," Averill replied with a spiteful smile. "I imagine she'll return for the evening meal. Like you, she never misses a chance to gorge at the trough."

"Averill, idle gossip is a trait of the lower classes," her mother said with a slight frown.

"I state facts, Mama," Averill countered, her smile turning impish. "It's not gossip if it's true, is it?"

"Yes, it is gossip," Elspeth said before her stepmother could reply. "And it is most unkind."

Averill rolled her eyes. "Will you be such a nag the whole time you're here? Should you not be at your husband's townhome this time?"

"He's still in the Highlands," Elspeth admitted. "I came on my own."

"On your *own!*" Susan repeated, incredulous. "Elspeth McGregor, that's no journey for a lady on her own!"

"I was well provided for," she said stiffly. Just incredibly miserable and lonely. "And I have a maid with me. I didn't mean I rode bareback the whole way."

That remark made Susan look as if she were about to faint.

Elspeth took that as her cue to go to her room and unpack. This time she had plenty of luggage—more than she'd ever owned before. The maids managed to pack things Elspeth hadn't even remembered receiving from the seamstress, so who knew how big her wardrobe actually was? There was barely anywhere to put the clothes. Had her room always been this small and…there was no other way to put it…sad?

Though she'd kept it clean and neat as pin, the walls ought to have been painted years ago, the rug on the floor was a castoff put away up here so visitors wouldn't see the holes, and none of the furniture was from the same century. The truth was that this room wasn't good enough for houseguests…but it had been considered good enough for Elspeth.

Why hadn't anyone objected?

No, she thought. Why hadn't *she* objected?

Why was Elspeth so happy for scraps?

* * * *

Later, Elspeth found her father in the luxurious chamber he used as sitting room, office, and bedroom. He was closing the door behind him when she called out his name. He turned, displeasure on his expression. "I must prepare for dinner. This isn't a good time to talk."

"Is it ever a good time?" Elspeth asked.

"We're preparing for your sister's wedding. You ought to have some compassion and understanding."

"Forgive my surprise, Father, but how would I have ever dreamed you would spend so much effort on one daughter when you simply handed me off to a stranger in lieu of payment?"

His eyes flickered as he took in her words. "He agreed you should not be told."

That was it. No sympathy, or expression of regret. Nor even the grace to look ashamed at being discovered. Just annoyance at the other man for breaking an understanding. Elspeth's feelings did not enter into it at all. "He didn't tell me. I found out through other means. And indeed, that's not important at the moment. What I want from you is an explanation."

"Explanation of what?"

"For why you did it!"

"I should think that would be obvious. I had some faint hope that the bastard would die in the war, for then everything might have been much easier. But he did come back, and he was most insistent on executing the terms of the loan. Had the gall to tell me I ought to have known what was coming, since I had extra years to gather the funds. As if it's so easy to find money lying about!"

"You can hardly resent a man who asks you to fulfill the bargain you yourself agreed to," Elspeth said. "But my question is why you decided that I was an acceptable substitute for cash?"

"An even more obvious answer than the first, you silly girl. Disfigured as he is, the man would've had the devil's own time pursuing a wife on the marriage mart. Yes, he's wealthy as sin, but hideous. I only mentioned marriage in passing, because he asked why I was spending so much money. But I could tell even then that it was something the man feared. And one that he would be most willing to manage via other means. It was all in all a most modern and painless exchange."

"Painless? It took me away from the only family I know! Do you forget that I was not even permitted to meet him before the day?"

"Be reasonable, Elspeth. If you had seen him, would you have gone through with the wedding? Of course not." He answered his own question with the only reply he could understand. "I saw an advantageous business transaction, and I took it. That's what a practical man does."

"You speak as though it was not a *person* involved in your so-called transaction. How could you treat me so callously?"

"Callously? It is an odd complaint you make, when I have secured for you a comfortable life with an income that will support you until your last days."

"With a man that you yourself consider hideous."

He shrugged. "What did you think you were entitled to? Are you some princess in a fairy tale, and it is my role to find you the most handsome prince?"

"That's what you're doing for Averill."

"That's different."

"How?"

"You weary me, Elspeth." He stalked toward his bedchamber.

She said, "All I wish to know is why you offered me up in marriage. Why not Mairi? Or Averill?"

"Mairi is always spouting off about the rights of women and other distasteful subjects. Any man unlucky enough to end up with her will likely need to exercise some strenuous physical discipline to bring her to heel. And as for Averill, it would be absurd to even consider that I would do anything to upset Susan's hopes for her."

"But *I* am your daughter. Or have you forgotten my mother so completely?"

He whirled around, his eyes blazing as he advanced upon her. "Don't ever speak of your mother to me! She was a jewel among women, and if not for you, she would still be alive today!" Then he struck her across the cheek, hard.

Elspeth stumbled back, away from his wrath. Her cheek stung worse than the burning from the fire.

Yes, she had always known that the death of her mother in childbirth had been a profound tragedy in their household. And she always feared that on some level it was the reason why her father treated her in a more distant and condescending manner. She had always hoped that, by being the perfect daughter, she would prove to him that his first wife's death had not been in vain, for her ideals would live on in the form of Elspeth, who rarely took an action or said a word without first asking herself if it was something that her mother would endorse. But to hear him say so baldly that he blamed her for her mother's death was like ripping open a wound she had thought long scarred over.

* * * *

Mairi came home just before dinner, and at least she was legitimately overjoyed to see her sister. But it wasn't until late at night that Elspeth and Mairi could speak in private, both of them sequestered in Elspeth's bedroom, the door closed with a chair slid in front of it to prevent surprise arrivals. After Mairi applied a cool cloth to Elspeth's stinging cheek, the two young women sat together on the bed in the corner of the room opposite the door, their heads close together.

Mairi said, "It's been horrific living here since I discovered the truth. Of course, I never said anything to him directly, but I fear he's got some inkling that I know. But in all honesty, both Father and Susan are so bound up in the preparations for all the festivities that they have ignored everything else, including me. But that won't persist beyond the wedding breakfast."

"Oh, she's getting a wedding breakfast?" Elspeth asked, her stomach turning at the idea.

"She's getting *everything*. But I suspect Father's creditors will visit the next morning. Or evening. For his lenders seem like the type who rely on the cover of darkness."

Elspeth couldn't help but wonder what time of day it had been when her father traded her to Struan. If she were still speaking to Struan, she might ask him. Then she let out a short laugh, contemplating the absurdity of inquiring of her husband exactly when he had purchased her.

Mairi gave her a strange look, and Elspeth waved her bout of levity off. "I agree we cannot trust to Father's better angels. Have you decided on any course of action?"

"Well, the League is composed of women who are sympathetic to my situation. They had the usual suggestions of finding a position as a governess, or a schoolmistress somewhere. Scotland is fortunate to have a great proliferation of schools now. However, the fact remains that I'm legally in Father's care while I'm unmarried, so he could force me to either marry some man I've not met, or ship me off as an indentured servant—whether formally or no—to a location I would have no say in. My only sure escape is to flee the country, or disappear from public knowledge."

Elspeth said, "Linneliath is such a vast house that I honestly believe I could tuck you away in an upper floor, and no one would even know you were there."

Mairi shook her head with a sad smile. "Your husband's home is no better than this house, if he is of the same mind as our father, and believes that women are chattel. I must say, I thought—I'd hoped—he was better than that. He seemed better than that when I spoke to him at the wedding."

Elspeth was bitter as she spoke. "Oh, Mairi, how I wish I had listened to you these past few years, when you were attending your meetings and trying to get me to come along with you. I trusted that if I acted the part of the perfect lady, I would somehow be rewarded with a lady's perfect life. You saw what I didn't."

"It's a hard truth to learn. And I wasn't the most welcome of messengers. I was so confident in the obviousness of what my society was sharing that I never took the time to view the news from the perspective of anyone else."

"Perhaps the ladies of your society should start a fund," Elspeth suggested, "to provide aid for those women who must strike out on their own, without the blessing of their fathers, or husbands, or brothers." She spoke in jest, but part of her wished there was some alternative other than capitulation.

Now, Mairi laughed. "Perhaps you could ask your husband to donate. He's wealthy enough."

"I doubt he would be sympathetic to the cause. I could sell my jewels to become an initial funder—not Mama's pearls, though, of course. Jewels do belong to a woman outright, if they have been given as a gift. I brought some jewels with me, you know, because of all the parties and things. They're surely worth a great deal."

"And what would happen to you when your husband learned of it? While you may theoretically have the right to sell them, it would be foolish to think there would be no punishment for doing so. And I fear that selling jewelry in haste leads to a poor return." Mairi got a guilty look on her face. "I attempted to sell a few pieces of my own jewelry already. The offers I got, even from reputable businesses in the city, were shockingly low. Perhaps one fifth of what one would expect the price to be as a buyer of the same jewels. Other offers were closer to a tenth. We can't buy our way out of this predicament."

"I'm not giving up. It's too late for me, but not too late for you. Speak again to the ladies of your society. One of them may have some fantastic idea that will prove the perfect solution."

"I may as well wish upon a star to meet the perfect man at my stepsister's celebrations," Mairi grumbled.

"It could happen," Elspeth said, feeling hope, that intimate enemy, rise in her chest. "It's an era of enlightenment, is it not?"

"My darling Elspeth, I envy your gentle heart. How is it that you can be treated so shabbily, and yet maintain your cheerful air?"

"Practice. Isn't that exactly what I have done my whole life?"

Mairi laughed, then said, "Well, show me all your new things. I see we're surrounded by fripperies."

Elspeth showed her everything. Day gowns, evening wear. Sumptuous ballgowns in fabrics too priceless to touch. (She touched them anyway.) A stunning blue satin empire gown with jet beads. A pink velvet gown with a flour-sack train that trailed eight feet behind her. A ballgown rendered in golden silk, somehow holding all the light of a sunset within it.

"These are…" Mairi whispered, shocked into speechlessness.

"Wasteful? Symbols of woman as mere object?"

"Art." Mairi's tone was reverent. "You didn't say you have the wardrobe of a Persian empress."

"I didn't know! I've never seen half of these before. Struan did tell me he paid for a whole new wardrobe for me but…"

"These must have arrived later than the first items, and you never had a chance to wear them up there. And everything just got sent down here together. Pest, you will be the best dressed woman in the isles."

"I don't want that."

"Well, you have it anyway. Best make use of it while you can. Averill is holding half a dozen events. Outshining her at every single one will be amusing, if nothing else."

"She'll be enraged," Ellie noted. Then she smiled. "Perhaps it will build character. After all, if she were in *London*, there must be a risk of running into a better dressed lady."

"Ah, London!" Mairi trilled. "If only she could go back there…forever."

"She'll be married to Mr Farquhar soon enough. She'll be out of your life within weeks."

"I count the breaths," Mairi muttered. "Well, let's plan your outfit for the first party. What gown will make Averill the angriest?"

Chapter 27

IT HAD BEEN NEARLY A fortnight since Elspeth had left the Highlands.

Struan had come to the city because Linneliath was unlivable without Elspeth there. It made no sense. She hadn't lived there long in the first place, and it was *his* family's ancestral home, but somehow she had made it into her home in the blink of an eye. And he didn't know what he was going to do if he had to keep walking those halls and going into rooms that she was never in.

So he came to Edinburgh. Not because Elspeth was in the city, but because he simply wanted to, damn it. And of course, he'd discovered instantly that she ignored his advice to stay in his townhouse. Damn it again. Fortunately, the other men were still in town as well.

Thane, Calan, and Duncan all had homes in the city. Kai was staying in his family's house in apparent contentment. Struan wondered if it was Kai's way of recapturing his own childhood, and finding a return to a more innocent way of life after experiencing years of war. He'd been extremely young at the beginning. It was one of the reasons the other men had decided they ought to look out for him. Though Kai turned out to be a remarkably mature and capable person, there was still an air of boyishness about him. No wonder his mother kept cooking all his favorite meals and baking special treats. It was a celebration every day, because Kai was still alive.

Struan couldn't object, partly because he was now eating a blackberry tart baked by said mother. The men—Kai, Struan, Thane, Calan, and Duncan—sat in the dim but incredibly comfortable parlor of the house. Struan liked how dark the room was. It made it easier to pretend that the other men couldn't see the shame on his face.

"It's time to talk," Calan said. "I got your letter from a few weeks ago, and both Duncan and I have been watching the McGregor house to see that the other sister is all right. Which she seems to be, by the way."

Struan nodded. In fact, the same day Ellie had ripped out his soul by revealing the truth Mairi had somehow learned and wrote down in her letter, he'd sent a request to Calan by the fastest method he could think of. The request was simple: *Will two of you watch over Mairi McGregor. Will explain later.* He knew they'd follow the instructions without question.

"Look, before I can explain what's going on, I need to tell you the truth about how I acquired Elspeth."

"Acquired?" Kai asked.

"Let him speak," said Calan.

Struan told them, in fits and starts. It didn't take long according to the minute hand on the clock. But it felt like hours before he got to the end of the brief account.

"You don't look surprised," Kai told Calan.

"I was given a head start on the news of Struan's wedding," Calan said. "He tried not to tell me how it all happened, but I am, as you know, sometimes insistent on getting to the truth of a thing."

"Did you hurt him?" Thane asked, alarmed.

"No! Jesus." Calan sighed.

"I had to talk to someone," Struan said. "Calan was handy. And he did help me with preparing for the wedding. He really didn't tell you anything?"

Duncan shook his head. "Calan keeps his mouth shut. But we all knew there was something strange about your marriage. I wasn't able to uncover anything specific."

"Uncover? You were *looking*?"

"Of course I was looking. You went from confirmed bachelor one day to bridegroom the next, with no courtship in between. We'd never heard of your new wife or her family, and you absconded from the city the same day as the wedding."

"I didn't abscond. I just left."

"No, he's right," Kai said. "You definitely absconded."

"Fine. I…I wanted to get home."

"With your pretty new wife," Thane added.

"Who has since left me," Struan reminded them. "And so I'm back to where I started. Figuratively. And literally."

"And now you need help to get her back."

"I just want to talk with her."

"Hhhm," Calan murmured.

"So she believes that her selection is solely due to the unpaid loan?" Kai asked. "You didn't tell her anything else?"

"For example," Calan suggested, "you didn't tell her you care about her."

"Of course I care about her."

"But did you *tell* her so?"

"I tried." Struan put the remainder of the tart down. It tasted sour now. "I'm not good at that sort of thing." Though apparently he was good at doing terrible, torturous things to Elspeth and then sending her away. That was probably not the best way to convey how much he cared about her.

"And she's also in Edinburgh now," Duncan said. "We were watching the house when she arrived, and that surprised the hell out of me. Good thing you included a letter to be carried on the same ship she sailed on."

"A brief letter," Calan added. "Not much better than the first scribbled order."

"I'll give you the details now." He told them the rough outline of what had happened when Ellie announced she was returning to the city, though he did it with a minimum of emotion. He did not, for example, say how her departure and the way she'd looked at him left his stomach in knots and his chest heaving. He did not say that he nearly ran after the carriage as it left so that he could stop her from leaving him. He did not say how he'd gone into Elspeth's bedroom and lay face down on her bed just to inhale the scent of the sheets.

He didn't say any of those things; he didn't have to. These were perceptive people and had gleaned secrets from men who were better actors than Struan.

"The main thing is to get Struan in there, so he can talk to her," Kai said at last.

"Listen," said Calan. "Women are always willing to talk, eventually. So write her a letter, let her know you're here. You just need to be patient and keep asking her if she's ready to talk."

"But they didn't have an ordinary fight," Kai pointed out. "This isn't a tiff over what china pattern they've decided to buy. This is a revelation about the truth of how she ended up at this place."

Struan nodded, thinking that Kai had the better insight into Elspeth's frame of mind, even though Calan was usually more in tune with the mysteries of women's thoughts. "I handled the whole matter in the worst possible way. But I really believed that if I had simply told her the bare truth, she would have been just as hurt."

Calan took a bite of his tart, chewed slowly, then said, "There was probably a way to tell her the truth without hurting her feelings, but I agree that it doesn't matter now. The fact is that she did learn the truth, and she learned it from someone other than you, so she believes that you can't be trusted."

Struan said, "If she won't trust me to tell the truth, how can I expect her to want to talk about the truth?"

"Women have been known to change their minds on occasion." Calan smiled with a confidence that Struan envied.

"So what do we do about it?" Kai asked. "On a practical level, I mean."

Calan said, "We need to make it possible that our man can have a quiet chat with his woman. Struan, you said that Elspeth is in town on the occasion of her sister's engagement…festivities, whatever that means. I assume there will be events, and there will be people coming to those events. So prepare yourself to be a guest."

Struan said, "There's only one small problem with that plan. I'm not invited to anything."

"Who cares? You're the husband of the sister of the family who's planning it all. The other guests won't question it, and the family would never make a fuss in public. We know what McGregor is now. He's a desperate social climber. He wants more than anything to have the respect of those in the city who are above him. He would rather die than embarrass himself, and I'm sure that includes not being humiliated at a party."

It was logical to assume that McGregor wouldn't make a scene if Struan showed up at his house. He knew too well that Struan could reveal the unsavory truth that he had been willing to trade a daughter to end a debt. The baldness of McGregor's avarice would scandalize the very people he wished to become his peers.

"I'll find out when the next gathering connected to this engagement will be," Struan offered.

"It seems odd," Kai said suddenly, "that McGregor is spending so much time and money on *this* daughter's engagement when he clearly didn't care about the other one. Why do you think that is?"

"Who knows?" Struan replied. "He thinks of no one but himself, as far as I can tell. Averill is actually his stepdaughter, so perhaps it's his wife who's propelling all of the nonsense surrounding the engagement."

Calan stood up. "Well, I've got somewhere to be. Let me know the moment we learn something new. I think it would be best if I also attended the first event. Moral support, and all that."

Kai shook his head. "You just want to go because you know there will be unmarried ladies there."

"How dare you suggest such a thing?" Calan looked wounded. "I'm going for the married ones."

* * * *

Reconnaissance revealed that Averill McGregor was planning not just a single party, but a sort of campaign of attrition upon all of Edinburgh's polite society. She was holding a string of events over the course of a few weeks, all intended to raise her profile and then crown her as the most desirable debutante in the country, only to be immediately taken off the marriage mart with a well-timed proposal at the final party. The fact that everyone knew the proposal was imminent did not seem to detract from the suspense.

"They say Mr Farquhar is totally enchanted by her. He would have proposed months ago, but she insisted that it be done this way. Poor man, he'll have to take her in hand once she's his wife," one observer noted at the club where Struan had been inquiring.

The consensus seemed to be that Averill McGregor was

beautiful but ruthless, qualities that the ton admired. She was providing a spectacle, and society loved nothing more.

Once Struan and the men understood that, it became clear just why McGregor borrowed so much. It was expensive to launch a young lady into society the usual way. This would be ten times as much.

On the night of the first party they were aware of (though not the first party in Averill's onslaught), Struan prepared for battle. He dressed in standard kit for evening, as did Calan. They had decided collectively that the others needn't show their faces yet.

Getting into the event was surprisingly easy—he told them he was Elspeth's husband. Calan just smiled, the bastard. He got in wherever he liked.

The party was a success by any standard, and Struan hated it from the moment he stepped inside. All he wanted to do was see Ellie, but it was difficult with so many damned people around.

And then he did see her.

She was dazzling. She wore blue satin that looked like the night sky. But although she was the most beautiful woman there, her smile was stiff and she looked uncomfortable. She was also wearing her hair in an odd style, with a curtain of blonde waves swept over one side of her face, covering most of her left eye and cheek.

Her stormcloud sister, Mairi, was close by. Mairi wore her hair the same way, so perhaps it was a new trend. However, he couldn't help but notice that she was like a guard dog keeping any gentlemen from getting too friendly with Ellie, and Struan blessed her for it.

"Are you going to talk to her?" Calan asked quietly.

"With Mairi ready to bite my legs if I get too close?"

"She does resemble some of the irregulars we had to fight down on the Peninsula. Not the paid mercenaries, you know.

I mean the ones who fought to see the blood."

"Let's hope it doesn't come to that," Struan muttered. "I don't think I'll be able to talk to Ellie tonight."

"I can distract Mairi."

"No, I mean that I don't think I can do it. She hates me."

"You can at least tell her how you feel."

Struan watched Ellie from a distance. "Not in front of all of these people. I need a minute."

"You need to talk to your wife."

Then Struan saw McGregor. "Now *him* I have a burning desire to speak to."

Calan sighed. "Go after him if you're afraid to go after his daughter."

"It's important." Struan glared at him.

"I'm sure. But you can't avoid your wife forever."

Struan left the room and followed his quarry. McGregor managed to get to the small room at the end of the hall and inside, but Struan prevented him from slamming the door shut by dint of his massive frame, and the fact that he simply pushed the door all the way open, in the process dislodging McGregor and forcing him a few steps backward.

"What do you think you're doing here?" McGregor demanded. "We've no more business and you can't collect any more from me."

"I could re-collect the original payment," Struan said. "After all, she's here in this house."

McGregor shook his head. "We didn't think that she would come back for the festivities. It was a formality to invite her."

"You didn't intend to invite your own daughter to her sister's engagement and wedding? That seems most unfamilial."

"What would you know about it?"

"I know nothing about it, and I care even less. I'm here

for Elspeth."

"And if she doesn't go back with you? What then? You can't threaten me, sir. If you reveal the details of our little arrangement to the public, it won't merely damage me. It will damage your own reputation as well. There aren't many in the city who would look kindly on a man who accepted a person in lieu of payment for a debt."

"No more than they would look kindly on one who would *offer* a person in lieu of payment," Struan pointed out in a low voice. "However, you have made an error in your logic."

"And what is that?" McGregor asked.

"You're assuming that I give one ounce of shit what other people think. Do you imagine that I care what a society matron, or some gentleman in New Town thinks of my actions? I don't live in Edinburgh. I live in the Highlands. I live as a veritable hermit. So any rumors or scandals that could possibly arise are absolutely meaningless to me. I've already got what I want from my time in the city. I've got a wife, and there is no legal recourse anyone can take which will ever change that fact."

McGregor's jaw worked, but nothing came out.

Struan went on, "However, you're the man who spent a daughter's worth of money in a vain effort to climb the social ladder. You're spending even more now for this other daughter's wedding and dowry. And since you're not borrowing from me, I wonder who you are borrowing from… and if they'll be as understanding and flexible as I was."

Finally the other man blustered, "Perhaps you will regret accepting that first payment. Because Elspeth is back at home now, and I have a mind to keep her here! No one will wonder at it after they get a glimpse of you. I'll explain that she is fleeing her monster of a husband, and that she's all too happy to resume her old duties as a daughter of this house. In truth, the place hasn't been run so well since she's left. I didn't really understand her role before. Servants are only as good as the overseer. Without a firm hand and a sharp eye, they grow lazy. So I think that it is best for me if Elspeth remains here. You shall not have her back."

"There is no force on earth that will keep me from Elspeth," Struan said, the words bursting out of him louder than he intended. "You sold her off. Now she belongs to me. And if you do anything to prevent me from taking her back, you will regret it."

Chapter 28

YOU SOLD HER OFF. NOW she belongs to me. And if you do any-thing to prevent me from taking her back, you will regret it.

Elspeth pressed herself against the wall in the darkened hallway, and prayed that no one could hear her heart hammering in her rib cage, or her too-short breaths.

It was eagle-eyed Mairi who'd seen Struan in the ballroom first. She'd alerted Ellie in a low voice, but by the time Ellie really believed that he was here, in Edinburgh, at her family's party, he'd suddenly left the room. It had taken a little while to escape the room and follow him, but at last, Ellie had heard his voice down a hallway. The sisters advanced as much as they dared, and then hid in the next room, listening hard.

She didn't know what they were discussing until the last moment when Struan raised his voice and declared her his lost property. She couldn't hear her father's response, if he made one. All she knew was that Struan would not see reason. He obviously rethought the choice to allow her to return home, and was now intent on dragging her back.

They held perfectly still as they heard the door slam shut and heavy footfalls moved down the hallway. Struan was leaving.

She turned to Mairi, whispering, "Did you hear that?"

Mairi nodded. "It was hard not to. That is a man who could be heard across the city."

"What am I to do?" asked Elspeth. "I don't want to go back to his house, but I have no choice. I was so naïve! I wanted so badly to believe. I wanted it so much that I ignored better sense, which would have told me that such a thing only happens in fairy tales."

"I read all your letters to me. You thought you *were* in a fairy tale," Mairi pointed out. "You praised him to the skies."

"Yes, but that was before I knew the truth. When I was still trying to be an ideal wife, imagining that I had an ideal husband."

"Well, to be fair, it sounds as though he was ideal in many ways. You wrote that he was kind and attentive, and treated you well and even indulged you with gifts and other kindnesses, which you have certainly not had an excess of in your life."

"You're taking his side?" Elspeth asked, aghast.

"I am merely repeating what you wrote. You sounded very much in love."

"That was because I didn't know he'd essentially purchased me as if I were a side of beef at a market."

"Oh, you're so tender you would surely be veal."

Elspeth smiled despite herself. "You know what I mean. He kept me ignorant because it made me more biddable."

"You were always biddable," Mairi said. "You prided yourself on how you leapt to obey virtually any order or even request."

"I am as God made me," said Elspeth.

"No, you are as *you* made you. Over the course of a lifetime and with Father's reinforcement, yes. Even when you were little, you always looked so happy to be told what to do. I would sit and scream, and have tantrums and say no, no, no. But you, my sweet sister, simply stood up and said yes, yes, yes. It's really no wonder why our father offered you as the bride. You're the one who would never object. But as it happens, maybe this was an inadvertent favor on Father's part. The man you describe in your letters, and even who you talked about once you got here again, seems to be a rare example of a man who thinks he's not above a woman."

"He thinks he's above me if he claims he can pick me up and drag me back to his home."

"Would it be more pleasant if he knelt at your feet and asked nicely? Yes. But he's correct in that both the law and the rules of our society will uphold him in every instance. And he came here, Pest. He followed *you*."

Elspeth sighed in frustration. "We must find some way to escape, both of us."

Mairi gave her a sad smile. "We'll think of something. Stay here a moment, will you? I want to have a few words with Father. You can slip down the hallway once you hear the yelling."

Ellie waited until she heard Mairi address their father in an imperious voice, then pull the door closed.

She took a deep breath, counted to ten, then stepped out of the side room…only to run directly into Struan.

"What the…" he muttered.

He'd taken hold of her shoulders by instinct, but Ellie knew the second he realized it was her.

He tightened his grip as he glared down at her. "What are you doing here?"

"This is my family's house. What are *you* doing here?"

"I had a few more things to say to your father."

"You'll have to wait for Mairi to finish now. Besides, it sounded like you said enough before."

"You were listening?"

"You weren't exactly discreet as you were demanding your property back."

His lips twisted. "Never mind what I told him. We need to talk."

Ellie tried to shrug him off. It was impossible. He was already directing her back into the darkened side room, kicking the door shut with his foot after he moved in.

"I don't want to talk to you!" Elspeth insisted.

"Too bad."

"We have nothing to talk about. You made yourself clear the last time we spoke. You don't care about me in the least, and you never want to see me again. And yet, you followed me. Why?"

"You know why."

Part of her—most of her—prayed that this would be an apology. An abject recusal of everything he'd done before. A begging for forgiveness.

She should have known better. The man standing in front of her now knew exactly what he'd done. But not a flicker of remorse showed in his face. He was simply retrieving his stray.

"You told me I could come back home," she whispered. "You told me to go."

"Aye, I did." He looked her over, and seemed to take in her appearance for the first time. He moved one hand to toy with the sapphire necklace she wore.

"It was in the jewel case in my trunks that got packed," she said, as if he were about to accuse her of stealing it. "I didn't know about the case till I arrived here. They belong to you, I assume. Your family…"

"I didn't come here for the stones," he said shortly.

"Then what?"

But he was still tracing the line of the necklace…until his fingers dropped a few inches lower to the edge of her bodice. "This is one of the new dresses you ordered."

"And you paid for. Does it meet with your approval?"

"In part." His gaze drifted down to her décolletage, and Elspeth felt the heat in it. Her body responded instantly.

"What's wrong with it?"

"It's covering what I want to see." He cupped her breast, his hand burning through the fabric, his thumb finding her suddenly hard and aching nipple and circling once.

Elspeth's reaction was embarrassingly needy, a moan ripping up her throat as she arched her back to press into him. Why did his touch feel so perfect? She hated him, but she wanted this touch, this intimacy that no one else could offer.

"You like that, wife? Or are you just playing a part?"

"Not playing… Oh, God, when you touch me," she gasped out as he continued to tease her breasts.

"What do you want? Say it."

She closed her eyes, hating her weakness, her desire for him.

"Say it, Ellie," he told her, his breath on her ear, his voice deceptively soft, even gentle. "You want me. Say it."

"I have not forgiven you. This is only…fucking," she gasped out between desperate breaths as he pleasured her relentlessly, his mouth hot over her exposed skin.

"Then fuck me," he told her, yanking her skirts up to get access to her throbbing core. He cupped the triangle of curls between her legs.

Elspeth's heart pounded in anticipation.

"Do you want to be fucked, Ellie?" he asked.

"Yes!" she hissed. "Yes, I want you to fuck me. I need to feel you." She needed to hear him call her that sweet name again, the one he'd decided to use for her.

He exhaled, and she realized how tense he was, how ready to snap. *He wants me too*, she thought.

Struan moved his hand slightly, slipping a long finger between her legs, stroking with maddening slowness.

Ellie practically cried out at his touch. She was so

aroused that it was almost painful as the tip of one finger slid over the nub at her core.

"Fuck, you're dripping," he said, the words coming out as a growl.

"I…am." She could confess that. It was undeniable. "Don't make it be for nothing."

He'd been working at his own clothing until he could free his cock. He pushed toward her, not entering her, just pressing his length between her legs, sliding along that slick fold, teasing her with all that hardness.

She bucked her hips, trying to capture him somehow. As if she could ever make the giant pinning her down do anything other than what he wanted. "Struan, please. No more torture."

"Is that what it is when I don't fuck you? Torture?"

"It's torture either way, so we may as well do what we both want."

With a low sound, he shifted so he could slide into her, filling her so that she nearly cried out as the pleasure burst through her. And then he braced her against the wall and took her.

It wasn't elegant or measured. It was pure carnality. And it was exactly what her body craved.

She reached her peak so fast she wasn't ready, and almost cried out.

Struan covered her mouth with his to keep her quiet, his kiss rough and hot, without a trace of tenderness.

He finished a second later, his whole body hard against her own. She was pressed between him and the wall, and it wasn't comforting or comfortable, and she didn't care. She'd needed that release so badly.

"Fuck, Ellie, you feel so good," he said then, his voice raw, his breath fast and his heart thudding so she could feel it when they were pressed so close together.

He took a deep breath, then seemed to come to his senses. He withdrew, then set her down on the floor again. She could stand, barely. Her dress was in complete disarray, and she could only imagine the state of her hair.

Struan put his hands on her head, her face, as if unable to stop touching her. When his fingers grazed her bruised cheek under her hair, she winced.

He saw her reaction, frowned. Suddenly, he swept her hair away from her face before she could stop him.

He went still when he saw what her hair had been hiding. "Did I…just now?" he asked, confused, alarmed. Then he registered that the wound was older, already healing. His eyes narrowed. "Who."

"I got into an argument with my father," she explained hastily. "I goaded him. He's never struck me before."

"He never will again." Those words were practically bitten off.

"I won't give him a reason again."

"No. He won't do it again because I'll fucking kill him if he does. And I'm telling him that now." He looked to the door.

"Because I'm yours?"

"Yes, you're mine. And he's an ass. Go to your room and pack some things. You're leaving this house with me."

"No."

He turned back to her. "What?"

"I can't go with you. I don't want to."

"Ellie, he hurt you."

"So did you."

That hit its target. She saw the fire go out of his eyes, even as he said, "I could make you go."

"Then make me. If you want to bring your lost property back to your house, if that's why you're telling me to be obedient and follow you like a whipped dog, *make* me."

She was shaking as she spoke, sure she'd gone much too far. Would he just pick her up and stalk out of the house with his prize, like some ancient Viking warrior? Defiant was the last thing she wanted to be, but the only thing she could be now.

Struan just stood there for a moment, maybe also stunned by her refusal, maybe just unsure of who to be angry at first.

Then he turned away. "I'm hunting down McGregor. If you insist on staying in this hellhole, at least freshen up before you set foot outside the room. We wouldn't want people to think we were up to anything." That last past was said with a sneer.

And then he left.

Ellie almost called him back, but bit her tongue. She'd reached the limit of her newfound courage. If he returned and once again told her to follow him, she undoubtably would. Lord, she'd just offered him her body because she couldn't endure a few weeks without him. How could she pretend she didn't still have feelings for him?

Chapter 29

THE MCGREGOR HOUSE WAS QUIET the morning after the party. Elspeth woke early, mostly because her mind was in turmoil the whole night. But though she lay in bed till nearly nine, she was still the only person partaking of the breakfast on the sideboard at ten. That was when a footman entered the room.

"Apologies for interrupting, ma'am, but there's a message for you." His tone clearly said that *no* message ought to be delivered before noon.

"Oh? Where is it?"

"It's not written down," he explained. "If you will come downstairs, ma'am. The messenger is waiting…"

"Yes, of course."

She couldn't fathom why they hadn't simply written a note. In the hallway next to the kitchen, a towering man stood stiffly to one side. He looked more like a prizefighter than a footman.

"That's him, ma'am," her own footman muttered. "Said he'd speak only to you."

She sighed and greeted the visitor. "I'm Elspeth McGregor. You have a message for me?"

The messenger looked nonplussed. "Um…"

Oh, dear. Had the footman roused the wrong daughter of the house? That would be embarrassing all round. "You do have a message for me, do you not? Are you in the right house? Who is your employer?"

"I work for Mr MacInnes, ma'am."

"Ah." Well, that explained the complete lack of respect for the unwritten rules of social discourse.

"The message is for Mrs MacInnes," he went on.

"I'm afraid that's me after all."

He stood up straighter as he delivered his message. "I have instructions to convey you to Mr MacInnes's town-home, along with whatever luggage you may care to bring with you, the rest to be sent for afterward."

"Excuse me?"

The footman glanced at her, uncertain. "He said you would understand that it is for the best."

"Ah," she said again. No wonder Struan had sent this hulk to collect her. He'd probably been told to grab her and haul her away bodily if she made a fuss.

"Your message is clearly stated," she said, smiling at the man. "If you will kindly wait while I just go put a few things in my bag and give a message to my maid."

The footman nodded, apparently relieved, and she turned to go back upstairs, with no intention of coming back down.

She was seething. Struan was acting like a cad. Yes, perhaps she'd succumbed to a bit of physical weakness last night. But she'd already told him that it didn't mean anything, and she certainly wasn't going to leave her home for his. A few moments of wildly passionate, mind-melting intercourse was no solution to their actual problem, which was that their marriage was a sham and a shambles, and she would not continue the charade.

Instead, she would write some instructions of her own, and the hulking footman could carry *that* back to his lord and master.

"Miss Elspeth!" Agnes said, hurrying up to meet her. "Is

something going on?"

"I'm just writing a note to my husband. Come, you can take it downstairs once I finish. I'm barricading myself in my room once I'm done, lest that footman try to drag me out with him."

Agnes looked like she was about to faint at the very idea.

In the small chamber that her father used as an office, she sat at the desk, which was covered in half-done letters and half-paid bills. What a mess. She found an unused sheet of greenish paper and dipped the nearest pen into the inkwell. She had better stationery in her own room two floors up, but she was damned if she'd walk up and down that many more flights just to waste it on him. After scrawling her incredibly short note, she folded it and walked over to the table where they kept all the supplies for the post.

She jumped when a dark shape streaked over her slipper. "What was that?"

Agnes also gave a yelp, and spun about as she tried to stomp on the creature. "A mouse! Ugh!" She utterly failed to vanquish the rodent, but she did manage to catch her sleeve on the edge of the desk, sending items to the floor in a clatter. "Oh, no!"

"We *never* had mice before," Elspeth said, bending to pick up some items. "What is this house coming to?"

The maid hastily gathered all the scattered papers. She handed the green one on the top to Ellie. "Here you are, ma'am."

"Thank you." Ellie quickly folded it into a smaller square, addressed it to Struan's townhome, and dropped wax onto it. "Where's that seal?" she asked, looking around. A brass seal always sat on the tabletop near the wax.

"Oh, I heard it clatter, ma'am. Let me look." The maid got onto her knees, peering under the furniture. "Where did it go?" She shook the curtains, and continued to shuffle around the floor.

"Never mind," said Ellie. "The wax is already dry. Just take this downstairs to the waiting footman. Tell him it's the only thing he'll be escorting from this house."

"Yes, ma'am." Agnes got to her feet, shook off dust, and took the sealed letter, tucking it into a pocket in her apron.

Ellie remained in the room, looking over the disarray. There were half-completed letters and notes everywhere. How did her father accomplish anything when he couldn't even keep his papers organized? No wonder he was terrible with money.

Automatically working to tidy it all, she saw another piece of identical green stationery lying askew on the blotter. She put it at right angles, as she remembered it being before, and then put a small pink scrap on top, as it had been before. She read the words on the scrap before she even realized what she was doing: it was the street direction for some gentleman she'd never heard of. Mr Lister. Was *he* a creditor too? She looked away before she could see anything else. It would never do for her father to know that she'd been using his things. He'd accuse her of snooping. She picked up the last few items that had gotten swept off the desk in the wake of the mouse sighting and slipped out of the room before she was noticed.

And not a moment too soon. Her father was tromping down the stairs, calling for a footman to attend him. "I've errands to be run. Where is *any*body in this house?"

In her own room, she flung herself on her bed, deeply annoyed at Struan. So she had a moment of weakness last night. It wasn't as if she'd reversed her opinion on everything that had happened and now she was going to sink into his thrall again. Why would she, especially since he had suddenly become so demanding, ordering her to *his* townhouse. A house she'd never even set foot into!

She almost heard Mairi's voice in her head: *He's doing it because he can. He can do whatever he wants. He's the man. You're just the wife. The ornament. The bearer of his future children.*

Ellie closed her eyes, putting a hand to her forehead. Lord, what if that moment last night was what made her fall pregnant at last? How ironic. Just when she'd declared herself done with him. He'd be insufferable if he thought a baby was involved.

But it was just the one time since she'd left the Highlands and his home and his bed. It was unlikely that one brief encounter would result in her bearing a child. Struan had been concerned he couldn't have children at all, and he'd said it often took more than once. Though of course they had done it *far* more than once at home. But the last time was weeks ago. She'd know if…

Ellie's thoughts suddenly stopped short and crashed. When had her courses last come? Definitely the one time before they'd first slept together, for she'd cursed the timing of her body, getting in the way of what she'd hoped would be the actual consummation.

But since then? Had she bled at all?

She groaned in frustration. She'd never been able to rely on her supposedly monthly courses arriving when they ought to. She'd always envied Mairi's certitude about her own. *I won't go out today*, Mairi had said more than once. *I've marked this Tuesday as the first day of* you know. *I shall be indisposed.*

Ellie had usually been surprised when she saw her courses arrive, each time.

But counting back, going over each day at Struan's home, she realized that after the first time, there hadn't been another.

Still, that didn't mean anything. She was irregular and

always had been. She could wake up tomorrow and learn that her body was just the same as usual.

But it wasn't really the same, was it? She'd been awfully sick on the passage back to Edinburgh, and frequently nauseous even after arriving home. She'd blamed her family, her upset mind, and the change in weather.

Maybe it wasn't the weather.

What other symptoms did breeding women have? She tried to think. Feeling sick to the stomach. Yes. Weight gain? Yes, she'd definitely filled out. She put it down to rich food and less housework. But again, perhaps that was foolish. Oh, and her breasts. They'd had also been so tender lately. She'd once heard a maid talking about that as a sign.

"Oh, Lord preserve me," she whispered. How did one know such a thing for sure? Who could she talk to about it?

Ellie curled up onto the narrow bed, tears now streaming down her face. She had not been prepared for this revelation, and she was ill equipped to deal with it. What she wanted was to cry and scream, and throw herself into Struan's arms. But tears were cheap, ladies did not scream, and she was no longer depending on Struan. Why then did her whole heart ache for him now?

Perhaps it was because despite his utterly mercenary acquisition of her hand in marriage, and then his continuing silence on the truth of the matter, he was a person who—at least for a short time—she had found such a profound peace with. He had literally saved her life once, and had indeed offered his name and his home and his life to her.

Not without subterfuge, but every time she had sought comfort, he had done his best to provide it. Now while she was alone on her bed, Elspeth could remember with perfect clarity the many times they had lain together, with him holding her in an embrace so solid it may as well have been a fortress.

Was her own rejection of Struan in essence any different from her father's rejection of her?

Though the situations were not at all similar, the fact remained that Elspeth had rejected Struan, and left him, ostensibly for a short visit, though she couldn't deny the many times she had considered the possibility of never returning to his home.

It was a fantasy, for she had no illusions about her ability to live independently, nor about Struan's tolerance for an errant wife. Good Lord, what would he do if he knew she was with child? (*If* she was with child!) He certainly wouldn't have allowed her to leave Linneliath, and if he knew her state now, he would come storming over to retrieve her personally. Struan had been clear what he wanted from the marriage: children. He wanted an heir, as so many men did. In truth, Elspeth ought to write to inform him of her suspicions, if only because that fact might soften his displeasure at her defiance.

Unconsciously, she dropped one hand to her belly, which was still the same shape it had been before. There was as yet no obvious outward sign of her condition. If that *was* her condition. Nothing was proven.

And yet she felt that her guess was right.

Elspeth spread her hand across her stomach, knowing that whatever decisions she made, she was not making them only for herself. She had to think what was best for her son or daughter, and she must be willing to endure more pain if it meant their safety and comfort. She thought of her father again, and wondered how he would greet the news of his first grandchild, and the first grandchild of his late wife. Would his hatred continue for another generation, or would that child be fully forgiven, Elspeth having taken on all of its sins?

The next thought rose unbidden and unwelcome in her

mind. What would happen if she herself died in childbirth as her own mother did? Would Struan hate his son or daughter for that?

Whatever happened, her child would require a guardian, and Struan was the only possible choice. He would treat their child well, even if there was no love between him and Elspeth. Once again, it seemed her only course of action was to put aside her own hazy dreams and desires and think of others. It was what she had done her whole life, and now as a mother-to-be it was the only rational choice.

There was a soft knock at the door. "Pest?"

Elspeth didn't answer, but a moment later the door pushed open and her sister slipped in the room. "I knew you had to be awake. But what's wrong? You're crying."

And then Elspeth told her what had transpired between her and Struan, and her fear about being pregnant.

"We could run away together," Elspeth said desperately. "I do have all those jewels, and I don't care how low a price they fetch. We could make it work. You could be a schoolmistress and I could be a seamstress. We could go to London, or perhaps Dublin. We could save money for passage to America...."

Mairi sat on the bed and reached out a hand to hold Elspeth's. "If you're right about your condition, it's not just the two of us. And I would never destroy your life or that of your child because of my own fear about my future. But you, my darling Pest, you must think of your child. If you flee, and he knew you took his child with you, he would pursue you to the ends of the earth."

"Oh, God. I almost wish he would," Elspeth whispered, clinging to her sister.

"Do you, Pest?" Mairi asked, stroking her head.

"I don't know! I don't know what I want. I'm a wreck, Mairi. Everyone wants me to be something for them, and there's none of me left to be something for me. And now there's a baby…maybe…and I must be something for them."

She burst into a new round of sobbing, and her sister— her prickly, stormy sister—soothed her with whispered words that solved nothing, but still built a bulwark between Ellie and the world.

* * * *

The hulking footman's name was Michael, and he'd also been to war. Struan had hired him because he needed work, and the fact that he looked more like a bodyguard than a footman hadn't really occurred to him until that day.

Michael reported to him in the parlor. "She refused to come, sir. She wrote this for you." He offered Struan a folded note on green paper.

Struan opened the letter, his heart pounding at seeing his name in Ellie's handwriting in dark blue ink. The note inside, written in the same dark blue, was brief, even brusque.

If you wish to discuss matters, be at St Giles at one. If you are not waiting outside the main doors when the clock strikes, I will assume that no arrangement can be reached and we shall place our wagers where we stand.

He frowned. That didn't sound like Ellie at all. The lettering was sloppier than on the outside, and it looked like she broke the nib off at one point. She must be enraged, he thought, to have written something in such a haphazard way. And she hadn't bothered with a seal. That was a mark of disdain, and he felt it keenly. But at least she had written. That meant something, didn't it?

There wasn't much time to alert the other men, prepare, and get to the church she'd mentioned. So Struan sent off a hurried note to Calan and the others, asking them to join him at St Giles, but not to interrupt if they saw him and Elspeth talking.

Struan arrived at St Giles and stood outside as he'd been told. Why had Elspeth picked this place, of all the possible spots in Edinburgh? It wasn't the church where they'd got married. This cathedral was more atmospheric, though. Done in a gothic style, the dark stone and lofty height of the building set an ominous tone.

None of the other men had shown up yet, at least as far as Struan could tell. He waited anxiously for Ellie to arrive. He assumed she'd come in a carriage, but every time one stopped in the street and someone emerged, he was disappointed.

He wanted to pace, but the note had been clear: be by the main doors. A wedding was taking place inside, and he could hear the rustle of the guests. He hoped the outcome of that wedding would be better than his own.

Then the clock tolled one, just a single, startling peal of a great brass bell. He looked up to the bell tower, and that was what saved his life.

Darkness was hurtling down toward him, and it was as if he'd never left the battlefield. He leapt away from the spot he'd been standing, heard a thunderous crash, and then rolled several yards further until he ran into a low wall near the street. He looked up past his arms, which he'd brought up to cover and protect his head, just as he'd done in the army when the shelling started.

But this was a churchyard, not a battlefield. And it wasn't a shell that struck, it was a statue.

He got up slowly, taking in the ring of shattered stones that had so recently been a…gargoyle? He looked up and noticed an empty spot on one side of the bell tower, where a line of carved statues was now incomplete.

A few people strolling near the church had cried out when

the crash happened, and they ran toward Struan, fearing the worst. He was able to wave them off, saying there was no harm done. They drifted away, still glancing back. The doors of the church opened, and the first of the wedding guests began to stream out, chattering happily.

Then Calan and Kai appeared, both looking confused.

"What's the matter?" Calan demanded.

"Well, I'm fairly certain someone just tried to kill me."

"*Fairly* certain?"

"I'm still alive. If someone was serious about it, they probably would have tried harder. Perhaps it was an accident."

Calan glared at the loose stones and rubble lying on the path. "Ah, yes, one of those accidents when statues that have perched safely on the top of a building for two hundred years suddenly fall at the same moment a distinctive and recognizable man walks beneath them."

"You make a good point." Struan looked up again, assessing. "Whoever was up there is going to be impossible to find by now. He'll mingle with the crowd from the wedding, or slip out a side door."

"And they must know that you survived the attempt. Which means they'll try again."

"Maybe we should leave the area," Kai suggested. "Just in case the man has another weapon to hand and hopes to end the business quickly."

The men retreated to Struan's townhouse, and sent word for Thane and Duncan to join them there as soon as possible. When they'd all gathered, Struan gave a short recounting of what happened.

Calan stood up. "Hear me out before you reach over and strangle me, but…this was obviously orchestrated by your wife."

"No!" Struan snapped. Then he sighed. "When Ellie

wants to crush me, she simply tells me the truth. Besides, she'd never stand for a murder like this, with debris everywhere. She's very tidy."

"It's rather touching that you know her habits so well, with your marriage still so new," Duncan said dryly.

Struan knew far more than her habits. He knew the exact texture of the skin on her inner wrist. He knew how she smelled after a bath, when her hair was still wet and shining. He knew which shift in her breath signaled that she'd fallen asleep.

He knew her heartbeat.

Did he *know* if she was capable of killing?

"It wasn't her," he insisted.

"Then who?" Thane said. "You don't have any enemies… other than the French, and that's not personal."

"It's her father, yes?" Duncan asked. "There's no one else it could be."

Struan grunted. "That feels like the most logical answer. I spoke to him at the party last night. Twice, actually. The second time was more harsh."

"What brought that on?" Thane asked.

"He struck Ellie."

The sudden quiet in the room was ominous.

After a long moment, Duncan said, "I'm slightly surprised that he survived the second chat."

Kai suggested, "It would have provided incentive for him to make certain Struan didn't live for long after that. Maybe he panicked."

"You're *sure* your wife couldn't be involved? Death is simpler than divorce after all," Calan said.

"I don't believe she'd participate. She'd probably just be pleased to learn I was dead."

"You're being mean," Duncan said flatly. "I was watching their house this morning, and I happened to see her go out with her sister. She didn't look overjoyed."

"Well, she doesn't know Struan's still alive," Calan said.

"Not funny," Duncan snapped back. "It's one thing to think her father is the culprit—his debt is a strong motivation, especially with the threat to his reputation added in. But he'd never tell his daughter of the plan beforehand."

"To spare her feelings?" Calan sneered.

"No," said Struan, suddenly certain. "Because he wouldn't bother. He tried to kill me because of what *he* wants, not what she wants. He's never cared about what she wants."

"That's disheartening," said Kai. "I bet he also didn't tell her because she wouldn't have condoned it. She would have stopped him if she knew."

"You've got too much faith in women, Kai," Calan told him.

"You love women," Kai objected.

"Of course I do. But I don't have faith in them. There's a difference."

Chapter 30

ELLIE COULD HARDLY KEEP TWO thoughts together over the next few days. Mairi had reached out to one of the women from her League, with the result that Ellie was able to have a private consultation with a doctor and a midwife, both of whom confirmed Ellie's suspicion. The midwife, seeing her reaction, calmly asked if Ellie wished to do anything about her condition, explaining that she still had options.

"I have to think about it," Ellie said.

"Don't take longer than a fortnight, dear. Earlier is safer. But no matter what you choose or when, come to us if you have questions."

Ellie thanked her, and left with Mairi.

"I know you won't end the pregnancy. So when will you tell him?" Mairi asked.

"I should probably do it before it's obvious."

"Probably," Mairi said dryly.

"I'm terrified."

"Of his reaction?"

"Of my state. I don't know what to do, Mairi. I'm about to be a mother…soonish anyway. And I don't have a mother to speak to."

"I know." Mairi embraced her. "It's not fair. For what it's worth, you do have a sister."

"Thank you. It's worth a lot."

"You could speak to Aunt Rosalind?" Mairi offered tentatively.

"I thought about that, but I would hate to trouble her with my…trouble."

"She's a mother herself. She'd understand."

"Maybe I'll be able to speak to her at the next party."

"Ugh. Another party. I wish Averill would just elope. Run off to London again."

"Darling London," Ellie cooed, mimicking something Averill had said the day before. "The sound of the bells at sunset!"

Mairi snickered.

The sisters were again confronted with Averill the moment they came home. "Where have you been?" she demanded.

"Out," Mairi snapped. Ellie said nothing, not wishing to explain *any*thing about their errand. "Why do you suddenly care about what we're doing?"

"I don't. I just wanted to know what you're wearing for the party."

"What does it matter?" Mairi replied with a shrug.

"Not tonight's party," she said scornfully. "I mean for the masquerade."

Of course Averill had insisted on a masquerade for her final party. It was the most potentially dramatic, and afforded her the best opportunity to overawe the attendees with some spectacular costume, and then the most astonishing reveal of her identity at midnight, when all masks came off.

Elspeth and Mairi understood that to even think of competing with Averill was a sin in the their stepsister's eyes. Mairi didn't have much interest in the idea of a masquerade anyway, and thus announced that she intended to dress as Hypatia of Alexandria.

"Who?" Averill asked blankly.

"Exactly," Mairi told her. "It will be easy to fashion a costume in the style of an ancient lady and I can wear a crown—"

"What!" Averill cried.

"A crown of *laurel*," Mairi said, "to signify my role as a scholar. A simple mask of white linen will do. And I shall carry a scroll."

"How dull." Averill was clearly delighted with this decision. She looked at Elspeth. "And you?"

"I'm not sure. I thought I might try to be some figure from a fairy tale. Cap o' Rushes, perhaps." Elspeth always identified strongly with that particular tale.

"Who?"

"Cap o' Rushes is a girl who works in the prince's scullery." Elspeth neglected to add that Cap o' Rushes was also a princess in hiding from her own king. Wasn't Ellie sort of in hiding herself?

"What does she look like?" Averill demanded.

"She has dirty skin and tangled hair and she wears a cloak and cap woven of rushes—" Ellie began to explain.

"Excellent," Averill approved, cutting her off. "I'm sure that both your costumes will create…comment." By which she meant mockery from the other partygoers.

"What are you going to be, then?" Mairi asked.

"I shall be Aphrodite, clad in the purest white silk, with gold adornments!"

"I can't wait," Mairi muttered, rolling her eyes so only Ellie could see.

* * * *

Not long after, Ellie was in the long, narrow room in the family home that served as a sort of shared library-parlor-sitting room. Bookshelves lined one wall. The books on those shelves were a mix of pristine and unread (the pages on many hadn't even been cut), less pristine because they had been read (mostly novels, travel guides, and reference books that appealed to Averill and her mother), and completely fake (wooden panels carved to resemble a row of book spines). The fake ones were placed on the high shelves where no one was likely to try to pull them off. Her father felt that a gentleman ought to appear well read, even when he never read.

She confined her attention to the lower shelves of real books. The travel guides and memoirs were the most interesting. After all, she wanted to be anywhere but here. She spotted *Walton's New Traveller's Guide to London and Environs*. How funny that both Struan's and her family's libraries contained the exact same guide! As she scanned the book, especially the few engraved plates illustrating famous sites, she saw the description about Covent Garden again: *This remarkable space is truly magical at night, when the glow from the lanterns among the trees is nothing less than otherworldly.*

She heard the words in Averill's voice. She'd said those very words, multiple times during the endless morning visits of social acquaintances. Had she simply not come up with her own way of describing the sight?

Ellie quickly flipped to the part of the guide covering shopping: *The exquisite shops of Bond Street, lined up like so many cakes, contain delectable wares.*

Another too-familiar phrase. That was strange. Averill was no creative spirit, but why would she be pulling lines from a travel guide when she could have simply shared her own memories of London?

Mairi walked in. "What are you doing? Trying to decide where to flee from scandal?" she asked jokingly.

But Ellie's eyes dropped to her torso, and she inhaled as an idea overtook her. "Mairi! Read this."

She showed her sister the lines in question, then asked, "Why does Averill never say anything original about London? Why does she never talk about what the family did or who she saw? Why is it only this patter?"

"Because she wasn't there," Mairi said, looking up as the idea clicked in her own head too. "But if she wasn't in London, where was she? And why lie about it?"

Ellie tapped her belly meaningfully. "She's always been a flirt. What if she did more than flirt, and got into trouble, but left it too late to bring it off that way the midwife suggested I could do?"

"She'd have to hide it. And her mother must have helped."

"I'd bet Father is the one who decided everything," Ellie said. "Susan and Averill both know to not get in the way of his plans. And his plans depend on Averill marrying well. And that means not a breath of scandal."

Mairi snatched the book out of Ellie's hands. "I'm going to find out the truth."

"How?"

"Leave it to me, Pest. We all excel at something."

* * * *

The weather had turned, unsurprisingly. Scottish weather was dependable only in the sense that one could depend on it to change, usually for the worse. Rain pelted down at a sharp angle, obscuring the details of the buildings on the other side of the street. The trees planted at the corner might as well not exist. Elspeth peered out the window, the glass smudged with her fingerprints and the spot where she'd leaned her forehead against the cool glass.

She needed the cool, since every fireplace and grate within the large house was roaring at full blast in an attempt to drive out the dampness that had come in with the storm. Averill threw a tantrum the moment her hair started to frizz, crying that she would be *ruined* if people saw her hair in such a state. Nothing less than mirror-smooth locks would do, and Averill blamed the sky itself for trying to thwart her future happiness.

Mairi had left the house in protest, saying that the League met regardless of weather and that she'd rather brave twelve thunderstorms than another one of Averill's *childish* tantrums. (This statement, perhaps by design, set Averill off again.)

Elspeth had felt too queasy to dare the out-of-doors, so she retreated to her room, hoping that everyone would simply ignore her until she had to emerge this evening.

The party that evening was straightforward, in that it merely required guests to sparkle and shine in the usual way. Ellie was surprised that so many people came to each party—she hadn't realized Averill was so well-known in society. Or perhaps they all just liked an excuse to be seen.

Elspeth wore a burnished silk gown, one that looked like a sunset at sea. It was fashionably cut with a high waist and a low neckline, so Ellie was happy to cover the expanse of her chest with a necklace that consisted of several chains of gold links punctuated with topaz stones so that it looked rather like a halo of sunlight.

She got a hard look from her father when he saw her ensemble, and she was glad that she'd listened to Mairi when her sister suggested hiding the jewels Ellie had unwittingly brought with her. They'd removed all the pieces from the beautiful mahogany case and wrapped them carefully in some old fabric that was destined for the rag pile. They then concealed each small bundle in various places in Mairi's room, while the case itself remained in Ellie's room, locked up to conceal the fact that the jewels had been replaced with pebbles from the garden.

Ellie hadn't dared bring up the matter of Struan's presence in town with the servants, who'd normally be intersected to keep unwanted people out. What could she say? Only Mairi knew that they'd had a fight, and she had her reasons for not wanting to spread that knowledge further. But she could hardly tell the footmen to bar Struan from entering the house. It would raise even more questions if he showed up at the door and was denied entry.

Maybe he wouldn't appear at all tonight. Maybe last time he just wanted to prove that he could, and now he'd leave her alone.

She couldn't even tell herself that without laughing.

At the party, she noticed after a while that she seemed to be getting more than the usual amount of attention…the usual being none.

"Why is everyone looking at me? Is it the dress? Is it too revealing?"

"It's the height of fashion," Mairi said bluntly. "You look perfect."

"Then what is it?"

"I'll find out."

Mairi stalked off, leaving Ellie standing by the side of the room. She dared not move, lest she draw attention to herself even more. Then Mairi was back.

"What did you find out?"

"Two things. First, Struan just arrived, with his men at arms."

"Oh, no. What does he want from me? Wait, what's the other thing you learned?"

"I don't know precisely how it started, but people *are* talking about you. They've heard, somehow, that your marriage isn't going well."

"I didn't tell anyone!"

"Someone guessed, maybe. You arrived in Edinburgh without him. And now he's here, but you're staying in different houses."

"There are lots of ways to explain that."

"But only a few of those ways are interesting to boring people who want to think the worst of others."

"What am I to do about it?"

"Well, you could appear with him in public, and look happy about it," Mairi suggested.

"He's not the type to play along with a charade like that." Besides, Ellie wasn't sure she could deal with being next to Struan and pretending that nothing was amiss. She was so bad at acting, and he'd sense something was happening. "Maybe I can persuade him to leave the house before anything gets worse. And I'll say I have a headache and go upstairs and then Averill can just pretend I don't exist. And…"

"Oh, God. That's Mr Malloch. It's out of our hands now," Mairi muttered.

"Who's he?"

"The one in the garish pink coat. He fancies himself a major wit, though he was just talking to Father, which I'd think he'd think was beneath him. But now he's got his eyes on Struan. He loves nothing more than humiliating his chosen victim in as public a way as possible."

"I would think any hostess would strike him from the guest list," said Ellie. "People stand for that sort of cruelty?"

"Are you joking? They adore it. It adds spice to the evening. I bet Averill invited him especially."

Ellie watched in growing horror as the dandy began to stalk his prey through the wilds of the ballroom. He had curly, dark blond hair and sported a severely trimmed goatee. He greeted Struan and his companions civilly enough, but even she could see that the crowd was shifting around the small group. Like jackals awaiting the kill.

Malloch said loudly, "Since we have to wait for the happy announcement of one daughter, we must content ourselves with considering the success of another. You do consider your marriage to the older McGregor sister a success, don't you?"

Struan looked like he wanted to throw Malloch across the room. The man named Calan Shaw interjected smoothly, "What an odd question, considering that both husband and wife are here in the same room. Is *your* wife in attendance, sir?"

"Alas, I am not so blessed yet," the dandy replied with a smirk.

"Then my opinion of the ladies of Edinburgh has improved," Calan responded, so calmly that it took the dandy a moment to realize what Calan just said.

Rather than seeing the parry as a warning to retreat, he viewed it as a further reason to dig in.

"To achieve my aim," Malloch announced, "I must study previous victors. Tell me, Mr MacInnes. You are a married man, and thus have run the gauntlet of the marriage mart, and all the scrutiny of matrons and their daughters." The dandy looked incredibly pleased with himself as he spoke to Struan. He clearly heard some inkling of the reality of the situation, and knew that Struan had not spent one day in the drawing rooms of the Edinburgh matrons. "If you will enlighten us, please explain how you settled upon a wife, when you surely had so many to choose from."

"As a matter of fact," said Struan, "I did not have many to choose from." He paused. The silence of the room grew uncomfortable. Then he said, "The moment I saw Elspeth McGregor, she was the only conceivable choice."

The words were technically true, and yet Elspeth winced.

Conceivable, indeed.

"Is that so?" the dandy went on, oblivious to the murderous glances being sent by the other men of the company. In particular, Calan had a glint in his eye that Elspeth felt was more fitting in the eye of a wolf.

"It is," Struan snapped.

"You are a man of great perception, then," Mr Malloch said. "Clearly you knew what qualities you were seeking in a wife, and stuck to your principles, even when wandering amid the garden that is all of Edinburgh's marriageable beauties. So tell us, sir. What is the prime quality that a man requires in a wife?"

Struan looked directly at Elspeth when he spoke next, and she could not pretend to misunderstand his response, nor the very particular meaning it held for them.

"Frugality."

Chapter 31

"YOU SAID WHAT?" THE DANDY'S jaw flopped like a fish.

"You heard me." Struan's attention was locked on Ellie, who'd obviously not forgotten what the word meant to him. To them. He'd said it because it was something only she'd understand. Because he needed her to know that he wasn't going to just mope in the Highlands while she was down here. And he definitely wasn't going anywhere until he found out if she was involved in the attempt on his life.

Malloch was upset because his little set piece wasn't going as planned. Struan was supposed to have embarrassed himself, or just run away in shame or something. Instead, he'd done the unexpected. Malloch said, "I heard you, but I don't understand."

"That fine, because I'm not married to you." Struan pushed past the dandy. "If you'll excuse me, I ought to rejoin my beautiful wife right now. I'd hate to think anyone would entertain rumors about us based on the sole fact that she has been observed living an independent existence. As if she were her own person."

Mairi, who was standing close to her sister, actually smiled at that. Ellie was still regarding him with flushed embarrassment.

He moved through the room, instinctively glancing at all

the corners. He saw McGregor watching him. He looked annoyed, but not guilty. Or particularly scared. But then again, he had plenty of reinforcements here, on his chosen ground. Christ, he hated thinking that every place could be a battlefield.

Of course, it was. Even after slaying that stupid dandy, he was still in enemy territory. He had to get to Ellie and get her alone to talk.

He reached the two sisters. "Miss McGregor, I'm afraid I'll have to leave you alone here while I go have a chat with my wife."

Mairi looked to Elspeth. "I'm not going anywhere, not if you don't want that."

Ellie reached for her sister's hand. "Perhaps we'd better make ourselves scarce for a little while. Until the guests find some new entertainment. Struan and I will talk in the back-yard. Meet us there in a quarter hour."

"Half hour," Struan said firmly.

"Twenty minutes," Ellie told Mairi.

"Or sooner if I hear a scream," Mairi said.

Ellie sighed and told Struan to come with her.

The backyard wasn't open to guests. It was the same area where Struan had first seen Ellie doing laundry with the ser-vants, a lifetime ago. At night, the area was lit only by the illumination from the windows overlooking the space, and a half-moon trying to escape a cloud.

"What's happened?" she asked. "You look serious."

"I always look serious."

"No. You often look grumpy. And frequently forbidding. But now you look serious. So tell me what's caused it."

"This may be awkward."

"Oh, goodness, we've never had an awkward conversa-tion before."

He hadn't often experienced Elspeth being sardonic—but

he had to admit he liked it. Still, this was no time to get distracted.

So he said, "I believe someone tried to have me killed. Possibly your father."

Elspeth rocked back on her feet. "*What?*"

He repeated himself.

"Oh, my Lord, Struan. When did this happen? Why didn't you tell me? Were you hurt?" she gasped. "What did he do? Did anyone else get hurt? How do you know it was him? Oh, my God, he's no longer sane. That must be it. He couldn't have tried to kill you if he was in his right mind. Because if that were so, he'd be…evil. He'd be…" The color drained out of her face as she ran through the litany of questions. "He'd be…just as he always was. Oh, God—"

As he listened to the flood of words, several things became clear.

First: Ellie was stunned by the news. She wasn't behind the attempt, nor had anyone told her of it.

Second: she asked if he was hurt. Which meant she cared a little bit. He clung to that.

Third: she had no trouble at all in accepting her father as the culprit.

"I didn't get hurt," he told her, breaking her string of questions. "No one did."

"Oh, thank God," she whispered, her eyes closing.

He explained in detail what happened, including receiving the note with the instruction to meet at the cathedral. He showed her the paper.

Ellie was already shaking her head. "I didn't write that. I *did* write, but not that."

"What did your note say?"

She winced, then whispered, "Go to hell."

"Ouch. But the paper looks familiar?"

"I got it from Father's desk… Oh, God."

"I don't *know* it was him," he admitted. "Not with perfect certainty, but…"

"But the paper matches. And you'd threatened him the night before, after you left me, didn't you? He was scared and desperate, and desperate men do not have scruples. Not that he had scruples before."

"I'm sorry, Ellie. I know he's your father."

"And he has never forgiven me for being his daughter." Ellie sounded older, colder than she had before. "Well. What do you intend to do about it? Will your friends handle the matter?"

"My friends?"

"Yes. Calan, and Duncan and Thane and Kai. Any one of them could intimidate my father into compliance. All together, they'd cause his heart to stop."

"I don't want him dead," Struan said. And truly he did not. Struan was sick of death. "But I can't let him roam about trying to kill me again. Or trying to hurt you."

Elspeth gave him a sad smile. "He's done his worst to me already."

The marriage. Struan felt the words like a slap in the face.

She must have read his reaction, because she gasped and added hastily, "Oh, I didn't mean when he gave me to you. Or even when he struck me."

"No?"

"I meant my whole life. All I wanted was for him to recognize me. To like me a little. He didn't even have to love me. I would have settled for some fondness."

"Don't you dare." Struan had her in his arms before he knew what he was doing. Elspeth had been fed scraps all her life. Scraps of affection, little leavings of love. Her sister Mairi adored her fiercely, true, and that was perhaps the only thing that had made Elspeth's life tolerable.

Struan might be a miserable bastard now, but he remembered endless amounts of love from his own parents, and the people around him. He'd found friends in the army, whose love was real even if they never called it such.

She cried silently for a few moments, her chest heaving. But then she recovered herself and stepped away. "Thank you for informing me of the murder attempt. I know you were under no obligation to do so. Tell me what will happen next. Then I can prepare the rest of the family."

Even now, even faced with the appalling news that her father meant to be a murderer, Ellie still thought of serving others.

"I plan to talk to him. That's all," Struan said quietly. "Alone at first, but with the men if he needs to hear…multiple voices. To make it real to him."

"What will you make him do? Confess?"

"There's little point to that, especially since the attempt failed. All I want is to convince him that it was a foolish idea that should not be repeated."

She looked skeptical. "How will you do that?"

"I'll make him understand that he'll not benefit from my death. Nor will he benefit from your death. Or your life as a widow, for that matter. He needs to understand that you will never again be a source of income for him."

"I'd never give him anything."

"Yes, you would," Struan said. "You're softhearted and generous, so you would give it. Eventually. And it would never stop."

She looked down, and he heard the telltale sniffle that heralded more tears. She mumbled, "Everyone knows that about me, don't they? They call it kindness, but it's really weakness, isn't it?"

"It's not weak to have a good heart, Ellie. Oh, and one more thing. I want you to come live at my townhouse. If your father is…not rational, then it's not safe for you here."

But Elspeth was slowly shaking her head. "If it was Father behind what happened, we shouldn't let him know we know. And me suddenly going to live with you after I went through all the trouble of running away from you...it's too sudden a change. And if Mairi goes...he'll know *we* know."

Chapter 32

Ellie looked over to where Mairi stood. She'd been so focused on Struan and his news that she didn't even hear her sister open the door to the backyard.

"Our father's done something awful."

"You'll have to be more specific," Mairi said dryly.

"Can we please continue this conversation anywhere but here?" Struan asked. "If anyone else joins us, we may as well talk about it on the dance floor."

"There's a park not too far away. I can get the gate key," Mairi offered.

"And who else has one of those? I'd prefer to talk in private."

"Where?" Elspeth asked.

"My townhouse." He held up a hand before Ellie could object. "Both of you will come and both of you will be free to leave after we talk. Christ."

"Good. I'll call a carriage."

Ellie jumped at the new voice, which turned out to be Kai, who stood there with Calan, Thane, and Duncan.

"Is anyone actually still at the party?" she asked.

"Too many," Duncan replied. "We thought we'd be of more use out here, though. Since we're supposed to be watching…things," he finished awkwardly with a side look at Mairi.

Luckily, she didn't seem to notice. Since Kai was already hurrying down the narrow passage to reach the main street to hail a hired carriage, Struan ordered Thane to return to the house and make sure no one had remarked on their absence.

"Then what?"

"Keep an eye on McGregor."

"Lucky me." Thane disappeared into the house.

"Ladies." Duncan offered his arm to Mairi, who allowed him to lead her to where Kai had just gone. Struan offered his arm to Elspeth. Calan stalked behind them all like a tiger.

"I'm sorry you don't have a cloak," Struan told her. "But I'd rather not have you go back in alone and I don't know where to look for one."

"Just don't allow anyone to steal the necklace," she said. "Since it's yours after all."

"It looks better on you."

She couldn't help but laugh, then quickly promised, "We're not friends again. I'm still mad at you."

He sighed. "I know."

Struan's townhouse was more like him than Linneliath was. They gathered in the library, and Ellie wandered around, looking at all the books until everyone sat down. She noticed a whole shelf of books on mining and geology.

Finally everyone took their seats by the fire.

"Are we all aware of the whole situation?" Struan asked.

Ellie shot one panicked look to Mairi, because there was certainly *one* aspect of the situation that Struan didn't know. She hoped.

Mairi shook her head slightly.

"I know what you've told me and that's enough." Duncan stood. "Why don't we leave you three to talk. We'll be in kitchen if you need us."

"You're hungry again?" Kai asked his friend.

"I'm always hungry."

The soldiers left, and Struan sat down in the large, worn leather chair. He looked tired. "Miss McGregor, as I told your sister earlier tonight, I think your father tried to kill me." He explained the situation to an utterly unsurprised Mairi, then said, "Was there anything you wanted to ask me?"

Mairi said, "Do you think that he wants you dead to cancel his debt to you? Since I assume there's no written agreement that says Pest will be suitable payment."

"None. There is a record of the original loan, though it's safely back in Linneliath."

"I suppose it's worth asking if you have other disgruntled customers. I didn't think that you were a money lender."

"There's no reason you would. It's not typical for those in my class, is it? My family has been well off for generations, and most of my predecessors felt that it was duty to assist others, which could mean financial assistance in the form of either loans or small gifts, depending on the situation. Typically the loans were to longtime tenants or neighbors, people who are vouched for or well-known to the lender. My father drilled it into me that I ought to carry on all of our family traditions." Here he looked pained, though Elspeth wasn't sure why. "So I naturally continued the practice of lending money when needs arose."

"But I don't understand," she said, "because wouldn't that mean that you knew my father previously?"

"That was my mistake," he said. "It would be more accurate to say that I *thought* I knew him, based on his claim that he knew my father. In my defense—and it's a weak defense—I was young. I had in fact only just turned old enough to manage the funds myself. I suppose I was trying to live up to the family name. And it is true that one of the initial loans that I made was to your father, who couldn't get credit from any other reputable lender, a fact I discovered too late. I wouldn't have done it if I had known."

"But you did," said Elspeth. "And then you extended the term of that loan."

"I was at war," he reminded her. "There was little I could do while on the Continent except for short times of leave. It was unwise to have the loan go unpaid for such a long time, but it couldn't be helped. And the sad fact is that your father is terrible with money. He doesn't view a loan as an opportunity to earn more money with an initial investment. That's what a loan should be. He instead views it as some sort of windfall, a magical pot of gold unconnected to the ordinary rules of men and finance. He thinks he's found treasure each time, and he spends all the money as fast as he can. That's what he did with the loan I gave him, and what he had done with other loans in the past, as I've come to find out."

"I think it must be a sort of sickness," said Elspeth.

"That's a good way to think about it. I don't want to say that it's not his fault, because he made the choices that he did over and over again, even knowing the consequences. But it is true that he seems to feel some sort of compulsion that warps his good sense, and turns it into a type of greed. Gamblers are like that. The kindest thing to do would be to never give him a coin again."

Mairi smiled, though without mirth. "He wouldn't think it a kindness."

"Even if I forgave the entire amount that he owed to me," Struan said, "there are other lenders in the city to whom he owes a considerable amount. I'm afraid that debtors' prison is probably his future. It will leave your family in ruins, destitute. Other than Ellie, of course, so long as she chooses to be my wife."

Elspeth understood that he had no intention of stepping in

and playing hero in order to save her father or her stepfamily. It would do no good to save them, because they would not view it with gratitude. They would merely take it to mean that all of their choices were ultimately the correct ones, with fate keeping them afloat yet again.

"I think that debtors' prison will probably be a rude awakening for him, and while I can't say that I am entirely unsympathetic to my stepmother or Averill—"

"I am," Mairi muttered.

"—it's true that everyone besides Mairi was perfectly content to treat me as a servant and not offer much in the way of support, whether monetary or bonds of family love."

It was painful even now to admit all of that. Elspeth had spent such a large portion of her life pretending that was not so. She had desperately wanted to believe that if she worked hard and didn't cost her father anything, and didn't make a fuss, she would somehow be considered worthy in his eyes, an acceptable compensation for losing the person he truly loved.

But the truth was he never thought about her enough to even consider whether she was worthy or not. She had saved him the trouble of having to do so by being so self-effacing that she disappeared as a person. All she had been was a useful pair of invisible hands, hands that made sure they cost nothing to keep.

But she could perhaps salvage something out of her disaster of a marriage.

Elspeth said, "I have a proposal for you."

Struan raised his eyebrow. He said, "I thought we were past proposals. The first one didn't work out so well."

"A business proposition, then," she clarified. "The truth is, I need your help. *We* need your help."

He sighed. "If you need help, you could just ask. You're my wife. Whether you like it or not."

"It's not me who needs help. It's Mairi."

"What?" Mairi asked, not prepared for this.

"She seems to be a capable young woman." Struan looked at Mairi suspiciously. "Please don't tell me you're going to blow up Parliament or something like that. I happen to know that the League for the Advancement of Scottish Women does not condone violence."

"I've never blown up anything," Mairi protested. "Yet."

Elspeth shook her head. "We know Father's loans are now with men far less reputable than you, and once again, Father is unable to make the necessary payments. Mairi is concerned that Father will attempt another…non-monetary form of repayment, since it worked for him in the past."

He nodded. "I suspected that possibility as soon as you read me Mairi's letter. I sent word that day to tell Calan and Duncan to keep watch."

There was a beat of silence. Then Mairi said, "Watch *me*?"

"To keep you safe, yes."

"Without telling me."

"They didn't impede your daily life, Miss McGregor. You didn't even notice them, did you? And you never would have, unless something occurred to force their hand. Only then would either of them have stepped in, and only to ensure your safety."

Mairi looked furious, but she said nothing.

Elspeth said, "I don't think we should wait to see if my father will do a terrible thing twice in row."

"So what is your proposition?"

"Fund Mairi's travel to some destination where she may start her life over, out of the reach of our father."

"Where?" Struan asked Mairi.

"I've no idea. London? But it may be still too close. Perhaps Paris. The more adventurous option is to go westward, likely to New York City or Philadelphia, where I may find a community in which I can thrive, continue my political activities, and feel safe from Father."

"He is at heart a selfish person," Elspeth said. "It took me far too long to accept that, but I believe that if Mairi simply disappears, he won't pursue the matter, largely because it would be costly and time-consuming. And his attention span is a short one."

"I could fund her journey to whatever destination she chooses, but how is that a proposition? It sounds to me like a simple request."

"I didn't think you would listen to any request I made."

"And yet you have just made one, and I have listened. But I'm curious to know how you would've sweetened the pot if I didn't agree."

"Oh," said Elspeth. "I planned to say that if you helped Mairi escape, then I would return to you and play the role of wife."

Struan expression went cold. "I do not want you to play the *role* of wife."

"I didn't mean it like that."

"Then how did you mean it, Elspeth McGregor?"

"I just meant, that is to say…I would resume acting—no, not acting—I mean that I would live with you again. But I suppose you do not want me to live with you anymore."

The way he looked at her made her heart stutter. He said, "The few months that you lived with me were the happiest ones in all my adult life."

Mairi said, "I should go."

"But it's not the same now, is it?" asked Elspeth, ignoring her sister's sudden discomfort.

"No, I fucked that up, royally," he said with a dark laugh.

"I don't know how to get you to agree to help Mairi."

"As I said before, you could simply *ask*. You seem to

think that I am a monster who must be bargained with rather than someone who wishes to do the right thing."

"So you will help Mairi?"

"I don't think I need help after all," Mairi said. "Other than help leaving this conversation."

"Then what will you do?" Struan was saying to Ellie. "Live on your own somewhere? I'll pay your annual expenses if you do."

"It wouldn't be much," said Elspeth. "I can manage any size household, so managing for myself, and one other will be no challenge."

"Wait. Who is this other to be? Mairi will be far away. Am I to pay the expenses for you and some lover to keep house together?"

"Of course not! I already have one husband."

"Then who's the lucky person you intend to shelter and keep?"

Elspeth said nothing, biting her lip as she looked away. But her silence was information enough.

"My God, you're pregnant, aren't you?"

"Well," said Mairi. "It is definitely time for me to find the men in the kitchen and see if there's any food left before I have them take me back to my loving home. Good luck, Pest."

"Mairi!" Ellie watched her sister's retreat, feeling abandoned. But then again, it was her problem. She turned back to a furious, shocked Struan.

"Well?" he demanded.

"Well, yes. I'm going to have a child. Your efforts have borne fruit, as they say."

"And you weren't going to tell me?"

"I didn't know until I'd already got to Edinburgh. I couldn't confirm it until…well, today, honestly."

"And you weren't going to inform me until your sister

forced the matter. It's *my* child too, Elspeth. Any child of mine is my responsibility." He inhaled. "Oh. I understand. So you were planning to hide them from me so that you could raise them on your own. My God. Do you hate me that much?"

"I made no plans at all," said Elspeth. "It will be six months or more before the child is born. I have no idea where I'll be in six months."

"If you would listen to reason, you would be at home with me where you'll have everything you need to be ready to bring our baby into the world. You wouldn't be boarding with your socially obsessed father, who's already proven that he would sell a human being as quickly as a sack of onions. I can't believe that you would keep this from me."

"I know you want an heir," said Elspeth.

"I don't want an heir, I want a family!" he burst out. "If you want to hurt me far more than I've hurt you, all you have to do is to keep our child away from me. Knowing that I have a wife and child somewhere in the world and I'm not able to see them or be with them or share anything about your lives… That's hell for me. And it's up to you whether you want to put me in hell."

"You're a man. You're my husband. You will be our child's father. All the power is yours," she declared.

"What good does that power do? What sort of home will it be to live in if you don't want to be there? If the only reason you're there is because the law makes it so? And what is the point of having my child there if my wife isn't also there? Could you seriously expect me to raise a child without their mother? No, *you're* the one with the power. And you're the one who will make the choice about all our lives."

"I can't do that!"

"Can't? Or won't? People have taken advantage of you all your life, Elspeth. It must get to be a habit after a while.

Thinking that you have no control and that you have to listen to what other people say, that you have to obey their orders."

"Have you been talking to Mairi? You sound like her."

"Have you been listening to her? Sounds like she's talking sense," he said. "Anyway, I refuse to have you in any place you don't wish to be. But I won't let you abdicate now and then play the victim later. You have the choice of what to do with your life and my life and our child's life. You're the one who has to make it."

Struan turned to walk away, but Elspeth grabbed his arm. "Don't you *dare* leave me like this."

"Like what?" He surveyed her as she spoke, and she couldn't deny how his mere presence made her forget everything else. He dominated her attention.

"Alone. You're the reason I'm in this condition. You and your desire."

"My desire?" He was looking at her in that way that left her skin tingling even without him touching her. "I seem to recall you showing a lot of enthusiasm for the game as well."

"Only because…you showed me." Elspeth was having trouble getting her breath. And her skin felt uncomfortably warm.

He noticed, raising one hand to her cheek. "Flushed, Ellie? Embarrassed to admit you loved being fucked by me? Or are you missing the blindfold from our early nights? Or the time you stormed into my bath, curious as a cat? Oh, you remember all that, wife." He ran his fingers under her chin, tipping her face up to his. "If I felt between your legs right now, you'd be wet and ready. Yes? Tell me the truth."

She nodded, then whispered, "Are you going to torture me again?"

He went still. "That last time we…not the last time, I mean the last time before you left. I'm sorry I did that to you."

"You mean when you tied me to your bed and pleasured me all kinds of ways except penetrating me because you wanted to prove a point?"

"Yes, then. And all the things I said to you during and after. I was lying about all of it. I had to lie to make you hate me."

"I know why you did it," she said.

"You don't. I was just being a bastard."

"Because you were afraid. Are you really sorry for everything you said that day?"

"God yes."

"Good. I said horrible things too. I'm sorry for them. I didn't…I'm not good at being mean, and I might have overdone it."

He laughed, disbelieving. "God, Ellie. You're marvelous at being mean. You cut me into pieces."

"Thank you? But I didn't like it. I don't want to do it ever again."

"And I'll never do what I did again."

"Actually." She took a deep breath. "The truth is that while I hated everything you said, I liked everything you did. Tying me to the bed. Pleasuring me with your hands and keeping me on the edge.…"

"Christ, Ellie." His breath had grown harsh. "Keep talking like that and I'll drag you to my room."

"Do it," she said breathlessly.

His room was one floor up and on the opposite side of the house, which might be far enough to prevent anyone hearing them. He didn't have to drag her—she was eager to get there. Struan didn't bother with a tour. He led her directly to his bed.

She told him what made her most excited and desperate, all while he worked to remove her gown and shift, though he left the necklace on. Clearly, he had no intention of repeating their last rushed encounter. He lay her down naked on his bedsheets, then started on his own clothing. He gently pushed aside her attempt to help. "I like looking at you like this. So impatient and bothered. You look like you want something from me."

She licked her lips when he revealed his stand. "I want that. Inside me."

"You'll have it." He ran his hands over her waist and her thighs and her bottom, making approving sounds when she raised up her hips and begged him for more.

"In me," she pleaded. "I want you inside me."

"Soon," he promised, his hands moving up her torso, regarding her breasts with hunger. He squeezed one, and she let out a startled gasp.

"What?" he asked, his eyes clouded.

"I'm just very…tender now."

He bent his head and kissed her gently where his hand had been, and then he slowly took her nipple in his mouth and circled the pebbled part with his tongue until she forgot all about the previous discomfort.

"Better?" he asked, taking a breath.

"Yes," she breathed. "Don't stop."

He suckled her with a level of devotion that left her panting, and even while he did, he eased two fingers between her legs. She convulsed when the pleasure hit her, arching her back as she moaned his name.

She was more than ready for him, but he continued to play with her, teasing her with his fingers, drawing out more moans and pleas as he drove her to distraction.

"You're so close, aren't you?" He almost purred in his satisfaction at her need. He slid his fingers in slowly and pressed his thumb over the hard nub. And he flicked his thumb softly. Rhythmically. Relentlessly.

The pleasure built fast, and she was crying out within

moments, utterly under his spell.

"Watch me, Ellie," he ordered as her eyes fluttered closed.

She opened her eyes and found him staring at her, his gaze locked on her face as he worked her body to a peak that left her shaking and limp, her nerves singing, her muscles clenching around his fingers as she flew apart. But he still ordered her to keep her eyes open and focused as he withdrew his fingers, raised them to his mouth, and licked her juices off.

"Now watch me take you, Ellie."

He was standing at the edge of the bed. He gripped her hips and pulled her down so he could position himself between her thighs, angling until he was pressed against her still-throbbing core. He licked his lips, relishing the moment.

Then, with a slowness that was both tender and torturous, he slid into her, inch by exquisite inch.

"Eyes on me, Ellie," he said, his voice low, commanding but somehow comforting.

She kept her attention on him, skimming over his face and body. All the skin, all the scars, everything that made him who he was.

He moved one hand from her hip and slid it across her belly, not even rounding yet. "You're so beautiful, Ellie," he said with a raw note emerging. "Inside and out."

"So are you," she gasped, meaning it. She loved every inch of him. "Struan. I'm…getting close again."

"Are you? Even if I go slowly?" He grazed her most sensitive spot with every languid, lazy thrust. He was bending half over now, his head closer to hers as he tested new angles. Still he watched her, and made her watch him. She'd never felt so vulnerable.

"Yes. It feels so good." She saw the sweat on his temples, heard his breath tighten. He was on the edge. The knowledge made her own breathing speed up. How could this feel so painfully sweet, like it was the first time?

"Ellie," he said, his heart in his eyes.

She reached up and put her hands on his shoulders, pulling him down so his chest was inches over hers. "Together now. No more holding back." And then she deliberately took him in deep and held herself tight around him, keeping her eyes on his face.

He inhaled once, then let out a low, almost soundless moan as he stiffened and released his seed inside her. She felt it even as another orgasm rippled through her core, spreading out to her limbs in a slow wave. She relaxed under him, sighing as all the tension drifted away.

Struan waited a moment before withdrawing, and then rolled onto his back beside her, his chest still rising and falling heavily.

She wasn't sure how this exchange altered anything—though she couldn't pretend it was meaningless—when Struan spoke.

"How long will it take a maid to pack your things?"

"Pack for what?"

"You're moving here, to the townhouse."

"I don't know if I'm ready for that."

He rolled his head to the side to look at her. "I thought we just confirmed that you're very ready for that."

"Oh, Struan. What you make me feel when we're…"

"Fucking."

"Yes…that's not life. How I feel in a bed…or wherever… doesn't solve all the problems outside of the bed."

"But if we're in the same house, we have a much better chance at working those problems out."

"And you can more conveniently get me into bed?"

"Well, there's that."

"I won't be seduced into being…"

"Safe? Happy? Cared for? Christ, Ellie, what sort of seducer could I ever be? I'm not trying to lead you into sin. We're already legally married."

"Through deceit."

He sighed. "I should have been honest from the start, but I never knew how to begin telling you the truth. At first it seemed like it would be an unnecessarily cruel shock. And then, as you settled into your new life, I told myself that maybe it didn't matter how the marriage was arranged, if you were content with the results. I was afraid that I would hurt you, and then I hurt you anyway. Everything that happened was my fault. I told you that, or I tried to."

"Did you?"

"Not well, I admit." The backs of their hands brushed, and he took her hand in his. "It was stupid of me to think that I could maintain the secret, but I hoped that I would somehow be able to. Because telling you wouldn't just hurt you, it would hurt me too. I was already falling for you, even before we got off the ship. Before that, actually. When I first saw you, doing the laundry."

"No man has ever fallen in love looking at a woman doing the washing."

"I did. It was your laugh. It was so pure and full of joy, and I wanted it. I wanted you."

She was silent, hearing the truth in his words, knowing he was holding nothing back now.

"I had this idea that we could have a real marriage," he said quietly. "That you saw me as a real person. That I wasn't just a collection of old wounds and a way out of your previous life. I thought that if I could just make it through a few more months or a year before telling you, it would soften the blow. I hoped that I could prove to you that my love for you was real and that was all that mattered."

"I should've asked more questions." Elspeth shook her

head. "My father knew that I wouldn't. Mairi would have worn him down with questions and arguments and proclamations. I just nodded and asked when I should pack. Agreeing to the marriage was my fault as much as yours."

"I never would have let it happen if I hadn't seen you and wanted you. And now I don't know how to let you go." Struan looked devastated as he spoke. "I don't think divorce is possible at this point. Especially if you're with child. But I know that you can't maintain the fiction of our marriage, so tell me how you wish to live, and I will make it possible."

Elspeth wanted to protest. It was on the tip of her tongue to say *No I don't want to leave you*. But that was precisely what she had done, wasn't it? And despite what just happened, that momentary madness they shared, Struan seemed resigned to the idea of her leaving him, if not relieved. And Elspeth wondered how he could know what she wanted when she didn't know herself.

"I suppose it all comes down to the child," she said.

"What do you mean?" he asked, anxiety sparking in his voice.

"I mean that until our child is born, it will be impossible for me to make any decision about the rest of my life. I'd like to nurse the child, at least. But I know you don't want me around any longer, and—"

"I didn't say that," he countered. "Christ, of course I want you. I only said that we can't live a lie. There's no point in forcing you to pretend to be happy when you're miserable. And you would be miserable with me."

She'd be miserable without him too.

Struan looked so defeated that Elspeth wanted to put her arms around him, and tell him that he was being foolish, and that there was no need to assume the worst. But weren't they already at the worst? Their marriage was in rags almost as soon as it had begun. And while, yes, Struan could expect an heir soon enough, it seemed the only person who actually derived any satisfaction from the arrangement was Elspeth's father.

And now *he* had gone and gotten himself into exactly the same situation that the marriage was meant to get him out of.

"I suppose I might die giving birth," Elspeth said, indulging in a moment of morbidity. "In that case, at least I won't have to decide where to live afterward."

"I won't let that happen!" Struan rolled to cover her, displaying that massive figure that she almost didn't think about anymore. But he was intimidating, and he was un-ignorable. He looked as though he would personally fight off Death if it came to her bedside, and she half believed he could do it.

"How could you stop it?" asked Elspeth, gently pushing him off as she sat up, clad only in his heirloom necklace. "If it's my fate to die while giving birth, that's simply how it is."

"Bullshit. You're not your mother." Struan suddenly stood and crossed his arms. "You'll have the finest doctors, a midwife, whatever is needed. People say death is inevitable, but half the time it was because they didn't want to bother saving somebody's life. Cheaper to let them die. So they'd administer some opium to quiet the screaming, put on a sad face, and say it's inevitable…but really they didn't want to fail. They didn't want to spend time and resources working to save a life only to have the life slip away, or to have the life be saved, but the body mangled. There's no point in saving half a man."

"Wait!" Elspeth knew Struan had forgotten the original conversation and was now talking about the past. She slid off the bed and stepped up to him, putting her hands on his arms to get his attention. "Stop doing that. Listen to me. The war is over. You're done with it, and you are a whole man. Anyone who says differently is an idiot."

He didn't react for a moment, not even to show any

awareness of her touch. Instead, he stared in front of him, his eyes unfocused, unless they were focused on some point she could never see.

Elspeth tightened her grip on his arms and tried to shake him, with about as much effect as a butterfly shaking a mountain. So she leaned against him, putting her head against his crossed forearms, pressing her cheek into his skin. And it felt so perfect. She always wanted to touch him and be near him. Because she loved him.

Of course she loved him. She tried to convince herself otherwise. She tried to pretend he didn't love her. But he did. Everything he'd ever done for her or to her was done out of love. And his one error—hiding the truth behind the marriage proposal—he'd done to shield her from a harsher truth.

Ellie squeezed her eyes closed to stop the tears. Admitting that she'd allowed his mistake to hurt them both would be difficult. But she had to do it. How?

After a moment, he lifted his arms slightly to loop them above her head and pull her into an embrace. He didn't even seem aware that he was doing so, but Elspeth cuddled against his body and slid her arms around his torso to keep him close.

"Struan? Talk to me."

He didn't talk at first, but he did raise one hand to her head, and began to play with a lock of hair, twisting it and twining it around his fingers like a solitary game of cat's cradle.

"I wish you wanted me as much as I want you," he said. "Ellie, is there anything I can do that will make you come back?"

"You know," said Ellie with a wild thought. "You never actually proposed to me. I mean, when I first saw you in the church, it was already our wedding. I knew that I was going to marry you and you had no reason to ask."

He sounded a little perplexed. "So? If I had asked that day, would you have said yes?"

"Of course."

"Not that that means anything. You didn't know the truth then. You do now."

"I know much more than I did then," she said. "I know what it's like to be married, which I had no notion of before. And I know *you*, which of course I didn't know before. I like to believe that my decision would be much more informed if you were to ask me now."

Elspeth looked at him expectantly, but he didn't respond. She tapped one foot and prompted, "Well? Are you going to ask or not?"

He swallowed nervously, and she couldn't help but smile. Struan was such an intimidating figure most of the time, except to those people who knew him. Seeing him nervous was rather sweet. She said, "This moment cannot be the most terrifying thing you have faced in your life."

"It's more terrifying than you might think," he said, though with a faint answering smile that told her she had broken through the first barrier.

"Please ask me. It's traditional. And I think we are, despite everything, both rather traditional people."

Struan took her hands in his, running his thumbs over her knuckles, as if to ensure that she really existed. He cleared his throat, then said in a low tone, "Elspeth McGregor, I need you. I can't imagine any other woman at my side. I want to be the kind of man you deserve. But the only way I can do that is if you allow me the chance. I love you so much that it scares me. Will you be my wife, not because somebody else wants it, but because you want it?"

Elspeth's heart pattered beneath her ribs. She rarely glimpsed such raw emotion in Struan as she did in that moment. He didn't have to ask her to be his wife. He had everything already, according to the law. And yet, he asked anyway. Because she wanted him to. And she could say no to his question, and destroy him. But all she wanted was to say was, "Yes."

"Yes?" Struan echoed, hope in his eyes.

She'd loved him before, but it was the simple, adoring love of a rescued stray, so eager to be valued that she'd give him everything he asked for and much of what he never asked for, just so that he wouldn't discard her as a worthless thing.

Now she knew her worth.

Now she knew why she was answering the question.

"Yes. I love you. I want to be part of you. And have you be part of me. If you'll forgive my own mistake. I should have let you explain. I should have trusted you."

He kissed her forehead. "Do you trust me now?"

"I trust you as much as I love you. Completely."

Chapter 33

STRUAN DIDN'T SLEEP MUCH. HE wanted to. He wanted to stay in the same bed with Ellie until…well, until forever. But she was sleeping soundly and he didn't want to wake her with his restlessness.

He hated that Ellie found out she was pregnant on her own. That sort of news should be joyful, not terrifying. He vowed that he'd do everything in his power to ensure that she and the baby would thrive.

Breakfast would probably be a good start. He dressed quickly, and made his way down to the kitchen, surprising the cook and maids. He asked for a tray of bread, butter, and jam, with tea. Nothing that took extra effort.

"I'll take it upstairs myself," he informed the maid who assembled it. He didn't want more people than necessary bothering Ellie while she was in a new place.

Sunlight was peeking through the drapes when he returned to his bedroom. Ellie stirred when he sat on the edge of the bed.

"Good morning," he said, reaching for her hand, lying on the pillow next to her unbound hair. He liked the scene, and hoped to see it again, possibly every day.

"Did I sleep too long?"

"No. But I did bring you up some breakfast. If you can

eat in the mornings?"

She wrinkled her nose, seemingly taking stock of her body's temperament. "I think some bread would be all right."

"Luckily, that's what we have."

She sat up and ate carefully, slowly. She was pale, and certainly didn't have much appetite, but she didn't get sick. After she finished, she said, "I'm afraid I have no clothing other than my gown from last night, which is hardly appropriate."

"I had some of your new clothes sent here when the seamstress finished them," he admitted. "You've got plenty. And I hope you'll be sending for the rest of your things later today."

"I will. And I need to speak to Mairi! And you may want to summon your friends again. I assume everyone left last night."

"They did, shortly after we, um, went up here last night. The men would have taken Mairi back home and one of them will have kept watch."

"I still can't believe you just told your friends to watch Mairi, and they did it without asking why."

"They're soldiers. They know that when one of us asks for something to be done, we have a good reason."

"Hmm. Well, she handled the news better than I thought she would. But maybe call off the dogs today?"

"I'll call them off when it's safe, and not one moment before."

* * * *

A hour or so later, in the warm, wood-paneled parlor, a now properly clad Elspeth found a another copy of Walton's guidebook.

"You seem to be interested in London," he said dryly. "Was that the plan before you let me in on the secret?"

She looked serious. "Speaking of secrets, Mairi and I might have uncovered something about Averill," Elspeth told him. "It explains my father's obsession with guaranteeing she's successfully married, and why he's spent so much money on her."

"Go on."

She held up the guidebook. "When Averill was sixteen, she visited family in London for the better part of a year. The idea was to allow her to see the city and get exposure to the social graces she'd need after her debut and then on the marriage mart."

"All right." None of that sounded particularly groundbreaking.

"After she returned home, she would go on and on about her time in the city. She'd talk about her favorite places. The glow of the colored lanterns in Covent Garden." Elspeth opened the book to a page she'd marked. Struan read it and, yes, there was the same description.

"Now go to the page about Bond Street." He did.

"I'll tell you what it says," she announced, her eyes closed. "'The exquisite shops of Bond Street, lined up like so many cakes, contain delectable wares.'"

He frowned. The same phrasing as in the book. "Did you memorize this?"

"No, but Averill did. She said these things," Ellie explained. "*Exactly* these things. She never varied, she never added to the descriptions. If anyone asked, she might say something vague and change the subject."

"What's your point?"

"She *never* was in London. She bought Walton's guidebook and read it to memorize enough to convince people she was."

"Where was she, if not London? And why lie about her location?"

Ellie's hands dropped to her stomach. He understood immediately.

"Holy Christ. She was with child? That's why she vanished for a year?"

"Yes. But not to London," Ellie said. "Mairi did some snooping. She was at a cousin's in the countryside in County Monaghan. Remember I told you my father's family was from Ireland originally? It was out of the way enough so she could hide her pregnancy."

"And the child is still there?"

Ellie shook her head.

"Oh, I'm sorry. Did she miscarry? That must have been awful."

"No. Let me clarify." Elspeth's jaw tightened. "From what Mairi was able to find out, Averill bore a healthy baby but had no interest in keeping it. She demanded it be given up in such a way that it would never be traced back to her."

Struan's own muscles tensed. Averill's callousness shouldn't have surprised him, and yet… "And then what?"

"Then she came back to Edinburgh to prepare for her social debut and this engagement…gauntlet. Just as if nothing ever happened." Ellie shrugged, but it was clear she was deeply upset by the story. "Maybe it's better. For the child, I mean. Maybe they'll have been taken in by a family that truly wanted a child…" She trailed off. "I'm being naive again, aren't I? It'll be an orphanage or a workhouse for them. Assuming they're still alive."

Struan wished he could tell her differently. "These are the most likely outcomes, I'm afraid. But now that we know, we can discover the child's fate, good or bad. We owe them that much."

"But what's to be done? The child could be practically

anywhere in Ireland or even England now. If they're still alive."

"Let me put my resources to work."

"I know you'll spare nothing." Elspeth nodded, then added, "I'm very disappointed in Averill."

He fought a sudden urge to laugh. Coming from Elspeth, that seemingly meek phrase was more on the order of a vile curse.

* * * *

By afternoon, Struan had sent word to the other men to meet at his home. Ellie (accompanied by Michael the footman) traveled to her house to retrieve Mairi so she could join the planning. Struan didn't relax until both women returned. He didn't trust McGregor at all. Luckily, after their mutual revelations last night, Ellie had finally decided to stay with him—hopefully forever. And he hoped to hell Mairi would see reason too, since she was also at risk. Struan was sure the man would marry her off or sell her at the first opportunity.

So when he saw Michael helping both sisters out of the carriage, he sagged in relief then hurried to the front door as if he were the footman.

"Get in here," he barked ungraciously.

Oddly, Mairi smiled at this. "I wish it to be known that while I am independent, I'm not an idiot. We'll all be safer here, won't we?"

"Yes," Struan agreed, shutting the door behind them as they entered. "Thank you for your practicality."

"It's my one virtue," Mairi said.

"Not your only one," said Ellie. "Plus Father is so consumed with the planning for the masquerade that he wouldn't notice if we danced out the door. Come, Mairi."

Ellie showed her sister up to a guest room where she

could settle in.

Shortly after, they all met in the parlor, and Ellie had naturally taken on the role of hostess, pouring tea and cutting up a poppyseed cake the cook baked. Kai and Duncan were both enthusiastic about the cake. Calan was more interested in the coffee. Thane brooded.

"How much of the situation does everyone know?" she asked Struan in a low voice. "I mean, do they know about the origins of our marriage?"

"Just recently, yes. I had to tell them."

"You mean since you followed me to Edinburgh?"

"Well, as a matter of fact," Struan said. "Calan knew the truth the whole time."

Ellie glared at Calan. "Really."

"'Fraid so," Calan replied, having overheard them. "People often confess things to me."

"But you didn't tell me the truth when you first met me at the church so long ago."

"It wasn't my truth to tell."

Ellie took the plate of cake away.

"What?" Calan protested.

"Can I have another slice?" Kai asked. "It's delicious."

"Yes, of course," Ellie said, bestowing a smile on him. She served him another slice...which he then slid over to Calan.

"Kai was quartermaster," Struan explained to an outraged Ellie. "It was his duty to make sure his men got provisions."

"None of you deserve cake," she muttered.

"Wait, what about me?" Duncan asked.

"You're fine," she allowed. "You're helping watch over Mairi after all."

"So is Calan," Duncan pointed out.

She wrinkled her nose. "Technically."

"I don't need watchers," Mairi said from the doorway.

"Especially now that I've decamped to this house. Thus far, no one has even attempted to kidnap me into a life of slavery." She was wearing a lovely maroon gown. Her hair was pulled back in a loose knot, as casual as if she were at her own home.

"You sound disappointed," Struan said, unfazed.

Mairi accepted a gigantic slice of cake from her sister. "Not really. After all, if I ever want to experience slavery, I could always get married. Is that coffee? Could one of you lot pass down the pot, please?"

Calan rolled his eyes but slid the tall silver pot down the table.

Struan looked over the group. "Thursday evening is the masquerade, when Mr Farquhar and Averill McGregor will announce at midnight that they will be married."

"Farquhar will have propose to her first. They're not engaged yet," Ellie said.

"They're not?" Duncan asked, surprised.

"Averill wants a public proposal, as a spectacle. Big scene, him on one knee, all of the theatrics. And then they'll announce a date for the wedding at Farquhar's family church. It only seats about sixty, so everyone present at the party will hope that *they* receive an invitation to the ceremony and then the wedding breakfast."

"Sorry you didn't have a wedding breakfast," Struan told Ellie.

She waved it off. "It saved the household extra baking. The fancy cakes take forever."

Calan leaned forward. "So this party is the finale, and once Averill McGregor is safely engaged, we can expect that her father will do anything to pay off his debts. Including selling another daughter, or succeeding at killing his son-in-law, in the hope of getting his hands on whatever inheritance comes to the widow."

Struan nodded. "So I'd like to surprise him during the party somehow. Catch him off guard, well before he's ready to move. Any suggestions?"

"Do you want to be subtle?" asked Kai. "Or are we interrupting the festivities?"

"I don't care."

"If you spoil Averill's evening, *she's* liable to kill you," Mairi warned them all.

"Never mind Averill," Ellie said. "My concern is that there is little to confront my father with. It's all hearsay and whispers. Yes, he has debts, but that's hardly unusual. Or are we going to tell the world how he paid off his first debt to Struan?"

"No," said Struan. "I won't allow your name to be dragged through the mud as a result of this."

"It's our biggest advantage," Thane said. "He has to keep that secret. We don't."

"I won't have Ellie talked about that way. I may have blustered to McGregor about it once, but I can't really let it happen."

"Does *he* know that?" Calan asked. "Or would he believe you'd expose him?"

Ellie burst out, "Of course he believes Struan will expose him! That's why he tried to kill him!"

Duncan stabbed a piece of cake with his fork. "So he might try again. But probably not during the biggest night of his family's social calendar."

"All right." Calan stood up. "We have one evening to neutralize McGregor and ensure he won't try to do something stupid. We could attempt to remove him from the main party and have a little chat with him in some secluded spot in the house. Where's a safe place for that?"

"My bedroom on the top floor," Ellie said. "No one will be on that floor because the servants will be working. And he never goes up there, so he won't have any advantage once you get him in there."

"What are you dressing up as for the party?"

"Cap o' Rushes," Ellie said.

"I'll be Hypatia of Alexandria," said Mairi. "And I made Catriona agree to come too, to counterbalance Averill's vapid friends. She already owns a black cat mask and a black gown."

"And Averill?"

"Aphrodite, goddess of love and beauty," Ellie supplied.

"She's not subtle, is she?" Calan asked.

"Her outfit certainly isn't," Mairi agreed. "I imagine *you'll* appreciate it."

Calan ignored that jibe. "Struan? What's your costume?"

Struan hadn't thought about it. "I don't have one."

"He doesn't really need one. Lots of guests will simply wear silk or lace masks to match their gowns or suits," said Ellie. "And I expect none of you gentlemen will want to be encumbered by extra props."

"Correct," Duncan grunted. "Unless it's a sword."

"So don't worry about what you're wearing. Worry about what you'll do."

Struan said, "I think our best plan is to find some opportunity to get McGregor alone, then escort him up to the top floor where we can have our talk."

"There are enough of us to keep an eye on him all evening," Calan said. "We'll watch and give a signal if any of us sees a chance to divert him."

"I could say I found a cache of silver coins upstairs," Mairi offered. "Or something like that."

"Keep that idea handy," Duncan said. "I'd hate to use such an obvious lure unless we have to. But we may have to."

They continued to discuss options and possibilities. Struan caught Kai's eye at one point and both men stepped away to another part of the room.

"Kai," Struan said. "After all this is done, I need you to find something for me."

"Of course. What is it?"

"A child."

It was an indication of just how well Kai had performed his duty as quartermaster that Struan thought him the best person for the task, strange as it was. And to Kai's credit, he barely paused before saying, "I assume you mean a particular child, so I'll need details."

Struan gave him what he could. A now deeply upset Kai absorbed it all, and said, "And the mother's getting engaged Thursday night in front of the whole city?"

"So we are told."

Kai, normally so mild-mannered, gave a thin little smile. "Let's make it a night to remember, then, shall we?"

Chapter 34

THE EVENING OF THE MASQUERADE arrived.

Ellie did dress as Cap o' Rushes, having found one absolutely correct gown in the infinite number of trunks that now seemed to be in her collection. The costume required only a simple mask and the addition of a rustic-looking burlap overdress, which she sewed with the help of Agnes, who'd come over to Struan's townhouse as well.

"Can you see any of the gown underneath?" Ellie asked anxiously.

Agnes pursed her lips. "Mmmm, only little hints, if the light falls just so. In the ballroom, amid everyone else trying to be showy, you'll not be noticed at all until you choose to be."

Ellie nodded. "Good. The ties on the overdress will be easy to loosen, and I'll yank the overdress off just at midnight when the unmasking will be announced."

The crowd was even bigger than the previous parties, and Ellie soon wished she could run away. Alas, they were stuck there till at least midnight. Averill had insisted that both families must stand together during Mr Farquhar's proposal, as a show of approval.

She stood near Mairi most of the evening. As far as she could tell, almost no one identified them, and certainly didn't associate them with the hosts. Catriona Ross joined them early on. She was a striking figure, since she had black hair, a black gown, and a beautiful black satin cat mask complete with ears and whiskers. She made a habit of hissing at any gentleman who dared ask her for a dance, which caused her and Mairi no end of mirth. Ellie was rather awed by Miss Ross.

"Everything all right?" a man in a lion mask asked them as he walked by.

"Splendid," Miss Ross snapped back. "Keep your eyes on McGregor, Thane. We're doing just fine."

He growled before he moved off.

"If Mr MacPhearson asked, would you dance with him?" Ellie ventured.

"Perhaps," Miss Ross said with a wicked smile. "If I'm in the mood. He *is* a good dancer," she added. "My aunt once bullied him into dancing with me."

Before Ellie could ask for details, Mairi murmured, "Our men are circling like wolves."

"Where? Who?"

Her sister pointed out a slender gentleman wearing a feathered mask with a long pointed beak. "Mr Buchanan is the stork over there—bit on the nose, I fear. And there is Mr MacKenzie as a bear. Appropriate." Ellie nodded, seeing Duncan in the corner.

"And Mr Shaw as…the Grim Reaper?"

"I think he's a monk," Ellie corrected her, though she had to admit that Calan's costume was rather off-putting. The long dark robe and the pointed hood completely concealed his appearance.

"He's holding a *skull*."

"A contemplation on Death," Struan murmured, joining them. "Hermits do that sort of thing." Struan had opted to not wear any costume, and even his black half-mask didn't do much to hide his identity to those who knew him—the scarring on his cheek and neck was plain to see. Ellie was privately pleased with his choice. Struan had no need to hide anything about him, and she was impressed that he wasn't attempting to conceal his appearance.

"Better than a scythe," Ellie said. "I thought he would look…merrier." She was surprised he'd pass up a chance to charm a lady.

"He's not here to have fun," Struan said. "Calan takes serious things seriously."

Mairi made a skeptical noise, then said, "Our father hasn't left the ballroom all evening. He's glad-handing any-one he sees. I don't think you'll have much chance to pull him away from the crowd."

"We have time," Struan replied.

"Not that much. The unmasking is at midnight," Ellie said.

They all looked to the large clock standing at one end of the room. Midnight was in less than an hour.

Averill was, of course, the center of attention, in her scandalously thin silk gown and gold headdress. If she were to appear on a public stage, she'd be arrested for violating the indecency statutes. But because she was a lady of society, celebrating her triumphant impending marriage, she was called an original, and garnered all praise. (The men were especially willing to praise her. It was a *very* thin silk gown.) Ellie noticed that Averill kept glancing to a man wearing a leafy green mask and a green velvet jacket over his darker green satin waistcoat. She smiled every time she caught his eye.

"Who's that man in green?" Ellie asked Mairi. "That's not Mr Farquhar."

"Who? Oh, no, certainly not. Farquhar is wearing some medieval getup. He's Prince Somebody-or-Other. I don't know who that man is. Why?"

"Averill keeps flirting with him."

"She flirts with every man." Mairi shrugged.

Time raced forward, and soon the clock chimed midnight.

"It's time! It's time!" Averill called out. "On the last bell, reveal yourself!"

Ellie took a deep breath. "Here we go."

"Good luck," Struan told her.

She and Mairi moved to the central platform, where they were expected to be for the next event of the evening.

Mairi untied the mask she wore and stepped up to the platform. "Hypatia arrives," she said dryly to her father and stepmother.

"Where's your sister?" McGregor asked.

Ellie undid the ribbons keeping the tattered overdress bound to her. As it started to fall to the floor, she grabbed the messy wig she wore over her real hair and flung it away too, letting the blonde waves cascade down her back. Finally she pulled off her mask. "Here!"

She stepped forward, her cloth-of-gold gown catching all the candlelight and throwing it back.

"Elspeth?" her father asked, as if he'd never seen her before.

"Yes, it's me," she declared. It was her, Cap o' Rushes, the scullion who worked her hands raw for a household that never bothered to thank her. It was her, the hidden princess in the fairy tale, decked in gold.

* * * *

Struan gazed at Ellie, in her dazzling ensemble that had been hidden until just a moment ago. Everyone in the room was struck silent for just a few seconds. Ellie was the brightest thing in the room, and the loveliest.

"Miss McGregor. I mean, Mrs MacInnes. I mean… Please. Allow me." The stuttering Mr Farquhar took her hand and helped her up the last few steps with the sort of consideration he'd not shown his presumed fiancée a moment prior.

"Elspeth!" her stepmother said. "You're like the sun!" Her tone was full of surprise and delight, and Ellie glowed at the words. Struan happened to agree with the woman's assessment, but how had anyone taken *this long* to notice that Ellie was pure sunshine?

Averill did not have the same reaction. "This is *my* party," Averill hissed. "Everyone's supposed to be talking about *me*. And you pulled a trick like that."

Ellie looked at her and replied calmly, "What trick? I told you I was dressing as Cap o' Rushes. It's your own cross to bear if you don't bother to learn what that means."

Mairi, in her own learned costume, smiled.

Struan took his mask off and stepped up as well. He would support Ellie on this stage or any other.

"Well, go on," Averill muttered to her intended.

Mr Farquhar cleared his throat and slowly, with some evident discomfort, bent down on one knee before Averill, who preened in delight as everyone's attention fell upon her.

Before Farquhar could say anything, though, an unknown voice boomed out, "All hail Aphrodite! Queen of Love!"

The audience applauded politely, and Averill smiled even as her brow furrowed. She looked over the crowd. Obviously, the *all hail* was not planned by her.

Then a man moved to the low stage, parting the other guests around him to make way. "Ah, my goddess! Have you forgotten your longtime worshipper? Before you continue, Averill darling, I wish to make a toast."

Everyone looked at the man who'd spoken up. He was handsome, in the way that many men in their twenties are handsome—dark-haired, nicely groomed, well-dressed. He didn't have a costume as such, only dark eveningwear like many other gentlemen present. He held a velvet half mask in his other hand. Struan didn't recognize him, but he saw Averill go absolutely dead white.

"Scott Lister," she gasped.

The newcomer turned to the crowd at large, holding up a champagne glass. "My toast is to this young lady, the one who everyone here rightly hails as a goddess and a beauty and a star among the many women who have put themselves on the marriage mart this season. But what the good people here do not know is that this shining star has a secret."

"Don't you *dare*," Averill said, her voice weak but her eyes blazing with hatred.

Farquhar stood up and stepped back, confused at this turn of events. "Who's this man?" he muttered, clearly baffled.

"What would I not dare for the sake of the truth?" Mr Lister returned mockingly to Averill. He looked over the rapt crowd. "Not long ago, this lovely star shone so bright that she grew bigger and brighter, and soon enough there was another little star shining too. And the second star looked just like the first, isn't that true, Averill?"

"Averill, what's this about?" asked Farquhar. He was already edging away from her, because there was little question what it was about. Farquhar's own mother was frantically signaling him to come to her, as if Averill were a venomous snake.

"It's nothing! It's lies!" Averill said. "Robert, stand with me. You are to be my husband!"

"This is not yet decided," he replied.

"And he's never been alone with her!" his mother added with relief in her tone. "So he is not at fault for any past indiscretions."

"I am pure!" Averill shrieked.

The newcomer, Mr Lister, laughed cruelly. "An immaculate conception, darling? That's not how I remember it."

"Get out of my house with your slander, sir!" McGregor shouted, stepping up to the man. His face was nearly purple with rage.

Mr Lister looked smug. "It's not slander if it's true, and after all, I can prove it. You yourself gave money to me on account of the little star."

"After you refused to do the honorable thing," McGregor snapped, evidently forgetting that he had first denied the whole situation.

"She didn't do anything to preserve her honor. Why should I?"

Averill hurled a wineglass at the man, who dodged so nimbly that Struan decided he must be used to having drinks thrown at him.

The crowd was absolutely buzzing at this point. If McGregor failed to join the level of society he sought, he had succeeded at entertaining them.

"Oh, Lord," Ellie whispered. "What is happening?"

"The truth is coming out," Struan said in a low voice. "And as we both know, that can be a tumultuous process."

"If you'd continued to pay, I wouldn't have to ruin your party," Lister was saying. "*You* failed to uphold your end of our agreement."

"I tried, but *you* ignored my letter!" McGregor blustered. "And if you'd read it and followed the instructions, we wouldn't be here now."

"You mean you wouldn't invite me to the festivities?" said Lister. "When I am such an intimate friend of the family?"

More gasps.

Struan put the last pieces of the puzzle together. "You wouldn't have been invited because you'd be dead," he informed the man.

"What?" Lister looked alarmed for the first time.

McGregor was already shaking his head. "Nonsense. Complete balderdash."

"I believe *I* received the letter McGregor wrote to you, sir," Struan said. "A letter that instructed me to come to a certain church at a certain time. It was an invitation meant for you."

"Two unsigned letters, sent from the same house, but sent to the wrong recipients after they were shuffled accidentally by a maid!" Ellie added. She turned to Lister. "Repeat the content of the letter. I know you remember the words."

"It said *Go to Hell*," he announced, in a tone that suggested he'd never been so offended.

Ellie flushed, and Struan realized again how happy he was that her letter never got to him.

"Those words were meant for another man," she said. "But I can see how you interpreted it to mean that McGregor was no longer willing to go along with...whatever you'd arranged with him."

"The mix-up may have saved your life," Struan said. "Since I got McGregor's instruction to you, I happened to be standing where McGregor told *you* to be, and a heavy stone gargoyle plummeted to earth a breath away."

Lister's eyes widened, then he turned to regard McGregor. "Indeed?"

"Ravings," McGregor said. "You have no proof."

"Sadly, that is true," Struan said more quietly. "There was no witness to him being on the roof."

"It doesn't matter," Lister said. "McGregor will suffer anyway. Tonight is his downfall, and though the golden goose is now cooked, I've eaten enough golden eggs." He smirked, holding up his glass again.

"To golden eggs." Mairi lifted her glass as well.

"I *hate* you!" Averill screamed at Mairi, or perhaps the whole crowd. "I did what you told me. So did Mama! I was about to be engaged, to a man *you* picked!"

"At great expense," McGregor added, glaring at Averill. "I should have given instructions to leave you in Ireland with the baby!"

Gasps echoed throughout the crowd. Several ladies appeared about to faint—though Miss Ross was not one of them. Duncan was obviously covering a laugh, and Calan, who'd removed his hood, had a suspicious twitch to his mouth. He now stood behind the family, his movements so subtle no one even noticed he'd stepped up on the platform.

Then McGregor whirled on Mairi. "And you, you harpy! What good have you done to advance the family name? You forced me to rely on that piece of muslin!"

"You forget Elspeth, who made a fine match," Mairi said coldly.

"She married a monster, but at least she is married. You are a complete disappointment to your mother's memory."

Mairi lunged at her father, but Calan had somehow guessed where things were going and hooked one hand around her arm, pulling her back. Ellie couldn't hear what he said to Mairi, but despite her sister's flaming eyes, it must have kept her from attacking her father.

McGregor was shouting at the footmen to close the doors, as if restraining the guests would stop the gossip. Mrs McGregor took two steps forward and suddenly collapsed. Duncan and Thane rushed forward to help her while McGregor jumped down from the platform and ran for the doors.

Struan quickly headed him off. "You can't leave your own party, sir. What will people think?"

McGregor jumped back as if Struan had physically threatened him. "Get away from me! None of this is my fault. It's Averill that's to blame. Everything that happened is because of her!"

"Father!" Ellie snapped. "You can't blame others for your own actions! You made her give up that baby. And Averill, why did you..." Ellie looked around. "Wait, where is Averill?"

Everyone looked.

But Averill was gone.

Chapter 35

DUE TO THE ABRUPT END to the masquerade, there was an embarrassing amount of uneaten food in the house. So Ellie told the servants to distribute as much as they could to whoever they thought needed it. But there was still more, and thus the next day she was serving an odd breakfast to those who were present—caviar and cake not usually being part of the meal.

"Your father finally confessed what happened," Struan told her after a long sleepless night watching McGregor. "Mr Lister, the father of Averill's child, was blackmailing McGregor, demanding increasing payments to keep quiet and not destroy Averill's reputation before she was safely married off. McGregor paid more than once, but he resented every pence, and then he got the idea for his blackmailer to meet with an unfortunate accident. But things went awry, and I was the man who came to the designated spot where the stone was to fall. So I thought your father was trying to kill *me*, when in fact he was trying to kill another man, to protect an entirely different secret."

Ellie sighed. "And since he stopped paying, Lister revealed the truth about Averill at the party. I would scarcely believe it if I hadn't seen it," she murmured. "I knew my father was a selfish man, but I never thought him murderous."

"He thought he'd found a way out of his problems."

The men had gathered after a long night of trying to discover where Averill had gone, and with who. They'd partially succeeded.

Calan entered the room. He looked haggard, which was not to say he looked bad. But he collapsed into a chair and reached for a cup of coffee. "Nothing. She slipped out in the chaos, along with that gentleman dressed in green. I spent most of the night and morning down at the harbor, trying to find out if they boarded a ship. But no one saw anything that I can tell."

Duncan shook his head. "The harbor was a long shot. I visited each posting inn I could think of that has southbound routes, asking for passengers of their description. No luck."

"Nor for routes going westward," Kai chimed in. "Without knowing who the man was, it will be hard to trace their path."

"They could still be in the city," said Ellie.

"Possibly," Struan said. "We'll keep looking."

"And Mr Lister?"

"He's currently a guest of the local magistrate, blackmail being a crime. Whether he'll actually be punished for it is another matter. And McGregor certainly won't get any of his money back—he's in dire straits now."

"The McGregor name is utterly ruined," Ellie said with a sigh.

"Good," Mairi muttered.

"Not just socially, Mairi," Elspeth cautioned. "The moneylenders will fall upon Father now. They've no reason to delay. This house and nearly everything in it will be seized to pay what is owed."

"I can live in a garret."

"You may, but what of Father? Our stepmother? Averill, once she returns, as she inevitably will?"

"Who cares about them?" Mairi asked.

"I do! They are family, no matter what."

"Ellie, you're impossible! They don't deserve your love."

"Love isn't about deserving." Ellie smiled. "And I will not let you live in a garret."

"Don't ask me to live with you at Linneliath. I can't live there, Ellie. I'll visit, but I can't live there. It's at the end of the earth. I need a city. I need people. I need…noise."

"I know," Ellie said softly.

Struan said, "I'll ensure that you're provided for here in Edinburgh. The others as well. I won't repay McGregor's loans. His many mistakes are his own. But I'll provide lodgings and board and a reasonable income to ensure comfort, if not luxury."

"You have no duty to do so," Mairi told him.

"As your sister said, love isn't about deserving. I love her, and she wants you all provided for, so I will do it for her sake."

* * * *

Three days had passed. Averill had not surfaced. Her mother was in a state of shock.

Mairi said, "She hasn't left her bed since…well, since it happened. Her lady's maid says she hasn't eaten a bite, and she doesn't even really sleep. She just lies in the bed and stares at the ceiling."

Ellie stood up from the floor, where she'd been packing up a few more items she intended to take to Struan's townhome. "I didn't realize it hadn't improved. We must go to her."

Ellie and Mairi entered the room, followed by a maid, who was carrying a tea tray. The maid placed the tray on the table, and both women waited until the servant had withdrawn to speak.

Her stepmother was propped up in bed, but otherwise no attempt had been made to look at all engaged in the world. She was staring at the tea tray rather than at Elspeth, so much so that Elspeth asked if she ought to pour, the impulse to serve never far away from her.

"Only if you wish. I don't want any," Susan said dully.

But the mere presence of the tea piqued her interest. Elspeth walked over and poured three cups, then handed one to her stepmother. "Please drink a little. It will give you strength."

Susan took the cup, but said, "I have no strength. I never did."

"Don't be silly. You've had a shock is all. We will discuss things and decide what to do about it. Together. For we are family."

The woman stared at Elspeth. "How can you say that? After how I've treated you? I don't deserve your pity."

"The incident at the party wasn't your fault," said Elspeth.

But her stepmother was already shaking her head. "I don't refer to last night."

"It was three nights ago," Mairi reminded her gently.

Susan looked surprised. "Has it been so long? Anyway, I mean my shame at my behavior over the many years I have been mistress of this house. It will be a little comfort to you, Elspeth, but I would rather have the words spoken late, instead of maintaining silence any longer."

Recognizing the seriousness in the other woman's face, Elspeth remained silent.

"Your father had…intense feelings about both you and the loss of your mother. When I first married him, I didn't understand the depth of his grief at losing his first wife. And Averill has always been most demanding of my attention, and I'm afraid that I found it all too easy to turn a blind eye to you and your sister. In truth, I was selfishly grateful for your natural attitude of calm, and what I had assumed to be an inborn desire to ensure the comfort of others. My life was spent managing both your father and my daughter as well as my own inadequacies, so I treated you as an afterthought." She shook her head. "It was most unkind of me. Especially in the last few months, I found I could no longer pretend that my previous actions were right."

Elspeth had always assumed Susan to be flighty and shallow and self-absorbed, like her daughter, for whom she exerted herself to no end. It seemed that her stepmother had hidden depths.

Ellie confessed, "For twenty years, I held the belief that I could earn my father's love by obeying every rule he set out and anticipating every wish he expressed. But no one can force another's love, and he was determined not to love me. I can hardly act surprised when I learn that my refusal to ask for anything for myself would result in anything other than people ignoring me entirely. I suppose I learned the opposite lesson from your own daughter."

Her stepmother smiled sadly. "Averill knew from the cradle how to demand the attention of the whole room. When she was a baby, it was through crying. As she grew older, her methods grew more sophisticated. I must confess that I aided and abetted everything she did. I love her dearly, she is my own flesh and blood. And I only want her happiness. But I do realize that for her, happiness doesn't look the same as it does to me. By appeasing her whims, I wasn't giving her happiness. I was merely teaching her that there were no consequences. I should have been more alert, but by the time I knew she'd been…involved with Mr Lister, she was already carrying a babe. Your father insisted she hide the pregnancy and abandon the baby. But Averill didn't protest. She was barely more than a child herself."

Elspeth said, "Well, now some new man will have the task of ensuring her happiness. I do hope that he will find the task to his liking, for her sake as much as his. Do you know who he is, the man she ran away with?"

"No," her stepmother said. "But I'm sure she'll contact me soon. I'm her mother."

Ellie and Mairi shared a look, neither of them certain how to tell the woman that Averill seemed to have entirely disappeared. Finally Ellie said, "She will come to you in need."

"Yes, when in need she is most appealing." Her stepmother took a sip of the tea and looked steadily at Elspeth. "But that's not what I need to talk about. I wanted you to know that I am aware of the conversation you had with your father, about the…circumstances of your betrothal."

Elspeth flushed with embarrassment.

She went on, "I was so appalled. I promise you I had no notion of what he had done to alleviate that particular debt until a few weeks ago. I knew that he had borrowed, I knew that he had done so for years. He was never prudent about money, and it was a failing I was willing to overlook again and again, because I was weak."

She looked at Elspeth with eyes newly hardened by experience. "The truth is that I was so grateful to have a comfortable home, and an income and pin money. It meant whenever I needed something, I didn't delve too deeply into how he maintained our living. He always told me not to worry, and that he had everything in hand. And that everything he was doing was to ensure my happiness and the security of him and his own family. But what he did to *you*, that was unconscionable. If there is anything at all that I may do to alleviate your distress, I will endeavor to try."

"I'm not in distress," Elspeth assured her. "It's true that when I discovered exactly what happened, I was terribly hurt. And frightened. I had been lied to not just by my father, but by my husband as well. That's the reason I left the Highlands to return here, because I was angry, and also because I feared the same fate might befall Mairi."

Elspeth took a deep breath. "However, Struan isn't a beast. He is the best man I have ever known in my life. His initial action was a mistake, but I understand now why he did it, and I believe that his motives were always good. In any case, we have weathered the storm, and I believe we will be happy together now that we're being honest with each other."

"I'm relieved to hear it," her stepmother said. "Though I'm all too aware that your circumstances are the results of good luck, for I know that your father did not take Struan's goodness into account when he made his bargain. He should be ashamed of himself. And he should be ashamed of himself as a father, blaming you for the death of his wife. As women, we know that there is always a certain danger in bearing a child. And we accept it, those of us who wish to become mothers."

Elspeth nodded, restraining herself from touching her belly.

Susan continued, "But the fact is that life is uncertain. She might have died from a fall from a horse, or eating something she ought not to have, or simply from getting ill in a cold winter. Would he then blame the stable boy who saddled the horse? Or the meal? Or the season?"

"We must accept fate," said Elspeth.

"*He* never did, not about his wife. And we've all suffered for it. I felt your mother's presence in this house. Not a ghost; I never felt she hated me. But I always felt my own inadequacy, when I knew in his mind I was only a pale replacement for his perfect first love. He married me in haste, out of wild grief, and I hoped that I could fill the void in his heart. I was too young and foolish to understand that at the time. And after the wedding, it was far too late."

"It was too late for all of us," Mairi agreed.

"I threw myself into raising Averill," said Susan. "But part of me always knew that he never moved beyond that first awful phase of mourning, and what's more, he never wanted to. I think eventually he came to enjoy his misery and his rage at the world. By hurting you, he felt in some way he was getting back at Death. I don't say this to excuse my own actions. I should have defended you more often, and I should've been a better mother to you and your sister. I suppose it is too late now."

"No, I don't think it is," Ellie assured her, her heart cracking for the woman's newly revealed pain. "There will be a time soon when I will need to consult with a mother."

"Truly?"

"Yes. I hope," said Elspeth slowly, "that I may call on you should I need…wisdom."

"Always. And I hope I can offer any wisdom at all."

Epilogue

IT WAS EARLY SEPTEMBER. SUMMER was fading into an early autumn. It was warm during the day, but sometimes a chilly north wind would rush through the streets of Edinburgh, causing ladies to shiver and men to hold the brim of their hats.

Further north, the same wind filled the sails of the ship Elspeth and Struan had boarded to return to the Highlands. Ellie was visibly pregnant by now, and Struan had been torn about whether to remain in the city where excellent doctors abounded, or go home. It was Ellie who insisted that they go to Linneliath. "It's only right for our child to begin at the place where they will live so much of their life," she had said.

"But your health is paramount."

"You do know there are midwives throughout Scotland," she had said. "And if you must, you could pay a doctor to attend me when my time nears. And I know that I will be stronger if I'm at home in Linneliath."

Now, they stood on the deck of the ship, watching the shoreline to the west as the prow cut cleanly through lapis-colored waves. Struan clasped her hand tightly and raised it to his lips to kiss her fingers.

Ellie smiled, thinking of all they'd endured since the last

time they sailed north.

The aftermath of the final masquerade took weeks to settle. In the end, the creditors seized nearly all of the McGregor wealth—or all of it they could *find*. Averill had managed to spirit away her finest stones when she fled, while her mother must have hidden some of her collection with a trusted friend. And Mairi had already handed over what *she* possessed to Elspeth while she had been planning an escape. No creditor would dream of confronting Struan MacInnes or his wife, so those small valuables were safe.

The house was sold to the highest bidder after being stripped of almost all the furnishings, draperies, carpets, and art. (Elspeth did purchase her old desk, which now resided in the MacInnes townhome.)

Thanks to Struan's quiet contribution of funds, the remains of the McGregor family now lived in a modest but comfortable set of rooms close to New Town. Mrs McGregor had been shattered by all the events and could not live alone, so Mairi had rather surprisingly agreed to live with her and step in as daughter. McGregor himself was technically also a resident, but he was rarely seen at his new home, since he spent more and more time in the grimmest gambling dens of the city. No one who was anyone would give him the time of day.

Averill was…somewhere. Rumors abounded. (Rumors would circulate about Averill McGregor for years, in fact. She had achieved a notoriety and fame that no marriage would have given her.) She might be in London. Or Edinburgh. Or Dublin. Or New York City. What the rumors agreed upon was that she was accompanied by a man who *wasn't* Mr Farquhar, the man who'd nearly proposed that fateful night, *nor* Mr Lister, the man who'd fathered her child, but rather some unidentified *third* man, the one who'd been dressed in green.

The gossips were in heaven.

Struan had offered to find out the truth for Mrs McGregor. But she insisted that Averill would contact her when the time was right, and not sooner. Ellie had offered to bring her stepmother to their home in the north, but was immediately refused. "Averill needs to know where to find me," Susan had said with the desperate hope of a lost soul. Ellie knew there was no arguing with her until she was able to come to terms with events, and pressed no further. Mairi quietly promised to keep a careful eye on the situation. They both hoped that sometime in the new year, Mairi might bring their stepmother to the Highlands for an extended visit, with the allure of a new baby to brighten her days.

And not just the baby, since Kai had located a certain young child in Ireland and was even now traveling there to escort them to Linneliath to be a ward of Struan MacInnes. Ellie was excited to see how raising children would change their daily life.

She leaned against her husband, loving how solid he felt. "We'll be home by this time tomorrow," she said, delighted at the notion.

His arms went around her waist, lightly clasping her above her rounding belly. "At the risk of sounding like a bad poet, I am at home wherever you are."

"That *is* bad," she said, laughing. "But I love it."

"I love you." He dipped his head kiss her cheek softly, but then remained to nibble her ear. "If you would accompany me to our cabin, wife, I could show you how much I love you."

Heat shot through her, proving that her current condition did not at all dampen her desire for the sort of activity that got her in this condition in the first place.

She tilted her head to catch his lips with hers. Then she said, "Would you also permit me to demonstrate some frugality?"

He made a low sound that sent her pulse racing. "Please."

"Afterward, I may grow faint, husband. You'll have to attend me all night long."

"Done."

"You will have to do whatever I demand."

"Your servant," he promised.

"Mmmm. Well, then, my love. If we are both determined to express our baser natures and our mutual carnal needs, we'd best begin as soon as possible."

"Lead me, love."

The End

Author's Note:

As far as I know, there have never been gargoyles on the top of St Giles. But it never hurts to look up.

ABOUT THE AUTHOR

Elizabeth Cole is a romance writer with a penchant for history. Her stories draw upon her deep affection for the British Isles, action movies, medieval fantasies, and even science fiction. She now lives in a small house in a big city with a cat, a snake, and a rather charming gentleman. When not writing, she is usually curled in a corner reading...or watching costume dramas or things that explode. And yes, she believes in love at first sight.

www.ingramcontent.com/pod-product-compliance
Lightning Source LLC
Chambersburg PA
CBHW020907060726
47591CB00004B/1132